CW00447484

THE WAYWARD HAUNT SERIES

THE BONE GRIMOIRE

CAS E. CROWE

Author: Cas E. Crowe

Editor: Kristin Scearce, Hot Tree Editing

Book Cover Design: Miblart

Title: The Bone Grimoire

Paperback ISBN: 978-0-9756135-2-8

Hardback ISBN: 978-0-9756135-3-5

Ebook ISBN: 978-0-9756135-1-1

THE BONE GRIMOIRE

Book Four

THE WAYWARD HAUNT SERIES

CAS E. CROWE

- YUKOVSLAR
- IDRA
- JUBRIS
- GALVAC
- TARAHIK
- BRENDLASH
- PORT SERRES
- DARTHMUSK
- STAZIKA PALACE
- ESSIDA
- GOSHENIENE
- GONZAVREE
- CUBAIS
- OTTURIN CAVES
- SCARMOUTH
- VALDAVAR

NAVASK

SARGROSSIO SEA

THE FROZEN SEA

●TARAHIK

BASSINGER STRAIT

EDRADUS ●

● THE BONE TOWERS

ASKIVNA
●

ISLA NECROPOLIS ●

THE SEA CAVES ●

HELMS POINT ●

MUIREN

BECCSTRAIT

NORTH ALANRIC OCEAN

• EDRADUS

• ASKIVNA

• ISLA NECROPOLIS

THE SEA CAVES •
• HELMS POINT
MUIREN •

VUKOVAR

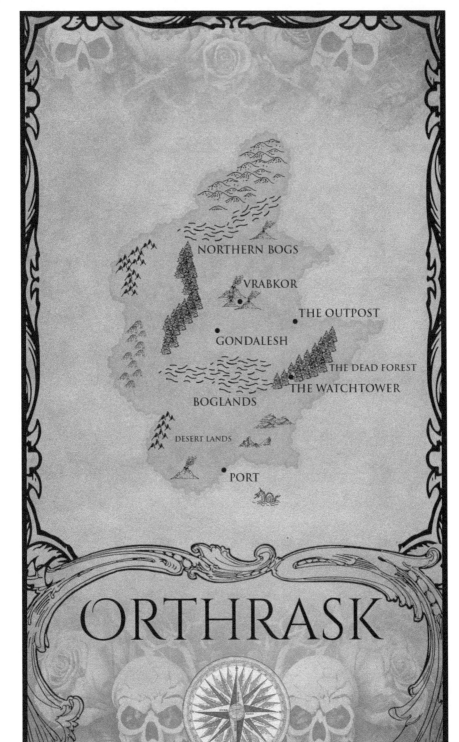

NORTHERN BOGS

VRABKOR

THE OUTPOST

GONDALESH

THE DEAD FOREST

THE WATCHTOWER

BOGLANDS

DESERT LANDS

PORT

ORTHRASK

CHAPTER 1

I was blinded by light. After hours, maybe even days of being trapped in darkness, the shocking luminance made my eyes water. I squinted, fighting the dots that stabbed at my vision. I didn't like cages, which was ironic considering I'd often wound up in cells. This one was all white walls with no apparent entry or exit. The door, wherever it was, had been concealed by magic.

Great. A glamour is in use.

I rolled sideways off a steel sleeping shelf that, now that I had the ability to actually see it, looked more suitable for a morgue. Maybe it was from a morgue. Nothing would surprise me at this stage.

My bare feet touched the cold floor, causing a chill to sweep up my body. Everything in this cell was sterilised and stainless, the fluorescent light making the white walls gleam in an irritating way.

I honestly had no idea how long I'd been asleep. Correction: how long I'd been in an induced sleep, because I was certain that was what Toshiko had ordered. After her betrayal, she'd had three of her loyal servants move me from the ship's deck down to the lower cells, which, judging by the vibrations that rattled through the floor, were a level above the engines.

To be honest, it was all kind of hazy. I was truly at a loss as to how much time had passed since Toshiko had kidnapped me and had the Black Palace set alight. The Council of Founding Sovereigns were dead. Killed on the very hour they were meant to sign the new accords. Accords that would have abolished conscription to the Haxsan Guard. For the first time, casters would have had a choice to join the armed forces or not. A powerful surge of bitterness swept through me at the thought of how close we had been to making real, visible change. Toshiko had destroyed that opportunity. She had ruined everything.

Is everyone in the Black Palace dead?

My brain conjured an image of the sovereigns burned to crisps on their thrones. Macaslan and Darius reduced to chunks of ash. Marek and Talina holding each other as the fires consumed them. Annaka glaring at the onrushing inferno in outrage that this was to be her end. Bronislav closing his eyes, accepting his cruel fate. Macha petting her bird affectionately, ignoring the tendrils that circled around them like a lover's embrace.

I swallowed, feeling sick for an entirely different reason.

Jad?

We hadn't exactly left things in a great place. I had absorbed the Bone Grimoire's magic, but I'd paid a terrible price to receive it: Jad's love. It still pained me to see the loathing that had taken form on his face when I grabbed his arm and forced him to talk to me in the hallway that day. That's all I'd wanted to do. Talk. But touching him had burned his skin like fire. He couldn't be near me without being physically ill. I had suddenly turned from being the most precious thing to him to a curse.

The last thing I remembered was Jad walking away, never wanting to see me again. At least, that's what I imagined he was thinking.

And now, he might be dead.

They might all be gone.

The light couldn't be blamed for the haze in my eyes anymore. My tears were entirely at fault.

A metallic announcement reverberated around the cell, echoing off the stark walls, seeming to come alive from every direction. "The door is opening. Please stand back."

I would have snorted if I had more energy.

Stand back? I don't even know where the door is.

A creak filled the cell, like a rusty gate swinging shut. To my left, a part of the wall opened, and Toshiko emerged. Stabbing rage flared inside me. She was dressed in a black-and-red kimono, her dark hair pulled up and held by a scarlet comb, her white make-up flawless. At first, I thought the red patterns along her kimono were embroidered roses, until she neared me and I saw what they really were. Leafless trees. The branches were on fire.

How fitting.

Those gold cat eyes—eyes I had once thought beautiful but were now only malicious and spiteful—stared at me with little concern. "Good, you are awake."

She spoke the words as though I were a teenager who'd reluctantly climbed out of bed at midday.

"Awake?" My voice was croaky, another indicator I'd been here for a long time. "Please don't pretend you have nothing to do with my wacky sleep pattern."

The corners of her lips tilted slightly. "You are correct. Spells are being pumped through the ventilation to keep you asleep, as I please."

"Why?"

"Why not? You are my gift to the new sovereign. In just under an hour, we will be arriving at Orthrask. I need you to look presentable." She scrunched her nose. "At present, you are not fit to be seen."

3

Orthrask. Morgomoth's kingdom.

We're that close?

I had been afraid before, but now that fear burrowed into my blood, making me cold all over. By receiving half the Bone Grimoire's magic, I had spoiled Morgomoth's plan. If he learnt the spell to merge the Larthalgule and Neathror blades, then he would create the ultimate weapon. I still didn't fully understand what that meant, but by taking half the book's power, Morgomoth couldn't complete the spell. Would he make me surrender the necromancy I had taken so he could acquire it, and become the most powerful necromancer to ever exist?

Of course he will, you idiot. And he'll make the process painful.

Toshiko snapped her fingers. One of her loyal soldiers appeared. He laid a set of clothes on my sleeping shelf and then hastily retreated.

Toshiko waved her hand. Another door appeared in the cell, leading to a private bathroom. "Clean yourself up. The water will last for five minutes once you turn it on. I will be here waiting."

Despite my anxiety, a shower sounded like heaven. I'd be able to wash the grogginess away and formulate a plan. Necromancers were never entirely alone. I could summon Lunette, or any other ghost whose soul had been bound to the ship. It was a warship, after all, and had likely seen many battles. There would be more than a few ghosts on board. I'd conjure them and force them to help me.

Toshiko's voice startled me out of my thoughts. "You have no magic in this cell. This prison is unique. It rids all power from the detainee. In here, you are practically human." She pronounced *human* with the same level of disgust one would have about rodents. "Your ghosts cannot help you here."

Her lips remained in a firm line, but in her eyes, I detected a toxic smile. Toshiko might have passed herself off as the dutiful guard dog at the Black Palace, but really, she was a feral wolf with razor-sharp teeth.

The revelation was terrible news, but it also confirmed something I'd struggled with since she appeared in the cell—her type of magic. Toshiko was a mind-reader. It made my heart tangle into a knot. I couldn't trust myself to say anything. I couldn't trust myself to think with her around. She would know my deepest thoughts and plans the moment they crossed my mind. Now I understood how Toshiko had managed to fool everyone in the palace. She knew everyone's intimate thoughts.

I grabbed the clothes the soldier had left for me and hurried into the bathroom. I had to get away from her. Just being close to Toshiko made me feel contaminated.

Could she plant thoughts in my head?

Twist my emotions?

I knew nothing about mind-readers. Lainie was a harmonist, and she had the power to change people's moods. I suspected mind reading worked in a similar way.

The bathroom had been supplied with soap and shampoo. There was an oval mirror on the wall. Toshiko wasn't wrong. My appearance was terrible. Back at the palace, before she had it set alight, I had been dressed as the sovereigns' necromancer, ready to make an appearance at the court and stand firm as the new accords were signed. The sovereigns had wanted me to look intimidating. My dress had been a stunning gown of black satin and silk, my eyes painted dark and smoky. Now, it was torn and crinkled, dark smudges ran down my cheeks, and my eyes were bloodshot. My skin had also taken on an unhealthy paleness. My dark auburn hair, which had been braided to perfection, now hung in messy clumps. I looked like a dark queen, dethroned and waiting for her head to be chopped off at the guillotine.

"Ten minutes," Toshiko snapped. She watched me through the door.

I briefly toyed with the idea of smashing my fist into the mirror, grabbing a sharp piece, and impaling it into her side. Her smug glare alerted me to the fact that she'd read the thought in my mind. I slammed the door, distancing myself as far as possible.

I climbed into the shower, relishing the heat of the water, until I remembered Toshiko's warning that it would switch off after five minutes. I scrubbed my body with soap and quickly washed my hair, wishing I had more time and more privacy to come up with a new plan.

Can Toshiko read thoughts between the walls, or does she have to look directly at me to know what I'm thinking?

I closed my eyes, hoping she was wrong about my necromancy being cut off. I had never heard of a cell that could strip away a prisoner's magic, but I supposed anything was possible. I calmed my breathing, forcing my mind to reach out for any souls that could be on the ship, but everything came back blank.

Damn it. Damn it. Damn it.

I tried again.

Lunette. Are you there? Please. I need your help.

Radio silence. The connection I had with Lunette, my most loyal ghost friend, didn't exist. Either that or she didn't want to see me naked in the shower. I suspected it was the former.

The water shut off.

Dabbing myself dry with a sorry excuse for a towel, I slipped into my new clothes. Khaki cargo pants, a long-sleeved trekking shirt, and a mountain jacket that fit snugly. I recalled the image I'd seen in the portal at the Isla Necropolis. Morgomoth's kingdom had been an island of volcanoes, a wasteland of fire and steaming craters. Was this gear to protect me from the elements?

I suppose I should be grateful Toshiko has given me proper clothes.

She could very well have given me nothing but a modest shift.

I stepped back into the cell, the door to the bathroom disappearing in an instant. The glamour smoothed over it, making the wall appear just that—a sturdy, inescapable wall.

"Are we going hiking?" I mocked.

I might have been a prisoner and utterly terrified, but at least I still had my self-respect and the ability to be sarcastic.

Toshiko pointed to a pair of hiking boots that must have been brought in while I'd been in the shower. The boots were exactly my size and had excellent grip. My feet sank into the cushioned insoles.

I eyed her suspiciously. "Where are we going?"

The expression in her gold eyes lightened. "Orthrask is no longer a mere island. It has grown and continues to do so. The port is some distance from the citadel. The clothes will safeguard you from the harsh terrain."

The port?

Citadel?

It was another sign of how far Morgomoth and his new kingdom had advanced. His land was growing, along with his power and control.

Toshiko inspected my appearance, a hint of relief crossing her face. "Once we make port, I will be back to collect you. Some *dear friends* who you know well will greet us and accompany our journey to the castle."

Dear friends?

Was one of them Lainie? No, I didn't think so. Lainie hadn't been able to look at me when she'd left me to die at the Isla Necropolis. She wouldn't arrive at the port with welcoming arms. I didn't think she'd advanced in the ULD's ranks to entitle her to the position either. If anything, Lainie was a scared little girl, trapped and regretting her decision. No, the people meeting us were high up.

Oh providence. Not Vulcan and Hadar.

My mind was scrambling now, clogged with panic. I couldn't think clearly.

Is Toshiko doing this, using her insidious mind power to scatter my thoughts?

"See you soon." She left the cell, her ominous words resonating across the walls.

The glamour reappeared, smoothing over the door. There one instant, gone the next. I hurried over to the wall and ran my hand across the stone. It was solid. I didn't know why I'd expected to slip through. It was another sign of how desperate and afraid I'd become.

Cool air touched the back of my neck, my damp hair sending goose bumps over my body. The ventilation had turned back on, and with it, the spell that kept me groggy or asleep.

No. I have to stay awake. I have to plan. I have to find a way out.

My eyes were heavy. Weakness tugged at my legs. If I continued to stand here, I'd tumble to the floor asleep. I forced my feet to take two hefty steps toward my metal sleeping shelf, but my legs buckled, and I had to use my arms to drag me the rest of the way. My arms soon gave out too. I became a useless heap on the cold floor. I shut my eyes, paralysed. The only thing that moved was the increasing beat of my pulse.

Jad, I wanted to scream, wishing he was here.

But Jad was likely dead, along with the rest of my friends.

I gasped, my parched throat burning. Tears streamed from my eyes.

I can't let Toshiko do this to me.

I can't let her win.

But she already had.

My mind provided me with one last operose thought before sleep finally took me in its clutches.

Uncertainty is the worse.

8

I STARTLED AWAKE, expecting Toshiko or her henchmen to shake me out of my stupor, but instead, I was… in a throne room.

What the…?

My eyes slowly settled, my inertia fading away. No, this wasn't a throne room. Not exactly. I'd been here before, only last time it had been crumbling apart, huge chunks of debris falling from the ceiling at the same time the floor had caved in. Now, the place was solid and seemed untouchable. The decorative chamber was adorned with frescoes, the columns inlaid with carved marble. Runes glowed on the ceiling, reminding me of the constellations in the night sky. In the centre of the chamber was a macabre plinth, not made of stone but of a series of humerus, radius, and ulna bones, which had been moulded together to form two giant hands. Phalanx bones had been shaped as fingers. Held secure between them was the Bone Grimoire.

An astonished gasp worked its way out of my throat.

No. Not possible. I'm dreaming. I have to be.

There was no way I could actually be back at the Isla Necropolis. It had been destroyed. The Bone Grimoire had gifted its magic to both Morgomoth and me. No longer containing power, the book had disintegrated into ash.

And yet, here it was.

The fact that I had dreamt of this bizarre scene wasn't the only alarming puzzle. Standing behind the book were five robed figures. When they raised their cowled heads, I saw only darkness.

Their voices carried across the chamber into my mind as one, intrusive and commanding.

"Welcome, Zaya Wayward."

CHAPTER 2

I gritted my teeth, pain radiating through my head at the sound of their hollow voices. Every muscle in my body strained. I was like a rubber band pulled tautly. Any farther and I would snap.

"Zaya," one of the robed figures repeated. *"Look at us."*

My eyes travelled to them. There didn't seem to be anything under those blood-red cloaks, which moved softly in the cool air. The creatures' forms were not solid. Whenever their robes moved, revealing what should have been a flash of skin or at least a hand, there was nothing. It was like watching someone hold bedsheets attached by strings, playing ghosts.

I shivered, the fine hairs along my arms erect. I couldn't be certain if I was seeing faces beneath their cowls or an illusion. Shiny and bone-smooth, they might have been skulls, but the shadows never allowed me to see clearly. The one thing that was present and that couldn't be denied was the stitching over their lips, thick and black and crusted over by age.

"Who are you?" My voice carried across the chamber in an endless echo. This was my dream. If they were going to intrude, they could damn well tell me who they were and what they wanted.

"You are here because we summoned you." They all spoke as one, vocals rising from a soundless whisper into a resonating cry. I had half a mind to dub them Hell's Choir.

"We are the Grand Masters."

I swallowed, doubt lingering inside me. "There were ten Grand Masters. There are only five of you."

"We five are your guides."

I shifted on my feet. In the short time I'd spoken to these people, they'd seemed to grow twice their size, and me smaller. "This place was destroyed. I watched it collapse to the ground. If this is a dream, then why does everything look and feel so real?" I pointed to the Bone Grimoire. "That doesn't exist anymore. I absorbed its power. The book is gone."

"You possess half its power," the robed figures corrected, their voices rising in a ragged chorus.

"Yeah, thanks for reminding me. Now, if you could send me back—"

I stopped, their words suddenly taking on meaning. "You five are with me? Does that mean I gained your powers?"

"Yes."

"And Morgomoth...?"

"Obtained the magic of our brothers and sisters. They serve him."

"Serve?"

I didn't like the sound of that.

"They are part of him now, as we are part of you."

I didn't like the sound of that either. These people were part of me? What exactly did that entail?

"We are in your mind, your soul, your magic."

Great. How intrusive. Now I had my own personal shrinks who could apparently summon me to imaginary places.

"You created this place."

A tap dance of fear shimmied up my spine. "Did you just read my mind?'

"We are in your mind, your soul, your magic," they repeated, as though I hadn't heard them the first time.

Their voices carried across the chamber, resonating along every surface in a ghostly caress. A tingling shiver skirted over my skin.

I shut my eyes and exhaled a breath. "The acoustics in this place make your voices"—*eerie as hell*, I wanted to say—"difficult to understand. Could one of you speak at a time, please?"

"We speak together. We are one."

Right. This entire situation was starting to feel useless.

"You must escape Toshiko and her men. You must not set foot on Orthrask as a prisoner. We have seen your path should this happen. You will die."

"I don't exactly have a choice. The cage I'm in has stripped my magic."

I felt a stab of fury at my own weakness.

"You will not always be in your cage."

That was true. At some point, Toshiko was going to have to let me out and hand me over into the custody of these *dear friends*. Would that be the time to, say… summon wrathful ghosts to do my bidding? I didn't like using the dead as a weapon. It had made my heart almost collapse with guilt when I'd resurrected fallen soldiers outside the Isla Necropolis. Granted, I had been trying to save the living, but still, it had left a sting inside me that had never entirely faded. The departed were meant to be at peace. Using them made me no better than Morgomoth.

"The dead will never be at peace while Morgomoth reigns. Flee the ship. Learn to summon the Neathror and Larthalgule blades and unite them as the Interitus blade."

"As what?"

"It is the blade of necromancers. It has never been wielded before."

I had been cold in my cage. Now, my body was running on ice. My hands trembled, my blood pounding in my ears. "And I'm supposed to just... what? Summon the blades at the tip of my fingers and create this Interitus blade? I wouldn't know where to start. I don't even know what this weapon does."

"*Neathror is the bringer of death. Larthalgule gifts life. Combined, the Interitus blade is capable of controlling both the dead and the living. Neither can ignore the commands of the blade's wielder.*"

My mind raced, the realisation striking me with terrifying clarity. "That was what Darius meant by the ultimate weapon."

I recalled the words the senator had spoken to me back at the Black Palace, before it had been burned to the ground. "*We need the Bone Grimoire, Zaya. Morgomoth cannot obtain it. If he learns the spell that merges the Larthalgule and the Neathror blades, then he'll create the ultimate weapon. If that happens, there will be no defeating him.*"

My heart contracted. "If Morgomoth gets his hands on the Interitus blade, he controls the living and the dead?"

Smiles curved the Grand Masters' pale lips, the stitches stretched taut. They looked dryly amused. Their silence was answer enough.

I choked back my gasp of despair. No wonder Morgomoth wanted the blade. He'd have control of every mind, living and dead. No one would have the ability to speak or even think clearly. They'd all be his subjects. He'd have no opposition. No force against him. It would be his word and nothing else.

Another, calmer insight settled in my mind, and I took my first easy breath since I'd woken in my cage. "Morgomoth needed the Bone Grimoire to find the spell that would combine the Neathror and Larthalgule blades. Without the spell, he can't create the Interitus blade. Right? The Bone Grimoire was destroyed. The spell is gone. He can never find the spell."

The Grand Masters' laughter filled my head. I couldn't tell if their cackles were directed at me with sarcasm or pity.

"The Bone Grimoire was not destroyed. It was absorbed by you and Morgomoth. Your minds are connected to it. Where do you think we are right now?"

"I thought we were in my head." I froze, panic climbing inside me again. "This is my dream, right?"

"This is your mind inside the Bone Grimoire."

I turned to the plinth where the spell book rested. "Then that means the spell is in there."

"Yes."

"And if both Morgomoth and I are linked to this place... then that means—"

Deadly shrieks tore through the chamber. They were the screams of something neither human nor caster, something monstrous and wicked.

I turned around, already knowing what I was about to see, but was still shocked by the unsettling reality before me. Shadows and smoke, as thick as ash clouds, rushed toward me with unnatural speed. The torches sputtered, the darkness closing in, leaving me in a moment of confused blindness. A violent flash of light erupted from the smoke and shadows, and my eyes settled on Morgomoth's cruel face.

Great. He's upgraded his storm of shadows with lightning.

Does that mean he's grown stronger?

I decided I really didn't want to know.

Bolts of shocking white forks struck the chamber floor, cracking the mosaic tiles. The light illuminated the horror of what Morgomoth had become. Blackened bones, charred, broken teeth, dark blood running through exposed veins. It reminded me of oily tar.

What had happened to Morgomoth to make him the creature out of a nightmare?

My breathing halted, fear seizing me the way it always did when he approached. He had no real body. The wraiths who swirled in and out of the smoke and shadows were what pieced him together. Their gnarled hands reached out for me. Pain and sorrow reflected from their blood-red eyes, and whenever they cried, their despair and madness came through their wailing cries.

These souls were trapped. There was something different about some of the wraiths, though. Five of the ghosts were hooded, their mouths stitched. Whenever I caught sight of their wispy faces beneath their cowls, their expressions were set with feral rage.

The Grand Masters.

Or what was left of them.

These were the poor masters whose necromancy had been obtained by Morgomoth. They were a part of him, a network of necromancy and the dead.

Morgomoth must have seen the naked terror on my face because he smiled. He made his way to the Bone Grimoire like a storm darkening the sky.

"He cannot obtain the book," the Grand Masters shouted, their breathless cry a long lament through my head. *"Take it. Now!"*

I dived, running as though my life depended on it. Maybe it did depend on it, because the storm of darkness swept through the chamber, chasing me like a tsunami.

I'm never going to outrun this.

No matter how much training, pain, and hardship I had pushed through as a cadet, after everything I had been through and managed to survive, I knew in that moment that I would never be strong enough to match Morgomoth. I could feel the darkness coming for me, ready to pummel me into minced meat. I was playing a fool's game to think I could ever beat him.

"That's not true." The Grand Masters' voices became an

unearthly scream in my head. *"Grab the book. Learn its magic. Learn the spell."*

The terror in their tone, as though they feared what might happen if I didn't save the Bone Grimoire, spurred me on. I couldn't let Morgomoth win.

Not now.

Not ever.

Swallowing a steady stream of curses, I lunged for the book. My hands clasped it.

Mine, I thought, feeling a small moment of triumph.

There was a pause, like everything had frozen in time. My elation dropped. I looked up to see the shadows closing in around me in a cresting wave. My heart thundered with horror, seeming to climb all the way up to my throat. Morgomoth's animalistic eyes were fastened on me. He reached for my hand, perhaps intent on breaking my wrist. No, he was going after the book. His lips, which were horribly scarred, like they'd been sewn together and ripped apart over and over, parted with a snarl.

That's when I saw what he held. Neathror. Somehow, in the blink of an eye, he'd summoned the weapon, the same athame-sabre I had struggled to conjure for months. Another sign of my weakness.

Lightning flashed, reflecting on the blade, making it appear as though it were made out of starred jewels, momentarily beautiful until it sliced the air, singing as Morgomoth drove it down. I quelled the urge to scream.

This is a dream. Wake up. Wake up!

The blade was nearly at my neck.

My heightened senses pulled me to action, and I lunged out of the way, Neathror barely missing my throat.

I dropped onto a cold, sterile surface.

Wait, what?

·I was on the floor in my cell, gasping for air, like I'd just woken from a nightmare.

A very real frigging nightmare.

I could still hear Morgomoth's high-pitched roar in my ears. The savage and unforgiving tone left me shaking and sweating. I crawled up onto my hands and knees, finding small comfort in the white walls that lined my cell, almost grateful that the fluorescent light burned too brightly. Anything to forget that terrible, suffocating darkness.

Was that all a bad dream?

Or did it really happen?

In my head?

No. In our *heads.*

The Grand Masters' necromancy was divided equally among Morgomoth and me. That meant their magic linked us. We had both been in that place. Our minds were connected.

I don't like this. I don't like this at all.

My head filled with white noise, and the walls started to blend together. Even the floor tilted, leaving me so disorientated that I had no idea what was right or upside down.

Calm down. This is just anxiety playing tricks with your mind.

I scrambled backward from the spinning walls, taking comfort in the centre of my cell. My hand landed hard on something behind me, and I gawped, too shocked to do anything else.

How is this possible? How is this here?

The Bone Grimoire had somehow followed me.

I touched the smooth ivory surface. It freaked me out a little that it was bone, melted down by stagma fire and moulded into a hardcover. Two skeleton hands had been laid decoratively on top. Where the backs of the hands should have been, exquisite sculptures of the sun and moon had been etched. I looked at the bones that lined the spine, a squeamish tumble rolling in my gut. Finger bones.

"Did you follow me here?"

Or had I somehow… taken it?

I shook my head.

No. Not possible.

The book doesn't exist anymore.

I recalled the words of the Grand Masters. *"The Bone Grimoire was not destroyed. It was absorbed by you and Morgomoth. Your minds are connected to it."*

"Have I somehow taken you out of my mind?"

I had to say it out loud to hear how truly crazy that sounded.

The book, of course, didn't answer.

Maybe I've finally lost it.

But just in case….

My fingers shook as I gently opened the spell book, not entirely sure what I wanted to find inside.

All my muscles spasmed.

The pages were empty.

I cannot frigging believe it.

I flicked through every vellum leaf, but not a single word, rune, or image leapt out at me. I shook the grimoire, hoping something might fall out. Nothing.

What is the point of having an empty book?

Are the spells hidden?

And if they were? How would I ever find the enchantment I needed?

A key rattled, shocking me back to reality. A part of the wall to my left slowly creaked open.

The Bone Grimoire dissipated into wispy smoke, which flew straight to my chest. I gasped, startled by the cold rush of air that bit into me like icy razors.

The book was hiding itself… inside me?

The door opened fully and Toshiko emerged, accompanied by six soldiers. Men who were no doubt loyal to her and had betrayed the Council of Founding Sovereigns and the Haxsan Guard. Judging by the bandages wrapped around their left hands, they'd cut the symbol of the Infinite Eye from their palms, the only magic that would have kept them bound to the Council and the sovereigns.

How long had Toshiko been working in the background, establishing her own lethal force?

Her golden cat eyes were lit with molten rage when she looked down on me. "Get up. We are nearly at the port. Something has happened. His Highness is upset."

I assumed *His Highness* meant Morgomoth.

Oh providence.

The coldness in my chest tightened, as though the book inside me sensed what was occurring.

I knew exactly what Morgomoth would be unhappy about.

And I knew "upset" would be an understatement.

CHAPTER 3

Toshiko's men bound my wrists in what appeared to be thick, ironclad manacles but, on closer inspection, were made out of the same substance as the walls in my cell.

Wonderful.

Toshiko wasn't taking any chances. She would make sure I was stripped of my magic the entire way to Orthrask.

I wondered where this unusual substance came from. I'd never heard of any metals—gold, silver, or bronze, or any minerals, for that matter—that could deprive a caster of their power. It must have been new alchemy. Had such sorcery existed before, the Council of Founding Sovereigns would long ago have employed it.

Alchemy.

I knew of only one alchemist who could accomplish a binding like this. She enjoyed experimenting with magic and producing twisted monsters and weapons. What would stop her from creating this?

Hadar.

"This way," Toshiko demanded, her gold eyes flaming.

I was led out of my cell and through the sprawling prison block, the guards surrounding me: two in the lead, two behind me, and one on either side. I had no chance of escaping. I experienced a small semblance of satisfaction when I saw that each man had his hand secured tightly on his weapon, which meant they weren't 100 percent convinced my manacles would hold. And to bind me in manacles in the first place meant Toshiko and her men were afraid of what I was capable of. It inspired me to hope.

I kept my head down, refusing to make eye contact with Toshiko, fearful it would give her direct access to my thoughts. I still had no idea how her magic worked.

They don't know that I have the Bone Grimoire inside me.

Granted, the book was empty, and I had no idea how to use it, but still….

Morgomoth won't hurt me if he knows I have the book. He'll want to trade it.

Toshiko hurried ahead, leading us up a flight of thin stairs and through various identical passages in the ship. I hadn't seen a good deal of the vessel when I'd first woken from my drug-induced sleep on the deck. I'd been too traumatised by seeing the Black Palace alight, the building shooting jets of flame into the city of Muiren. And the screaming. I'd never forget the horrible wails that cried into the night, chilling me until my very bones felt solid with ice.

Thinking about it, despair filled the pit of my stomach. It took all of my effort to not cry. My friends were likely dead. Jad was likely dead. I had no one left. Nothing. All I had was the knowledge that I had to destroy Morgomoth and stop his deadly reign. I had to do it alone. And I had no idea where to start.

And that's only if I escape.

A grisly cry from the guard beside me made me jump, his shout right at my ear as he fell. His leg had been cut at the back of the knee. Blood soaked from the wound, running like a broken fountain onto the concrete floor. He stared at me with brazen horror.

I shrugged. "Don't look at me. I didn't do it."

Toshiko spun around, her painted face a perfect mask of outrage. "We're not alone."

Her men instantly drew their weapons, but they weren't fast enough. Something struck them, cutting at arms and legs. The slashes weren't deep, but they were serious enough to send blood flying into the air, the walls stained with red dribbles. My entire body trembled with the effort to duck the falling bodies, the men wailing as they were hit with more abrasions from behind. I'd seen some terrible injuries in the past, but death by a thousand cuts seemed to be a horrifically drawn-out way to die.

What the hell is going on?

It's almost like something invisible is attacking.

Attacking them. *Not me.*

Toshiko grabbed my arm, her black nails biting into my skin. She was panting through her gritted teeth, reminding me of a wild, snarling animal. Something collided into her, and she screamed as she tumbled backward like a knocked-over bowling pin. She kicked and thrashed on the floor, her eyes widening in dismay. Something had her in its grasp. She was gurgling and making horrible whimpering sounds, and I realised with a stab of fear that she couldn't breathe. Whatever the thing was that gripped Toshiko by the throat, it was suffocating her. And not just her. All the men had lost consciousness; they were slumped on the floor like a pile of discarded carcasses.

I ran, horror registering in every fibre of my body. I didn't get far before I slammed into something solid. And fleshy.

"Ouch. Watch where you're going."

I flinched, startled by the familiarity of the voice.

A friendly face materialised from the thin air.

"Annaka."

She brought a dirty, bloody finger to her lips, urging me to be quiet. Her grin was huge. A pirate's smile. "You didn't think we'd let Toshiko kidnap you, did you?"

In her hand was an athame-sabre, still wet with the guards' blood. She motioned behind me.

Appearing as though they'd stepped through an invisible portal were Marek and Bronislav, keyed up with battle fervour. Marek was sweating, his short-clipped hair spotted with blood that was not his own. Bronislav had a few purple marks on his face, showing he'd met someone's fist at some point. There was relief and exhaustion in Marek's eyes when he saw me, his smile genuinely warm, but it disappeared the moment he focused on the unconscious soldiers. Bronislav just looked like he was hell-bent on causing destruction, his face a mask of icy rage. Both men's athame-sabres were red where the blood dripped, making sickening splashes on the floor.

"What the hell?" I spat, having no other words to describe my shock and joy at finding my friends alive.

"I made us invisible," Annaka explained, her voice crisp but edged. She grabbed my arm, leading me down the passage with quick footsteps. "There are more guards coming, and we need to keep moving. Our plan didn't exactly work out."

"Plan?"

I glanced over my shoulder. Marek and Bronislav kept up behind us, their eyes examining every passage we passed.

How many more of Toshiko's guards are they expecting to spring at us at any moment?

"How are you here?" My emotions were both a whirlwind of elation and fear. "I thought you were all dead."

"We are very much alive," Annaka said. "We fled the Black Palace and snuck on board the *Crown of Glory*."

The Crown of Glory. *So that's the name of this ship.*

"I've been keeping us invisible throughout the voyage," she

continued. "When I've been too tired to control my magic, we've been hiding out in the prison, trying to find a way to break you out of that cell."

I stared over my shoulder. Despite my blood still thrumming with adrenaline, I smiled at Marek and Bronislav.

They were alive. And, for the most part, okay.

A part of my elation crumbled.

Where is Talina?

Jad?

We had sprinted around a corner when Annaka halted suddenly, nearly causing me to topple right into her. The stillness in all her muscles told me she was listening intently. I cast an uncertain glance at Bronislav, questioning if his supersensitive hearing had picked up on the same sounds Annaka detected. His heavy breathing turned silent, which meant something was coming. It must have been big. And dangerous.

I couldn't hear a thing. If the person, creature, or monster that approached was dead, my sixth sense would have picked up on it, but I still had the damn manacles on, and they numbed all my magic.

Up ahead, the lights flickered once, twice, and then went out.

"Oh providence." Annaka's voice sounded small and afraid.

It was the awful, high-pitched wheezing that shook me to the core. Detaching itself from the dark, a figure hobbled into the passage. Its clawed hands scraped the walls, making its entrance with dramatic effect. The creature stopped, sniffing the air. For a moment, it looked like it might have stumbled back into the dark again, but then its overly large nostrils caught a whiff of us. The creature turned its head.

I swallowed, a spasm of nausea shooting through me.

Chak-lork.

The creature's milky eyes settled on us, gleaming from the ship's fluorescent lighting. It was one of Morgomoth's water demons, judging by its appearance. Its body was soaked. Fat, watery splodges dripped off its carcass, only to be sucked in like a sponge through its feet as it advanced with lumbering footsteps.

Another of the chak-lorks emerged. Then another, and another, until an entire mass of the drowned dead barricaded the passage.

Hideous giggles resonated down the passage behind us. I whirled. More chak-lorks had arrived, barricading each exit. The scent of them was horrible—the odorous reek of dead fish, left to float in the hot sun.

We're trapped.

"Make us invisible," Marek hissed. His face was tightly strained, his smooth skin now tense from worry, making the scar that ran across his cheek to his half-slashed ear that much more apparent.

"I can't." Annaka was pressed up against the wall. "They've already seen us."

It was almost comical the way the chak-lorks approached so slowly, like they really had just stepped out of a watery grave and were getting their bearings. I knew they could advance with alarming speed in a heartbeat, though. Their jagged, stumpy teeth chomped down, causing their own lips and gums to bleed. Their sparse hair hung around their faces in wet strings. They knew we had nowhere to go. They were savouring this predatory moment.

"You're kidding me, right?" Bronislav stared at Annaka with bewilderment.

"No, I'm not. I don't have any energy left to make us invisible." She was smiling, which was more disconcerting than anything else I'd witnessed since I'd woken on this cursed ship. "I'm using all my strength to keep *him* invisible."

Gruesome shouts echoed down the passage. I crammed my bound hands against my mouth, sickened by the image. The chak-lorks were being sliced apart, as though an invisible blade were shearing neatly through throats, arms, and torsos. Dismembered body pieces skittered across the floor before liquefying into thin, watery blood. They never morphed back into solid forms. Whatever was destroying the creatures was making a permanent job of their demise.

Him?

I dared not hope, but my heart betrayed me anyway, beating faster with anticipation.

When the last chak-lork was disembowelled, the four sections of its hacked body collapsing into a mess of gore, Annaka let go of a relieved breath. Her invisibility charm vanished.

Jad appeared like a summoned spirit, as imperious and intimidating as any dark prince. The athame-sabre by his side burned with fire magic. Never in my life had I seen a blade like that. It reminded me of a blazing torch, ready to melt anything it touched.

It's actually made of fire.

My tongue locked up when I looked at him—really looked at him. I couldn't swallow, let alone speak. Jad had moved like a silent assassin, and for a painful moment, I feared I was seeing Trajan Stormouth again, but his eyes were dark, not red, and my panic dissipated. We stared at each other across the space that separated us. He was assessing me, perhaps scanning for injuries. I could have sworn there was something that almost appeared to be regret in his eyes, but the illusion passed. He was as aloof and intimidating as the day I first met him.

His gaze turned to the others. "Keep to the plan and get on deck."

Marek had traded his athame-sabre for a cast-shooter. He loaded the weapon. "What about you?"

Jad ignored him, striding toward the watery mass of chak-lorks that was gaining upon us from the other end of the passage. He turned to me, the colour in his cheeks fading the closer he neared. I was poison to him, and I saw the animosity on his face, the way his hollow eyes flamed from the discomfort of being close. He raised his athame-sabre.

Oh providence. He's going to strike me down. He really does hate me.

This was the price of the Bone Grimoire. There was no doubt or second-guessing. Jad's love had turned to loathing.

Before I could scream or even shout a protest, the blade came down, the heat chafing my wrists. My heavy manacles clattered to the floor, as black and crispened as toast where the weapon had sliced them.

I stared at Jad, my heart stopping dead.

He gave me a look that felt capable of shattering my bones and walked away, ready to take on the band of swarming chak-lorks. "Get her out of here."

Was it our muddled romantic past that made him act so cold, or was my presence truly disgusting to him?

There was so much I wanted to ask.

What happened to you?

When did your revulsion for me start?

But this wasn't the time nor the place.

A slow grin swept across Annaka's face. "Let the fire-wielder do his thing. We, on the other hand, need to get the hell out of here." She removed the cast-shooter from her holster and cocked the weapon. "Let's go, Sleeping Beauty."

"I'm not asleep anymore," I bitterly fired back.

We hurried out of the passage, stepping over the watery chunks that had once been chak-lorks. Marek and Bronislav kept close behind us, their weapons raised for anything, either dead or alive, that might jump out. The heavy lines of their shoulders were tense. They must have been anxious to get on with the plan, whatever that was. I stole a glance down the passage at Jad, reluctant to leave him behind. He was already making quick work of mutilating the creatures, their macabre shrieks piercing and guttural.

"Don't worry about him." Annaka's tone was firm. Her eyes were fixed ahead on the stairs. "He'll be fine. It's *you* we need to get out."

There was no point turning around to help Jad; he'd just shoot me another frosty glare. Judging by his stealth and speed, his athame-sabre practically singing as he swung it through water-logged flesh, Annaka was right. He'd be fine.

We sped up the stairs and down various passages where the lights flickered so badly, it was almost a strobe light party. Even the ventilators, which circulated cool air, switched on and off.

What's going on outside the ship to cause havoc inside it?

The floor bucked suddenly. The four of us were thrown against the wall, then tossed onto the floor, the ship shuddering like it was in the epicentre of an earthquake. We stood, wobbling to steady ourselves. Air rushed through my throat in a whoosh. The pain in my chest sharpened enough that breathing hurt.

What the hell is happening this time?

Fierce vibrations rippled up my legs, but there was another kind of motion too. A judder. And it felt familiar.

Marek lifted his head, his lips turning pale. "Did the ship hit something?"

"Typical bloody amateurs," Annaka spat. "They must have collided with one of the Bone Towers."

I managed to clamp down my slew of angry cuss words, but Annaka let every expletive out.

Bronislav's olive skin shone with sweat. "Are we sinking?"

Annaka snorted. "Probably."

"Not again," Marek moaned.

The sinking of the *Velorosa* had been a traumatising experience. I didn't fancy a replay either.

"Let's move," Annaka insisted.

She seemed to know exactly where she was going, which made me wonder how long this plan had been in motion. How many days had my friends been hiding, invisible and silently plotting? An invisibility charm of that power would have taken an immense amount of energy on Annaka's part. I was surprised she was still standing.

"This way." She led us up a stairway to the upper levels. Red warning lights flashed and sirens blared, instructing everyone to evacuate immediately.

Yep. Definitely must be sinking.

My muscles were still cramped and ached from lack of movement, but my necromancy senses had come alive and were ticking. A rancid smell filled my nostrils. It was the scent of decay and festering wounds, of earth burning, and the terrible aroma of ash and fire meeting the sea.

Annaka pulled back the double doors to the deck. Whether it was my necromancy or the Bone Grimoire inside me, I sensed darkness, vast and unyielding. Coldness drove into my skin like needles.

I looked out at the world beyond. Orthrask, Morgomoth's kingdom, was a land of darkness, lit only by fires. Ash rained down like snow. There was no greenery or lushness to be found. Everything was just rock, dust, and rivers of lava. Far in the distance—maybe several days' travel, judging by the outcroppings and jagged peaks that protruded from the land like sharp teeth—was the ring of deadly, cataclysmic volcanoes, all belching smoke and flame. They surrounded one large volcano in the centre.

I didn't have the gift of super sight, but even from here, I knew the edifice built into the crater was Morgomoth's castle. His kingdom of death.

CHAPTER 4

I swore, my heart hammering against my ribs.

How could they have built a castle of such enormity so fast?
Dark magic. It has to be.

Again, it was another testament of Morgomoth's power. Even
the land, which was as barren as a desert, was shifting. Large rocks
and heavy peaks rose from the sea. It made the Bone Towers look
like decrepit tombstones.

Orthrask was what the Dark Divide looked like when it was
unleashed into the living world. This land was born of evil and
corrupted by it. Whatever trees had tried to grow here were
burned to mere husks. I couldn't see any wildlife. No creature
would be stupid enough to live in this poisoned environment,
surely?

A guttural howl ripped through the air.

Hot anger laced Annaka's shout. "Duck."

We'd barely made it out the door when a large projectile of
fire came tearing toward us. *No.*

I stood corrected about wildlife in Orthrask, because it wasn't
a weapon that nearly burned us into cinders. Unless stagma could

be referred to as a weapon. The magnificent but deadly creature dived, opening its massive jaws to belch a jet of fire across the deck. Heat licked my skin, every hair on my body feeling as though it had been singed. The bridge was incinerated in an instant, the screams quickly wiped out by the whooshing flames. I didn't want to think about what condition the *Crown of Glory*'s crew would be left in. If there was even anything of them left.

I kept low to the deck, following Annaka as she swerved through the falling debris and fire, often throwing terrified glances over my shoulder to make sure Marek and Bronislav were behind us. Smoke hindered my vision, and all I could do was trust that Annaka knew where she was going. Even as prepared as my friends had been for this rescue, they could never have planned for this.

Up in the sky, the stagma pivoted, flying in for another attack. Its leathery wingspan was twice the length of any carrier-hornet, its black scales glinting against the flames, making its body appear coppery. Barbs ran all the way down its spine, continuing along its long tail, which ended like a spiked mace. This time it went for the stern, shooting a stream of fire at the *Crown of Glory*'s lower deck.

I watched, gobsmacked, as another stagma, this one redder than the lava that streamed through the land, joined its companion. It dived for the ship, then at the last second rose, using its gigantic talons to swoop down on Toshiko's loyal soldiers. It grabbed them in fistfuls, squeezing tight. Even from this distance, I fancied I could hear spines cracking and veins popping. The soldiers' screams only seemed to encourage the creature. It soared into the air to drop the men and women from a great height. They either fell into the infernos that raged across the ship or hit the water like concrete.

We weren't sinking at all. And we'd never collided with a Bone Tower. Stagma were attacking the *Crown of Glory*.

Why would they attack? They work for Morgomoth?

The Bone Towers had been their home.

And yet...

Maybe they aren't impressed that they have an intruder in their midst.

Maybe... they haven't sided with Morgomoth at all.

A slimmer of hope spread through me.

Maybe they're fighting the ULD.

Another of the vicious creatures appeared, blasting more heat and flames across the ship. This stagma was an impressive green, its scales shining like emeralds. Smaller than the others, possibly female. Which made her more vicious. Her green eyes were alight with hunger, and I recognised the determination in that beautiful, wicked expression. She nose-dived straight into the *Crown of Glory*, the ship's middle breaking apart in an explosion of timbers, molten metals, and burning wreckage. The stagma sliced through every level until she reached the ocean, projecting deadly waves across the sea. Ripples of destruction travelled over the deck, the surface beneath me tilting dangerously.

Marek grabbed me before I lost my footing. "Move. To the lifeboats."

The bow was rising, becoming more vertical each second. I could just make out the stern through the smoke, which was a mirror image of us. I imagined the propellers lifting out of the water, slicing like a helicopter's blades through the air.

"Jad," I shouted to Marek, my voice hoarse. There was so much noise, so much choking fumes that I couldn't be certain if he heard me.

Marek gripped my wrist, forcing me to the handrail. Our feet were starting to slide out beneath us.

I made the mistake of looking down. Toshiko's soldiers were tumbling off the deck, plummeting into the water. They disappeared under the surface, never rising. No doubt suction had pulled them under.

Annaka and Bronislav were already climbing over the rail. Annaka shouted something. I think she may have said, "Jump."

So much for getting onto a lifeboat.

I was grateful when Marek helped me over the rail but ashamed of how much I relied on him. Whatever spell had been pumped into that cell had weakened me.

"We can't leave Jad." My voice was hardly a croak.

Providence, Jad had been right where the green stagma dived into the ship.

No.

Annaka and Bronislav leapt, tumbling precariously down the side of the ship. They barely made a splash in the sea, meaning either it didn't hurt or we were so high up that anything from this distance appeared small.

I clung to the railing. My head was spinning. The dread in my body had drilled right through the bone to my marrow.

"Zaya. Jump." Marek whacked me on the back.

I lost my grip. My breath sucked out of me, I fell for what felt like forever, the horror of every second dragged out. I hit the water, my body overcome with agony. Suction dragged me down, an unrelenting pull not even the current could fight. I couldn't see anything. There was nothing but darkness and suffocation. Stupidly, I opened my mouth, an instinctive response to breathe. Water rushed into my throat, my already-whirling head going dim.

Kick, you idiot. Get to the surface.

I thrashed, the muscles in my legs protesting from the strain. Light appeared above. I forced my arms to reach for it, swimming frantically upward. I sliced through the surface, so close to the ship that the air was unbearably hot, my skin burning. The back of my throat felt as though it had a razor cutting through it.

"Zaya." My name sounded distant, though I suspected it was shouted right at my ear.

I swivelled around. Even that slight movement was an effort.

Marek grabbed my shoulder. His eyes were red, possibly from the seawater, and the scar that ran across his cheek to his partly severed ear was wet and shiny in the firelight. "Swim. Before the ship pulls us under."

I forced my arms and legs into a freestyle, following him through the waves. I supposed I should have been grateful that the sea was relatively calm, but that could change in a heartbeat, more so when we were this close to Orthrask, where I suspected the weather was unpredictable and always dangerous.

A lifeboat floated ahead. Annaka and Bronislav were already on board. They pulled Marek up, his shoulder muscles straining against the force. Groggily, I summoned the last of my energy and reached the boat. Annaka and Bronislav tugged me aboard, letting me drop in exhaustion on the small deck.

I looked up into the sky, wishing I could see the night stars. It was so dark, it had to be night. But maybe the sun never shone in this part of the world anymore.

Providence, help me.

Jad.

I clambered up to sitting, aghast at the horror silhouetted against the smoky sky. The ship was sinking, both severed parts plunging into the sea.

"No." My voice was no more than a whisper.

No.

"Jad," I rasped, my voice so quiet, I didn't think anyone heard me.

The *Crown of Glory* had vanished forever. The sea flattened out, undisturbed, as though it hadn't just swallowed an entire vessel and everyone on board.

"Zaya, it's all right." Marek was in front of me. He wrapped a blanket around my shoulders and rubbed my arms, trying to keep me warm.

All right?

How could any of this be all right?

Jad was....

I couldn't think it. It hurt too much to acknowledge that Jad might be—

"Zaya."

The new voice startled me. I recognised it. Through all the darkness, a shred of relief floated inside me seeing her safe and well, though I couldn't find the words to say anything to her.

Her jade eyes watched me. Her voice sounded distant when she spoke to the others. "She's in shock."

I'm not in shock, Talina.

I was past shock. That had come and gone months ago. Very little could astonish me now.

But grief was another thing. Grief chiselled deep in my heart, creating a hole that could never be filled. Not with courage, or hope, or love. I'd lost so much in the past. I didn't think I could take it anymore.

Talina settled on her knees in front of me with a first-aid kit. She flicked a lock of her honey-blonde hair over her shoulder.

"Drink this." She handed me a glass phial filled with a clear liquid.

"Will it knock me out?"

I really hoped the answer would be yes.

"No, but it will lessen the shock."

That works too.

I grabbed the spell and swallowed it down, the taste minty and not at all what I'd been expecting. Normally, healing potions tasted foul.

I briefly wondered how long Talina had been on the lifeboat.

She must have been hiding out here this entire time, considering there were rucksacks at the boat's bow.

Yes, my friends definitely had this planned.

"Better?" Talina watched me with a mixture of uncertainty and alarm.

I nodded. The potion had worked fast. My trembling hands had stilled, and my breathing had slowed. Even my chattering teeth had stopped.

"Jad?" I looked at them all for answers. "He could be dead."

Why aren't any of them in as much anguish as me?

Marek tilted forward on the balls of his feet. "It will take more than that to kill him. Jad's changed. I'm still not entirely sure what happened after the Isla Necropolis. He's more… lethal, somehow. Darker."

I looked at the lieutenant, stricken by his words. I wasn't sure if it was seawater or tears that still hindered my vision.

Before I could ask Marek to elaborate, a heinous shriek tore across the sea. It was a cry filled with such loathing, such hostility and aggression, that my stomach twisted into a knot.

Talina swallowed heavily, her emerald eyes wide. She was looking at the expanse of land that made up Morgomoth's kingdom.

Shielding my eyes from the glare of flames, I scanned the cliffs and the beach. The sand was black. Even the dock was made of volcanic rock, which was gleaming so harshly that it caused spots to burst across my sight. Wails, cries, and snarls filled the sky, this time followed by the unmistakable whinny of a horse. A flash of lightning illuminated the Four Revenants at the end of the pier, mounted on smoky, black horses.

Old friends indeed.

They'd upgraded since I'd last seen them. The revenants wore dark cloaks, giving me the impression that I was looking at four medieval depictions of the Grim Reaper. They tore on the reins,

36

the powerful horses beneath them rearing on their muscled back legs. I imagined riled frustration coursing through each of the wraiths. They must have watched the *Crown of Glory* sink. Hopefully, they thought everyone on board had drowned. If they reported to Morgomoth that I was dead, then perhaps it would buy me some time to come up with a plan, because right now, I was running on empty.

Please turn around now. Please go away.

But the Four Revenants never left the pier. Their cloaks wouldn't allow me to see clearly, but I quickly realised from the movements of their cowls that they were scanning the sea. Searching for survivors.

Searching for me.

Fear roared in my veins. "We need to be invisible. Now."

Marek responded with a grave nod. "Annaka," he whispered. His astounded gasp alerted me that something was wrong.

I spun around. Annaka was lying facedown at the bow near the rucksacks. Bronislav scrambled forward and gently took her in his arms to turn her around. Her head fell back, her long cornrows trailing over his arm. Her beautiful ebony skin was saturated in sweat, and her lips were colourless.

Bronislav stared at me with unabashed terror. The sight of it made my own blood run cold. "She's burned herself out."

Annaka had passed out. Bronislav gently slapped her cheeks, urging her to wake up with a soft whisper, but the pirate remained motionless.

It's going to take her time to recover. Time we don't have.

"Duck," Talina hissed, her teeth tightly clenched.

A trail of light spanned across the sea—a spotlight searching for us. We flattened ourselves to the wood planks. The board and oar beneath me were cold and wet, but the discomfort was nothing compared to the shock of the light that sped past, the smoky air momentarily lit up.

Please don't see the lifeboat.

An empty lifeboat just drifting would look suspicious.

The boat dipped, sloshing water the only sound. Marek was biting down on his lip, his eyes squeezed tightly, as though he were hoping that by not looking at the light, it would go away. Bronislav was shielding Annaka with his body, his startled face searching the sky. The beam of light trailed over us again, reminding me of a beacon from a lighthouse. Talina pressed a hand over her mouth.

The longer we remained suspended in fear, the more uncomfortable I grew. My lower back muscles spasmed. My upper body was twisted in an awkward way, thanks to me diving for cover. My right foot began to tingle. If I remained like this, pins and needles would attack me all over.

Go away. Go away. Leave.

But my plea went unanswered.

Light beamed down onto the lifeboat, so bright that I could see nothing but a luminous glow. I shut my eyes, feeling that burn linger on my skin, unbearably hot, like I'd gotten too close to a hearth. A trickle of sweat flowed down my temple. Another worked a circuitous route over my cheek, finding its way onto my upper lip.

They've seen the boat.

Everything went quiet. Even the sea had fallen silent. The air felt strange. Luck wasn't on our side, and I imagined our boat in the midst of a terrible electrical storm that was about to rain havoc upon us. A dead scent clung to the air. It smelt like… chaklorks. I had an image of the waterlogged creatures rising from the sea, swarming onto the boat like a mound of skittering insects and pulling us under the surface. I tried to shake the vision away, hoping it wasn't a premonition.

The light never left. It continued to bob spottily on us, the seconds painfully slow.

There was a sound, like the tide coming in but on a massive scale.

Every part of me went numb. That sound....

I'd heard it before on the night the Four Revenants were raised from the seabed. Water rising and churning, cresting over in a single, destructive wave.

Four wretched shrieks sliced across the bleak sea.

They've found us.

CHAPTER 5

Marek was the first to move. "Grab an oar. We need to row."

Row? We can't outrow them.

I scrambled up to sitting, following Marek's order regardless, and took one of the oars. It barely made a splash as I lowered it into the water, and I had to hold on tight to prevent the sea from ripping it straight out of my hands. In the time since the Four Revenants had found us—what seemed to be the space of a heart-beat—the ocean had become a raging monster. Tumultuous waves threatened to capsize us. Talina and Bronislav struggled with the oars. My upper arms and chest ached. I'd been built for athame-sabres, cast-shooters, and combat, but a rower I was not. Annaka was still unconscious at the bow, mercifully oblivious to the chaos around us.

Marek shouted over the roar of the waves. "We need to make shore. There are caves we can hide in."

He pointed somewhere behind him, but against the white-wash of waves, the smoky air, and bursts of white lightning, it was difficult to make out any land.

We're travelling blind.

Talina's face went stark white, her features set in grim horror. I risked looking over my shoulder. The Four Revenants were advancing. They travelled across the water, their horses sprinting through the waves, powerful hooves beating in time with my raging heart. Too late, I recalled how they could manipulate water. The sea seemed to ebb and flow around the revenants, the waves under their spell. The wind had tossed their cowls aside. They were just as terrible as I remembered. Wraiths made of nothing but bone and scales, held together with seaweed and the sharpest seashells I'd ever seen. The revenants wore golden war horns around their necks, which they took to their mouths. The endless, piercing cry from the instruments made me feel like spiders were crawling all over my skin. I didn't know if the sound was to elicit a war cry or if it was to signal that the revenants were on the hunt.

The sea around us bubbled, the fountaining jets morphing into new forms. Fear crackled through all my veins.

Chak-lorks.

When they raised their heads, their lips were grinning. Their bodies were fish-bitten and slimy, and I questioned how many weeks they had been drifting in the water.

"Not these guys again." Marek's fingers strained on the oar as he pulled and pushed in rotations.

Bronislav's astounded gaze settled on him. "You've met these horsemen before?"

The revenants were gaining on us too fast, the chak-lorks on all fours like wolves, tearing through the water toward us. They really did look like some kind of ancient hunt reborn into the world to cause terror.

Even if we make it to shore, we'll never outrun them. It's impossible.

The Four Revenants' depthless eyes met mine. Inside them, I saw nothing but primitive, animalistic hunger. When they smiled, their bared teeth ended in fine points, filed down to be more menacing.

It was a miracle we had escaped them in the past, but it was obvious our luck had run out. We'd never make it to the shore. I didn't even know where the shore was, period.

A wave lifted us on the starboard side, nearly capsizing the boat. Talina screamed and dropped the oar. I clung to the edge, gripping on for dear life as the port side went under. Water inundated me, a shock to my nose and lungs. My chest burned, pain spiralling into the back of my head as the pressure built into my ears.

But there was another sensation too. Sorrow and torment crushed me. Something was suffering far below near the seabed. Something that was dead. A soul trapped in a broken body, incapable of moving on. My necromancy felt it acutely.

The current pushed the lifeboat back to the surface. I gasped, sucking in mouthfuls of air, my nostrils stinging as water trailed out. I searched for my oar, but regrettably, I must have dropped it.

No, no, no, no.

Now we were down to two oars.

"Zaya." Marek's shout was barely audible over the destructive waves.

I ignored him, forcing my magic to concentrate on that terrible, agonised soul below. Whatever it was, the creature was large. It had to be for me to be able to sense it at this magnitude.

What are you?

More importantly, can you help us?

I sent more of my necromancy magic into the sea, diving deep, feeling for the cold spot that meant a wraith was present. The poor thing was so panicked, so broken down and lost, that I sensed the soul flinch.

No. I had got it wrong. It wasn't a large beast. It was a humongous ocean dweller. It had to be at least fifty metres if my necromancy was correct. Judging by its suffering, it had died from numerous wounds. A very painful and slow death.

"Don't be afraid," I mind-spoke, trying to keep the soul calm. *"I will help. I'll guide you to the otherworld. But first, I need you to help me. And... I'm sorry to have to do this to you."*

I hated using the dead. I hated controlling them the way Morgomoth summoned and used wraiths for his bidding, but we needed saving, and this was the only way I could think to do it.

"Rise," I instructed.

Marek and Bronislav had stopped rowing. Their gazes were frozen on me, their faces perfect expressions of horror. Talina scrambled away, her pale cheeks now a shade of green. She let out a dismayed moan and buried her face in Marek's shoulder, no longer able to look at me.

I stared at my hands. Dead hands. My fingers were pale and ringed with black veins, as though I myself had just crawled out of a grave. I could only have imagined what my face must have looked like. This had happened to me once before, back on the Scarmouth beach when the Four Revenants were first resurrected. I suspected it had happened many times since then, but on all those occasions when I had controlled the dead, I'd simply never been aware, too focused on the sheer amount of necromancy I had to summon in order to wield it.

This was the cost of necromancy. My own heart stopped beating in order to command the infinite magic. No wonder Morgomoth had the permanent appearance of death. He was practically a wraith himself because he tapped into the boundless magic.

There was no time to explain it to my friends, because at that moment, the soul I'd conjured erupted from the sea with an ear-splitting roar, the creature's wet, shiny scales glinting from the fires that raged across Orthrask. I nearly fell out of my seat, startled by how large the beast truly was. A sea serpent. I'd once read in a history book that the sea serpents were believed to be related to stagma, but it could never be proven. The serpents tended to stay in the depths where they remained undisturbed. No one could get close to one, unless a serpent rose to attack a ship, and then... well, the result was always death.

I understood the theory now. This magnificent creature had a similar head and facial shape to the stagma, but its mouth was definitely that of a snake, only it had ten fangs that protruded from its mouth.

The serpent dipped and dived in the waves, its impressive body flexible enough to twist in knots—knots I imagined could break apart a ship. Long barbs that sliced through the water ran down its spine. The serpent had terrible suckers along its belly and large fins that doubled as wings.

Providence, save us. It can fly.

It shot out of the water, fins expanding into leathery wings, which flapped gracefully in the sky. The serpent bellowed a roar that was part wail, part aggression. It stared at me, milky eyes not seeing but waiting for instruction. The creature was definitely dead, animated only by my necromancy. Some of its scales had started to decompose, and where I spotted flesh, it was slimy from decay. An awful slash made a terrible mess of its side, allowing me to see some of its black insides. This was what had killed it. A wound that had slowly drained it of blood.

"I'm sorry."

The serpent didn't respond, only waited for my next command.

Please, it seemed to beg. *End this. Let me move on.*

I swallowed, guilty that I couldn't grant the serpent its wish. Not right away, at least. *"Attack them. Stop them from gaining on us, and then you can pass on to the next world. I promise."*

I didn't have to put much sentiment into my request. The serpent dived. The attack was brutal, a cacophony of screams and shrieks that were unnatural to the world as its humongous teeth bit into the chak-lorks, chewing them up like gum and spitting out limbs. The serpent went for the Four Revenants next. It was the first time I'd seen the wraiths appear rattled, their horses now rearing because of fear. The serpent twisted around them, its massive jaws coming down in one effortless chomp. Just the sound of it rattled my own teeth.

"Row," Marek shouted.

The serpent was giving us the time we needed to flee. I didn't know if the Four Revenants were dead. I didn't think so. You couldn't kill what wasn't alive, but you could distract them.

I scrambled across the boat and grabbed the oar, helping Bronislav row through the tumultuous sea. Talina and Marek did the same next to us. I refused to look up, concentrating only on the oar, trying very hard to not listen to the unnatural combat taking place on the sea.

"I will be back. I promise I will be back once the revenants are gone."

I didn't know if the serpent heard me. I only hoped that it didn't think it had been abandoned.

My head was pounding, either from all the magic I was using or because of the adrenaline running through my blood. Salt spray lashed at my skin, the stings along my face and hands indicating that I suffered from more than a few abrasions. The shore was nowhere in sight. Either Marek had gotten it wrong and we were rowing out to sea, or the heavy smoke provided too much cloud cover.

A wave struck us from the side, nearly toppling our little boat. Another wave crested, the surge pushing us with freakish momentum.

We're in the surf.

Talina cried out. The powerful swell had gained another oar. She looked at her empty hands, outraged by our bad fortune, but that was nothing compared to the look of dread that suddenly appeared across Marek's face. His eyes went impossibly wide.

I turned, terror clutching me. The next wave was the height of a house.

Marek's shout teetered on hysteria. "Grab the rucksacks and hold on."

There wasn't time to do either. The wave peaked, a wall of white water crushing us like a fist. I had no idea if I'd been thrown from the boat or if the water had simply inundated me. The sea pulled me from one direction to another, as though it had a vendetta to rip me in two. My body was stretched and bent in impossible positions, and I was tossed over and over again in what felt like a never-ending explosion of force.

I washed up on the shore, the strength knocked out of me. It hurt even to breathe. A twinge started in my chest, which then escalated into a relentless throbbing, and I bent over and vomited water. It had a strange taste. Not salty but rather metallic and bitter.

The volcanoes. They've unnaturally affected the sea.

We didn't stand a chance of finding fresh water on this island. The rivers, the lakes, the streams—if there were any—would likely be acidic and liquefy our insides the moment it touched our throats. Orthrask was an unnatural blight on the world. I knew from the amounts of dead fish and other sea life that had washed up on the beach. The smell was horrendous.

Marek hobbled out of the water not far from me, his arms wrapped around Talina. Bronislav carried Annaka out of the shallow waves and gently laid her on the black sand.

She stirred, her eyes slitting open from their sleepy haze. She slowly leaned on her elbows, gazed at her surroundings, and then looked at each of us with a heavy sigh. "Do I even want to know what happened?"

"No," Marek and Bronislav said in unison.

Talina was holding her arms, shivering. She pointed to the waves. "Our rucksacks."

They had washed up in various spots on the beach. We retrieved them and inspected the contents inside. I was grateful that the packs had been protected with magic. Despite the sopping-wet exteriors, the interiors remained dry.

My friends had packed well. There were blankets, torches, and cans of dry food. Camping cooking gear, too, though I doubted there would be an opportunity for us to hunt and catch animals on this island. Not ones that would be safe to eat, anyway. There were also weapons.

We each took a rucksack. One remained, which looked neglected and forlorn in the wet sand.

Jad.

I looked out at the sea, where the serpent was still attacking the revenants and the army of chak-lorks. Through the smoke and rippling explosions, I could just make out a flash of scales, the serpent still hard at work to destroy our enemy. Was Jad out there still? Marek didn't seem overly concerned about his captain's welfare, which made me think something else—of the dark magic kind—had occurred with Jad.

Not Trajan.

I stabbed him with Neathror.

Trajan is dead.

But I had no actual proof of that, and when I thought back on it, the way Jad had looked at me on the *Crown of Glory*, as though he wanted to crush me like an ant under his boot, well… that hatred had felt familiar.

Not Trajan.

A stab of ice punctured through my gut. I could deny it all I wanted; it didn't stop it from being true.

Talina's voice was heavy with worry. "What now?"

Marek's gaze wandered to the cliffs that towered over the shore. "We stick to our plan and find the caves."

The caves?

My eyes roamed across the sandy beach to the dramatic cliffs that stretched as far as I could see. They seemed to jut out of the sand like a huge barrier wall, preventing armies from crossing into Orthrask. The puzzling geology was a combination of dark basalt columns, jagged crags, and granite peaks. The height was vertigo-inducing.

Marek's shoulders were slouched under his rucksack. He looked as though he wanted to do nothing more than curl into a ball and go to sleep, but he lifted his head with resolve and stared at the towering cliffs. "We need to find the entrance to the cave. It shouldn't be far."

I dug my heels into the sand. "What about Jad? He's still out there."

When no one immediately answered, I couldn't deter the desperation from seeping into my voice. "Please. Will one of you just tell me what is going on?"

Why are none of you worried about Jad?

Marek's eyes glinted like marbles, his impatience growing. "Once we find the caves, I'll tell you. It's not safe for us to be out in the open. We're too exposed. We need to move. Now."

He stared at the cliffs again, his Adam's apple bobbing when he swallowed. I followed his line of sight but couldn't see anything in the sweeping expanse of the crags, and yet I experienced that awful sensation that I was being watched. Could the others feel it too?

Talina angled her head, studying the flat expanse of beach. Annaka reached for the cast-shooter in her holster and frowned deeply, her teeth clenched. Bronislav had already drawn his athame-sabre, his hand a knuckle-white fist around the hilt.

Yes. They sensed it.

Marek began the difficult ascent up the beach. "Come on. Annaka, Bronislav, keep your eyes on the water. Talina and Zaya, watch the cliffs."

Talina ran haphazardly after him, struggling in her wet boots across the sand. "What are we looking for?"

"Anything that moves."

I stared at the cliffs, imagining all manner of monsters watching us from the cracks and shadows. A shiver slithered down my skin.

"I'll come back," I told the serpent. *"I'll set your soul free. I promise."*

There was no response.

I couldn't even hear the battle anymore over the waves, and there was too much smoke and spray in the air for me to see beyond the shore.

We walked in silence, my panic not once dissipating. I felt like a taut wire, all my muscles straining, ready for fight or flight. The lack of typical sounds at the beach was deeply unsettling. No seagulls or birdlife. No gentle lapping waves—just roaring ones—and no sand crunching underfoot.

My thoughts went where they always did when I was alone and afraid. To Jad.

What happened to him?

Why is Marek avoiding my questions?

I'd become so consumed in thoughts of Jad that it took me a moment to realise the black sand around my boots was shaking. Fierce vibrations rattled up my legs, causing my knees to tremble.

Talina's narrowed eyes met mine at the same time an indescribable wail rolled across the beach.

No. Not across it.

From underneath.

It burst from the sand, the force tossing us all backward. It moved so fast that I could barely comprehend what I was seeing through the displaced waterfall of sand. I clambered onto my feet, my bowels turning into water. It was a gigantic sandworm. The creature's reddish-brown skin secreted a foul-smelling mucous. The worm's breaths fluctuated in and out through its skin and bristle-shaped appendages. I couldn't detect any eyes, but that didn't seem to matter when it turned its peculiar, shovel-shaped head toward us. The monster's nostrils flared, detecting us on smell alone. Its lips pulled back, revealing a walled tube where its last meal was still coated in saliva. Several tongues scraped over the meaty chunks to push them into the oesophagus.

"Run!" Marek screamed at the same time jagged teeth protruded from every surface of the worm's mouth.

CHAPTER 6

We sprang out of the way as the worm dived, all its teeth acting like massive pincers. The creature burrowed through the ground, black silt raining down on us, the beach we stood on becoming as pliable as quicksand. We hurtled across the shore, not seeming to have any clear direction. Self-preservation was the only thing guiding my way, and judging by the speed of the others, I wasn't the only one with that goal in mind.

But where are we running to?

The sea wasn't an option, and even if we did find this mysterious cave, I doubted that would stop the worm.

I risked a glance over my shoulder. The creature had reared its ugly head from the sand. Its long body soared to an immense height, blocking out the dull glow in the smoke that might have been the sun.

Annaka, Marek, and Bronislav were ahead. Talina and I, in our sopping-wet boots and heavy rucksacks, found it difficult to make any headway up the beach. A shriek escaped me when I felt a rush of hot breath over my shoulders, reeking of decayed meat and blood. I grabbed Talina, jerking us both out of the path of the worm as it plunged, the impact shooting sand into my eyes and mouth. We lost our footing and collapsed into the supple sand. I struggled to get back onto my feet, the lurching ground knocking me down over and over again. Talina's aggravated cry told me she was having as much success at keeping upright as I was.

"It's coming back," she yelled.

The worm's long, reptilian body had disappeared, but I knew from the way the sand rippled toward us that Talina was right. The worm was not dead. I had no control over it, and the small cast-shooter I'd retrieved from my rucksack wouldn't have the fire-power to destroy a monster of this scale.

Marek was running, grappling his way toward us, his heavy boots sinking in the sand.

What can he really do to save us?

The beast shot out of the sand, jaws gaping wide. The roar deafened me. Several tongues emerged from the creature's mouth, slimy and forked.

Talina buried her face in her hands, accepting the inevitable. I snapped my head from side to side, trying to find an escape, teeth clenched to breaking point, the tension inside me making all my thoughts sluggish. I knew it wouldn't work, but in the face of death, I raised my cast-shooter and fired anyway, a last resort for survival.

An explosion of fire erupted. The worm elicited a roar powerful enough that I hit the sandy beach so hard, my bones groaned. Blood splattered from a gaping hole in the worm's side, the flesh cooked right through. I stared, stunned that my cast-shooter could cause that much damage. It hadn't deterred the worm, though. Only enraged it.

The creature slid toward us. I aimed the barrel of my weapon, determined to shoot round after round if that's what it took. Before my finger could squeeze the trigger, though, another blast of fire hit the worm, shattering blood and flesh from its mucous-coated face.

No. Not my measly cast-shooter.

This was fire magic. And the only person I knew who wielded it was...

Jad appeared from the smoke and haze, his hands aglow with flames. His eyes, ringed in red, burned with lethal intensity. As graceful as an athlete, he tossed the fire, which sliced through the air like projectiles to wedge into the worm's skin. The creature's thunderous bellow split my ears. It no longer cared about Talina and me. Jad had its full attention. It slithered toward him, slits for nostrils flaring as it inhaled the captain's scent.

Jad conjured more flames, effortlessly sending them like meteorites into the worm. Each blast packed a tremendous punch, the aroma of burnt meat and sizzling flesh so overwhelming that I nearly bent forward to empty my stomach.

Jad was playing with the worm, distracting it to buy Talina and me time to escape. I grabbed her arms, trying to heave her from the sand, but with the way the ground shook beneath us, we were like two skaters clinging onto each other, the surface as slippery as ice. My own wrists felt like they might snap from the tension. Talina's leg was wedged to the knee. She cried, tears swimming in her eyes. I tried with more force to get her out, but our connection broke and I fell backward, the sand sinking over my own arms and legs. We were both trapped. Again.

The sand will drown us.

A growl that was unlike anything I'd heard from a living animal before ripped across the beach. Jad scrambled out of the way of the worm's chomping teeth, skilfully dodging its vicious strikes. He leapt onto its back with more strength than was possible and ran up its long body until he stood firmly atop its head. Jad drew his athame-sabre, which was imbued with the same fire I'd witnessed on the *Crown of Glory*.

I realised then that Jad was the predator and the worm the prey. He drove the blade down into the creature's head. Blood squirted, staining the black sand red. The monster let out a final, defeated roar and, like a spring uncoiling, flopped onto the ground with a heavy thud.

Trembling and light-headed, I gasped for air. I had hoped that Trajan's death had killed the lycanthor power inside Jad, but looking at him now, his glittering eyes like red flames, I knew that had been an impossible dream. Jad wiped the worm's blood from his face and smiled like a wolf. I could feel the dark magic radiate off him.

Marek and Bronislav lifted me and Talina out of the slit. It took them a few attempts, but at last, we were freed. Marek cradled Talina in his arms as she loudly wept. I realised now why Marek and Bronislav hadn't been able to help before. There was a line of ash burned across the beach. Jad must have put up a fire-wall to prevent them from aiding us.

No. To prevent them from getting killed.

My legs heavy, I plodded away from the group, from the blood-soaked sands that had trapped me, and from the worm, hating the stench of its charred meat. What was left of its mangled body was either burned or covered in blisters. A feast for the seagulls, if they ever visited Orthrask's shores.

I stopped a small distance away from the water. My mouth was thick with black sand, and I unceremoniously spat it out.

Let it go. Forget it.

But all I could see was the savagery on Jad's face and the joyful satisfaction that had surfaced in his eyes when he'd killed the worm. The visual had left an imprint I couldn't blink away.

"Zaya, are you okay?" Annaka latched a hand on my shoulder. Her thick lips were uncharacteristically pale.

I nodded, but all I wanted to do was barf. "I just need a minute."

Jad's voice reached me across the beach, as sharp as a whip. "There's no time for a minute. The cave is that way. You passed it. We need to take shelter before more of these earth diggers arrive."

More worms?

Providence, help us.

Jad had been talking to all of us, but I could feel his negative energy directed toward me only.

"Let's go," he snapped, his voice somehow more vicious, still full of battle fury.

Wet and miserable, I followed the captain and my friends up the beach. I wished I could get closer to Jad, figure out what was going on with him. Even though he'd saved Talina and me, I didn't want to risk his wrath. His hatred couldn't be denied as he checked over his shoulder. He didn't tear his toxic gaze away from me.

My gut reaction was to draw away, but not because of that look, as terrifying as it was. The wind had picked up, and mixed between the smoky air and volcanic gases was the lingering scent of death. But not the worm's death.

No.

The scent was coming straight off Jad.

IT WAS no wonder that we had passed the cave. It was just a slit in the rock, hidden away by two stone pillars. It wasn't even a cave, really, but an endless tunnel, the perfect size for a large worm to slither through.

"Is this a good idea?" I whispered to Marek.

He remained beside Talina, his arm looped around her waist, keeping her upright. She was still too shaken to walk properly. It worried me that the shock hadn't worn off yet. She was our healer. If anyone was injured, we'd be relying on her to mend us. Shock screwed around big time with a caster's magic. I hoped she'd recover quickly.

Marek's blink was the only sign of his exhaustion. "Jad says we'll be safe in these caves. At least for a little while."

A little while.

The captain was some distance ahead, using his athame-sabre to light the way down the tunnel. I could feel the flames even from here, feel that unleashed storm of tension brewing around him.

"What happened to Jad? And don't say you'll tell me later," I insisted, seeing the hesitance in Marek's eyes. "I want the truth."

"Tell her," Talina pleaded. I hadn't even been aware she was listening. "She needs to know."

The sadness in her voice made me freeze up.

Marek winced, his face draining of colour. "You stabbed him with Neathror. I'm not sure if he's ever quite... healed from that. His magic is stronger. His lycanthor strength... it's unparalleled to anything I've seen. Neathror... it did something to him. Changed him somehow."

The words were unsettling. Neathror took life, and I could acutely sense now that there was death lingering around Jad.

Had a part of him died? Was that why my necromancy was going haywire? Because it could sense something dead inside him?

I wouldn't know for sure without getting close, and that was the one thing I couldn't do. I was a curse to Jad. I'd gone from being his greatest desire to the most hated object in his existence. I couldn't get near him without making him physically ill or burning him. No wonder he was keeping his distance from me.

The separation made me feel so alone.

Marek must have guessed what I was thinking because he squeezed my shoulder, a comforting gesture. Or a gesture to remain strong.

But inside, I was falling apart.

WE FOUND a cavern large enough for our group to rest in. It was dry and dark, the ground soft with sand. Our flashlights were the only source of light, but at least here it was sheltered and away from the hot winds and turbulent sea.

Jad's heavy gaze scanned us all. I wondered what he thought of the beaten-down people in front of him, because he raised his brow and exhaled a sharp, unimpressed breath. "I'll be farther down the tunnel, keeping watch."

He gave me a murderous look as he left, his silhouette blending in with the shadows. I glowered into the dark, hoping he could feel my wrath just as deeply. When I could no longer feel death lingering in the air, I dropped into the sand and just... stared. It was the first time I could breathe easily since the episode with the worm.

Talina took out a sleeping bag from her rucksack and settled down to go to sleep. Her face was drawn, her emerald eyes swollen from crying. She saw me watching and zipped the bag right up, cocooning herself inside. I wondered if she regretted coming to rescue me.

Marek, Bronislav, and Annaka set up a small gas cooker and began stirring what must have been a large batch of canned soup. I was famished, surprised I could still feel anything when my stomach growled.

I watched them, cold and hollow. "What now?"

Annaka stared at Marek with quiet question in her eyes but didn't say anything. A muscle flickered in Marek's jaw. Bronislav simply watched the bright flames beneath the gas cooker.

"You rescued me," I persisted. "So, what happens now? Surely you had a plan beyond salvaging me from the *Crown of Glory*."

What madness had they actually dreamt up?

Annaka elbowed Marek in the side. "You better tell her and not delay the inevitable. She's going to get mad anyway."

My throat clogged up with emotion. "Why will I get mad?"

The lieutenant rubbed a hand across his tired eyes. He looked at me, the resolve on his face as hard as granite. "Darius and Macaslan knew what Toshiko was planning. They hoped to providence that they were wrong, but when you went missing and the Black Palace was burning, they bribed the guards to let us out of the prison. Darius sent us with clear instructions. We were to sneak onto the ship and remain invisible. Once we neared Orthrask, the plan was to rescue you, find shelter, and then decide the next move."

I stared, not entirely sure if I was even breathing anymore. "You don't know the next step."

"Oh, we know it." Bronislav was guzzling down his soup, watching my every move. "It's to help you destroy Morgomoth. It's up to you now. We follow your direction."

I stood up, but my head started swimming, and I reluctantly had to sit back down again. "Absolutely not."

Annaka's smile was not a pleasant one. "We knew the risks."

"And so did Darius and Macaslan." I couldn't believe the senator and the commander had been willing to send my friends on this suicide mission. I couldn't hold back the snap in my voice. "Where are they now?"

In hiding, I bet.

Marek pressed his lips into a grim line. "Now that the sovereigns and the Council are dead, Darius and Macaslan are ruling the city, or what's left of Muiren. They have command of Vukovar's entire Haxsan Guard forces. They're the highest authority left."

"They're planning to attack Orthrask in five days." Annaka was heating a second batch of soup. She stirred the hot liquid, preventing it from spitting. It seemed entirely strange to see her fussing over a domestic duty. "The ships should be leaving Vukovar now."

I didn't say anything for a long time. This was beyond anything I had imagined. Haxsan Guard forces sent to Orthrask? Morgomoth would obliterate them all, then raise the dead army for his own. The Council of Founding Sovereigns would never have allowed it if they'd been alive.

An unpleasant thought struck me. I didn't want to believe it, but I knew it was true before the question even left my lips. "Darius and Macaslan let the sovereigns die, didn't they?"

I knew Darius and Macaslan were ruthless, but I didn't realise their measures were so cold-blooded and heartless.

An uncharacteristic crease formed in Marek's brow. "I don't know, but they certainly didn't seem sad to hear that the sovereigns and the Council were dead."

It must have been a horrible night for my friends when the Black Palace burned. One filled with panic and chaos, but still, I didn't approve of Darius and Macaslan just leaving the sovereigns and the Council to their fate because it removed an inconvenience from their plans.

Annaka nudged Marek. "Tell her the rest."

"There's more?" My lips wobbled. I wrapped my arms around myself, feeling cold despite the warmth from the cooker.

Marek gave me a strange look, imploring almost, as though he were seeking forgiveness before he started. He took out a mapographic from his rucksack. It was unlike those I'd seen before. He powered it on, and the device immediately started scanning, building shapes and forms which I soon realised was Orthrask's terrain.

"This is a prototype," he explained. "The only one of its kind so far. The alchemists at the Black Palace were working on this and setting their sights on making more before…."

He didn't need to finish for me to understand.

Before they all died in a wave of fire.

"Darius gave it to me," he continued. "It's scanning the island now, sending images by satellite to the Haxsan Guard ships, updating them twenty-four-seven. That way, Darius, Macaslan, and the other generals can coordinate a precise attack."

I shook my head, furious with myself for falling for Toshiko's nice girl act, furious for getting caught, furious at the measures Darius and Macaslan had taken.

My voice teetered. "Attacking Orthrask is suicide. *He'll* defeat them all. Darius and Macaslan are sending everyone to their deaths."

How could everyone be okay with this plan?

Annaka's lips curled up into a roguish smile. "That's why we need to help you vanquish Morgomoth first. Then the Haxsan Guard might have a chance of destroying the ULD for good."

I dropped my head into my hands, using my thumbs to gently massage circles into my temples.

Great. More pressure.

Now I'm responsible for ensuring the entire Vukovar Haxsan Guard makes it to Orthrask's shores.

I let out a frustrated groan. "I could strangle the pair of them."

Bronislav raised his eyebrows. "I'm not sure about strangling, but you can certainly talk with the senator and the commander if you wish."

I angled my head, too tired to even look up. "How?"

Marek took out an oval hand mirror made of what might have been gold. "With this."

CHAPTER 7

We had gathered around the mirror. I'd held my breath as we'd patiently waited for the senator and the commander to pick up our call. Marek explained to me how this technology worked, but I didn't really understand it. It used the same principle as the human's ancient telecommunication devices —something they'd called phones.

So strange.

This mirror was also a prototype, an object an alchemist had probably painstakingly put together, working long hours and late at night, but I didn't care about that as I snatched it from Marek's hand.

"What the hell are you both thinking?" I snapped the moment Darius's and Macaslan's drawn faces appeared in the reflection.

I was trembling all over, my chest unbearably tight.

Darius's grin was a serpentine smile. "I'm happy to see you, too, Zaya. You're looking well."

I was pretty sure that was sarcasm. "Explain to me how this

scheme you've cooked up is meant to work. All I can see it resulting in is death."

"I'm glad you haven't lost that feisty spark." Darius was still smiling, but he sounded tired. He brushed his fingers through his white-blond hair. Maybe it was the lighting from the mirror, but the senator looked like he'd aged since I'd last seen him.

His fierce eyes held mine. "From the moment Orthrask was created and Morgomoth made himself a new throne, it was inevitable that this would happen. We cannot let him and his forces get stronger. We have to be the first to strike; otherwise, he will attack Vukovar and the remaining continents. And we will all fall to his rule, just as Navask has."

He leaned forward, his voice low and conspiratorial. "Our ships will arrive in five days. Find a way to kill Morgomoth before then, and we stand a chance."

My throat turned taut to the point of pain. "I don't know how… and to kill him… that means I would have to go to his kingdom."

I looked at my friends, at the sombreness on their faces, and realised this was part of their mission too. To journey across volcanic terrain, where the land was unstable, divided by streams and rivers of lava, where vents of steam shot out from geysers, and where a foot in the wrong place could melt it right off. No easy feat.

In the mirror, Darius looked like he had more to say, but Macaslan cut him off. Her grey eyes pierced mine, and in her voice, there was no kindness or comfort. "You are on a tight schedule, Zaya. By now, Morgomoth will know you escaped the *Crown of Glory*. He'll have all manner of creatures, alive and dead, searching the island for you. If you're captured, then it's all over. Morgomoth will take your power, and he'll have the ability to unite the Larthalgule and Neathror blades. None of us will stand a chance against him if this happens. You must defeat him. You must unite the blades first."

Darius, quiet and observing, cleared his throat. "You must be the one to wield the Interitus blade, Zaya."

I just stared, probably resembling a doe caught in headlights.

Darius must have briefed everyone on what the Interitus blade was before they'd boarded the *Crown of Glory*, because no one said anything or seemed surprised.

Everyone was relying on me. Me! I felt useless and inadequate for the task. The Bone Grimoire was inside my body, and I had no idea how to access it, let alone find the spell that would enable me to unite the Larthalgule and Neathror blades. I was certain Darius was right. Joining the weapons was what it would take to defeat Morgomoth. The Interitus blade, which he sought for ultimate control, would also be what would destroy him.

No wonder he's hunting me.

He doesn't want me to get anywhere near the spell to unite the athame-sabres.

And if that's the case, then Morgomoth must think I'm a big enough threat to achieve it.

I squared my shoulders, trying to make myself appear brave. "Okay."

"Okay... you'll do it?" Darius raised his eyebrows in curious anticipation.

"It's not like I have a choice, is it? I won't just let everyone *die*." I threw acid into that final word.

Darius let out a dark laugh, but I detected a trace of ire roiling in the good humour beneath his eyes.

Macaslan glared at me through the mirror so hard, I was surprised it didn't shatter the glass. "This is a war. And war means making difficult decisions and sacrifices. We did what we had to. We saved your friends so they could rescue you. We chose you, Zaya."

Each reprimand was a punch to the gut.

Me over the Council of Founding Sovereigns.

My importance didn't make me feel any better. It just triggered more guilt.

Macaslan's voice was as hard as a sharp-edged sword. "That will be all. Call us when you need to. And keep us updated on what's happening in Orthrask."

That last part was directed toward Marek.

The lieutenant silently nodded.

The senator and the commander disappeared; the signal cut off.

I stared at the mirror for a long time. The girl in the reflection looked back with the entire world's struggle in her eyes.

I DIDN'T SLEEP WELL. The sand under my sleeping bag was uncomfortably warm, and I fretted over what was running beneath the island to make the ground insufferably hot.

Lava.

Could the tunnels and this cavern fill with it?

Was this in fact a lava tube?

I shuddered at the thought.

Everyone was asleep. I wondered how they could appear so peaceful, seeming to be lost in pleasant dreams. Me? If I did manage to drift off, I was positive the only thing visiting my dreams would be nightmares.

I tossed and turned and tried to fluff the end of my sleeping bag into somewhat of a pillow, but I still ended up staring at the ceiling, looking at all the grooves and hollows. I wondered if there were monsters staring down through the cracks, waiting for the right time to pounce.

"You promised."

The ghostly caress was a whisper across my skin.

I bolted upright, searching the black earthen walls. We had started a small fire and left it going to provide light and to conserve the magic in our flashlights; otherwise, we wouldn't have had a chance of seeing anything in the dark. Now, flickering rays danced across the cavern walls, casting moving shadows across the rocks.

Just a trick of the light.

Not wraiths.

And yet, despite the heat, I felt a cold presence around me.

"You promised."

All the hairs on my arms stood on end. It felt like ice had run down the back of my neck.

I had hoped it was Lunette or even Adaline. Hell, I'd even take Violetta, but the voice was far too guttural and hoarse to be any of them.

"You promised."

The voice floated around me, always moving so I couldn't be sure where it came from.

Fingers, icy to the touch, stroked my cheek and I leapt out of my sleeping bag. She sat next to me, her long brown hair floating around her, concealing her eyes. There was something unsettling about not being able to see her face. Her lips curved into a cruel, impish smile. The abrasions around her neck where the rope had cut were red and weeping, spotted with purple welts that still bled. The longer I stared, the faster the blood seemed to run down her neck and across her exposed skin, staining her white dress.

"You swore to help. Do not break your promise."

The serpent. That was who she meant.

I'd told that poor creature I'd be back, and yet so much had happened that I'd forgotten and abandoned the sea serpent.

A wave of guilt threatened to drown me. "You're right. I broke my promise, but I can't get back. There are worms on the beach."

"There is a way." The wraith clicked her bony fingers together in a gesture to follow.

She glided through the passage into the tunnel, her white dress floating behind her, somehow both ethereal and terrifying at the same time. I didn't know whether to pursue or not. On the one hand, I really did want to keep my promise and help the serpent move on to the next world, but on the other, this ghost had smothered me in my bed once. That was not something I could forget. Granted, blocking my airways and making me lose consciousness had taken me to Isgrad's memory, where I'd finally learnt who Morgomoth really was, but still. Surely there were better ways to have achieved that.

"Damn," I muttered, knowing leaving the safety of this cavern and venturing down the tunnels in pursuit of a wraith was one of the stupidest things I could do, but I had made a promise.

I am not like Morgomoth.

I don't manipulate the dead.

I summoned every ounce of strength into my aching legs and hurried after the wraith, my insides quivering. We turned down tunnel after tunnel, exploring the underground network. She was a beacon in the dingy shafts. Every so often, smoke wafted from vents in the earthen floor. I sidestepped the apertures, the stench of sulphur overwhelming. Steam permeated the air, and when I breathed, it felt like my lungs were melting.

I thought of my friends, asleep and unaware of the dangers that waited in the tunnels. I thought of Jad, who had separated himself from the rest of us, alone in the dark.

"Are the tunnels safe?"

The wraith twisted her head around, too unnatural for any living human or caster to have achieved. I swallowed, reminding myself that her neck had snapped when she'd been hanged, which was what gave her that… flexibility.

"Do you not recognise this place? Does it not feel familiar?"

It did, actually. I paused to examine the strange environment. I thought the black rocks were the result of gushing lava at some point in time, but when I touched the surface, it was cold. My fingers ached from the burning chill.

I pulled away. "It's the Dark Divide."

The wraith silently nodded. I wished she hadn't. Her head looked capable of rolling right off her shoulders. *"The Dark Divide is now part of the island."*

"Is it safe? Can we remain down here?"

What I really wanted to know was if we could make our way to Morgomoth's kingdom without having to rise to the surface. If the Dark Divide was beneath the entire island, it would provide us with a secure way to travel.

"These tunnels are dangerous. They are used by chak-lorks and lycanthors. You linger too long down here and those monsters will have a better chance of picking up your scent. Many of these tunnels are now lava channels too."

So that was a no.

"Come," the wraith urged.

We wandered down several passages until we came to a hewn stairway. The rock was rutted and difficult to climb. I was fit, but even my leg muscles strained from the exertion, my knees popping. The farther I scrambled up the steep ascent, the more the rock face became vertical. I was forced to use my upper-arm strength to scale the rocks, my fingernails digging into silt.

The light shifted above. Brighter. I clenched my teeth, pushing upward to the oculus. I crawled out of the shaft, entering Orthrask's stifling atmosphere.

Heat licked my skin, causing sweat to run down my face. A suffocating sense of misery struck me. We hadn't travelled inland.

No, the tunnels we'd taken must have run parallel to the coast. To my right, Orthrask was a wasteland of fire and craters, dotted with bogs and barren as a desert, all life sucked away. This part of the earth was just an empty husk. Even looking at it burned my eyes.

I veered left and walked to the edge of the cliff, focusing on the sea below. The serpent was floating on the surface, the waves washing its mangled body closer to the beach. Large birds—not seagulls or crows, or even vultures, but something that was a mixture of the three—pecked at the serpent's scales, tearing into flesh and sinew. Even from up here, the stench of it made my nose feel like it was about to bleed.

The birds fought and squawked over the helpings, their raucous cries aberrant. It was further proof that the wildlife here was not natural but mutated by the dark magic that stained the land.

The wraith's white dress rustled as she hovered above the dead reeds. *"Do it. Keep your promise."*

I shut my eyes, unleashing my necromancy into the dark world, like rays extended from a lighthouse. I located that lost, anguished soul easily enough. The hard part was what to do next. The serpent was still trapped in its body, desperate to get out and to be free of the pain that death made it suffer. I focused on my magic, feeling it wrap around me with gentle arms, lighting up my skin like the sun.

"This way," I called in mind-speak.

I wasn't sure why—perhaps it was an instinctive response in me—but I imagined myself as a beacon of light, opening a doorway to a place beyond. I sensed the serpent's soul drawing closer, slow at first, then approaching at a swift pace. A ripple of cool air struck me, and I knew the serpent had made contact. I was the door.

My heart beat faster as I experienced the creature's acute despair, its agony and torment, before all that suffering dimmed

THE BONE GRIMOIRE

and there was nothing beyond the veil but warm, sultry air and a turquoise sea. I remained perfectly still, watching the serpent fade away into those sunlit waters. When I knew it was at peace, I mentally shut the door, the night closing in around me again.

I gasped, my eyes fluttering wide. Searing, burning pain erupted through my abdomen, and then, like a light flickering out, it was gone.

So, this is what it actually means to be a necromancer.

To be the literal doorway to the otherworld.

"Interesting way to meditate."

I jumped at the harsh voice.

Jad was stationed by a large boulder, his shoulders and back leaning against it. His arms were crossed as he watched me with an intensity that matched a stalking beast. He looked every part the dark prince in a kingdom of eternal flames. It hurt that he kept his distance, but then I *was* poison to him.

"Not meditating." I couldn't keep my voice from sounding firm. His presence was unsettling. Again, I caught the whiff of death in the arid air and wondered exactly who or what I was dealing with.

"It's dangerous to be on the surface." There was a hint of irritation in his tone.

I opened my mouth to explain why I'd come up here, but...

Why should I?

He won't care about the serpent.

A flush crept over my cheeks. "Is that why you're here? To keep watch?"

Silent and brooding, his stare was simmering with reprimand. "I saw you wandering the tunnels and followed. You need to be kept safe. You can't just disappear from us."

He spoke the words as though being my personal guard was disgusting and beneath him, as though I wasn't worth the effort or the risk.

"How noble of you." I wished I could summon my own fire-ball and burn the hostility out of him.

"We're going back underground," he growled. "Follow me. And keep your distance."

He moved to the crater, his back to me.

"Afraid I'll make you sick again if I get too close?"

He turned, the searing rage on his face rooting me to the spot. "The very idea of you being anywhere near me makes me *sick*."

His voice was a cold, sharp slap in the face.

Ouch.

I blinked back the angry tears that started to haze my eyes and dug my feet into the black earth, refusing to move. I knew it was dangerous. We were too exposed out in the open, but damn if I would let him get away with this insolent behaviour any longer.

"What happened to you?" I snapped. I tried to speak in what I hoped was an assertive tone, but I was trembling so hard, it might have come out sounding flat. "I get that the Bone Grimoire has changed things, but this hostility has to stop."

"You know damn well what happened to me," he roared, the sound very much like the snarl from a lycanthor. His eyes shone a blistering red, brighter than even the flames that erupted from the volcanoes. "You stabbed me. You sacrificed me to get that damned book. You did this."

His pointed finger felt like a blade in my heart.

My mouth felt too dry to speak, but I forced an answer out. "You weren't yourself. You were Trajan."

Why couldn't he understand that letting Morgomoth retrieve the grimoire and absorb all its power hadn't been an option? I had thought over my actions at the Isla Necropolis. I had punished myself for hours, questioning if there had been something else I could have done, but I always came to the same conclusion. Stabbing Trajan had been the only way.

"I did what I thought was right." The tears I had been holding back broke from their well, flooding my cheeks. "I'm sorry. What more can I say or do?"

Jad was breathing hard. I could see the rapid rise and fall of his chest through his black tunic, the way the veins in his neck corded. "I'm only here because Darius and Macaslan asked me to; otherwise, I'd be on a ship like the rest of our Haxsan Guard soldiers, preparing for the war that's coming." He pointed to Morgomoth's stronghold far in the distance, which seemed to be staring back at me with vindictive enjoyment. "Once this is all over, I never want to see you again. I hope you die in that place."

I staggered back, the admission crushing me. Like an arrow straight in the gut.

This was not Jad. This was something else. Something wicked and vile and spiteful had taken over him.

He started making his way back to the crater.

A small, broken sound cracked inside me, but I had to be certain.

"Trajan," I called, terrified of how he might react.

He stilled, then turned slowly, his lips parting in a caustic smile. "You killed him, remember?"

That might have been true, but that depraved monstrosity Hadar had created, that man who had butchered and slayed casters and villages... he was not gone. Now I understood that lingering scent of death. Trajan was still in there, corrupting Jad's heart, poisoning it from the inside. Jad might not have loved me anymore, but that hatred was all Trajan.

"Move," he bellowed so suddenly that I jumped.

I did, but not because he demanded it. I walked right up to him, feeling a level of satisfaction when his cheeks turned green and he looked like he might bend over right there to be sick.

There was a terrified pounding in my chest, but I would not back down. "Don't talk to me or anyone else like that ever again. And don't bother leading me back to the cavern. I know the way."

Not true. I had no idea what tunnels led to the cavern, but by this point, I was so angry, I'd prefer boiling lava over his company.

I descended the steep shaft, only allowing my wrenching sobs to spill when I was deep underground.

When there was no chance of Jad hearing them.

CHAPTER 8

M oody, arrogant, egotistical… well, there were many creative names I could have come up with for Jad as I made the long hike back to the cavern. *Long* because I had no recollection of the way I'd come and was likely going around in circles. It wasn't until my mysterious guide appeared in a beacon of white light—not angelic in any way, more like a will-o'-the-wisp extending a slight radiance through the dark—that I made it back. Without her, I'd still be a mouse running through a maze.

The wraith had told me that the tunnels weren't safe and we couldn't remain here, but seeing my friends resigned in that much-needed sleep, their faces chalk pale from exhaustion, I couldn't wake them.

Coldness trailed up my neck. The ghost hovered beside me, her mouth right up to my ear. *"Make the journey up to the surface tomorrow and never return down here. For tonight, you are secure in this cavern."*

Was that because she was here, keeping watch?

Or because….

I shuddered thinking about it. Nothing would pass Jad and

his lycanthor strength, that's for sure, especially when he had that puzzling athame-sabre.

He must be back in the tunnel by now. Even that's too close.

I turned to the ghost and meant to ask for her name, but she'd vanished.

Resigned to the fact that I wasn't getting any answers, I dropped into my sleeping bag and tried not to think about what Jad—no, what *Trajan* had screamed at me, but the memory of our argument refused to be buried.

"Once this is all over, I never want to see you again. I hope you die in that place."

The hostile rage in those eyes, the slew of aggression he'd thrown at me from those perfect lips, that handsome face creased into a snarl... well, that was something I never wanted to experience again.

I can't talk to him.

I can't even look at him.

Not when he's like that.

It would be best to avoid Jad at any cost. I'd keep my distance.

That shouldn't be too hard. I'll burn him and make him sick the moment I step too close. Actually, now that I think about it... but no, I couldn't.

I wasn't in the business of intentionally hurting people, no matter how much they deserved it.

At some point, I must have drifted off to sleep, because when I opened my eyes, I was no longer in the cavern. At least, not in the one I'd gone to sleep in. I recognised the silver-thorned witch's underground lair. A familiar cauldron bubbled at the fireplace, the potion inside as bright as melted sapphires. Laid out on a working benchtop were knives, potions, and herbs. What appeared to be pieces of animals—spindly legs, mucous tongues, and claws twice the size of any wolf's—had been scattered around the bench.

A pull, like a magnetic force, drew me forward before I even knew he was there.

Isgrad was sitting at a desk, rifling through paperwork, making notes in a journal.

Another memory, then.

He ran his fingers through his hair, which was longer now. It was almost down to his shoulder blades. He hadn't been looking after it, the blond strands oily and resembling straw. His face, too, had changed. He was older now, maybe early thirties, but his eyes, which were as cold and blue as a frozen lake, held decades of knowledge and experience.

A shadow appeared across the wall. Isgrad looked up to see the silver-thorned witch hobble in on a walking stick. I couldn't prevent my jaw from dropping. She'd aged considerably. Her once silver-white hair had turned dull and grey. Her hands were spotted, the long fingers bent in an arthritic hold on her cane. Her skin had also become wrinkled and leathery. She shuffled across the cabin to her favourite rocking chair by the fire.

Isgrad shook his head with sad disappointment. "Why do you remain in that form? I can see that it pains you to move around. You could make yourself young and beautiful again with just a snap of your fingers. Why not do it?"

The witch eyed him with a stare that was as hard and unbreakable as stone. "Youth isn't everything, Isgrad. I am old. Ancient. Sometimes it's necessary to change my appearance to youth to achieve the spells I need, but other times, I prefer to be me." She sat and peered into the fire, as though the flickering rays held all the answers to the mysteries of life. "You will learn that over time. As the decades and the centuries pass, and the more beauty you see in this world, the more content you will be to simply... be."

Isgrad bristled, his glare as sharp as steel. "I am 145 years old. I've seen what this world has to offer. There's no beauty in it."

He's 145 years old?

When I'd first been brought to these memories, Isgrad had

been a teenager during the ten-year winter. That merciless decade of ice and snow had taken place a century and a half ago. I had no idea what period of time I was in now, but something about the way Isgrad held himself, his shoulders slouched as his hand sped across his journal, and the level of wisdom in those eyes, told me he was much older than his thirties.

But... 145 years!

I did the calculations. He had to be around fifteen when I'd first seen him in the memory. Subtract that from his present age, and that meant this memory was taking place twenty years ago.

Isgrad had been alive all those decades. Doing what? Spying on his brother? Secretly working against Willieth to bring the leader of the ULD down? No. Willieth would have become Morgomoth by now.

The two brothers' life sources were linked to each other. The necromancy that had been born into the world that evening had made them both immortal. It was the only explanation for their long lifespan so far.

I shivered, dread scraping across my bones. It was another revelation that Morgomoth was powerful. He'd had a century and half to learn and wield his magic.

Me? I'd had less than a year.

The silver-thorned witch watched Isgrad with a disapproving frown. "She's outside. She has been this last hour."

Isgrad flinched. A pained expression crossed his face. "No."

"She wants to see you."

Isgrad let his pen drop from his hand with equal resentment and frustration. "Again. *No.*" He spat the last word with icy venom.

The witch traced her thumb across the handle of her walking stick, her gaze returning to the hearth with quiet contemplation. "She's been waiting out in the cold all this time, shivering yet determined. That is loyalty hard to find."

"Then she's a fool." Isgrad had started journaling again, but his handwriting wasn't nearly as neat as it had been. It was a frantic scribble.

"The snow is falling heavier. Any longer out there and she will freeze."

"Then make her leave."

"If you want her gone, then you must be the one to do it. After all, you created this mess."

The witch stood from her chair, ignoring the way Isgrad gritted his teeth at her. One hand on her walking stick and the other on her lower back, she rubbed at what must have been pain spasming in her muscles as she wandered into the shadows and… simply vanished.

I swallowed.

There was no bed in the cavern, only a small sleeping mat and a blanket on the floor for Isgrad, but it didn't appear to have been used. The place really was just an open living area and a kitchen. Where did the witch sleep? Maybe she didn't need rest? Maybe immortals never did?

I stared at the shadows again, wondering where the witch went when she crossed into the dark.

Isgrad shut his eyes, reining in what might have been a furious growl. Then he left his desk and stormed across the cavern.

I followed, struggling to keep up with his long strides. We walked in silence up the hewn stairs. Flames sparked to life in torches along the walls, illuminating the cave drawings. I remembered them from a previous memory, and it still unnerved me to see the detail in the ancient depictions. Animals and wicked beasts hunting humans, ripping into their throats with predatory hunger, the eyes lit with satisfied delight. It was a representation of the period just after the change, one of the few—maybe the only one—to exist now.

I followed Isgrad to the mouth of the cave, which had been

artistically sculpted with magic to resemble the jaws of a wolf, the stalactites carved into incisors. Isgrad walked across the snow-packed ground and leaned against a tree. He drew his cloak tighter, the hood casting his face in shadow. His jaw was tight as he waited.

She appeared from out of the dark woods, her footsteps soft and discordant in the mist-filled night. She had brown hair tied back in a braid, her cheeks and nose red from the cold, but her lips were rosy and plush. She was beautiful, even as she stood before Isgrad in her Haxsan Guard uniform, which revealed her slim build and toned body. The girl's dark eyes held a trace of playfulness.

She reached out for Isgrad, but her happy smile vanished the moment he pulled away.

The light in her eyes guttered. "What? What's wrong?"

Isgrad drew his hood down, eying her flatly. "I told you not to come here. It isn't safe."

"Nowhere in this world is safe." She embraced him, her arms around his waist, her voice silky and full of resolve. She rested her head on his chest, and her eyes started misting. I knew from just that expression that she was terrified of him pushing her away again.

Isgrad went as still as a waxwork. "No, Briya." He disengaged himself from her hold. "This isn't going to happen again. I made up my mind. The answer is no. Go home."

Briya only looked saddened by his lack of affection. "So, the past year meant nothing?"

She didn't sound angry, only surprised, like she didn't really believe him.

"It meant everything." Isgrad's voice shook, but not with anger.

I wondered how many times the pair had had this conversation, how many times they'd put themselves through this despair.

Isgrad stared out into the dark foliage. "I'm doing this to keep you safe. If my brother found out about us, he would use you as a puppet to control me. That isn't right. I won't let it happen."

"What would it matter if he knew?" Briya angled her head to look at him. "He doesn't know I'm a mole and you're an informant in his resistance. He thinks we're on his side. Why would he care if we were together?"

Mole? Informant?

Isgrad is working with the Haxsan Guard?

I thought he'd hated the Council of Founding Sovereigns.

Perhaps all the decades of debauchery, murder, and manipulation Willieth had cast on the world had made Isgrad reconsider his options. What horrors must Isgrad have had to endure or even inflict to spy on his brother?

Isgrad held Briya's gaze, as though this would be the last time he would see her. "Willieth resents me. He would rather burn me in fire than see me happy, but he cannot kill me. Our life forces are linked. While he lives and becomes more immortal, so do I. He makes me commit terrible acts because he knows it breaks me inside. If he knew about us, he would crush you like a flower."

"His name isn't Willieth anymore. Your brother is Morgomoth. If you hate him so much… if you fear him, then become a deserter. Come back to the Haxsan Guard base with me. We can leave it all behind. I love you, and you love me. Don't let Morgomoth destroy that too."

She grabbed his hand, intertwining her fingers with his.

Isgrad didn't pull away this time. Rather, he seemed to be savouring the feel of her skin on his, like he was memorising it for the future. "Go home, Briya. Return to the Haxsan Guard base. I cannot give you the answer you want to hear."

She stared at him for a long time, those rosy lips now pale and trembling in the snow. "What happened? What did you learn?"

"I didn't learn anything."

"You must have for you to act this way. Only a few days ago, you told me you loved me enough to want to marry me, and now you're acting like I'm a disease you're afraid of catching."

Her hysteria was rising, and tears began to flow. She wiped them away furiously with the back of her hand.

There wasn't a hint of sympathy or understanding on Isgrad's face. He hid his emotions too well. "You're not listening. I am immortal. My life is linked to *his*. I have spent years searching for the Bone Grimoire. When I find it and I absorb the book's magic, then my sole purpose is to kill my brother. Willieth's death will be my death too. I do not want you to end up alone. I'm not worth it, Briya."

"That's my choice to make, not yours." She was so passionate in her argument that I hoped Isgrad would reconsider. But I knew he wouldn't, because I suspected there was more happening here, a final piece of the puzzle that he refused to let her know.

He shook his head vehemently, causing some of the flecks of snow to fall from his hair. "It is not your choice to make. It's mine."

He turned away from her and swept toward the cave, ignoring the final desperate plea on her face.

"Don't come back here," he shouted, his voice resonating with sorrow.

Briya dropped to her knees, a whirlwind of emotions plaguing her face as she loudly wept. I wanted to comfort her, but this was a memory, and nothing I could do would make an impact. The only thing that was in my ability was to watch.

I hurried after Isgrad, following his swift steps down the hewn stairs back into the cavern. He paced back and forth, then punched a wall with enough force to fracture the rock. I jumped, startled by the intensity of his anger.

The silver-thorned witch appeared like a wraith from the shadows. She watched him with barely disguised scorn. "So, you broke her heart?"

Isgrad glared at the witch. "I saved her from a life of misery."

"Did you? Or were you sparing yourself?"

He opened his mouth, perhaps to shout at her, but instead, he dropped into a chair and held his head in his hands, looking utterly defeated. "The Bone Grimoire doesn't offer its magic freely. It comes with a price. And I know what that price is now. I can't stand the thought of losing her to that. The book would take her love away. She'd eventually hate me."

So, Isgrad had been sparing himself, as the witch suspected.

She merely nodded, though there was something about the way she watched Isgrad that made me think all his actions had been in vain. "I will make you a healing potion. For your hand," she clarified when he peered up, a question etched in his expression.

Isgrad's knuckles were bleeding. Bits of splintered rock were wedged in the abrasions. He remained sitting, just glaring at the fire in the hearth as though all his problems were entirely its fault.

"It was the right thing to do."

I didn't know if he was talking to the witch or himself.

I pitied him and the decision he'd had to make, but I was also envious. Isgrad had called the shots, breaking his love apart before the Bone Grimoire could shatter it for him. I had not been so fortunate. If I'd had the option to push Jad away first, to put distance between us, it would have made his hatred easier to bear.

I understood why Isgrad did it.

I would have made the same choice.

CHAPTER 9

"Zaya. Hey, wake up. We need to go."

My eyes slowly peeled open, the corners full of dry gunk. I'd been crying in my sleep, and at some point in the night, it had dried, becoming an irritating itch. My mouth tasted sticky. The back of my throat burned. I wondered if I was coming down with a cold.

"You all right?" Soot coated Marek's cropped hair, his skin patchy with dirt and sweat. He'd had more sleep than me, but he looked like he needed to curl back up in his sleeping bag and fall into a coma.

"Here." He gave me a bowl of cereal. Just cereal. No milk. I supposed that wasn't a luxury we could have in this environment.

"Eat up," he insisted. "Jad's waiting for us on the surface."

I stilled, feeling sick for an entirely different reason.

"Once this is all over, I never want to see you again. I hope you die in that place."

Jad might as well have stabbed me in the heart for the pain those words caused. The memory of our argument was still fresh in my mind. I dreaded having to see him again.

I ate my dry cereal and then packed my sleeping bag into my rucksack. The others were ready and waiting. Annaka had gathered her cornrows into a tight updo, revealing her drained face. Never one to admit defeat, her lips pulled into a cocky grin when she looked at me. Talina was rummaging through her first-aid kit, checking over healing potions and spells, and Bronislav was examining the tunnel with his flashlight, perhaps on the hunt for chaklorks.

Marek took the lead, never stopping to second-guess himself as we wandered down the endless shafts. I wondered whether he'd already spoken to Jad before the rest of us had woken and had memorised the tunnels. We soon reached the steep ascent I'd tackled last night. Our progress was slow, the climb seeming twice as hard. I was the last to reach the surface and was grateful when Marek took my arms and helped me onto the barren ground. I blinked, the heat causing sweat to break out on my skin, the air sticky. I felt like I'd walked into a soup bowl.

Marek had told me it was morning, but there was no way to tell. The sky was filled with purple-grey thunderheads, which churned all the way to the horizon, the landscape derelict and dry. There was not a spot of sunlight. Orthrask was an island lit by volcanic fire and lightning. Even the thunder sounded like it wanted to destroy us.

How are we ever going to reach Morgomoth's kingdom?
The elements will kill us.

"Let's go," a familiar voice snapped.

My shoulders hitched, but I dared to lift my gaze. Jad's eyes were blazing again with that deadly inner fire. Honestly, a nest of vipers had more mercy in their expressions. He'd kept himself a safe distance from the group—from me—and started walking into the bleak landscape ahead. "Follow me."

There was nothing friendly in his command.

"Wow." Annaka stepped up beside me. "I know something

happened between you two, but... wow, that was intense. He looked capable of skewering you with lightning."

She waited for me to elaborate.

"Later," I said, sharper than I'd intended.

Five days to the kingdom.

Five days till the army arrives.

Five days to figure out how to merge the Larthalgule and Neathror blades.

Five days to assassinate the most powerful necromancer in the world.

The thoughts played out in my head in a cruel taunt.

It didn't seem long enough, but after watching Jad storm ahead like a demon hellbent on destroying the world, five days felt eternally long.

I'm not going to be able to do any of this with him being such a brute.

But I had no choice.

THE MORNING TREK through Orthrask was a perilous journey. The ground shook whenever a volcano spewed fire into the sky, warning us to stay clear. Many times, we had to veer off track to avoid large geysers. The steam that wafted from the craters was so strong, I imagined it could melt skin from bone.

None of us talked out of fear that something unnatural and hungry would hear us, or because we were all too melancholy to try. This place sucked the strength out of you like a vacuum drawing in dust. I spotted Annaka behind me in the sand-riddled air. She was walking with her head down. Out of all of us, she seemed to be suffering the worst.

I drew back. "Are you okay?"

She raised her eyes and smiled, but it lacked strength. "Just tired. This is taking it out of me."

"Are you sick? Do you have a headache?"

She kept wiping at her brow and squinting. "I'm keeping us invisible. Otherwise, we'd be exposed out here."

"Then we should stop and find cover somewhere so you can rest for a while."

I scanned the environment. There was nothing but flat terrain for kilometres ahead. At some point, Jad must have adjusted our course away from the craters and geysers. I had no complaints about that, but here, there was no shelter anywhere. I'd been so lost in my own miserable world that I hadn't even noticed when the landscape changed.

Annaka shook her head. A bead of sweat dripped off her chin. "We can't stop. Jad was very insistent when he told us his plan aboard the *Crown of Glory*. We have to keep moving. The Haxsan Guard are depending on us to get you to the kingdom in time before they attack."

My throat bobbed. "But you can't continue like this."

"And we can't delay."

At her insistence, we kept walking, her footsteps becoming more languid and heavier. I grew anxious when she reached out for me with a gasp. I didn't make it in time. She collapsed to her knees, vomiting her breakfast onto the rocky ground. Her gorgeous russet-coloured skin now appeared yellowish, her palms pale. I realised with a sinking heart that she was about to faint. She toppled onto the ground like a collapsed tombstone, sending up a cloud of sand and dust.

Marek turned on his heel, and he sagged a little.

"She needs rest," I insisted.

He gently lifted Annaka from the ground, one arm wrapped around her shoulders, the other beneath her legs. "We'll have to move faster now that we don't have an invisibility charm shielding us."

"You don't look any better, Marek. You can't carry her all the way. We need to stop and take a break; otherwise, we'll all end up on the ground unconscious from exhaustion."

"Jad said we—"

"I don't care what he said." It took all my effort not to shout at Marek. "Jad has lycanthor strength, so of course he can keep going and not suffer from fatigue, but we can't."

Talina and Bronislav had stopped walking and turned to watch us. The pair either lacked the energy to get involved or they weren't interested in getting into an argument.

Marek's gaze focused on each of us. I wondered if he was silently assessing our physical appearances and needs. "Jad is about thirty minutes ahead of us, inspecting the land. Let's take half an hour. We can have something to eat and get our strength back. It will take him that long to return."

I didn't like how nervous he sounded.

Marek carefully laid Annaka on the ground, as though he handled a precious gem he was afraid would shatter. I didn't miss the tenderness that swept across his face as he gently brushed back one of Annaka's cornrows, which had come loose from her updo. Talina hadn't missed it either. Ireful colour bloomed on her cheeks, but her expression remained solemn.

Our group hadn't been settled long, eating dry biscuits and sipping from our water bottles, when Jad arrived.

So much for thirty minutes.

His fists were clenched by his sides. "What the hell is this? We don't have time for a picnic." His fury was directed at Marek. "You know the risks. This is a direct violation of my orders."

"Oh, get over yourself," I shouted. "We need rest. If you're so worried about the time, then go check the route ahead and make sure it's safe for the next leg of our journey."

I hated this person he'd become. Trajan's dead soul was making Jad vile and toxic. And it was my fault. I'd hoped the Neathror blade would kill Trajan, and it had, but the consequences far outweighed what it had been worth.

Somehow, and soon, I'm going to have to force Trajan's soul to move on, the same way I did with the sea serpent.

That would prove tricky. I couldn't even get near Jad without poisoning him.

And even if I do manage to vanquish Trajan, that still doesn't deal with the fact that the true hatred for me is coming from Jad.

Trajan was just amplifying the emotion.

Marek pleaded his reasoning and apologised.

I scoffed. "You have nothing to apologise for. It's *him*"—I aimed a hostile glare at Jad—"who needs to apologise to us."

Bronislav swallowed tightly and looked away. Talina focused on her food, avoiding eye contact with everyone. Marek's face slackened, either from disapproval or disappointment.

Annaka looked better now that she'd had water and something to eat. She wasn't the sort of girl to let anyone get away with talking disrespectfully, but even she knew the tension between Jad and me was not something to interfere with.

"Five minutes. Then we move." Jad looked capable of summoning flames and incinerating us on the spot.

"Once this is all over, I never want to see you again. I hope you die in that place."

Why couldn't I get those horrible words out of my head?

He sped away, his footsteps leaving burns in the earth.

My chest caved at the sight.

Just another problem to deal with.

I HAD no idea what time it was, or how long we'd been walking. My lips were dry and cracked, and whenever I licked them, my tongue trailed over small cuts that stung. My armpits were soaked. Pain dug into my toes and ankles, and I knew later when I took my boots off, I'd be greeted with oozing blisters. I wanted to sleep. I wanted clean water and something more substantial to eat. More than anything, I desperately craved a shower.

No one else fared any better. Our progress had slowed to a crawl, practically zombielike across the expanse of desert land. Jad moved like he was possessed by a demon. Many times, he'd stop to scrape the heel of his boot along the black gravel, hinting at his impatience for us to keep moving.

If Marek and the others were disgusted by his lack of compassion, they didn't say anything.

We hiked for a long time. After a while, my brain must have gone numb and simply focused on putting one foot in front of the other, because when I next looked up, the environment had changed. We'd passed the plain of nothing—what I called the empty flat bedrock that had stretched out for kilometres—and were now trekking across a red-orange sea of dust and sand. A jagged line of barren mountains rose in the distance, the volcanoes beyond them belching fire. No matter how often I looked at the towering black keep on the horizon, though, we never seemed to get closer.

"Are you okay?"

My neck tensed with the effort it took to turn around.

Talina walked beside me. I'd been so out of it that I hadn't heard her approach. She'd wrapped a spare shirt around her head, using it like a shemagh scarf to protect her from the scorching winds. It wasn't a bad idea.

I nodded, too fatigued to complain. "It can't be too much longer till sundown."

Not that I could see the sun, but surely even Orthrask had to cool on occasion.

We'd made an agreement to travel only during the day. That way, Annaka could rest in the evenings and keep us invisible while we travelled. Even just stopping for a sit-down sounded like a five-star luxury at this point.

Talina shook her head. She pulled her scarf down, her skin patchy with dirt, her lips just as chapped as mine. "I meant are you okay with what happened before? With Jad?"

I flinched. Just hearing his name made my stomach churn. "He hates me. There's nothing I can do about it, so I'm going to have to be *okay*."

I squinted against the hot blasts of wind. Jad was making easy progress across the rocks. It wouldn't be long before he turned around to glare at us all again.

I heaved a long sigh.

Jad. The environment. The grimoire. The task ahead.

It was all giving me a big fat headache.

"He doesn't hate you."

I was surprised by the conviction in Talina's tone.

"You could have fooled me." I hated the miserable sound in my voice.

"I'm being honest. Every night when we were on the *Crown of Glory*, hiding in the cargo hold behind crates, Jad would leave us to find the glamoured door to your cell. He'd never come back till the morning. One morning he didn't return at all. We found him asleep outside the cell."

"Meaning what?"

"Meaning he does care about you."

"He cares about his mission. Which is getting me to the kingdom of doom over there"—I pointed to the formidable castle on the horizon—"so I can kill Morgomoth. Or die trying."

"I hope you die in that place."

Again, the words tormented me, like someone had stabbed me in the gut to the hilt, slowly twisting the blade into my intestines.

Talina rolled her eyes. "Oh sure. Yeah, he really hates you. That's why he can't stop glancing this way. That's why he sat outside the mouth of the cavern last night, watching you sleep."

"He did not."

"He did. I woke and saw him, then buried my head in my sleeping bag so he wouldn't know. Don't give up, Zaya. It's the grimoire's magic making him behave this way. Beyond the anger and the madness, he does love you. Think what Jad must be going through. To love someone all your instincts are telling you to hate. It's so… tragic."

"Strangely, this isn't making me feel any better."

"Just saying it the way I see it." Her eyes wandered to Marek. A hint of regret flooded her face.

The lieutenant had his arm wrapped around Annaka's waist to help her walk. I knew it killed Talina to see it.

"Why don't you tell him how you feel?"

Her spine stiffened. "Absolutely not."

"Why? He likes you. We can all see it. It's actually painful to watch the pair of you skirt around each other all the time."

"He's interested in Annaka."

Now it was my turn to level my gaze skyward. "He's *helping* Annaka because that's the sort of guy Marek is."

Talina looked as though she were genuinely sorry to have brought the topic up. She tossed strands of her blonde hair over her shoulder. "There may have been a chance for us once, but I missed all the signs, and it wasn't until Annaka arrived on the scene that I realised… well, it doesn't matter now. She's interested in him. And he's interested in her. I'm not going to get in the way of that."

Before I could utter an objection, she broke away, her shoulders hunched as she pressed through the sweltering winds.

Someone snorted.

I glared at Bronislav as he walked past. "What?"

"Teenage girls," he muttered, but he was smiling—with amusement. "You are all so juvenile."

"We can't all be cynical bastards like you, can we? And you shouldn't have been eavesdropping."

He tapped his ear. "Supersensitive hearing, remember."

His smug expression faded the moment he looked at Jad's silhouetted figure ahead. "Talina has a point, though. Jad's heart rate increases every time he looks at you."

I just stared at him, not sure what to make of that news.

He shrugged and kept walking. "Thought you might like to know."

The revelation gave me mixed feelings, but I knew it was still hopeless. While I possessed half of the Grand Masters' power, Jad's feelings for me would continue to be aversion and loathing.

He and I were over.

No, you fool. You're not over.

Because Jad and I had never truly begun.

CHAPTER 10

J ad was determined to go on until nightfall. The others
reluctantly agreed. There'd been noises—horrible, whining
shrieks that I'd never heard from any living creature before—
that had echoed across the bleak landscape. Guttural, ripping
howls bounced off one rock to another so that we were never truly
sure where it actually came from. No one fancied stopping to rest
when there could have been animals out on the prowl. Hungry,
unnatural animals.

That had been an hour ago. Now the sun was setting to the
west. Amazingly, it could be seen as a pale, washed-out hue amid
the roiling thunderheads. Every part of me was drenched in sweat,
the sand and dirt sticking to me like honey. I needed food, water,
and sleep. And painkillers for my throbbing headache.

Talina's relieved cry stretched uncomfortably across the plain.
"Water. Thank providence. Look. Water."

She ran forward, energised by the new gift that waited ahead.

At first, I thought she might have been hallucinating, but no,
it was there. A pool about five metres all around, the deep blue
colour of the water making me salivate. We'd rationed our

supplies to ensure we had enough for the five days, but this was an offering from nature not to be refused. I ran after her, ready to bury my face in the small lagoon, too, to drink and clean away the filth I'd accumulated these past twenty-four hours.

I slowed. The ledge around the pool was stained with vivid red, green, and yellow soil, as beautiful as a rainbow.

Pools don't have that unless....

"Talina. No!"

She'd dropped to her knees, cupping her slender hands together, about to scoop water to drink. Then she yelled, my heart ripping through my ribs at the sound of that anguished cry. It had happened all so fast. Talina was flung aside, landing hard on the unforgiving ground.

I stopped running—hadn't even realised I'd started. It was Jad. He'd moved so fast, knocking Talina out of the way before she could submerge her hands into that burning water.

He scowled at her with a look so menacing, it could have cut steel. "Whatever pools or streams you come across on this island are not drinkable. Don't go near them."

He picked up a fist-sized rock and threw it into the pool to emphasise his point. The water fizzed. No, not the water. The rock itself was melting like an aspirin dissolving. Rising gas and steam bubbled to the surface before deceptively smoothing over again.

Tears streaked down Talina's cheeks, her face greyish.

I draped my arms around her shoulders, holding her tight. "It's okay. You're all right."

She shook so hard that I thought she may have been having a fit. "I hate this place."

"I know. I hate it too."

For the first time, I wished she hadn't been such a loyal friend. I wished she'd remained at Vukovar, where she would have been moderately safe. She risked too much by being here. They all did.

I gazed up at Jad to thank him, but he'd already walked away.

It felt like a dismissal, a rejection. Like it was my fault.

Talina's shock dulled a bit. I helped her up from the ground, fearful of letting go. Her legs were stable, but her knees were trembling. "Come on. Let's keep moving."

Getting away from that pool was the priority.

HALF AN HOUR LATER, we reached the end of the flat plain only to be greeted with a boiling mud bog that stretched far and wide. The roiling sludge was as black as tar, giving off the distinctive stench of rotting eggs as it gurgled and bubbled. The persistent *pop, pop, pop* made me queasy. Every so often, the rising muck would take on a perfectly round shape, like it was sending up eyeballs to look at us.

I covered my mouth with my hand. There was something else beyond that acidic, coppery reek. It reminded me of the bombing aftermath at Essida, when the air had smelt of burning hair and fat.

Talina let out a small whimper.

I latched on to her hand, realising what she'd seen. Bodies. Well... parts of them, churned over and over again in the soupy mud. There was a foot. An arm. Bones that might have once been a ribcage, not yet broken away from the spine. Now that I knew what caused the smell, I couldn't take it any longer. My lungs felt like they'd collapsed inside me.

Bronislav stared at the boiling slurry. Dark humour lined his face. "Well, at least now we know how Morgomoth is getting rid of the people who annoy him."

I knew it was a ploy to hide his shock, but no one appreciated the comment. Annaka eyed him with a sour face.

Marek sounded as though he were struggling to breathe. "What now? This bog stretches for kilometres."

It was a terrible blow to our progress. It would take us hours, possibly another day to get around the bog, but there was no other option.

Marek scratched his head. "This never came up in the mapographic." He sounded like he was apologising.

Jad had kept his distance from us. I didn't like the way he kept looking behind him. "It's possible it's been glamoured from technology. We need to find shelter. Now."

"Where?" My throat was too sore to shout, but he still heard me through the sweltering winds.

"There's a forest of sorts ahead. Not too far."

He started walking.

A forest?

He had to be joking.

Marek faithfully followed his captain, leading our team behind him. "Jad's right. I saw it earlier in the afternoon on the horizon. For a long time, I thought it was just rocks and mountains, but I checked the mapographic. It's a forest."

"Your mapographic was wrong about the bog," I said miserably. "What if it's wrong about this?"

A forest? In this environment? It isn't possible.

"What if it's a mirage?" I persisted. "A spell designed to trap us?"

Marek's entire body had gone rigid. "We have no other option but to take the risk."

I studied his expression, trying to figure out his true frame of mind. Before we'd encountered the bog, he'd been talking to Jad. The pair had conversed in private away from the rest of us.

I crossed my arms. "What's going on?"

He waited until the others were some distance ahead, but he kept his voice low regardless. "We're being followed."

I stared, not wanting to believe what he was saying.

My own voice was a whisper, held by an edge of fear. "By what?"

"We don't know."

I DIDN'T TELL the others. Talina was freaked out enough as it was, and Annaka was pouring her energy into keeping us invisible. She needed to keep her focus on that.

If this creature... thing is following us, then it must be relying on scent.

That freaked me out even more. How on earth could we hide when it was tracking us through smell alone? It would catch up to us eventually.

Jad must have a plan. He's far too calm not to.

If Bronislav heard the creature, if he was aware of what was going on, he didn't say anything.

IT WAS WAY past nightfall by the time we reached the forest, a very loose term for what it actually was. The trees had been reduced to husks. Branches and vines crawled across the foliage in spiderwebbing tangles. The entire area was a dense jumble of thick roots that made the trees appear to be standing on stilts above the mud—the same hot slurry from the bog. The forest might have been beautiful when it first started growing, but the dark magic of this land had corrupted it.

Annaka's fine eyebrows rose. "It's a mud... swamp."

Bronislav raised his shirt collar over his nose. "It stinks worse than that bog."

The better to hide our scent.

That, of course, had been Jad's plan all along.

We entered the dead forest. The roots were thick and sturdy enough to support our weight, but I wouldn't have liked to put a foot in the wrong place. The sludge below wasn't boiling, but I imagined it was still hot enough to leave nasty burns. The deeper we ventured, ducking and climbing over the roots and branches, the more I heard cries that sounded like the screams of the dying. Strange lights flickered in and out of the shadows. No one else heard the wails or saw the lights.

One of the wispy radiances drew closer. A wraith. He floated aimlessly, vanishing through the dark trees. The entire swampland was full of condemned souls, staring back at me with hollow eyes. Their sorrow-filled voices nearly broke me. They were suffering. This land was just as toxic to the dead as it was to the living.

It felt like we'd travelled all night, but Marek assured me only an hour had passed since we'd arrived. I detected the excitement in his voice and lifted my drooping eyelids. Ahead was a tower, some sort of fortified keep made of stone. Roots and crawlers had grown around the structure. Orthrask was a relatively new island to the world, and it startled me that a watchtower of this size had been built. What was more unnerving was that the dead plant life had managed to grow over it in such a short time.

Jad raised his hand, urging us to stay put. "Let me check it out first."

He kicked the solid doors down and crossed the threshold, disappearing into the dark folds inside.

Five minutes later, he reappeared. "It's abandoned. Let's rest here tonight."

I was too tired to voice my uncertainty.

Abandoned?

How could he be certain?

It was a watchtower.

The casters assigned to this post could very well come back.

And if it was abandoned, why had they left it in the first place?

Inside, the watchtower was empty and dry. There was no sign anyone had been here recently. Or would return. I stared out through one of the slitted windows, which I assumed was designed for casters to unleash a barrage of fire upon invading forces... or unsuspecting travellers. Again, I questioned why this tower was built. What were those assigned here meant to be keeping watch on? And why had they left?

The tower would have provided 360-degree views of the surrounding lands once, but roots and thorns had overgrown the building, eclipsing the outside world.

"It's cosy." Annaka sat down and took out her sleeping bag from her rucksack. "Beats sleeping in a cavern where lava could flood us."

She had a point there.

We're safe here. Protected by the dead forest.

So why did I feel so exposed?

We remained sullen and quiet as we ate. More dry biscuits, jerky, and desiccated fruit. I wished I could wash it down with water, but we had strictly divided everything into rations to ensure we had enough over the next four days. We had canned soup, but no one could be bothered to cook it. Jad remained outside, eating silently on his own. The tower wasn't a large edifice, which meant the proximity between us was something he didn't want to risk. I was both glad and annoyed by that. He was taking the first night shift. Marek would take the next one, followed by Bronislav. Annaka was excused; her invisibility charms were more important than participating in guard duty. No one asked Talina. She'd suffered the worst today when she'd nearly taken a boiling spa bath. And me? Marek insisted I needed to rest. I needed all my strength to defeat *him*.

Despite how bonetired I was, my mind wouldn't switch off. I listened to the sniffs, breaths, and coughs as everyone drifted into a much-needed slumber. It made me envious. They could sleep easily because they didn't have to take on Morgomoth. They didn't have to learn the spell that would unite the Larthalgule and Neathror blades.

Four days. That's all I had left, and I had no idea how to begin. Darius and Macaslan were relying on me. The entire Haxsan Guard forces were relying on me.

The answer is inside the Bone Grimoire.

And the pages are blank.

How am I meant to work with that?

This... *everything*... it was all an impossible task.

The dry wind outside caused the vines and branches to scratch against the tower, the sound reminding me of claws scoring stones. I sensed evil in this building. I felt it in the trees and the roots, in the wraiths who hovered in dark places, and in the very stones we lay on.

I focused on my magic, reaching out for anything that was dead and wanted to cause harm, but the only things out there were the wraiths.

Go to sleep, Zaya.

Just shut your eyes and don't open them till dawn.

I startled awake, sitting ramrod straight. No, that wasn't correct. I didn't recognise this place. It certainly wasn't the watchtower.

Am I... dreaming?

It was a large chamber made of black stone and crystal, the walls and ceilings decorated with mirrors, giving the impression that the room was twice the size it really was. It also made me feel as though I were in a hall of mirrors, where there was no certainty of the correct way out. But I knew the power pulsing in this room was darker and crueller than any mere carnival trick.

A perfect circle was etched into a jade marble floor. A swastika symbol was in the centre, which was held by a griffin and eagle. My mouth hung open, and I tasted bile in the back of my throat. Slowly, I looked up to the dais where an obsidian throne stood, as magnificent as the ones I'd seen at the Black Palace, only this one lacked the grace and style of royalty and was all sharp angles and jagged points. A young man with shoulder-length blond hair sat on the throne like a king presiding over the room. His volatile temper shone in his eyes. They were the same colour as the deepest, most dangerous oceans. His face was pale, more dead than alive, his handsome features spoiled by his heartless expression.

A small moan of terror escaped me.

This was Willieth. Before he'd become that burnt skeleton made of shadows and fire.

This is another memory.

Willieth's thin lips crept into a taunt. "At last, you arrive. I was beginning to wonder if you had abandoned me."

I stilled, my blood running thin.

No. He can't see me.

My relief was short-lived when someone entered through the open glass doors. Isgrad dropped to one knee before the throne and bowed his head. "You summoned me, brother."

"Indeed." Willieth's voice was cold, his expression pitiless. He looked down on his brother like he was nothing more than a begging dog. "We need to talk about Briya."

CHAPTER 11

Isgrad kept his expression blank, but in his eyes, I detected a flash of hesitance. It was gone in a heartbeat, and I hoped Willieth hadn't noticed it.

Isgrad gave his brother a puzzled look. "I haven't seen Briya in weeks. The last I heard, you had sent her to Jerasinum to assist your resistance there."

I was surprised by his level of composure. I was certain that inside, Isgrad must have had panic rattling across his bones.

Willieth's tone was flat and detached. "She has run away to the Haxsan Guard. Did you know she was a spy?"

There was a note of incredulity in Isgrad's tone. "No."

"Ah, brother. Do not look so dull. You and Briya were close, were you not?"

"We were… I believed us to be… friends. Working together to serve you and the ULD."

Willieth looked up to the ceiling and laughed. "Friends. Indeed. Then she has used and fooled you, but never fear, brother. Briya has fallen into my trap."

The hairs on my arms rose.

To his credit, Isgrad managed to keep his chin high—a soldier simply reporting to his lord. "Trap?"

Willieth drummed his fingers on the arm of his throne. His nails were long, like talons, a sign he was in the early stages of becoming the monster I knew and despised. "I had my suspicions about Briya. She was always far too keen to show her loyalty and prove her allegiance, and yet she never really did much. Just watched. I had Yarrock trail her these past several weeks, and he confirmed what I suspected. She is a Haxsan Guard soldier."

Isgrad maintained his closed-off expression. "You said you had set a trap?"

"I misled Briya about the attack we will strike on Saracta. She will provide the Haxsan Guard with the wrong time and direction of our assault. We will hit them hard after they arrive." He arched his eyebrow. "A cunning plan to sack the city and destroy the Haxsan Guard troops at the same time, is it not?"

Willieth actually sounded proud of himself.

"A wise decision." Isgrad's lips remained a neutral line. He bowed once more and turned to leave.

"I haven't dismissed you, brother."

Isgrad stiffened. He dutifully returned, submissive and yielding.

Willieth offered him a slow smile. "I have a task for you. The Council of Founding Sovereigns needs to understand what price they will pay if they dare think they can infiltrate my ranks through espionage. I cannot let spies—even the beautiful ones—go without punishment."

A bolt of panic went through me.

Isgrad went very still. "You are angry, brother."

"I am annoyed. It should be you who is angry. Briya used you. That is why I am giving you the honour of tracking her down and carrying out the assassination."

Isgrad's skin went a sickly colour in the subdued light.

Fear bombarded my mind, but there was nothing I could do. This was a memory, and I was here only to observe and learn the truth. At least, that's what I believed these memories were trying to accomplish.

Isgrad stared stonily ahead. "Of course. There will be nothing left of Briya once I find her."

His neck tensed with the effort to get those words out.

Willieth clapped his hands with wicked delight. "Oh, where is the fun in that? No, you are to bring me back her head. What is left of her, you will send to the Council of Founding Sovereigns. Preferably in pieces." He shone a triumphant smile at his brother. "You have one week."

Isgrad bowed and left. He couldn't have moved fast enough out of the throne room. I followed, my feet flying beneath me to keep up. He wandered down several passages, avoiding other dissidents who swept in and out of the halls, and found a private alcove where he dropped to his knees and cried. His long, heaving sobs broke my heart.

The scenery shifted. Everything around me blended like dark watercolours, morphing into a different scene and space.

I was in a new memory.

Isgrad hurtled down the long stairs and stormed into the silver-thorned witch's cavern, his face a mix of despair and urgency. "He knows. My brother frigging knows."

The witch was in her rocking chair, staring at the fire. Her eyes shifted toward him, taking in Isgrad's flustered appearance with a resigned understanding.

Isgrad moved across the cavern to stand in front of her. He stared, panting through gritted teeth. Something had dawned in his icy-blue eyes. "You knew this would happen, didn't you?"

The witch took a moment to answer. "I see many paths ahead. This is just one of them."

"Why did you not warm me? My brother knew all this time about Briya and me."

"Because it's not my place to intervene. I observe the past, present, and the future, but I do not manipulate it. I do not get involved in the choices that are made. I did that once, and it was a terrible mistake."

Isgrad placed his head in his hands, looking as though he'd been seized by sickness. "I've been put in an impossible situation."

"Sit." The witch pointed at the seat opposite. "Tell me everything that occurred."

Isgrad did.

When he finished, the silver-thorned witch settled back in her rocking chair and closed her eyes.

Isgrad had calmed down a little, but his impatience was climbing. I knew it by the way his fingers curled, his white knuckles looking capable of popping out of his pale skin. "What are you doing?"

"Thinking."

She opened her eyes. A faint smile played on her lips. "Your brother knows of your relationship with Briya. He's testing your loyalty. You must make him believe that you are truly his soldier. That your allegiance lies with him."

Isgrad stared at her with unabashed horror. "What are you saying? That I kill Briya? Do those… *things* to her remains?"

"Yes. You have to make Willieth believe it's true. There is a mass grave beyond my woods to the north. I will locate it precisely for you on a map. Bodies are brought there every morning and night. Find a corpse that looks like Briya. Mutilate it beyond recognition. Do exactly as your brother has requested. Give him the head and send the rest of the body to the Council."

In the firelight, Isgrad's cheeks took on a green tinge. "I can't do that. It would be disrespectful to the dead woman."

"You must. You're no closer to finding the key that will open the doors to the Isla Necropolis. Without it, you will never discover the Bone Grimoire and absorb the Grand Masters' magic. You must stay by your brother's side and earn his trust again. You must continue to spy and report to the Haxsan Guard. Lives are depending on you."

Isgrad stood, the line of his shoulders tense. He hurried to his desk. "I have to write to Briya. I have to tell her to go into hiding. She needs to know that she's been given misleading information regarding the planned attack on Saracta."

His pen remained poised above his notepad. He shook his head and made a disgusted sound in the back of his throat. "I can't."

The witch watched him. I had a feeling she'd already known whatever it was Isgrad had worked out.

He settled into his desk chair, looking utterly defeated. "It's another test. If I warn Briya about the attack and the Haxsan Guard divert their plan, then Willieth will know that *I* am really the one who's the informant." He threw his pen against the wall. It snapped, black ink running across the rock like blood. "He set me up."

"Then do not let him win."

Isgrad eyed the witch for a long time. "I can't be responsible for all those deaths. I could warn Briya. Let her know the truth. Willieth will hate me. He'll want me dead. But I'll run away, or stay here. I'll find the Bone Grimoire and return to defeat him."

"You are rambling words of madness," the witch spat. "Staying by your brother's side, earning his trust and the loyalty of the dissent rebels, is the only method you have to kill him. This plan can only work from the inside. Otherwise, you won't have the element of surprise. Your brother will easily defeat any attack you lead."

"Then what? I just let all those people at Saracta die?"

"You knew sacrifices would have to be made when you swore to kill your brother. This is one of them."

Something changed across Isgrad's face. A silent anger swept over him, his eyes filling with rage and wrath. The walls shook. Jars that contained herbs and spells toppled from their shelves. Glass shattered, exploding from some unknown build-up of pressure that played havoc with my ears. I gasped, struggling to keep my footing as the ground lurched beneath me. Terror ran into my belly, tingling and leaping. Fissures snaked their way across the cavern walls, the air becoming ripe with the scent of disturbed earth.

The witch stood from her rocking chair. "Isgrad," she barked, her eyes ripping into him with fury. "That is enough."

She slammed the end of her walking stick into the ground. The shuddering instantly ceased.

Isgrad was trembling, his eyes still alight with glittering frenzy, but slowly it started to ebb out of him, leaving him with nothing but shame and remorse. "I'm sorry. I… I don't know what just happened."

The witch hobbled over to the desk, knobbly fingers tight on her walking stick. She grabbed his shirt and sniffed.

Isgrad understandably flinched. "What are you doing?"

"You wreak of magic. Untrained. Dangerous. Magic."

"Necromancy?" I hated the mixture of hope and dread in his voice. "Is it no longer dormant?"

The witch let go of his shirt. She took out a map of her woods from a desk drawer and marked a spot on it with a pen. "There. That is where you'll find the mass grave. Write your note to Briya. Tell her to go into hiding, but that's all. Nothing else."

She avoided looking at him.

Isgrad surveyed the damage in the cavern. The walls had splintered. A large crack ran up the stairs. Furniture had been tossed aside or completely torn apart. It looked like a tornado had swept through the witch's home. "I'm sorry," he repeated.

"You never specialised, did you?"

Isgrad looked like he was about to be violently ill. "No."

She stared at the floor, at the ceiling, at her destroyed cavern. Everywhere but at him. Studying her, it occurred to me that the witch was deliberately not telling him something. Something that worried her.

At last, she turned to Isgrad with the map. "Go."

The memory changed.

Isgrad was standing at the edge of the mass grave. The courage on his face faltered. Below in the trench, bodies had been piled, waiting to be burned or buried. The stench was unbearable. Even the air tasted contaminated by the rot.

Isgrad carefully climbed down the disturbed soil. He grimaced when his foot made contact with pliant skin, which sent a wet, spongy sound into the night that did nothing to appease the roiling in my stomach. He squeezed his eyes shut, perhaps trying to pluck up his nerve. Not only was the trench home to bodies but maggots and worms as well.

Isgrad began his search, turning the dead over to get a look at their faces, scanning for the ones with brown hair. This one was too old. This one too young. A man. A woman. A child. Some burned. Some blistered. Too thin from illness or neglect, or inflicted with wounds that had never been treated, just left to fester and slowly poison.

I wondered how long Isgrad could torture himself like this, digging through the dead, getting pieces of them under his nails. He'd have to scrub himself clean under a shower for a very long time to remove that lingering scent of death.

At last, he found a young woman with dark brown hair. Her eyes were bulging, as though she were permanently surprised by her own death. He dragged her from the mound of bodies and hoisted her over his shoulder. Isgrad laid her out on the flat ground and examined her ashen face, her lips purple and bloodless. He'd brought a collection of knives with him, which he now reached for.

"I am so sorry," he sobbed.

I turned away, hating the sound of the blade cutting through flesh.

The scenery changed.

I'd returned to the black stone and crystal chamber. Willieth was sitting on his throne, inspecting his nails with boredom. His blond hair had been tied back with a gold clasp. He looked like a beautiful yet wicked prince. Such a contrast to the monster I was used to.

The doors to the throne room were thrown open and Isgrad prowled in, stalking forward like a hunted criminal. "Here."

He tossed the caster head. It rolled across the floor, the long hair trailing after it like a brown river. It hit the dais and was still.

Willieth looked at the severed head with less interest than he had with his nails. "Goodness. Did she put up a fight? I hardly recognise her."

I bit my lip, keeping in the wave of nausea that rose up my throat. Isgrad had been brutal. The nose was gone, the lips reduced to meaty pulp. What was left of the teeth were broken and hung loose. Even the eyes—oh, I dreaded thinking how Isgrad must have squeezed those eyeballs out. There was nothing left but black holes. Whatever flesh remained on that face had been cut beyond recognition.

"I did what you asked." Isgrad's voice was a callous echo through the chamber. "I know what this was really about. I am loyal to you and none other. Do not test my allegiance again."

Willieth clicked his tongue softly. "And the body?"

"Sent to the Council of Founding Sovereigns. In pieces."

He turned, retreating toward the door.

Willieth let out a hollow chuckle. "Not so fast, brother."

He snapped his fingers. The doors slammed, locking Isgrad in the throne room. I jumped at the enormous boom that resonated from the entry. It had sounded... final.

Willieth stepped down from the dais. He bent over and plucked the head from the floor, examining what remained of its face with mild amusement. His fingers wrapped around the long hair, letting the head dangle by his side. "I confess, what is left does look like Briya, but I must be certain. Killing a lover is, after all, no easy feat."

Isgrad was breathing hard. His chest rose and fell rapidly.

Willieth smiled, but it was devoid of warmth. "I will summon Briya's soul, shall I?"

I stood numb with fear. If Willieth did that, it was game over.

Is this how it ended for Isgrad?

Because I 100 percent believed that these memories were coming from him. I knew—no, I sensed he was dead. It was his soul sending me these little pieces of this life, letting me weave them together. He was trying to tell me something out of all of this. Something he couldn't say directly as a ghost.

It has to be.

Isgrad cleared his throat, speaking with a bravado I knew he did not feel. "Go ahead."

Willieth watched him for a long time, blue eyes assessing, burrowing right into Isgrad's soul. He advanced in one fluid movement and handed the head to his brother. "Go bury it. Or keep it as a trophy. Do as you wish. You have my trust, brother."

He rested his hand on Isgrad's shoulder, those slender fingers, fingers that could have belonged to an artist, squeezing. "I am sorry for Briya's betrayal."

Isgrad nodded and walked away. The doors were thrown open as if by invisible guards. He tore past them, the mutilated head still tight in his hand.

CHAPTER 12

I woke up… not where I expected.

Oh geez. Even in sleep, I can't rest.

I was at the Isla Necropolis. Tonight, the magnificent chamber was lit with torches, which sent dancing light across the walls. I'd never taken the time to look at the meticulous paintings. The frescoes were all depictions of the afterlife, casters making offerings to deities, the Sun God portrayed with light shimmering from his luminous skin as he accepted them with open arms. It was a recording, a documentation of an ancient way of life, far older than even the humans who had presided before the change. Even the monolithic columns had been designed like tall stalks with lotus blossoms, branches splayed upward to support the vaulted ceiling. It resembled an orchard, symmetrical and proportioned to the millimetre. At least, that's what I imagined. Magic rarely miscalculated.

"It is beautiful."

I flinched at the intrusive voices that swept in a phantom call through my mind.

The five Grand Masters stood behind the empty plinth, their

blood-red cloaks moving like running water in an imaginary breeze. The only things that seemed real about them were their bone-smooth jawlines and their lips stitched together with black thread. Whatever else remained of their faces was obscured by their cowls. I couldn't see their eyes. I had no idea if they even *had* eyes.

A sticky coating filled my mouth. "You summoned me?"

"No. You are here of your own volition."

"How can I be?"

My brain wanted to sleep. It wouldn't choose to be here.

"Your subconscious has the full resources of your mind when you sleep. You brought yourself to this chamber." They raised their heads, their faces still eclipsed by shadow. *"You have questions. We can smell them."*

That made me feel like I had spiders walking up my spine.

I pointed to the empty plinth. "The book is inside me?"

"Yes."

"How?"

"The Bone Grimoire contains our magic. Our magic is inside you. You may summon the book as you please."

"You told me to grab the book. Learn its magic. Learn the spell to unite the Neathror and Larthalgule blades. How do I do that? When I opened the grimoire, the pages were blank."

I couldn't help but look over my shoulder. I hadn't forgotten that both Morgomoth and I were linked to this place, and I became fearful that at any moment he would appear, ready to finish the task he'd set to accomplish.

"The pages are not empty. It is self-doubt holding you back, not allowing you to see what is clearly visible."

My heart thundered—with both anger and annoyance. "I don't have time for self-doubt."

"Agreed."

"Can't you just tell me what the spell is?"

"No."

"Of course you can't. That would be too easy, wouldn't it?" I let my sarcasm seethe.

They didn't answer.

I snorted, my eyes burning with unshed tears.

Four days left.

I was never going to make it. It was all too hard and complicated. Whenever I had an inkling of where to start, I was always met with a no for an answer. Self-doubt indeed. How could I ever overcome the widening hole that was forming in my heart, building from negativity and self-loathing? I wasn't good enough to do this. Fate had chosen unwisely. Jad would have been a better choice. Even Marek. Or Annaka. Not me. Pathetic, stupid me who couldn't even find a spell on a page.

"Do you think you are unworthy of the task ahead?"

The Grand Masters' voices only served to enrage me more. "How, then? Tell me how I'm supposed to do this."

"You already know the answer."

"I do not. I don't know anything."

Blinding fury coiled up from somewhere deep and dark inside me. Before I realised what I was doing, I slammed my boot into the plinth. Dark magic seeped out of me on impact, the plinth exploding. Bones shattered, looking like bits of desiccated coconut on the marble floor.

"Feel better?"

No. Absolutely not. I felt useless and stupid and pathetic.

I was breathing hard, my fingers tingling with pent-up magic. It was impossible to shove the anger back down; it had experienced the light, and it wanted to remain at the surface.

"A tantrum has never worked for anyone."

I threw full hostility into my stony glare.

The Grand Masters wisely shut up.

I wished there was someone who understood what I was going

through. Wished there was just one person, dead or alive, who could give me answers. Who knew what all this meant.

I stilled, furious with myself for not thinking of him sooner. "Could Isgrad help me? He learnt about the Bone Grimoire and the Interitus blade. If I summoned his soul, could he give me the answers I need?"

The Grand Masters were a part of me. I assumed they had witnessed the memories and knew who Isgrad was.

They didn't speak.

I crossed my arms. "Don't all answer at once."

Their blood-red cloaks billowed around them, and I wondered if power was pulsing through their wraithlike forms. *"How can you be certain these memories are coming from Isgrad?"*

I was just starting to feel my temper fray, a little bit of hope crawling in, but now it was drowned by doubt. "Who else would they be coming from?"

"The Dark Divide."

"The Dark Divide is controlled by Morgomoth. It's become Orthrask. That place only answers to him."

"Does it?"

I felt capable of spewing fire. "Of course it does."

"And yet it was the Dark Divide that first led you to the memories."

I remembered that terrible quake that occurred when I'd fled down the dark tunnels The mysterious door that had appeared, leading me to Isgrad and Willieth in their cabin.

No. It isn't possible.

I shook my head, not daring to believe it. "Are you saying the Dark Divide was trying to help me?"

Might still be helping me?

I almost laughed, cold and disbelieving.

"Zaya."

Trepidation ran in the Grand Masters' voices, making my skin instantly clammy.

"He senses you. You must leave. He is coming."

"Leave?" A knot of terror swelled in my throat. "How?"

How did one leave this place?

"Wake up."

Their voices were an amplified roar across the chamber, sending the echoing acoustics rattling across the walls. Wind tore through the chamber, the Grand Masters' cowls thrown back. I couldn't prevent my cry of horror. They had eyes all right. Eyes the colour of an underwater abyss, which bled black blood down their hollow cheeks. It burned their bony faces like acid; I smelt the sizzling stench in the wind. Pressure built in my head. Ringing filled my ears. My own eyes felt like they'd rupture into tiny, gory pieces—

I woke up.

I was back in the watchtower, my heart beating loudly, pumping anxiety through my veins. The impression from the dream continued to burn across my vision, as though it had been permanently imprinted on my pupils. It was hot inside the tower, but that didn't stop the cold sweat from running down the back of my neck.

Both my mind and Morgomoth's were linked to that place, and he had sensed me. It had been a risk going there. I couldn't return; otherwise, Morgomoth had every chance of obtaining the grimoire.

I clutched at my chest, wondering if the book was secure inside me. I still didn't fully comprehend it. The grimoire was no longer a physical item but magic that was part of my body. Something I could manifest into a material form.

I have to try.

I sat up and crossed my legs, imagining the magic flowing out

of me, pooling into a liquid onto the floor, moulding into something complete and physical. Turning into the book.

I opened my eyes.

There was nothing there.

That dark fire ignited inside me again. I cursed under my
breath, hating my weakness and my ineptitude to get anything
right.

"It is self-doubt holding you back."

"Do you think you are unworthy of the task ahead?"

"A tantrum has never worked for anyone."

*"Once this is all over, I never want to see you again. I hope you
die in that place."*

I fell back onto the stone floor, wishing I could sink into it
and disappear. My tears flowed freely, staining my cheeks, no
doubt making all the grime run. I had nothing left but my own
failings and self-loathing. The others were fast asleep and didn't
stir at the sound of my racking sobs. Bronislav and Marek must
have switched their night watch because the former wasn't present.
If Bronislav heard me crying, I hoped he'd keep it to himself and
not alert the others. I didn't need them to learn that they were on
a suicide mission. Not yet.

No. I can't let that happen to them.

Morgomoth is after me, not them.

*Darius and Macaslan need to keep communication with me, not
Marek.*

I knew the truth.

I knew what had to be done.

What the right thing was to do.

I was going to have to leave my friends.

I MUST HAVE FALLEN ASLEEP AGAIN—A dreamless sleep, thankfully—because I was roused awake, a hand shaking my shoulder.

"What the hell—"

"Shh."

Seeing Marek's alarmed face made me feel a shade paler. I crept up to sitting, a question on the tip of my tongue, but he beat me to it.

"Come on. We have to go. Get out of your sleeping bag."

"What's going on? Why are you whispering?"

The watchtower was empty. Only my rucksack remained.

Still half-asleep, I climbed to my feet.

Marek rolled my sleeping bag and mat up and stuffed them into my rucksack, which he tossed over his shoulder. Panic climbed in his eyes. "Outside. Come on. We have to be quick."

He grabbed my wrist and propelled me down the winding staircase.

"What's happened? Where are the others?"

I didn't like the way his thumb pressed into my skin. Something had seriously frightened him.

"They're waiting outside."

My legs struggled to keep up with his swift pace. The stairway was dark. Some of the roots and branches from outside had punched through the mortar and crawled up the stonework overnight. That in itself was startling, but it couldn't prepare me for the next shock I encountered. The vines had thorns, sharper than any plant I'd seen before. The barbs had scored into the stone, leaving behind scratches and indentations that appeared like some sort of prehistoric cave drawing. And there was blood running down the vines. It trickled over the stonework, making red pools on the stairs.

"Marek?"

He dipped under a branch. "So, it turns out this dead forest isn't actually... dead."

We slipped out the door into a spiked jungle. The forest *had* grown. Vines and creepers, as thick and heavy as snakes, had twisted and squeezed through the roots and trees, ascending to the heights of the canopy. Red liquid ran over their thorns and bristles, which looked capable of amputating limbs. The blood splashed into the bubbling mud below.

The forest is alive.

Its growth wasn't the only evidence of a thriving environment, though. Webs were interspersed through the foliage, some of them large enough to be the size of a house. The glossy silk threads could have passed for beautiful if it weren't for the animals trapped inside, their bodies wrapped a thousand times over in sticky sheet webs.

A viscid, coppery taste rose in my mouth. No, not animals. Body parts. Chewed and nibbled on, but still recognisably a foot, or an arm, or a torso here and there. There were so many pieces interspersed across the webs that it was impossible to tell how many people these parts had belonged to.

It had been a mistake to believe the watchtower was abandoned. The dissent rebels never left their post. They'd been eaten and wrapped up like leftovers.

Marek's fingers released my wrist and latched on to my hand. He squeezed tight, a signal to move. We climbed over thick crawlers and hunkered down behind a tree where the others were hiding. Bronislav had his finger hooked around the trigger of his cast-shooter. Annaka looked like she wanted to spit out a slew of curse words but remained silent. Talina's eyes were darting everywhere, round as saucers. I felt steam dampen my socks and boots. We were far too close to the boiling mud for comfort.

Behind a tree not too far to our right was Jad. He stood like a pillar of steel, his cast-shooter out as he silently watched and assessed.

But for what?

Marek opened his mouth to speak, but a wet plopping sound caught our attention. We stole a glance over the roots and crawlers that made up our hiding spot. I grew increasingly nervous the longer we waited.

There it went again.

Plop. Splat. Squelch.

Something climbed out of the mud ahead.

My muscles tightened with every passing moment.

It was a slimy mutant thing, half spider, half octopus. Densely packed hair populated its legs, the suckers leaving a viscous gloop in their wake. From this vantage, it appeared to be made out of flesh. Whatever it had been prior, though, this toxic island had changed it, made it into a creature that could swim in the mud and climb the trees. I was looking at an ecosystem completely new to this world, one that operated on savagery and darkness. It was further proof that Morgomoth's necromancy was unnaturally changing the balance.

"We're leaving now," Marek whispered. "Jad just gave the signal."

He returned my rucksack to me.

Slowly, we crept out of our hiding place, climbing across the network of roots that formed a pathway over the mud. It meant we would have to return to the bog and double back a few kilometres, but I preferred that over becoming webbed stew.

I kept my eyes on the creature. It leapt onto one of its large silk tangles, feasting on an animal with wings, not quite a bird or a bat but a mutant of the two. Hearing it eat was nauseating. The chomping of its teeth, the slurps and gurgles as it drank fatty juices, made me cringe all over.

Jad was leading. Bronislav and Annaka trailed after him,

followed by Talina and Marek. I wished they'd move faster. It sucked being the last in the line. Talina was struggling on the roots, some of the spaces between them too wide for her to jump. She slipped, banging her knee, her trouser leg eliciting a piercing rip into the night. To her credit, she didn't scream, but the sound of her scuffle had been loud enough to capture attention. I ducked behind the closest tree, daring to steal a glance. The creature raised its ugly head, eight median eyes staring at Talina and Marek with hungry resolve. I could imagine it was thanking providence at that moment for the fresh meat.

It charged, piercing fangs snapping.

"Run," Marek cried.

He gripped Talina's arms and forced her to her feet. They ran, but I knew they weren't fast enough. The creature would easily catch up and then—

Before I knew what I was doing, I sprang from the tree and picked up a dislodged root, throwing it with all my might. It hit the monster above the eyes, those black globes turning on me instead.

I gulped air, taking a moment to grasp that I was now the one who was going to have to hightail it. I hurtled back the way I'd come, discarding my rucksack to give me additional speed. The spider-octopus thing charged after me. I could hear its scampering feet, its suckers sliding over wood. There became nothing in the world but me and the distance from that monster. Blood roared in my ears. I wove between the trees, skilfully climbing over the roots and crawlers, my feet flying beneath me, but I wasn't fast enough. Never fast enough. The creature was gaining. The webs around me vibrated as it leapt from one tangled snare to the next.

Branches snatched at my hair and clothes. Thorns cut into my arms, slicing my palms as I pushed my way through the dead foliage. The blood was thicker the deeper I ventured into the forest, dripping like tree sap. It was slippery as ice too.

My scream rushed out of me before I even realised I was falling. I landed hard on a welter of dead leaves. The earth beneath me was damp, and a cry tore from my throat when I finally worked out what it was—hot, sticky blood. Pushing to my hands and knees, I threw every bit of my strength into getting back up, but the roots were moving, snaking around my ankles. They wrapped over my legs, then my wrists, pinning me down.

No.

No!

The spider-octopus thing appeared in the trees above, its pincers snipping. It opened its jaws, torrid breath powerful enough to knock me flat as it released a colossal roar. It seemed to watch me with a hideous, horrific smile.

I kicked and thrashed, but it was no use. The vines wouldn't let me go.

I looked up to see the creature lunge.

CHAPTER 13

I was suspended in a moment of terror. A moment that seemed both eternal and too quick. The creature opened its mouth, revealing black fangs that stank of such foul waste, it nearly knocked me unconscious right there. That would have been a mercy, sparing me from witnessing the yellow liquid that seeped from its venomous glands. There wasn't time to shut my eyes. All I could do was watch as I was about to become a meal for this vile monster.

A bright blur of motion exploded through the forest. The spider-octopus thing howled and snarled, pulling its legs inward. Four of the limbs had been gravely burned, the intricate layers of hair and suckers either singed or melted down. Another jet of fire struck from the trees, searing the creature's head. The heat alone was like standing too close to a hearth. Perspiration ran down my face, and an awful popping noise met my ears. Nausea rolled through me when I realised what that sound was. The monster had lost not one but two of its eyes, which had been as delicate as glass and unable to withstand the pressure of the heat.

It let out a shrill roar, forgetting me entirely, its focus now set on a new threat.

Jad dived from the trees, wielding his athame-sabre. The blade was alight, the flames moving so fast, they reminded me of a field of burning stars. He skilfully dodged its strikes, scarcely escaping those snapping pincers, bringing his sword down again and again as he hacked and slashed at the spidery legs. The monster dived and pounced, the suckers on its legs sliding over the sparks that rained down from Jad's blade. Everything was so dry, I was surprised the forest didn't ignite.

The spider-octopus thing sank back onto its haunches, poised to spring. It lunged at the same time Jad leapt forward. He ran straight for those pincers, slicing them off in one swoop, then drove the athame-sabre straight into the monster's ugly mouth. The creature teetered back, its piercing cry sending a wave of foul, sticky breath through the air. Jad's face contorted with animalistic fury, his red eyes alight in a killing frenzy. Panting and shaking, he extracted his blade and ruthlessly sliced across all eight limbs.

The monster bawled a final ear-splitting shriek and collapsed to the ground. Black blood oozed from the severed legs. There were cuts, punctures, and burns across its body, the smell thick and ugly.

I stared at Jad, grateful to be alive but shocked at the ferocity I'd witnessed.

He was still fevered by the intensity of the fight, his blood-flecked skin only heightening his look of ire. He stalked toward me, as though I, too, were an enemy he was considering cutting down. He raised his athame-sabre, which was still burning hot, and slashed the roots that had seized my wrists and ankles. They slithered away like snakes, disappearing into the boiling mud.

"Thank you," I said softly, the elation of being alive quickly fading.

Jad turned away from me and climbed back onto the ridge. I

saw the burns on his exposed skin and couldn't prevent a shiver of revulsion ghosting up my spine. They hadn't been caused by the creature he'd just destroyed. No, those wounds had been caused by *me*. Because he had gotten too close. Because he'd risked everything to save me.

Guilt cut deep, and I had to swallow the sting in my throat.

I climbed out of the pit. I was covered in blood. It was under my nails and in my hair. I could taste it on my tongue and across my teeth. Perhaps Talina would have mouthwash in that first-aid kit she carried.

Jad was staring at me from the trees. His red eyes glittered. "That was stupid what you did back there. You shouldn't have taken the risk. Out of all of us, you're the one who needs to remain alive."

A wave of frustrated anger swept through me.

How dare he.

"I saved Marek and Talina. Are you saying I should have let that monster eat them?"

The muscles in Jad's neck strained. "I would not have let that happen. I was about to save them. You intervened. You risked everything, like you always do."

Somehow, I managed to keep my voice firm. "I acted on instinct. I won't apologise for that."

"You acted without any thought for the consequences."

If there'd been any more of those spiderlike creatures in the forest, our argument surely would have drawn their attention, but at that moment, I didn't care. There was only me and Jad in the world and his fuelling hatred.

He gave me a long, penetrating stare. "Follow me. And keep your distance."

My breath was coming in and out in ragged gasps. I was trembling all over, but I managed to steady my aching legs and walk. I wanted to run right up to Jad and use my proximity to cause him physical pain.

Hurt him like his awful words had cut me. But I was also disgusted by the person he'd become, and I didn't want to be anywhere near him.

So, I did exactly what he asked and followed from a distance, keeping my eyes out for spindly legs or slithering tentacles. The journey through the forest was long and seemed twice as difficult as I remembered. We passed the watchtower, lonely and entangled in vines and branches. No one would ever be getting inside that keep again. I could no longer see the door.

We kept going. The creepers had grown, too, blood dripping off their sharp thorns, their barbs out to spike. Sometimes, in the corner of my eye, I thought I saw a root worming its way toward me, but when I glanced at it again, it was still. The forest was playing a game. It wasn't dead but a living, breathing organism. Anything that came in here, it devoured.

Don't think like that. Not when we're trying to get out.

I looked at Jad, at the cold, merciless warrior who had saved me only so I could die later.

"Once this is all over, I never want to see you again. I hope you die in that place."

Those words... why couldn't I drive them out of my head? Why couldn't I let them go?

My conflicted feelings were playing tug-of-war inside me, and I could no longer stand the empty silence between us.

"What happened to you?" I snapped. "I know the Neathror blade changed you, but where did that athame-sabre come from?"

After the events at the Isla Necropolis, I hadn't been able to see Jad's recovery. Toshiko and the other sovereigns had kept me locked in my chamber, and the servants and guards who did visit never shared any light on Jad's condition when I asked.

What had actually happened to him during that time?

How are you ten times stronger and wielding flames like they're nothing but simple parlour tricks?

Jad had winced at the mention of Neathror. He turned around, the shadows shifting across his face. For a moment, I didn't think he was going to answer, but he raised his athamesabre. The runes along the blade came alive with fire. He must have silently summoned the magic. The flames rose from those mysterious symbols, the weapon burning bright and illuminating the forest around us.

His voice dripped with derision. "When I woke in the Black Palace's infirmary, I was burning from the inside. The healers told me it was fever and that I'd recover, but I knew it was dark magic. Dead magic caused by Neathror. That necromancer blade changed my fire power somehow. It had made it stronger. And the more it ignited all my veins and seared my muscles, the more I began to despise you. *You,* who had caused the suffering and the pain when you stabbed that blade into my shoulder."

I flinched. My resolve to remain strong fractured into a million pieces and floated away.

His hateful eyes never left mine. "When I recovered enough to leave the infirmary, I was taken to the palace prison and left in isolation. Left to stew on nothing but thoughts of how much I loathed you. That went on for days. It wasn't until the night Toshiko committed her act of arson and Darius and Macaslan arrived to release me from the prison that I discovered how much my power had strengthened. Darius had brought me my athamesabre. As soon as it made contact with my fingers, it came alive with fire. I wanted to get out of Muiren, to leave for good, but Darius reminded me that I'd sworn to protect you. A magical oath that I *unfortunately* can't break."

"I hope you die in that place."

I could hear those terrible words in the silence afterward. That was the subtext of the conversation.

My cheeks were hot and clammy, the result of stealthy tears.

The shadows under Jad's eyes were so dark, they looked hollow. "That's the story. Satisfied?"

Before I could say anything, he continued his trek through the forest.

I followed, my steps slower and heavier. I didn't know what I had hoped for by pressing him for that information. Perhaps I'd wanted clarity? Or maybe I'd wanted assurance, a firm understanding that it was time to let go.

Yes. It's time.

I'd made a promise to myself to keep my distance from Jad, and now I had to honour it. I wouldn't talk to him. I wouldn't so much as even look at him. I'd carry on doing what I had to do—trying to discover the spell that would unite the Larthalgule and Neathror blades. I would put all my focus and energy on that, and once I achieved it and had the Interitus blade in my hands, I'd leave. I'd disappear when Jad and the others were asleep. I'd find my own way to Morgomoth's kingdom.

My friends shouldn't have to suffer. This is my task. Mine alone.

I glared at the back of Jad's head, wondering if he'd be happy if he knew he'd been released from his vow.

WE MET the others on the outskirts of the forest. If they sensed the aftermath of an argument between me and Jad, they didn't say anything. Bronislav looked uncomfortably at the ground. Perhaps he'd overheard our nasty words in the forest. I didn't care. I had settled into a place beyond fear or anger. The only thing I had left now was this task. Nothing else mattered.

As I'd suspected, we had no option but to backtrack the progress we'd made yesterday. It was a long, arduous hike, the dry dust thickening into a brown fog ahead. When we drew near it, I realised it was a sandstorm. Grit clung to every exposed fold in my skin, sticking to the blood I'd acquired from the forest. I must have looked a ghastly sight. I tasted sand in every breath and choked on it. Every once in a while, a larger object flew by: a rock, a dead branch, something that resembled dried bones.

I didn't know how long we walked with our heads bowed, trying to fight off the hot wind and the sand. Jad led far ahead. How he could even see, I had no idea. The heat and parched landscape were testing all my bodily senses. My stomach felt like it was eating itself from hunger. My ears were assaulted with an incessant buzz, and my eyes were watering so badly, I could barely pry my eyelids apart.

Marek was pointing at something in the distance, but I couldn't make out anything beyond Jad's silhouette. The lieutenant was talking to me. His mouth moved, but I couldn't detect the slightest sound over the howling gale. All I could offer him was a tired, disinterested shrug.

On we walked. And walked.

About a half hour later, I realised what had excited Marek—peaks, watery and ghostlike in the heat mirage. The closer we approached, the more their rocky shapes took form. We had arrived at a landscape of soaring pinnacles and craggy canyon walls. That dark place inside me crumbled further. The rocks would shelter us from the sand, but it would be a strenuous hike. We'd have to climb. No easy feat when we were already exhausted.

We passed towering spires and fractured rocks, the heat continuing to rise. It must have been nearly lunchtime, but that didn't stop Jad. On he went, forcing us up one more rock, down one more gorge, beneath one more arch. I was almost grateful when the sky changed, turning the darkest shade of plum.

Bronislav went very still. The strips of cloth he'd wrapped around his lower face to protect him from the sand and wind made his eyes stand out more brightly. All I could see was the fear in them. It made me shiver, something I didn't think would be possible in these sweltering temperatures.

"What's wrong?"

A series of green lightning forks streaked across the clouds.

I froze, smelling that wonderous aroma of rain, only there was an acidic taste in the air that made my skin crawl. Small plumes of dust rose from the ground, disturbed by sizzling spits.

Bronislav's shout shattered my ears. "Acid rain."

"Run." Marek's instruction was cut off by rippling thunder.

I turned, sprinting for the small cave I'd spotted only moments ago, the others right behind me. Spots of rain splashed on my arms, causing steam to rise off my clothes. We made it into the cave just as the deluge started. It burned holes in the ground, some so large they'd opened pits that could swallow a person whole. Steam wafted into the air. I imagined it was hot enough to melt someone down to the bone.

"Well, this sets us back." Bronislav watched the scorching downpour.

Marek checked his mapographic. "The rain will be here for a while. We're not going to be moving anytime soon. We may as well stop and rest."

He was pale, still shaking with the adrenaline it took to escape.

"Thank providence for that." Annaka dropped her rucksack. "I need food and sleep. Keeping you lot invisible is harder work than it looks."

She found a rock to sit on and retrieved a can of dried food from her rucksack. Marek sat down beside her. Talina reluctantly joined them. For the most part, Talina had made a point of avoiding Annaka and Marek, but perhaps she was too tired to even do that.

This is bad. We don't have time for delays.

Bronislav swore. "What do you think *His Majesty* is doing out there right now?"

I realised he meant Jad. His question was not directed to anyone in particular.

"Probably soaking up the acid," Annaka answered with her usual cocky grace. "Providence forbid he lose his spiteful attitude."

I stared at the torrent, urging my heart to calm down. Jad was out there somewhere. He'd probably found shelter, or maybe Annaka was right and the fire that burned inside him would counteract the acid rain. Maybe he'd just absorb it.

Don't think about him. He's not worth the pain.

I joined the small camp and accepted the dry food Annaka offered.

"We'll have to make the time up," Marek informed us. A fatigued despair had settled on his face. "Jad will have us travelling into the night."

No one said anything.

The deadline was looming, a time bomb ticking over all of us.

Four days.

But we didn't even have that.

CHAPTER 14

The rain kept up. I licked my lips nervously, tasting how cracked and scaly they felt. Perhaps Talina had ointment in her first-aid kit, or even beauty products. I wouldn't put it past her to have packed some, but when I turned to ask her, she'd already curled up on her sleeping mat and gone to sleep. Annaka had made the decision to rest, too, both girls looking far too young for the stresses and horrors we'd faced. They'd both lost weight. I had too. My waistband was a little looser than it had been yesterday.

"Get some sleep," Marek told me.

He was eating fruit from a can, something syrupy for energy, but from the way he scrunched his face, he could have been biting into a lemon.

I'd been so tense and anxious the last twenty-four hours—actually, I'd been this way since I could last remember—and I was desperate for sleep, but poor Marek had black beneath his eyes. He rotated his left arm in a wide circle, perhaps trying to release tension in his shoulder. Out of all of us, he'd had the least amount of rest.

"Why don't you sleep," I insisted. "There's no way anyone alive is getting through that rain without being melted. Is there any point in having one of us on watch?"

There was something unreadable in his eyes, and then he gave a harsh laugh. "You said *alive*. We're in the land of the dead. Acid rain wouldn't stop them."

He had a point. It wasn't worth the risk.

"Someone needs to stay on watch." Marek was shouldering the responsibility like it was some sort of sacred duty.

"You always seem to be on watch. Doesn't that bother you?"

He shrugged. "I'm the perfect person for it. Annaka needs the sleep; otherwise, she won't have the energy to keep us invisible. Talina is our healer. She needs her magic strong. We never know when one of us might end up injured."

I shivered at that less-than-friendly thought.

"And what about Bronislav?"

The soldier had stretched out on his sleeping mat, his cheek pressed into his pillow, his mouth parted slightly.

Marek rubbed at his bleary eyes. "Bronislav will take the first watch tonight. He needs rest now. We're relying on his hearing. How do you think we've managed to avoid dissent rebels?"

I hadn't considered that. Orthrask must have been swarming with Morgomoth's insurgents, yet we'd never come across one. I had Bronislav to thank for that. He'd been communicating with Jad the most. The pair must have been coordinating our journey based on what Bronislav was hearing.

A spark of emotion flickered inside me, but I quickly stamped it out. I couldn't afford to think about Jad. Otherwise, I'd hear those damaging words in my head again, and they had already splintered enough fractures in my heart. I would not let it sever me entirely.

"Get some sleep, Marek. Let me take the watch."

He released an exasperated breath. "Out of all of us, you're the one who really needs the rest."

He let the silent meaning drift between us. The echoes of uncertainty clouded my judgement again, my resolve taking a dive.

"It is self-doubt holding you back."

"Do you think you are unworthy of the task ahead?"

"A tantrum has never worked for anyone."

"Once this is all over, I never want to see you again. I hope you—"

No.

I would not allow myself to hear those last words. I had to stay strong. I couldn't spiral. Marek was right. I needed rest to remain determined, not just in the body but in the mind as well.

I unpacked my sleeping bag and rolled it out on the flat rock. "Thank you."

Marek nodded. He stared out at the rain, a mixture of resilience and hopelessness etched into his expression. I took a moment to really study him. He was always kind. Always looking out for others and putting everyone else before himself. He deserved so much better than this.

"Hey, Marek."

"Mmm."

"You should talk to Talina. She... she'd hate me telling you this, but she has feelings for you. And... based on what I've seen, I think you have feelings for her too."

Maybe it wasn't my place to say anything, but who knew what might happen tomorrow, tonight, in the next hour. I'd rather my friends had a chance for happiness, no matter how short that time might be.

Marek looked at me as though I'd changed his entire universe. Hope, in its purest form, lit in his eyes. There was no denying it. He loved Talina.

"I thought you should know." I dropped onto my sleeping mat. The deep thrum of the rain grew louder, almost soothing, lulling me to sleep.

"Zaya." Marek's tone was uncertain.

"Yes," I managed, my voice sounding far away.

"Pleasant dreams."

The dull grey light behind my eyes altered into darkness.

I DREAMT. No. I was pulled into a memory.

Isgrad stormed down the hewn stairs, the torches coming alive beside him, illuminating the dark conflict in his eyes. I followed, struggling to keep up, having to take two steps for each of his long strides. I hung back a little, actually, feeling the anger pulse off him in waves.

He entered the cavern and crossed the wide living area—repaired since that devastating display of uncontained magic—and prowled toward the silver-thorned witch. She was sitting in her usual rocking chair by the fire, knitting of all things. I took a moment to observe the oddity. A witch, capable of terrible and destructive magic, knitting. It was such a grandmotherly thing to do. It didn't suit her at all.

In the opposite chair, reading, was Briya. She tore her eyes away from her book, half joyful, half afraid to see Isgrad.

He stopped dead in his tracks. "What's she doing here?"

The witch stared up from her knitting. "Briya needed a safe place to stay. I invited her here to share my home for as long as she needs it."

Isgrad just stared. Then he turned to Briya, venom in his voice. "I told you to run."

The witch intervened before Briya could even open her mouth. "Do not blame her, Isgrad. I invited her for a reason."

"The same reason you invited me, I expect."

Was the witch playing matchmaker, trying to reconnect them? Isgrad might have been irate, but it was driven by fear. Fear of what his brother would do if he discovered Briya was alive. Isgrad wasn't being wrathful because he hated her. No, he loved Briya so much that pushing her away was the only option to keep her safe. I could see beyond the mask of rage, his face strained by inner conflict. Fear and love. I knew that if circumstances were different, Isgrad would drop everything to be with Briya.

The witch stood, studying him without reservations. "Something has happened to you, Isgrad. Your magic... it's off."

Those ocean-deep eyes turned on her. "No. It's finally working. I've never felt better. Stronger. My necromancy... it's woken. I can feel it inside me."

The witch harrumphed. She hobbled across the cavern with her walking stick, motioning for the pair to follow. The three of them gathered around the kitchen workbench. The witch cleared a space free of herb jars and dried bones. I didn't want to know what spell she'd been in the process of making. She took out a flatboard from a lower cupboard and placed it in the empty space.

I swallowed at the sight. It was a pendulum board for divination. There were none left in the world, or at least that was what I'd been told. According to the Council of Founding Sovereigns, they were far too dangerous in the wrong hands. Over the centuries, the pendulum boards had been collected and destroyed by the Haxsan Guard. I was likely looking at one of the last to survive.

The board was a beautiful display of craftsmanship. Gold scrollwork lined the edges, the surface decorated with runes and constellations. West, North, East, and South had been marked on the perfectly round panel.

This wasn't just a simple divination board but a compass.

The witch took out a necklace that had been hidden behind her silver robe. The pendant was a knife-shaped crystal made of pure quartz.

A smile bloomed on her pale lips. "Everyone believes scrying is the magic act of practising the unconscious mind and opening your soul to the second sight. What they don't know is that it also makes for an excellent locator spell."

Isgrad crossed his arms tight. "What are we tracking, exactly?"

"Your necromancy. It has left you."

His fingers curled, nails biting into his skin. "It has not. I told you—"

"That sad display where you ruined my cavern was not necromancy. That was your real power. Earth magic. You never specialised when you were young, but it was always there, waiting to come out at the right time. The necromancy that was dormant inside you blocked it. Now that the necromancy is gone, your true magic has made itself apparent."

Colour drained from his face and neck. "Gone? Gone where? I need necromancy to absorb the Bone Grimoire. Otherwise, I'll never defeat my brother."

The revelation sent a flurry of panic through him. He looked at the witch, then at Briya, as though he hoped one of them would contradict it.

The pair remained silent.

"Th-This can't be happening," Isgrad stuttered. "I was so close to the Bone Grimoire. Where has my necromancy gone?"

The silver-thorned witch watched him with pensive eyes. "I have an inkling that I know, but I need to make sure first." She handed him the pendant. "Cut your hand using the crystal. I need your blood for the locator spell to work."

Isgrad seemed to fumble for a response before he snatched the pendant and sliced the sharp point across his palm, not even flinching. The clear quartz soaked in his blood, the crystal turning into a vibrant, pulsing red. It now looked like a ruby kings and queens would fight for.

The witch snatched it out of his hand. "Time for the truth."

She dangled the pendant over the pendulum board. It began to swing, moving slowly in a wide circle, then veering to different runes, becoming nothing more than a blur. The runes along the board lit up, ebbing and flowing across the board, forming into a single coherent word.

Briya.

The witch caught the pendant with her other hand. She clasped the chain back around her neck, the quartz once again hidden beneath her silver robe. "It's done. The truth revealed. The necromancy has gone to Briya."

Briya was staring at her name lit in fire. "Me! I… that's not possible. I don't have it." She looked at Isgrad, visibly shaking from those blue eyes that glared at her with betrayal. "I don't have necromancy. I swear it."

"Not you, dear," the witch interrupted.

Briya backed away a step. "I don't understand any of this."

The witch pinned her with a long stare. "It is quite simple. You don't have the necromancy, but the infant growing inside you does. The magic that had been dormant for so long in Isgrad has found a new home. His child."

Oh providence.

The blood halted in my veins, making me dizzy and inept.

My parents.

Isgrad went very still. His eyes had become animal-bright in the firelight.

Briya swayed slightly. She gripped the bench. "That's not… possible," she argued weakly. "I would know if I was pregnant."

"Well, now you do know," the witch replied with little sentiment.

"But there'd be signs."

"Since the moment you arrived in my cavern, you have complained of nothing but headaches. And you haven't been able to keep food down. You are pregnant." She eyed the pair of them. "You should have been more careful."

Isgrad had collected himself, in the only way a man who received the news of a shock pregnancy could. He began pacing, visibly sweating. "How do I get the necromancy back?"

The witch scoffed. "You can't. The magic now belongs to your child. It will not be dormant inside her. She's been marked as Morgomoth's equal."

"She?" Briya clutched her stomach, as though the simple gesture would protect the growing bundle inside her.

The witch gave Briya a slow nod. "The scrying pendant revealed it. A daughter."

Isgrad shuddered. "Are you saying a child will have to go up against my brother?"

"I'm saying your *daughter* will. Her necromancy will become apparent in her teens. She'll then have to complete what you started and absorb the magic from the Bone Grimoire."

Isgrad let out a soft laugh full of disdain. "I can't let a child do that."

It irked me that he kept saying *child*, not *daughter*. Like I was something alien and not his.

The silver-thorned witch released a tense breath. Apparently, she wasn't pleased about it either. "Morgomoth always wanted you by his side. If he learns of this"—she pointed to Briya's belly —"he'll take your daughter and claim his niece as his own. He'll train her to be as twisted and dark as his own wicked soul. He'll use her only to make himself more powerful. To ensure that you always remain loyal to him."

Briya's eyes were still wide with shock. "That won't happen."

"No, it will not," the witch clarified. "Because she has two parents to protect her from that."

Isgrad's mouth tightened into a thin line. "No. Briya and the baby disappear. It's safest if I'm not involved. They should stay clear of me. Willieth will never suspect anything if I know nothing about the child."

Briya stared down at the floor, her face crimson with anger.

I kind of wanted to punch Isgrad on her behalf.

The witch gave Isgrad a stare that could have melted flesh. "Keep your daughter safe. When the time comes, she'll need to acquire the Bone Grimoire's magic and challenge your brother. You will need to be there to train her." Sadness seeped from her voice. "Your life source is linked to your brother's, as is your daughter's."

Isgrad stared in mute horror.

Briya—my mother—couldn't stop shaking. "What are you both talking about?"

A muscle twitched in the witch's wrinkled jaw. "Once Willieth is dead, both Isgrad and your daughter will die too. They are all connected to the one life source."

Briya released a shuddering breath. She started swaying, fingers hooked on the bench again.

The witch spoke, her tone dispassionate and direct. "Your daughter has been put on this earth to do one thing: to kill Morgomoth and then die." She hobbled back to the fireplace. "You're soon to be parents. I'll leave you both to figure out how you'd like to raise your daughter for the short time she has on this earth."

My parents looked at each other, the cavern filled with empty silence.

There had been an emptiness in my chest, but now it was filled with a growing ache.

My life source was connected to Morgomoth's.

"Once this is all over, I never want to see you again. I hope you die in that place."

I bowed my head, giving in to my sad, inevitable fate.

Jad was going to get exactly what he wanted.

CHAPTER 15

After I woke, the next few minutes were beyond strange.

Isgrad and Briya are my parents.

Correction: were *my parents, because they're dead.*

My life source is connected to Morgomoth's, who turns out to be my creepy, megalomaniac uncle.

I really am from a messed-up family.

I am going to die.

The certainty of it, the eye-opener to the truth, of who I really was and what I had been put on this earth to do, brought that emptiness back inside me. I felt nothing. Shock must have numbed all my senses. That was the only explanation for this… nothingness I felt. I kept repeating the words, *I am going to die, I am going to die, I am going to die,* but they had no impact. I couldn't push or suppress what it was. There was no wallowing in pain anymore. No denial. Just cold, hard acceptance.

I am going to die.

"Zaya." Marek was staring at me from the front of the cave. He'd slouched by a rock to keep watch.

Outside, the torrent still hadn't let up. Steam had eclipsed the terrain in an oppressive mist. The acid rain was so hot that the earth was sizzling outside. Clouds of condensation rose into the dust-riddled air.

Marek was still watching me, concern on his face.

My legs were cramping, and I grudgingly sat up. "I'm okay."

"Were you having a nightmare?"

I'm not sure.

"Yes."

"I get them too." A broken laugh erupted out of him. "I think it's this place."

Was that why Marek really chose to stay on watch so often? Because his sleep was disturbed by unimaginable terrors?

"Do you want to talk about it?" I asked.

His face turned resolute and hard. "No. They're just dreams, right? They can't really harm us."

I wished we lived in a world where that was true.

The others were still asleep. Bronislav still had his mouth open. I thought he might have been lightly snoring, but I couldn't tell over the heavy rain. Annaka looked so much younger when she slept, her gorgeous tanned-brown skin glowing in the flashes of lightning. Talina had curled up in a ball, hugging her knees.

I groaned, wishing I could sip water to soothe the burn in my throat, but we had rationed all of our supplies. We couldn't eat or drink again until the evening.

"How long was I out?"

A distinct line of tension travelled across Marek's shoulders. "About two hours. This rain is slowing us down. We're hours off our schedule."

I didn't say anything for a while, feeling the heavy thump of every heartbeat against my ribs. "Why don't you get some sleep, then? I can take the watch."

For a moment, I thought he'd say no, perhaps reminded by the nightmares that waited for him, but his eyes were so bleary and his face so drawn that the desire for sleep must have won. "Will you be okay?"

"Of course. Get some rest, Marek."

He looked out at the rain-filled landscape again. "Okay, but I'll sleep next to you. If anything happens, wake me."

He grabbed his sleeping mat and bag, rolled them out beside me, and settled down. He was asleep within minutes.

The deluge continued to fall for the next hour, as though the sky had drunk up the entire ocean and decided to cough it up in a river over Orthrask. I watched it, huddled against the rock wall, deliberating my next move.

I have to leave them.

I could not, would absolutely not, let my friends suffer this long journey. Not when the end result would be my death. Running away wasn't an option, though. Jad was a skilled tracker. He'd follow me, then scorn me for being stupid. No, I had to get in contact with Darius and Macaslan. I had to convince the senator and the commander to call the mission off and order my friends to return to the coast. Jad would be happy to do it. He was only here on some self-righteous quest of honour. Once he was granted permission to return, to meet with the Haxsan Guard forces on the beach, he'd order the rest of them to follow. Marek wouldn't dare disobey his captain. None of them could. Jad was in charge; they couldn't refuse his command.

If I can talk to Macaslan and Darius now and call this ridiculous suicide mission off, then I can leave as soon as the rain clears.

Feeling only a little snoopy, I gingerly crawled around Marek to his rucksack and pulled the zipper down. I found a bundle wrapped in linens and quickly undid it, relieved to find the oval hand mirror. It was made of gold and not simply gilded like I'd first thought. The mirror was smooth and clean, reflecting how ghastly I'd become. My cheeks were hollow and coated in grime. My hair hung in clumps, held together by sweat. There was gunk in the corners of my eyes and dried blood on my neck. My lips were in worse condition than I realised. They'd been bleeding between the cracks, making the surface overly large and puffy.

I turned the mirror over, wishing I'd focused more when Marek had dialled the senator.

How do I use this thing?

"What are you doing?"

I jumped at the voice, instantly lathered in a nervous sweat from the spiteful tone. I quickly wrapped the mirror in the linen and placed it back into the lieutenant's rucksack. It was nowhere near as neat as it had been. Marek would know someone had been looking through his things.

I turned around to face Jad. Annaka was right. The acid rain didn't affect him. It didn't even leave a mark. He simply soaked it up, his eyes becoming more crimson by the second, as though the acid was fuelling the hatred that was already inside.

I swallowed, unable to prevent the edgy shake in my voice. "Nothing. Marek left his rucksack open. I was just closing it."

Jad watched me, looking every bit like a warrior of darkness in the pouring rain, his black hair pasted to his head. The fabric of his clothes clung to him. The ridges of sculpted muscle were evident through the damp material, something I tried very much to ignore.

His gaze was predatory and focused. "Why isn't Marek on watch?"

I stole a glance at the sleeping lieutenant. "He was exhausted."

"We're all exhausted. It's no excuse."

I scowled at that. My anger fluctuated from anxiety to boldness. "We're not like you. Marek was tired, and I was awake. I offered to keep watch. There's nothing wrong with that."

Why did I feel like I was on trial, defending my actions?

The thought of leaving my friends had filled me with guilt. *Did* fill me with guilt, but honestly, I'd had enough of Jad's behaviour. Leaving him wouldn't be hard. And yet, the moment the image of me doing so crossed my mind, something inside me felt like it was being shredded in two.

"You were meddling with his things. What were you looking for?" The suspicion in Jad's voice was more than an undertone.

"If you must know," I said, trying to maintain my cool, "I was looking for the mirror. I need to talk with Darius and Macaslan."

There. I'd confessed it. There had been no point in denying it in the end. Jad could see right through me.

His handsome face creased into a frown of ire. "If you need to know anything about the mission, you ask me."

He pointed at Marek. "Wake him."

My temper rose, and I felt myself go white with rage. "Stop being such a brute. If having a watch is so important to you, you do the role from now on."

At least that meant we could all sleep and escape his hostile behaviour for a while.

He broke the friction between us with a cutting laugh. "I'm up every night, looking for a safe route for us to take through this providence-forsaken nightmare."

I crossed my arms. "Well, you did a fantastic job in the dead forest, didn't you?"

I caught a flash of something dark in his eyes and knew I'd gone too far. He'd been standing at the edge of the cave, keeping his distance, but at that moment, he stepped forward with unnerving swiftness, his breathing ragged. I flinched, startled by the level of feral hatred on his face. This time, I truly was afraid of what he was capable of.

No. He wouldn't.

He backed away, as though seeing the thought in my head. A glimmer of disgust settled in his expression, and he clamped down on what must have been a nasty retort.

I backed up another few steps. I didn't know Jad anymore. I

didn't know how far the darkness went in him. How far Trajan's dead soul had corrupted him.

"Wake the others and pack your bags. We're moving."

"It's still raining," I protested.

"Not for much longer."

He was right. A minute later, the deluge ceased. It was further proof that Jad's new fire magic was connected to Orthrask. He could sense what fire and shadow would do, and this land was made of both those things. Orthrask was a part of him, making him more toxic and lethal by the second.

I woke the others and rolled up my sleeping mat. There was much protest, but they grudgingly got onto their feet and collected their items.

Marek, not getting nearly as much sleep as he needed, watched me through groggy eyes. He noticed my trembling hands. "What's wrong?"

I couldn't stop shaking. I didn't think I'd ever stop being afraid in Jad's presence.

Marek glanced between me and his captain. Understanding seemed to gather in his expression. "What happened?" he whispered.

"I can't be near him" was all I answered.

"We will save him, Zaya. Have faith. We'll find a way to get the real Jad back." He might have looked confident, but his voice lacked surety.

That just made me feel worse. "*I* am the reason he's changed. *I'm* the one who cursed him."

"You didn't know this would happen. It isn't your fault."

"You try telling him that."

Marek didn't have a response for that suggestion.

I sniffled and wiped at my eyes, refusing to allow anyone, especially Jad, to see.

We left the cave. The acid rain had melted parts of the rock down, leaving the earth bruised and battered in its wake. Many of the pinnacles and towering arches were fragmented or completely burnt black. I couldn't help but think Jad suited the landscape.

"Are you okay?" Marek had remained by my side, no doubt to monitor me.

I nodded, but I felt far from all right. I had discovered a horrible, devastating truth about my heritage, my time was limited on this earth, and the person I loved the most would rather skewer me and leave my head on a stake than look at me. Those lifeless red eyes spoke volumes.

I muffled a curse. "Hadar succeeded."

Marek just stared.

"Jad is a monster," I emphasised and kept walking.

ON AND ON WE HIKED, time insufferably slow. I'd almost convinced myself that being dead would be better than this. There was pain in every breath, my head pounding from the beginning of a migraine. The wind beat at my face like invisible hands were trying to rip my skin off.

I knew I wouldn't last much longer without water and greedily guzzled it down from my bottle. I tucked into my dry food, too, eating as I walked. Screw it. And screw rations. If I was going to die, I wasn't going to hold back any longer.

Taking a page from my book, Annaka, Talina, and Bronislav did the same, giving in to their own craving hunger.

Great. I've started something.

Marek didn't say anything, but I sensed his disapproval.

"Eat," I encouraged. "If we don't, none of us will reach our next destination."

He reluctantly nodded and took out his water bottle. That

first mouthful must have tempted his thirst, because he drank as though it was icy water straight out of heaven. If such a place existed.

He wiped his mouth. "We're heading to an outpost just a little farther north. We'll stop and rest beyond its border there for the night. In the morning, a few hours before dawn, Jad, Annaka, and I will raid the place for food and water." His serious gaze focused on mine. "You're right. We're not going to last much longer on the rations we have, especially with the way we've just gorged ourselves."

"An outpost?"

He grunted. "Jad spotted it on the mapographic. It looks like a small military outpost."

"Is that wise? To go there?"

I didn't want to risk getting caught.

"We have no choice. There's nothing to eat out here. We're low on food. We need to raid their supplies."

A very long moment passed in silence.

"Okay," I said at last, not feeling 100 percent confident with the plan. At least Annaka would be able to keep them invisible, but they'd still have to be careful not to make a sound.

"Jad said you wanted to talk to Darius and Macaslan."

I nearly lost my footing.

He told Marek.

I nodded. "Yes, very much."

Marek sucked in a sharp breath. "I'll contact them this evening. I have information I need to pass on to them too."

I wanted a private conversation with the senator and the commander, but… well, I was going to have to push for that at a later time. I still had every intention of following my plan through. I was leaving. Going to the outpost would be a secret blessing. Once Jad, Annaka, and Marek raided the supplies and returned with food, I'd take my pickings when everyone was asleep—just enough to get me to Morgomoth's kingdom—and then I'd leave when we next made camp.

Not saying goodbye was going to be the hardest part of it all. They'd hate me, despise me even, but in time, they'd understand. I would make sure Darius and Macaslan communicated my reasonings clearly, because I, of course, wouldn't be coming back to explain it myself.

I'm going to die.

Die.

It didn't frighten me, what waited beyond. How it would happen did. I hoped that, when the time came, it would be peaceful. No pain. No suffering.

Three more days.

Find the spell.

Unite the blades.

Kill Morgomoth.

Die.

It sounded simple enough but would be far from easy.

Marek's startled gasp interrupted my thoughts. "Where's Bronislav?"

Annaka stepped up beside him and patted his shoulder. "Potty break. You didn't think that smell was just sulphur, did you?"

"Gross." Marek looked like he was trying not to breathe through his nose.

Annaka laughed.

I smiled.

What I planned to do was going to hurt them, yes, but they'd be okay. They'd have each other to get them through it.

CHAPTER 16

The sky was a stirring blend of shadows and storm. The ground lurched, trembling from quakes deep in the soil. Dangerous eruptions echoed across the land, almost like Orthrask was rasping deep laughter. There was too much cloud cover to see, but I knew the volcanoes around Morgomoth's kingdom were spewing fire into the sky. My theory was proven right a few minutes later when powdery black snow fell over us. Ash.

We continued our slog through the elements. The air became so humid, I thought my eyeballs might implode. My feet were soddened by sweat in my boots, and my armpits—I dared not lift them for fear of the smell.

Every so often, I thought I detected the sound of stirring wings. It couldn't be possible. It had to be an auditory hallucination of some kind, a sign of how seriously whacked my head had become. But there it was again. A bird chirping brightly and loudly. I scanned the skies, overcome when I witnessed silvery white wings taking flight. The bird was magnificent. Its incredible feathers shone an immaculate ivory colour, as though the embers and dust couldn't touch it. The bird soared and swooped through the air, song projecting from its impressive beak. It was swanlike, and yet, at the same time, I could have been staring at an albatross. Perhaps I was looking at a combination of the two. Watching the bird, a calming sense of peace settled through me.

I glanced over my shoulder, wondering if the others were seeing this or if I really had succumbed to madness. They were staring at the bird, too, mouths open in slight fascination.

Talina had a strange smile on her face. "It's beautiful. But how is it out here? Nothing lives here. Nothing can survive."

She was right. The bird was a mystery. It was too majestic, too supreme in grace and delicacy to have been created by Orthrask.

"It's a phoenix."

Jad stood on top of a large boulder, watching us like a king looking over his subjects. "It's been following us since we left the beach."

I recalled Marek mentioning that something had been trailing us. Something Jad sensed but hadn't left tracks for him to investigate. At the time, I suspected it had been something horrible and monstrous, but then the dead forest had happened, and the spider-thing, and the acid rain, and I had forgotten all about it. Looking back, Jad and Marek hadn't seemed alarmed about it these past twenty-four hours. I wondered now long they'd known a phoenix was in pursuit of us.

"Why?" I asked Marek. I refused to even acknowledge Jad.

The lieutenant shrugged. The barest hint of a smile formed on his face. "Who knows? Phoenixes are rare."

"Would Darius have sent it?"

Is the bird here to watch over us?

Marek looked as clueless as I felt. "I don't know. We can ask him later, but I doubt it. Phoenixes don't answer to anyone. They can't be tamed."

Who would want to tame beauty like this?

The creature dived, levelling out in the bitterly hot winds.

Jad's voice cut through the tranquil scene. "We have to keep moving."

I huffed out an infuriated breath but followed the group. Staring back at the phoenix, I silently wished I could be as free and at peace as that.

Hopefully, that's what waited for me in the otherworld.

THE SUN—WHAT could be seen of it in the constant gloom—had settled to the west when Bronislav went very still, listening to something the rest of us couldn't detect. Jad stopped ahead, his ears picking up on some hidden signal too.

Talina's face went bone white. "What? What's wrong?"

The pebbles beside my boot started shaking. I watched them, bouncing so fast that they scattered like marbles. Vibrations rattled through my feet. This wasn't an earthquake. It was far too unified to be caused by nature.

Talina grabbed my hand, a silent question in her eyes.

Before I could answer, Bronislav darted for the cliffs that over-looked the massive canyon-sized gorge we'd been walking by for the last hour. Jad sprinted after him. Seeing the captain alarmed… well, that just made my dread feel like it was tugging me in multiple directions. The rest of us scampered across the barren rock, flattening ourselves on our stomachs to look out at the expansive terrain beyond.

I had to hold back my gasp. An army of terrible proportion trekked across the gorge, so large that they were just a growing smear of black on the horizon. And this was only one division. Others were moving to the west and south. The forces were heading to the coast in every direction. Morgomoth knew the

Haxsan Guard were coming. He was sending his armies to repel the attack.

Not just to hold off but to destroy.

Chants and cries filled the air, beating in time with the clanking of armour and weapons. The march sounded like thunder rolling across the ground. My heart went into a gallop. The legions were too far away to see clearly, but I knew this was not only an army of dissent rebels but the dead. My necromancy had kicked in. The air was filled with the wails of tortured souls. These chak-lorks had been resurrected, their bodies controlled by dark magic.

A look of curious horror spread across Marek's face. "We need to warn Darius and Macaslan."

Jad sized up the unending army. "Let's go."

I knew he wasn't afraid of us being spotted. Annaka's invisibility charm kept us safe from that. No, we had to get to the outpost, restock our supplies, and keep moving. Morgomoth's forces would destroy the Haxsan Guard. I had to kill him before the two opposing sides collided with each other in a battle frenzy on the beaches. I had to take control of his dead army and call the war off.

Fear ebbed through me.

I had less than three days to achieve it.

WE KEPT WALKING, each step more agonising. My thigh muscles were being chafed by my trousers, which had been doused so many times with grit that the fabric had become tough and itchy. Honestly, it felt like my thighs were being scratched with sandpaper. The others didn't seem to be faring much better, but no one once pleaded for a rest break. Seeing that army, the sheer endless size of it, had spurred us on, even when we had little energy to give.

Marek had said the outpost was close, but there wasn't any sign of it. I was too afraid to ask. If he'd read the mapographic wrong... what might Jad do? I wouldn't have put it past him to rip out the lieutenant's throat with his teeth.

The outpost can't be far.

Our rations had reached dangerously low levels. My water bottle was empty. I had gluttoned myself on it before, and while it had given me the momentum to carry on, I was paying for it now.

Talina plodded heavily beside me, her shoulders slouched, unable to find the strength to keep them up. Either that or she was trying her best to shield her face from the scalding winds.

She snorted. "How could anyone fight for this place? How could anyone think this is right?"

I knew what she meant. "I imagine not many dissent rebels have seen Orthrask. What it really is."

Most casters had joined Morgomoth and his cause in search for a better life. Surely when they saw this, they'd turn on him. See him and Orthrask for the evil it truly was.

"And when they do?" Talina sounded sceptical. "When this place starts leaking its poison to the other continents?"

"That won't happen. We won't let it."

No. I'm the one who won't let it occur.

I had to remind myself that in only a few more hours, I'd be leaving them.

My task. My responsibility. Me. Alone.

"I hope you're right" was all Talina said.

There was more I wanted to say, but a shrill cry behind us took the words from my mouth. Annaka had collapsed to her knees. Marek was at her side, cradling her against him. She vomited into the hot sand. No, not vomit—blood. It created a watery-red paste in the grime.

"I'm sorry," she gasped when she was finished. She wiped at her mouth. Those beautiful thick lips that I'd secretly envied were blistered and now the colour of a dried-up bog. One of her eyes was red and inflamed. The other she couldn't seem to open. She no longer had the strength to remain upright and crumpled into Marek's arms. "I'm sorry," she repeated. "I have a migraine. My magic is spent. I can't keep you invisible any longer."

It took me a second to compute that we were exposed, in perfect viewing range, a target to anything alive or dead out here.

Marek gently brushed some of Annaka's cornrows from her face. "It's all right. Let's just try to get to the outpost. It's not much farther."

Bronislav gave a harsh laugh. "It's still an hour away, and she can't walk. Look at her."

He was right. Annaka's head had lolled onto Marek's shoulder. She'd either closed her eyes to go to sleep or passed out.

Talina groaned. "Stupid pirate. Why didn't she say anything before her migraine got this bad?"

She knelt beside Annaka and pressed her thumbs gently into her temples.

Marek watched her, growing more pensive by the second. "Are you healing her?"

Talina's face was like a storm cloud. "I'm trying to soothe her migraine. I'm too exhausted myself for my magic to work fully, but this should offer her some relief. When she wakes up, the migraine should be gone."

Bronislav fixed her with a confounded stare. "When she wakes up? Are you saying she's going to be out for a while?"

Talina didn't get on with Annaka, but her healing instincts to protect and nurse had kicked in, qualities that would always come before any grudges. She practically bared her teeth at Bronislav. "She's sick. She needs sleep. Then she'll need rest. Food. Water. Medicine."

"How many hours?"

I knew what Bronislav was asking. How many hours would we lose?

Talina sucked in a deep pull of air. "At least till the morning. She's utterly spent."

This was further proof why I needed to leave. This was too much on Annaka. Too much on all of them.

Marek lifted Annaka from the ground, resolved to carry her the rest of the way. "Let's just get to the outpost. We'll have to reconsider our plans when we arrive."

I bit my lip and winced at the unexpected tang of blood. We couldn't raid the outpost without Annaka's invisibility charms.

"Let's go," Bronislav ordered. "Before Jad comes back wondering why we've stopped."

I rubbed the crust from my tired eyes and followed.

"Not far now."

Marek had said the words at least five times in the last hour, but finally, I saw signs of the outpost. Lights, about a kilometre away. Twinkling in the distance, as beautiful and fragile as fireflies. All I wanted to do was find somewhere safe on its outskirts and sleep, but we had to talk to Darius and Macaslan and warn them of what was coming. And we desperately needed to get food and water. Without Annaka, I had no idea how we would achieve that. It was too much to hope that the outpost was empty.

Fighting the constant roar of the wind in my ears, I stilled, hearing something else in the gale. It was difficult to define at first. It could have been a trick, just the wind playing games with me. I almost hoped it was, but the longer I listened, the more it became apparent. Growls and hisses. I looked to Bronislav, wondering why he hadn't alerted us earlier, but I knew from the way he walked, his head bowed to defend himself from the wind, that he hadn't heard it.

I listened, turning every sound over in my mind.

Whatever it was that was coming, it was dead.

A sudden movement in the sky made my blood turn to ice in my veins.

"Hide," I shouted, the word an effort to extract from my parched throat.

The others looked up in time to see it. See *them*.

The Four Revenants had upgraded, becoming creatures of the sky. They rode on stagma, the beasts' leathery wings soaring through the air, the sound like thunder in their wake. Dead stagma, judging by their rotting scales. Morgomoth hadn't been able to control the wild creatures, and it angered me that he'd killed and resurrected them to do his bidding.

My friends hid behind a mound of rocks, which strangely looked like it had been built as a tomb, but it was large enough to conceal us, and there was no time to think about what it might or might not be. I dived, flattening my back to the pile of stone, pushing myself deeper into the fissured entry.

Bronislav was breathing hard beside me. "I never heard them."

"They're not of this world."

That didn't reassure him, didn't take away the guilt that caused heavy lines to strain his face.

"Keep quiet," I instructed, my voice deadly low.

Wings beat the air, sending fierce undulations rippling through the wind. I assumed one of the stagma had swooped right over us, because we were pelted with sand, which swirled around us like snowflakes, sticking to our sweaty skin. Horrible, grisly shrieks polluted the night sky, echoing from every direction.

I jumped when a stream of fire incinerated the rocks ahead of us into blackened crisps. Another blast erupted not far to our right, then one to our left. Hot tendrils whipped all around us.

The revenants were trying to smoke us out, which meant they couldn't be 100 percent certain we were here. Otherwise, they'd surely just snare us between the stagma's claws and drag us to Morgomoth's kingdom.

We had to wait.

More cries, screeches, and snarls. More explosive fires, the smoke becoming a barricade that eclipsed the landscape ahead. And finally, the heavy beats of wings fading into the distance.

We waited another twenty minutes, just to be certain the Four Revenants hadn't decided to turn back.

I held my hands together, wishing I could stop them from trembling. "Let's go."

I was really starting to hate those two words.

CHAPTER 17

We reached the outpost a little before midnight. Regrettably, it hadn't been abandoned. It was a hive of activity. Dissent rebels were stationed at their posts, all wearing hoods, which masked their faces in shadows. Lively noise and song bellowed from beyond the walls. Anyone would have thought there was a tavern inside, where everyone was boisterous and drunk. Perhaps there was. It was a sign that the rebels didn't fear attack, and even though it startled me that anyone could feel animated and sprightly in Orthrask, it did give me some comfort. Hopefully, when it came time to raid this place, most of the occupants would be out cold in an intoxicated sleep.

Marek and I sat at the edge of the ridge, studying the outpost from behind dried brambles. Bronislav and Talina had remained with Annaka in a cave we'd found at the bottom of the hill, and Jad had gone down to get a closer look at the outpost. He would return soon to report back. Until then, all we could do was watch and wait.

I thought about Annaka. She still hadn't woken, and it worried me that she needed more aid than Talina could give.

When I mentioned it to Marek, I couldn't help but grimace at his gaping mouth. It must have been a possibility he'd never considered.

What the hell will we do if Annaka really is sick?

"She'll be fine," he said at last, but I knew from the way his throat bobbed that he didn't believe his own words.

He returned his attention to the outpost. It was a stone building rising out of the cliff face, as though it were trying to swallow the mountain behind it. I studied it through the binoculars, grateful Marek had the foresight to pack a pair in his rucksack before boarding as a stowaway on the *Crown of Glory*. Made of solid black granite, the outpost had two towers and a large keep constructed as a viewing platform. The battlements along the parapet reminded me of stubbed teeth, the arrow loops like slashes. I wondered if we were just seeing the surface, if the edifice went much deeper into the mountain. I suspected that was the case.

We waited half an hour before Jad returned. He launched straight past us, refusing to talk until we reached our hideout. We descended the rocky, mud-slick slope. There must have been a hot spring somewhere. The sludge wasn't boiling, but it was still unpleasantly warm and difficult to walk on. Marek stumbled, heels slipping in the roiling muck. I recognised the telltale signs of exhaustion: the stiffness in his legs, the way he rolled his shoulders, trying to loosen the tension. I wondered if his vision was sliding in and out like mine was.

I released a silent breath. "Are you okay?"

Jad had made it abundantly clear from the moment he'd returned that we were not to talk or make noise, but he was far ahead, and I didn't think he'd be able to hear even from that distance.

Marek's bleary eyes settled on me. "Just tired."

"We'll be able to sleep soon."

"Not straight away we can't. Not me, at least." Marek's words were slurred. "I have to talk to Darius. Report what we've seen. I have to—"

His foot went out beneath him.

I tried to grab Marek, but he was a dead weight and we both hit the ground, barely avoiding a stream of scalding sludge. Rocks and loose pebbles bounced down the slope, the noise painfully loud.

My hand was lodged beneath Marek's arm. Grunting, I managed to wrench myself free, my fingers stinging from the friction. My hand came out bleeding, dirt and bits of stone wedged in the cuts along my knuckles. My breath rattled out of me. I was going to have to grab an antiseptic ointment from Talina.

But my suffering was nothing compared to what Marek must have been feeling.

I shook his shoulder. "Are you okay? Marek?"

No response. His face was deathly still. And pale.

I slapped his cheek.

Still nothing.

Oh providence.

Marek hadn't slipped. He'd passed out.

The terrible luck made me feel like a pit had yawned open beneath me. I couldn't carry Marek. Couldn't even drag him. I was weak myself.

"Back away."

I refused to flinch at Jad's unyielding glare. For the first time, he actually looked concerned—a glimmer of his former self—when he stared at Marek. "Move away. I'll carry him."

His words were laced with impatience.

I edged back up the slope, giving Jad the space he needed. He hoisted Marek over his shoulder like the lieutenant was nothing more than a rag doll and traipsed down the descent, making it almost impossible for me to keep up.

When we reached our hideout, I didn't go inside. It would put me in too close proximity to Jad, which would make me uncomfortable and likely burn his skin to a crisp.

On second thought, maybe going inside isn't such a bad idea.

Some minutes later, Jad emerged with the hand mirror. He sped past me, heading back up the hill.

"I need that," I cried.

There was a razor-sharp bite behind those eyes when he turned around. I had never seen anyone focus on me with such a cold calculation. "No, you don't."

"I need to talk to Darius and Macaslan."

"You need sleep. I'll report to the senator and the commander."

No. This is not going according to my plan.

"Please." I hated the awful desperation in my voice.

He stood there, glowering down at me, his eyes swimming with a regret I didn't understand. "No."

Jad continued his trek up the slope, disappearing into the shadows as though he were made of them.

No!

You arrogant, conceited....

I kicked a stone, so furious that it became an effort not to scream up into the night.

Shaking with either anger or frustration, I entered our hideout and set up my sleeping bag, seething the entire time. Talina was asleep beside Annaka. Bronislav slept with his hand curled around his athame-sabre, and Marek was so pale on his sleeping mat that he could have been laid to rest in a coffin. If I had the strength, I would have stayed up to keep watch, but I had nothing left in me. Only resentment for Jad. I wriggled into my sleeping bag, ignoring the way my stomach roared and my mouth salivated when my thoughts drifted to food.

Jad would keep watch. I was certain of it.

I was also certain of something else.

He'd deliberately taken the hand mirror tonight.

Almost like he knew what I intended to do.

Bastard.

I shut my eyes, waiting for sweet darkness to submerge me.

I LAUGHED BREATHILY without humour when I awoke. Well... awoke at the Isla Necropolis. The five Grand Masters were watching me. At least, I thought they were. I couldn't tell beneath those heavily lined cowls, but I remembered what I'd seen of their faces the last time I'd visited. I shivered, reliving that glimpse of burnt bone and sizzling flesh. I really had no problem with not witnessing that again.

I wrinkled my nose. "Wonderful. I'm back. What do I have the pleasure of your company for this time?"

"You tell us. This is your subconscious." Their voices were a ghostly resonance in my head.

Ugh. I didn't think I would ever get used to that. "I brought myself here. Is that what you're implying?"

I took their silence as a yes.

When I'd last been at the chamber, I had wanted answers about the Bone Grimoire. The book was inside me, and I wanted it out. I needed to find the spell.

It seemed my subconscious wanted me to know the answer too.

"Have you overcome your self-doubt?"

The Grand Masters' words were a mocking echo in my mind.

I didn't say anything for a long time. "Does it matter anymore? I'm not going to... survive."

That last word was difficult to swallow.

"If you cannot do this task for yourself, do it for others."

The dark anger I had swept aside returned, ripping my patience up like ribbons. "Everything I've done has been for others. I have always put everyone else first. Them before me. Always made sacrifices."

I was so, so tired. Tired of never stopping. Tired that my life wasn't my own to lead. It never had been; it had been preordained from the beginning. I had been born to finish Isgrad's task. And to die.

I crumpled to the ground, pinned like some weakling to the floor.

"Are you willing to make that final sacrifice?"

I lifted my gaze, staring at the empty, shadowed cowls. "Do I have a choice?"

"You always have a choice."

"It doesn't feel that way."

"You can run. Ignore your destined path. Live your life."

Was this reverse psychology?

Honestly, putting myself first for once was a tempting offer, but I'd always be running. Morgomoth would be in power, and he wouldn't stop hunting me. The world would fall under his dominion. There wouldn't be much of a life to live. And what of my friends? They'd die because they would never surrender to Morgomoth.

No, running wasn't an option, because that path would lead to a literal dead end.

"Then that is your answer. Use the book wisely."

I had been staring at the floor again and grudgingly looked up. My chest rose and fell, surprise flitting through me. The Bone Grimoire was resting on the plinth, which had miraculously put itself back together since my tantrum. I hadn't felt the book leave my body and knew I would never truly understand its magic. The series of humerus, radius, and ulna bones that had been assembled into two giant hands held the Bone Grimoire to the light as though the book was some kind of glorious, sanctified object. I suppose it was.

I bounded for it, imagining it disappearing like a puff of smoke.

It's real.

It's here.

The book was something tangible in my fingers. Air rushed down my throat, my eyes stinging with emotion. This chamber was not real but a place in my head, which meant the previous blockage to the book had been my own self-doubt. I had accepted my fate, and now the Bone Grimoire had made itself apparent.

You truly are a book of death and sacrifice, aren't you?

I opened the volume, the grimoire's magic tingling through my fingers. The pages weren't blank, but the language written on them wasn't in English either. My elation quickly faded.

I scowled at the Grand Masters. "More riddles?"

"The book is part of you."

"Meaning what?"

"Meaning you *must figure it out."*

As guides went, these guys were the most unhelpful I'd ever met.

I returned my focus to the grimoire. The pages were lavishly decorated with runes and geometric swirls, all of it dark and beautiful. This was ancient magic. I could feel its power thrumming against my skin whenever I gingerly turned a leaf.

My power. This book was a part of me.

Which means it has to answer my request. Doesn't it?

"English, please."

It would never be that easy, surely. But I watched with wide eyes as the intricate lines and scriptures changed, bleeding out on the page to form into English. I imagined the book could change into any language if I asked it to.

I could barely contain my squeal of delight. Finally, something was going right.

The book contained various spells and texts. There was moon magic and burial rituals. A section on spirit summoning, and another on astral projection to the otherworld. All magic that I wished I had the time to explore but would never have a chance. This was necromancy that was lost to the world and would remain so.

Impatience laced the Grand Masters' voices. *"You are wasting time."*

"I have to search," I protested.

"The book answers to you. Make it show you."

I rolled my eyes.

So cryptic. It's a good thing these guys never became teachers.

Would simply asking the book work again, though?

"Show me the spell that will create the Interitus blade."

The pages erupted into a flutter, as though an invisible wind had blown through the chamber. The grimoire stopped on a double-leafed page. I nudged forward, the temple falling deathly silent, like the walls and columns were holding their breath as well.

Salted water, a drop you will need
Earth and spirit, forced to bleed
Shadows and dark, summoned alive
Glimpse death to survive
Hope will come, pass, and fade
Create the almighty Interitus blade
Find the Kingdom to grieve and mourn
Where the dusk will meet the dawn.

I STILLED, feeling like I'd been plunged down into a bottomless void. "You have got to be kidding me. It's a frigging riddle. The spell is a riddle?"

I glared at the Grand Masters, wishing I had the power to burn them with my eyes.

I could just make out dark smiles beneath their cowls, the stitching that bound their lips pulled taut.

"The Interitus blade is a dangerous weapon. It can only be placed in the hands of someone who is worthy."

"You mean someone who's smart enough to figure this out?"

I read the riddle again, but there was no meaning to the words. "Can't you just tell me?"

"No."

Of course they couldn't.

I rubbed my tired eyes. I had run myself ragged trying to work out how to find the spell in the first place, and all it had achieved was another question.

Less than three days.

The sands in the hourglass were falling, drowning me with my impossible task.

"Zaya."

The Grand Masters' voices cut off my thoughts abruptly. There was something frantic in their tone. Something that bordered on fear.

"You've spent too long here. He's coming. Leave now. Wake up."

I grabbed the Bone Grimoire, cradling it to my stomach, hoping it might sink into me again, but it remained solid.

I squeezed my eyes shut.

Wake up. Wake up.

A tremendous dark pressure built into the temple. The walls shuddered, cracks running down the marble columns. Fissures snaked their way across the floor, and parts of the ceiling rained down. This was my dream. This was taking place inside my head, yet the doors had opened to an intruder.

A high-pitched buzzing filled the air, the whitewash of static reverberating through my brain. I moved behind the plinth to shield myself from the dull shadows that rose like smoke from the broken mosaic floor, forming into a substance that was thick and as dark as night. In that darkness, the faces of a thousand screaming wraiths took form, converging into one entity. It was a body made of shadow and glittering black veins, the bones pushing through translucent flesh.

Morgomoth didn't bother with civilities as he drew two blades that had been strapped to his sides. Power wafted from the athame-sabres, their heat chafing my face. The tether that had kept me calm snapped, replaced with paralysing terror. Morgomoth stood over me, a snake poised to strike.

How did he summon both the Larthalgule and Neathror blades?

Time slowed down as he swung the weapons, the sabres singing as they sliced through the air.

Wake up. Wake up.

But my body must have been too exhausted to even do that.

Sloppy with panic, I did the next best thing and imagined the Dark Divide opening its doors beneath me. If Morgomoth and I shared the Grand Masters' magic, if we were in fact equals, then it should have been possible for me to wield the Dark Divide too.

Freezing wind tore through the floor, which had yawned apart like an open grave. I glanced up as the aperture slowly closed. I heard Morgomoth's ferocious scream, saw his eyes ignite with fury as he watched both me and the Bone Grimoire fall away. And then the aperture sealed, plunging me into the dark.

CHAPTER 18

I landed hard on snow. Pain scraped across my elbows and upper back, but I pushed the discomfort aside. The aperture had vanished, the Dark Divide closing Morgomoth's access to me. It freaked me out that our minds were linked, that he could find me through dreams.

He possesses half the Bone Grimoire's power.

I have to be careful when I open the book.

Whenever I did, it would likely be a beacon to Morgomoth.

I gingerly climbed onto my feet, dusting off snow from my legs. The Bone Grimoire had landed next to me. I tucked it under my arm, refusing to ever let it out of my sight again.

Whatever world or dimension I was in, it was shrouded in ice. A freezing cloud of mist pressed down from the trees, the snow falling fast. Ice crystals hung from the thorny bushes. It was a bitterly cold and fiercely beautiful place, a nice reprieve from the toxic heat of Orthrask.

I jumped when I realised I wasn't alone. She was wrapped in a heavy shawl, leaning against the wet bark of a tree, her breath a cloud of white whenever she exhaled. Briya was staring at a constellation that burned bright and refused to be eclipsed by the snowstorm. I knew the name of that star thanks to Professor Gemmell's training back at Tarahik. Briya was staring up at the Zaya star. Ancient casters referred to it as the star of hope.

Briya put a gentle hand on the very distinctive bump on her stomach. I blinked. It was beyond strange knowing it was me growing in there. Perhaps not even growing anymore. Briya looked due soon.

I stared at the white landscape, which should have been impossible if I was calculating right. The seasons should have changed. Perhaps it was permanently winter in the silver-thorned witch's woods. That was the only explanation for the enormous snowflakes that flew at me.

The memory changed, darkness closing in like a theatre curtain rolling across a stage. I turned around, finding myself in the silver-thorned witch's cavern. And there I was, a tiny bundle in Briya's arms as she sat down by the fire. I must have been only a few days old, still red and swollen, my eyes closed but a blissful smile on my face, probably soothed by Briya's soft singing.

Isgrad sat in the chair opposite. There was no love in his eyes, only a haunted look of guilt. He was going to raise me so that I could die finishing the task that should have been his to complete. Briya watched him. She cradled me closer, a protective instinct that almost bordered on possessive. I knew at that moment that she had never given me up. I dreaded to think what Isgrad must have done to take me away from her.

Vulcan had said my parents were dissent rebels, but that was a lie mixed with a hint of truth. He had made me distrust my parents, made me loathe them, but there was love in Briya's eyes. I was her world.

She shot Isgrad a stern glare. "There has to be another way."

Isgrad leaned back in his chair. I wasn't sure if it was the flames in the hearth that caused his eyes to water or if it was fearful, anguished tears. "There isn't."

"I don't want her having any part in this. I want Zaya to have a normal life."

"She isn't normal," Isgrad insisted.

"No. She's exceptional, and she's going to live. I don't care what you do with your brother. Zaya lives. She has nothing to do with this."

"And you would let the world fall to Willieth and the ULD. She wouldn't have much of a life under his reign."

"She'd be alive, and that's all that matters." There was no fear on Briya's face anymore, just sheer determination and resilience. "I don't want either of you to die. You can't even be sure if the Bone Grimoire exists. Please, Isgrad. Find another way. I don't care how long it takes. We can hide in this cavern and raise Zaya while we find a way to kill your brother."

Isgrad smiled a bit, but his expression was torn. I actually felt sorry for him. He was responsible for what happened to Willieth. He'd taken his brother's life by accident and had created a monster when he'd begged for Willieth's soul to be returned. And now Isgrad was paying for it again with his daughter's life.

He stared at the baby asleep in Briya's arms. He straightened like someone had dragged a cold, invisible finger down his spine and drew silently forward, wrapping both Briya and the baby in his arms. "I don't want her to die either."

Shadows closed in. The memory was replaced by a new one.

I was still in the cavern but had jumped a year or two ahead. A toddler with dark auburn curls was sitting up in a wooden baby cot, playing with a toy horse, oblivious to her parents, who were studying around the kitchen workbench. Briya and Isgrad were reading spell books—ancient texts by the look of them. The silver-thorned witch worked beside my parents.

The hour was late. Briya rubbed at her tired eyes. She stared at the witch, who looked as pale as a wraith. "Thank you for finding these books."

The witch clicked her tongue. "I want you to understand that this might not work. It's never been done before. In time, we'll require the sovereigns' and the Haxsan Guard's assistance." Her wrinkled hand tightened on her walking stick. "I do not trust that either of them will do what's right. They may use Morgomoth's power for their own gain."

Isgrad looked up from his book. "But he wouldn't feel it, would he?"

The silver-thorned witch shrugged. "I wouldn't know. He'd be alive. Whether he'd be in paralysis, I cannot say."

Briya chewed on her lip. "We have to give it a try. We've come too far to give up now."

Isgrad took her hand. "We will."

The witch surveyed them with a clenched jaw. "Let me warn you both about this scheme. You're going against the plans of fate. What is meant to be will happen, no matter what you do to try and stop it."

Isgrad's blue eyes narrowed. "You told me long ago that we make our own choices."

"We do, but sometimes there's a destined path, and eventually, no matter how much one fights it, fate will steer them to follow it."

"Are you saying my daughter will die?" The muscles in his ruggedly handsome face went taut.

Briya released a shuddering breath.

The witch kept her face blank, but her voice was cold and direct. "I'm telling you that there are consequences for going against fate."

Isgrad looked capable of drawing blood. "Then why are you helping us if you believe what we're doing is wrong?"

The witch took in my mother's pale face and sunken cheeks,

then looked at my father, who stood resolved and stern, like no weapon on earth could cut him down. My heart thrummed from recognition. I was like them so much. I had inherited Briya's good-natured, complaisant charm, maybe even a little of her impulsiveness—okay, a lot of that—but I'd definitely taken after Isgrad more. The same defiance, the same maddening rage, the same willpower and strength of mind. How had I not seen it from the very first memory? I even had his eyes, deep and ocean blue.

"I'm helping you because you are parents," the silver-thorned witch confessed with a withering glance. "And parents should do everything in their power to protect their child."

Briya blinked. "Don't all parents do that?"

The witch let out a huff of amusement. "You would be surprised where cruelty can come from."

Neither of my parents said anything to that.

I thought of Jad and the horrors he'd suffered at the hands of his own father. Though I knew Jad would never confess it, it had haunted and scarred him.

The witch gathered two books and set them on the bench before Isgrad and Briya. The hexes looked complicated and difficult to follow, and I was glad I wasn't the one who would have to deal with them.

"Combining these two spells should work, but it will take years to find all the ingredients," the witch warned. "They're scarce. We'll need the fruit of a melencicata tree. I haven't seen that tree in years. I don't even know where we would find a seed."

"I'll find it," Isgrad announced, a hint of determination glinting in his eyes.

Briya's lips wobbled. "Years?"

The silver-thorned witch silently nodded. "Maybe a decade, if my calculations are correct. You can remain here in hiding with your daughter until the potion is brewed and ready."

Isgrad looked up from the spell book. "And what of my brother?"

"It will still take many years for him to come to complete power. Continue to be our eyes and ears in the ULD, and where you can, save casters from Willieth's terrible plans."

"It isn't casters I'm worried about. He wants to annihilate humans."

"And it will take him years to discover how to break the celestial shields down. The humans are protected, for now." But the witch didn't sound so convinced. She looked at them both with an expression of bleak honesty. "I know someone in the Council of Founding Sovereigns who will be willing to help once the spell is completed."

Isgrad clamped his teeth together. "You don't sound very happy about that. Do you trust this person?"

"Not in the slightest. But General Kravis is the only caster with the influence and manpower to help."

The world dropped out from beneath my feet. That was a name I'd never thought I would hear again. General Kravis. It made me nervous that he was connected to my parents.

Briya nodded reluctantly. "I've met him. I don't like him, but I agree. He would be the only one willing to contain your brother once we've spelled him."

Isgrad swore under his breath, but he took Briya's hand and squeezed it. "Then let's do this. We make the potion. And when it's ready, we strike."

Briya smiled, but it was a nervous grin. Her eyes travelled to me in my cot. At some point, toddler me had fallen asleep, the toy horse tucked beneath my chin. I was resting peacefully.

"The three of us together," Briya confirmed. "Alive, while Willieth sleeps."

"An eternal sleep," Isgrad reminded her.

A ghastly breeze tore through the cavern in a wailing omen.

All the candles sputtered and the torches along the stairs went out, leaving the three of them in darkness.

Isgrad cursed.

I quelled the urge to cry. My parents were intervening with fate. The silver-thorned witch was right. No one could fight their destined path.

I didn't know how yet, but my parents had paid the price for interfering.

I woke stiff and agitated. No one had bothered to light a fire, the darkness in the small cave suffocating. I unzipped my sleeping bag and sat up, brushing my unruly hair out of my face. What a mess it must have been. My stomach groaned in the silence. It felt like it was on fire.

"Are you okay?"

My eyes adjusted. Bronislav was sitting cross-legged against the wall, his hands hanging loosely over his knees.

I nodded, but I was far from all right. I hadn't been in a long time.

I sat in silence, processing what the memory had shown me. Isgrad had given up on finding the Bone Grimoire. That explained why it had remained at the Isla Necropolis. I'd thought Isgrad must have died on his quest to locate the book. It turned out he'd suffered a worse fate, but what that was, I didn't know.

My parents were the ones to curse Morgomoth to sleep.

Along with help from General Kravis and the silver-thorned witch.

I didn't know how to feel about that, but I desperately wanted to understand why my parents died.

When did they meet their tragic demise?

I realised Bronislav was watching me. "Can't sleep?"

He nodded. "Something like that. I'm contemplating how I'm going to wake Marek. We're raiding the outpost soon."

The lieutenant flinched at our voices but mercifully went back to sleep, the muscles on his face slackening.

"Please don't wake him," I insisted. "He's exhausted."

"We're all exhausted."

I stole a glance at Annaka. She didn't even look like she'd moved once since she'd been brought into the cave. "She can't do this."

After too long a time, Bronislav answered. "That's why I'm taking her place. We need to find a healing potion in that outpost. Talina wrote it down for me." He lifted a scrap of paper from his pocket, reading it slowly. "It's called rithanium. Jad and I won't be invisible, but at least we'll have killer super hearing." He smiled, but it was tight.

"And Marek?"

"He'll be our lookout. He'll remain on top of the ridge, reporting if anyone enters or leaves the outpost. He'll do it with the mapographic."

"The mapographic?"

"It's a prototype." He shrugged, as though that were an answer in itself. "That mapographic not only scans the surroundings but uses a thermographic camera that converts heat into a visual image. From the ridge, Marek will be able to know where everyone is in and around the outpost."

I contemplated this, navigating through the possibilities. "I'll replace Marek."

Bronislav's eyes shifted to mine. "I don't think so. You're the important one here. We're doing this to keep you safe."

I pointed to the three sleeping invalids on the ground. "They need food, medicine, and rest. It's me or no lookout at all."

This was it. My chance to leave. I'd take my rucksack with me to the top of the ridge, I'd watch and report using the mapo-graphic, and when Jad and Bronislav left the outpost, I'd steer around them, taking another route down to the building. I'd find my own food, medicine, and supplies, and then I'd leave. I was scared to hike Orthrask on my own, but I would do it. For them. To keep them all safe.

I have to.

My insides squeezed at the realisation that I would be leaving soon.

Bronislav watched with a look I couldn't read. It might have been curiosity. Or suspicion.

I kept my poker face up, trying my best to appear determined.

"Fine." He rubbed his fingers over his short-cropped hair. "Jad isn't going to like this."

I smiled.

No, Jad would thoroughly hate the plan. He wouldn't want to be anywhere near me.

I was counting on it.

CHAPTER 19

J ad went into a rage when he saw me. "What's she doing here?"

Bronislav and I had met him beneath the hill, a crumbling stretch of narrow rock. I kept my distance, feigning interest in the sky as Bronislav explained. It was an hour before dawn, not that we'd be lucky enough to see the sun in this place. Bronislav had explained to me on our way the exact nature and timings of our plan. Jad had it running like clockwork. He and Bronislav would be in and out before the sun rose, which meant in one hour, I'd be out of here.

I thought of the note I'd left beside Marek. I had written it hastily and hadn't given it the time and thought it deserved. It pained me thinking back on the words.

Please don't follow me. I need to do this alone to keep you safe. This isn't your responsibility. Hide for as long as you need and then make your way back to the beach. Leave this place when the Haxsan Guard ships arrive. By then, I will have defeated him. I beg you, don't come looking for me.

COLD, hard, and to the point.

I only prayed that my friends were smart enough to follow my direction.

After much scowling and heated arguments, Jad finally agreed to let me be Marek's substitute. I scoffed. It wasn't like there was an alternative option.

We climbed the tectonic slope, which seemed to have grown twice its height in the hours since I'd first been here. I hung back, scaling with uneven steps, keeping my eyes open for deep fissures. I barely missed scraping my leg across a jagged rock, the tip so sharp that it jutted out of the slanted ground like a knife. I was breathing hard not because of physical strain but because I was nervous. I kept expecting Jad to turn around at any moment and demand I go back.

"You shouldn't have brought your rucksack," he said, getting as close to me as he dared, his eyes as cold as a violent winter. "It's slowing you down."

I bit my tongue. "Bronislav brought his. I thought I'd need mine."

Granted, Bronislav had bought his rucksack so he could shove it full of supplies.

Screw it. Jad had riled my anger. "And I'm slow so I can keep a safe distance between us, *Captain.* Unless you want me to burn you alive."

I summoned every ounce of animosity in my voice, just to drive the point home: I could hurt him if I really wanted to.

Jad turned his head in a slow arc, his gaze cutting into mine.

Bronislav let out a low whistle. "You two are a barrel of laughs, aren't you?"

Neither of us answered.

"Keep moving," Jad instructed.

I wasn't sure if he was talking to me or Bronislav.

We reached the top of the ridge. The drop looked even more dangerous than it had previously. There was no activity in or around the outpost. The black granite built in the mountain was silent, like the edifice itself knew something was coming and waited with bated breath.

Bronislav wired me up and connected my earpiece to my radio.

"I don't like this," I said quietly. "It feels like this place has been made to look abandoned."

"They're in there." Bronislav tapped the mapographic. "Look at all the heat signatures. The rebels are asleep. Hopefully still drunk from their party last night. Should make our job easier." He tapped me on the shoulder. "Run this through with me one more time."

I talked through the plan. There was a large sewer drain that ran to a nearby hot spring. Jad and Bronislav would enter through the channel. From there, I was to navigate them through the building, using the mapographic and reporting through the radio. They'd grab what supplies they could from the kitchens and infirmary, and then they'd return, meeting me here. In and out. Simple.

A wobble hung in my throat, and I worried Bronislav would detect something was amiss.

"Good." He smiled, but it teetered at the edges. "Jad and I memorised the outpost's layout. We pretty much know our way in. We'll only call on you if we get stuck, okay?"

"Then why not just take the mapographic with you?"

I couldn't help it. I looked over at the captain. Jad was staring down the ridge, assessing the outpost. He was armed to the teeth, the scalding wind blowing his black hair behind him. He looked like a warlord about to bring down destruction on the world.

Had he changed the plan, making sure I wasn't too involved?

It both infuriated and reprieved me. It either meant he didn't think I was competent for the task or just wanted me out of the picture so he didn't have to deal with me.

Well, at least this will make it easier for me to sneak into the outpost when the time comes.

Bronislav swallowed audibly. "Jad memorised the route just in case."

"In case of what?"

"We get caught. If we do, and we're prisoners, you and the others will be able to continue."

I shook out my sore hand, my scabbed knuckles stretching, sending stabs of pain down my fingers. I didn't like the idea of Jad and Bronislav getting caught.

Jad checked his equipment and reconfigured his cast-shooter, prepped for battle. "Let's move."

"Keep to the plan," Bronislav reminded me. "We'll be back soon."

I felt sick watching them leave. Watching *Jad* leave. This would be the last time I'd see him. Yes, he'd irritated me these past several days and wanted nothing to do with me, but we'd been through so much together before that. My vision tunnelled, my emotions threatening to spill out. It hurt not being able to say goodbye.

Keep it together. Stay strong.

Once I died, would Jad be free of the curse? I certainly hoped so. I wanted him to experience life. Get married. Have children. Grow old. Those thoughts were enough to convince me that this was the right thing to do, but it still didn't prevent my heart from feeling like it had been severed from my chest.

I strangled the sob that burned in my throat and moved to the edge of the ridge, dropping onto my stomach in case there were sentries out. The outpost was still eerily quiet. I didn't like it. Not one bit.

I waited fifteen minutes, watching Jad's and Bronislav's thermal heat images move stealthily inside the building. Thank providence I had the mapographic. It would allow me to avoid them.

Okay, Zaya. Let's do this.

I scaled the uneven rocks, taking the same path Jad and Bronislav had only minutes earlier. Slick pebbles slipped out beneath my boots, causing me to skid. A few times I nearly went right over.

Concentrate. Stay calm.

But don't take this slow either. Move.

I bounded down the steep descent, careful where my feet landed, trying to move as fast as possible. When I reached the valley, I pushed through dead brambles and branches and came across the drain. It was a tunnelled vault with tightly fitted stone. Two walkways had been built on either side of the canal, which was just as well because the water was bubbling and polluted with sludge. At least, I hoped it was sludge. Falling into the canal would result in a very unpleasant mud bath, one that would slowly devour you in acidic juices. The smell was horrendous, but breathing just through my mouth wasn't an option. The air was so hot, it scalded the delicate flesh of my throat, my nostrils numb from the scorching steam. I lifted my jacket and covered my lower face, not soothing by any stretch of the imagination, but relief nonetheless.

The metal grill had been discarded beside the stream, warped like it had been melted down. Evidence of Jad's strength in action.

Thank you very much.

I slipped inside, careful where I stepped as I made my way through the dark, humid channel. My face was instantly coated in sweat, my hair sticking to my neck. Slithering sideways against the wall, I monitored the mapographic. There were two heat signatures moving fast through the building. Jad and Bronislav. They were heading for the kitchen. There were plenty of dissent rebels in the outpost, but none of them moved.

Again, that nagging tug that something wasn't right pulled at me. I feared that this could be a trap.

I have to keep going. I can't turn back now.

The mapographic led me through the murky drain, the constant spit and fizz of the water unnerving. I found a small stairway that ascended to a black door. The dragon-shaped handle was broken, courtesy of Jad. I slipped into the first-floor hallway, pressing myself against the wall, as if it could somehow defend me against a possible enemy. Secluding myself in a dark corner, I went over the plan I'd painstakingly memorised. As soon as Jad and Bronislav gathered the supplies and headed back to the drain, it would be time to make my move. Every minute and second would count. I'd collect what food and first-aid equipment I'd need from the kitchen and infirmary, monitoring Jad and Bronislav the entire time through the mapographic. It wouldn't take long for the pair to return to the ridge and discover I wasn't there. Bronislav would immediately call through the radio. I'd lie and tell him I'd gone back to our hideout, and that's when I'd make my way back through the drain and leave for good. It pained me to think what Jad would do once he found the note. He'd be furious. Bronislav would be stunned. The others would wake up, read the words I'd left them, and feel... what? Hurt? Betrayed?

This is the right thing to do.

The words continued to run through my head in a stubborn mantra.

I moved down the hall, as quiet and fluid as a wraith, listening for the approach of footsteps, but there were none. Again, I didn't like how quiet everything was in the outpost. There had been no one at the gatehouse or in the guardrooms. Surely everyone couldn't be sleeping off hangovers.

I slipped soundlessly from passage to passage, keeping close to the shadows. The outpost was a maze of corridors and stairwells, a place where anyone could appear from around a corner at any moment, but the mapographic showed that the halls and passages were empty. I deliberated whether I should hide in a room or take this chance to find some much-needed clothes when a figure stepped out at the end of the hallway. I sprang back around the corner, flattening myself against the wall.

Holding my breath, I checked the mapographic, hoping the rebel hadn't seen me. That he or she wasn't on their way to seize me as a prisoner. But there was nothing on the screen. The passage was… empty?

But that's impossible. I saw….

Cold air danced across my skin, sending goose bumps crawling over my arms. Not a rebel. Not even a person. A wraith. All my muscles bristled with tension, and my teeth wouldn't stop chattering as the temperature plunged. Except for the spectres I'd encountered in the dead forest, I hadn't sensed any ghosts at Orthrask. Not even Lunette, who threw her soul time and time again into danger to help me. She'd made herself scarce. I couldn't say I blamed her. Perhaps all the ghosts were too scared to make an appearance for fear they'd be trapped in Orthrask.

But this ghost?

This one is here for me.

It was approaching, the cool air seeping into my bones. I gripped my athame-sabre, not that the blade would do much good against a wraith. The hallway was freezing now. Ice crystals extended from the ceiling. A wintry fog rolled in, the walls instantly blanketed in frost.

I held my breath.

The wraith appeared around the corner, no more than a wispy mist that slowly solidified. His face was stark, but there was a twinkle in those familiar eyes. I recognised the tall, lanky young man with the mop of messy blond hair, still wearing his chunky platform boots and cowboy duster, a pair of aviation goggles around his neck. He'd died wearing his Haxsan Guard uniform, but even in death, he preferred his unique fashion.

I blinked back at the burn in my eyes. "Edric."

Guilt weighed me down. I hadn't spared poor Edric much thought since his death at Stazika Palace. So much had happened since then that we'd never had the chance to give him a proper memorial.

"I'm… sorry," I said at last. There was nothing else I could say.

Sombre emotion flickered in his eyes. The grief and pain that had ultimately made him decide to end his life was still there, but there was peace too. He raised his hand, the ends of his fingers disappearing in wispy tendrils, and waved for me to follow as he drifted down the hallway.

He'd been a friend. It's safe to trust him.

I hope.

I crept down the passage, the black stone icing over as Edric floated past. It made the floor difficult to walk on, my feet slipping out beneath me once or twice. He turned his head, making sure I was behind him, still staring with those sad, pitiful eyes. He led me past several doors built of heavy oak and then stopped by an entry at the end of the hallway.

Before I could open my mouth to ask him what was behind the door, he vanished.

"Edric," I half whispered, not appreciating the disappearing act.

Is he still here?

"Edric?"

No response.

I checked the mapographic. Beyond the door, there was a heat signature inside. And it was moving.

Go. Run. Now.

Edric had led me into a trap.

The snap of a lock being unlatched rattled through my ears. The door handle spun, almost in slow motion, playing out the terror just a bit longer. The door was yanked open, and I came face to face with Lainie. She stilled, shock radiating across her expression. She was dressed in dissent rebel regalia, a black cloak wrapped around her. Her hair was longer now, down to her shoulders, and eternally black, the red streaks long faded. The new look suited her.

But I didn't have time to admire Lainie's hairstyle choice. Hot rage pumped through me. I wanted to cut her down with my athame-sabre right there for the pain and heartache her betrayal had caused us. For all those long, insufferable nights that Talina had secretly wept. For leaving me to die at the Isla Necropolis.

But Lainie's words stripped the thought straight out of my head. "Good. You're here. I don't know how you found me, but we need to go."

She heaved a rucksack over her shoulders.

"Go?" I forced myself to moderate my voice; otherwise, I'd surely scream every foul curse I knew.

I looked at Lainie's outfit, her heavily packed gear, and the determined look in her eyes.

She snorted. "The rebels saw you arrive yesterday evening. Who do you think got them in the mood to drink themselves stupid last night? I'm putting them all in a sleep haze right now, but my magic isn't going to last much longer. We need to go. We need to put distance between us before they wake." She assessed my dirty attire. "But first, you need new clothes."

She dragged me into her room and shut the door discreetly. At her wardrobe, she started rifling through clothes, pulling out trousers and jackets.

Uncertainty tugged on my gut. "Wait. You're…"

Helping me?

She tossed me a dissent uniform. "Wear this. We'll have an easier time travelling across Orthrask if the rebels think you're one of us."

I stared at the girl who had betrayed me, who had left me to die, who had been tempted by evil. The girl who was no longer my friend.

I tried to restrain my uneven breathing, but the anger continued to hum through my veins like they were violin strings, the sound plucked higher and sharper. "Give me one good reason why I shouldn't shoot you here."

I already had my finger wrapped around the trigger on my cast-shooter.

.

CHAPTER 20

Lainie froze.

I wouldn't actually hurt her, and it didn't make me feel any better seeing her afraid either, but I elaborated on the question.

"You betrayed me and all of your friends. Give me a reason why I should trust you." I hated that I couldn't keep the weapon still. My hand was trembling, but at this range, if I did shoot, Lainie would be hard to miss.

Judging from the way her face blanched, she realised it too. "I… can't. All I can say is that… I was wrong. I hated the Haxsan Guard. I hated the Council of Founding Sovereigns. I thought the ULD would offer a better way… a better life, but *he's* just as wicked and cruel. *He's* worse."

Her voice hitched, and her eyes gleamed with unshed tears. I wondered what atrocities Lainie had endured in the time since she'd sided with Morgomoth.

"Please," she begged, taking a hesitant step forward. "I know you need to unite the Larthalgule and Neathror blades to defeat him. I can get you into his stronghold. I know where he's keeping the blades."

So Morgomoth *did* have the weapons. He hadn't just summoned them when our minds had linked.

My voice came out sounding deadly calm. "Swear it."

"What?"

"You left me to die at the Isla Necropolis. I think this is a fair trade. Swear you will help me on your magic."

She blinked, her eyes dilating from shock. "But if I fail… I'll…."

"Die," I confirmed.

I wouldn't let that happen. This standoff was a game. I'd release Lainie from her oath if there was a chance she was going to die, which was probable based on where we were going. But so long as she thought her life was dependent on helping me, her loyalty would remain true.

I nudged forward, keeping her in range of my cast-shooter, allowing her to see my finger ever so slightly curve around the trigger. "What's it to be?"

"I'll… I'll do it." Her face was pleading and full of panic. "I swear on my magic that I will get you inside Morgomoth's stronghold and to the blades."

"And you will never betray me again. Say it."

She nodded. "Yes. I swear it on my magic. I will not betray you."

"Good." I slipped the cast-shooter into my holster, my own pulse resuming a normal beat. "Then let's do this."

I changed quickly into the dissent uniform Lainie had laid out for me on the bed. I was grateful she'd turned around to give me privacy, because as I stripped down, I saw my reflection in the mirror. I flinched. I knew I'd lost weight, but I hadn't expected it to be so noticeable. Many of the cuts and scratches along my body had scabbed over. My skin was inflamed around the wounds, and patchy and sunburnt in other places. My lips were so badly chapped that it looked like they'd be run over with sandpaper. And don't get me started on my hair.

I desperately craved a hot bath, but that was a luxury I doubted I'd ever experience again.

I'm going to die.

The words cleaved at my heart, almost breaking my resolve again. Hands trembling, I sheathed my athame-sabre and hoisted my rucksack over my shoulder. I stole another glance at myself in the mirror, not recognising the girl who stared back. Seeing myself in dissent rebel regalia was an unnerving sight, but Lainie was right. It would prevent detection.

Lainie had managed to regain her composure. She released a breathy sigh of relief. "We need to move now if we're to find the others and get out of here before the rebels wake."

She opened the door and peered through, making sure the coast was clear in the hallway, and signalled for me to follow.

"The others aren't coming," I revealed. I pushed past her, slipping out into the hall. "I don't want them involved. *My friends* will remain out of this and safe. This is my task alone. And now I have a guide."

Lainie actually had the nerve to look upset, catching on to the subtle jab. "Okay. Makes sense."

I checked the mapographic. Two heat signatures moved with stealth through the building. I watched them descend into the drain. My apprehension spiked. My plan was already behind schedule.

"I need to get to the kitchen and the infirmary. I need supplies."

Lainie walked in the opposite direction from where we needed to go. My stomach twisted at the thought of betrayal, but she couldn't, even if she wanted to. She was loyal to me now.

She tapped her shoulder strap. "I have everything we'll need in my rucksack. I gathered food and first-aid supplies last night."

Fine. At least that's one good thing out of this mess.

"You're going the wrong way," I insisted. "We need to get to the drain."

She scrunched her nose. "There's a portal in the courtyard. It will take us out of here. Farther from the outpost than if we walked."

My stride slowed a little, and again I questioned Lainie's motives. "I didn't see a portal in the courtyard."

I had thoroughly looked over every detail through the binoculars when I'd sat atop the ridge last night with Marek. I would have remembered seeing a portal. The mapographic had never revealed one either.

"It's underground in the mountain." Lainie stopped walking, her delicate chin rising. She went very still. "Oh providence."

"What? What's wrong?"

I didn't like how whitish she'd become.

She turned to look at me with mute panic. "I just lost the hold on my magic. They're waking up."

I checked the mapographic. She was right. Heat signatures were moving. Some were already out in the halls, sluggish and unhurried. Some had moved into the kitchens and the infirmary. Apparently, Jad and Bronislav hadn't been as discreet as I'd hoped, because an alarm wailed through the outpost, the blaring noise stabbing at my ears.

"What is that?"

Blazing red lights flashed along the ceiling, causing staccato flickers down the passage.

Lainie grabbed my arm, dragging me down the hallway and around a bend. "Someone has sounded the alarm that there are intruders in the outpost. They'll search the entire area."

I scrambled beside her. "The area?"

She passed me a meaningful stare, and I knew in that moment that my plan had backfired spectacularly. My friends were in danger, and I was partially responsible for putting them in it.

I checked the mapographic. Heat signatures were swarming in and out of the building now. Two were in the drain.

I raised the radio to my mouth and pressed the push-to-talk button. "Bronislav, get to the others and run. They're searching the outskirts too." I finished the transmission before he could answer, and then I did the one thing I knew would make him and Jad instantly suspicious.

I turned the radio off.

The pair would continue to head to the ridge, and when they didn't see me, they'd think I'd travelled back to our hideout to warn the others. A quick glance at the mapographic revealed I was right. Jad and Bronislav were climbing the ridge. It almost made me feel guilty knowing how well my little scheme had worked. I shoved the mapographic and the radio in my rucksack. I didn't have time to worry about them anymore. I needed to focus on getting myself out.

Doors started opening. Sleepy dissent rebels poked their heads out, springing to action when they witnessed the rotating lights and heard the wailing alarm.

"Keep your head down and follow me," Lainie urged. "Walk fast. Pretend you have a purpose, but don't run. Otherwise, we'll draw attention."

We reached the double doors at the end of the passage. Lainie flung them open, revealing a grand stone chamber, the walls hewn into the mountain.

We really are underground.

We passed loitering guards who were too distracted to take much notice of us and hit the stairs. There were even more passages and tunnels deeper in the mountain. We avoided looking at any rebels we passed, keeping our faces concealed beneath our heavy cloaks. Thank providence Lainie had the hindsight to dress me in ULD regalia. Without it, I'd be a sitting duck.

"The portal is just down here," she whispered as we stealthily descended another flight.

"How deep underground does the outpost go?"

The siren sounded far away now.

Shadows flickered in Lainie's eyes. "It's deep. You don't want to know what happens in the lower levels."

I took her word for it.

My blood stopped at the sudden voice that rose from the darkness below.

"Please help."

Lainie stopped, too, only her brow creased with confusion. "What's wrong?"

"Help. Please. It hurts."

The voice was tortured, the tone laced with sorrow.

I jerked my chin to the darkness that swarmed the end of our flight. "Did someone die down there? Was someone executed?"

That voice. It was just like the sea serpent. Trapped and begging for escape.

Lainie brushed back a strand of her hair. "I don't know. It's possible. Please," she persisted, agitated by our delay. "We need to keep moving before someone gets it into their mind to shut the portal down."

"They can do that?"

She nodded, eyes pleading with me to get a move on.

We sped down the last of the stairs, the darkness coming alive with cerulean light. Lainie was right. The courtyard was underground, but it was more like a sunken pit. The earthen walls were smoothed by magic, as flat and uncharacteristic as concrete. In the centre of the courtyard stood the impressive portal. It was positioned above a podium, three steps leading up to the azure glow that rippled from the gigantic wormhole. The colours swirled and changed, sometimes indigo, sometimes silvery, sometimes an incredible dark teal, reminding me of the endless waves in an ocean.

Lainie moved toward it.

"Please," that torn voice begged again. *"Don't leave me here."*

I spun around, nearly losing my footing. There, tucked impossibly tight in the corner like an overly large cat, was a stagma. I knew the creatures' flexible spines allowed them to burrow deep underground in confined spaces, but seeing it was something else. This stagma was dead. Horrible abrasions lined its brown scales. There were holes ripped in its side, the blood on the floor dry and crusted. I couldn't smell death. I'd heard that when a stagma died, they didn't leave behind the stench of decay, but rather, thanks to the fire in their body, left a sweet, intoxicating scent. It was true—the courtyard smelt like firewood burning on a winter's night.

But this poor creature's soul hadn't moved on. It was trapped inside its broken body, desperate for a way out.

I swore softly, the moisture in my throat evaporating. "What the hell is this?"

Lainie, white-faced, looked at the creature. "It was probably brought down here to watch over the portal but wouldn't submit to the ULD. Not all the stagma have been compliant." She bristled, her spine seeming to lock up. "Rebels have been capturing the stagma and killing them. Morgomoth has resurrected most of the creatures so they do his bidding. I guess he hasn't reached this one yet."

Every last restraint vanished inside me. I didn't like how Lainie referred to the stagma as an *it*, as though the creature had no worth but was only a weapon to be controlled. This stagma hadn't deserved to die. The Bone Towers were its home. *Their* home. And Morgomoth and his dissidents had invaded, taking what they wanted when they wanted, creating a toxic wasteland. No wonder the stagma had attacked the *Crown of Glory*.

I sensed the creature was a male. "I have to help him."

"There's no time." Lainie pointed to the dark stairs. "They're coming."

My chest hollowed out, but I was determined to open that gateway into the otherworld like I had for the sea serpent. No creature deserved to be left in this pain.

I knelt beside the stagma. His scales were smooth but cold to the touch. The creature truly had been a magnificent beast, both beautiful and terrible. Broad shoulders, powerful muscles, and a large wingspan. It was such a tragic waste.

"Please," the stagma's soul cried again, begging for me to end his torture.

Lainie shot a despairing look at the poor creature. "Zaya. We don't have time. Come on."

An enormous crash came from upstairs. A heartbeat later, I realised dissent rebels were descending the stairway. Shouts and cries resonated down the stone walls. They were coming for us.

"Zaya," Lainie hissed. "We have to go."

I knew she was right, but I couldn't bring myself to leave. What had happened to the stagma, his life wiped out only so he could be resurrected as a monster, was cruel and a sin that someone needed to answer for. I did not want this creature to pass into the otherworld. I did not want this stagma to be dead. He deserved life. He deserved justice.

Something solid and alive with fire materialised in my hand, and on instinct, I thrust it into the stagma's chest. An explosion of light burst from the creature, throwing me backward. A high-pitched static filled the air as every surface in the courtyard turned into a white-hot furnace. I blinked, my eyes watering. The stagma appeared in the blistering rays, wings fully expanded, the beautiful leathery texture rippling with light. His scales glowed like halos. Gold glittered from his large eyes, the irises silver, like the colour of moonlight on a river at night.

I climbed to my feet, startled by the vast, powerful creature before me. A gold dagger was embedded in his chest. Somehow, fuelled by my own sorrow and desire for vengeance, I had summoned the Larthalgule blade. I'd brought the creature back to life. The athame-sabre dropped away, disappearing before it even made a clattering sound on the stone ground.

I felt it suddenly, like a claw digging in my heart—anger through my linked bond with Morgomoth. He knew I'd summoned the weapon. He knew what I had done. And he was not impressed.

A volley of caster-fire hit the wall behind me. I turned to see the dissent rebels emerge, silhouetted against the light that emanated from the stagma. They fired their weapons, round after round, me their target. Lainie wrenched me out of the path of the hex bullets. I felt them whoosh past my ears, but then there was a second sound, a roar of wind so powerful that it knocked Lainie and me to the ground. There was screaming. Screeches of bawling pain. Cries of madness. I got onto my hands and knees, trembling.

The stagma had joined the fight. The glorious creature was incinerating rebels where they stood, cutting down those who dared to fire at him with his talons. He was a whir of motion, claws, fangs, and wings. Blood splattered across the courtyard, bodies falling in charred heaps. The creature nipped and bit, making sure none of the rebels passed.

Is he… protecting me?

But it wasn't just the stagma fighting. I recognised the distinct male form that sliced his blade of fire through the foes. Jad was covered in blood; it streaked down his face and arms like he'd taken a shower in it. A wild savagery glazed his eyes. I had once again underestimated Jad's resilience. He had worked out what I'd done and had come back to get me. Granted, he couldn't physically touch me, but he would cut down every dissent rebel in the outpost to make sure I didn't come to any harm.

"Come on." Lainie tugged my hand, her palms slick with sweat. "The portal is closing."

I didn't want to leave the stagma. I didn't want to leave Jad. But they had the fight under control.

My task. Mine alone.

I ran, my feet slapping the ground hard, my new boots easily finding purchase. Lainie dived into the portal, gone in an instant. I clambered up the steps, the singing wind pulling me closer. At any moment, I'd be sucked right in.

"Zaya."

The voice sent fire through me, burning into my very soul. Jad had managed to pass the rally of dissent rebels. He was coming after me. He didn't care about the curse or what would happen if he got too close. Not anymore. He was spurred on only by battle fury. I detected it in those blood-red eyes. Seize and detain.

"Once this is all over, I never want to see you again. I hope you die in that place."

For a moment, I'd been frozen, but those words reminded me of Jad's true feelings—his real purpose in all of this.

"I'm doing this for all of you," I shouted over the wind. "To keep you safe."

I ignored the rage in those heated eyes and ran into the portal, tumbling into empty space.

CHAPTER 21

W ind tore at my body. The portal sucked me into its black hole like it was trying to rip skin and flesh from my bones. My heart flew up into my throat, my stomach sloshing into water. I screamed, gravity spinning me like I was a yo-yo. I would never, as long as I lived, understand why casters thought this was a safe way to travel.

I landed on a hard surface, the impact shooting up dust and grit. I felt it in my eyes and tasted it in my mouth as I coughed and spluttered.

Lainie hadn't fared much better. She tore herself from the ground, distaste lingering on her face when she peered down at her grime-sprinkled trousers. "Back away from the portal. We need to blow it up and break the connection to the other side."

She took out a hex-grenade from her cloak pocket.

Rolling to my side, I scrambled out of her way. "It'll take more than a grenade to destroy it."

Portals were protected by magic. Lainie was fooling herself if she thought she could take it down with a bomb.

She smiled at me, but it was grisly and fierce. "Not this one.

This hex-grenade has been imbued with fire magic, courtesy of Hadar." She pulled the pin and tossed the grenade with a strength that was impressive. "Duck."

A blinding incandescence hit the portal. A sound that was like thunder, shattering metal, and roaring fires wrapped in one erupted into the landscape. I shielded my face with my hands, the world suddenly filled with smoky air, my breathing turning ragged from the cinders. When I dared to look up, what was left of the portal was reduced to melted platinum.

Lainie shifted her stance, her gaze staring without blinking, astonished by the intensity of the hex-grenade. She angled her head, recollecting herself. "We need to keep moving. We've put four hours ahead of them, but they'll be coming now. They'll send word to the others to hunt us." She pointed north. "Morgomoth's stronghold is that way."

The portal had transported us to a desert wilderness of rocky outcrops, steep cliffs, and valleys. Blowing out a breath, I followed Lainie, the muscles in my back and thighs aching, my shoulders slouched beneath the weight of my rucksack. This was going to be a strenuous hike. The searing intensity of the wind already made me sweat underneath my cloak. Black material of all things. It sucked up the heat like a sponge, but there was no way I would take it off. It was the only thing preventing me from sustaining second-degree burns. Hell, even fifth-degree burns in this place. The landscape was nothing but hostile, lifeless earth.

Yes, we're definitely closer to Morgomoth's stronghold.

"How did they know in the end?" My voice sounded strained. I could still taste sand in the back of my throat. "That I was an intruder, I mean?"

Lainie hitched her cloak tighter around her ears. "I don't know. They might have only understood that there was an intruder in their midst at first, but after you resurrected that stagma, well... now they definitely know it's you."

As if to punch that fact home, a roar escalated across the barren rocks. Far ahead on the horizon, four dead stagma sped across the sky. Even from this distance, the undulations of those wings cleaving air could be heard. The coppery taste of fear polluted my mouth, spiralling right down into my gut. The Four Revenants were heading to the outpost.

Please. Please let the others have fled and be far away.

Hopefully, by now, Jad was taking everyone back to the beach and was in contact with Darius and Macaslan. I did not want to think about how furious the senator and the commander would be with what I'd done.

Lainie's eyes were riveted on the stagma. "Okay. That's good. He's sent the Four Revenants. That means no one saw you leave through the portal. They think you're still at the outpost. Or near it. They'll search the surroundings for a while. This is good. This gives us time."

She sounded like she was trying to convince herself more than me.

Lots of dissent rebels had seen me leave through the portal, which meant either the stagma I'd brought back to life had killed them all or Jad had. My money was on the latter.

"Why not come after me himself?"

Lainie bit her lip hard enough that I questioned how she didn't draw blood. "He can't. Morgomoth hasn't left his stronghold since the Isla Necropolis."

I regarded her with bafflement. "What do you mean?"

"He's physically weak. When you both absorbed the Bone Grimoire's magic... the half he took, it changed him. He's powerful with magic, yes, but he's losing control. His rebels are turning against him. Many have fled and are trying to make their way to the beaches. Some are still out there hiding, waiting for the Haxsan Guard to arrive. Others have been rounded up and killed, forced to continue serving Morgomoth in death."

I was silent, contemplating everything Lainie had revealed. It had never crossed my mind what the Bone Grimoire demanded from Morgomoth in payment. What he had valued the most that the book had taken away. Now, I knew instinctively what it was: his influence. Morgomoth prized power and authority over everything else. No wonder he was so desperate to find the spell that would unite the Larthalgule and Neathror blades. With the Interitus blade, everyone would bow to his rule. He would have no deserters. He would have unchallenged dominance.

I need to figure out what that spell means.

"How are you with riddles?" I asked Lainie.

Her expression pulled into confusion. "Not good. Care to elaborate?"

I didn't fear revealing what I'd learnt about the spell. Lainie couldn't betray me even if she wanted to. And I was confident she was on my side. She'd finally seen Morgomoth's true colours. Apparently, many rebels had.

Lainie was quiet after I finished explaining. "I've no idea what it means," she confessed with a heavy voice. "Perhaps you could ask the Grand Masters for more clues?"

"Perhaps," I agreed, though I didn't like my chances. The Grand Masters were a riddle themselves.

"Whatever you do, you'd better work it out quickly. Morgomoth's stronghold is just beyond that ridge." She pointed to the steep, rocky outcrop ahead. Forked lightning erupted from the volcanic ash cloud that filled the sky, thunder ricocheting through the smoky plumes.

The hairs on my arms rose, feeling the static electricity even from here. "How can we be that close?"

Lainie had said we were only four hours away from the outpost, and Marek had revealed on the ridge that evening that we'd still had days to travel.

She shut her eyes, squeezing them tight. "I forgot. Stupid of me." She dug into her rucksack and took out a small, smooth black pebble. "It's black quartz. Hold it and take another look."

The gem was unnaturally warm, almost burning, when she dropped it into my palm. I looked again to the ridge and nearly choked. Towers and spires protruded from soaring pinnacles of molten rock. It was a castle of obsidian and metal, overlooking rivers of black clouds and lava. And it was close. Lainie was right. We had maybe a day's travel ahead of us.

She declined when I tried to return the gem. "You keep it. You'll need it more than me."

"What is it?"

"There's a spell on these lands. It causes Vrabkor to always appear distant, no matter how close you are, unless you have a gem to counter the curse."

"Vrabkor?"

"It's what we call his stronghold. The Vrabkor Citadel."

I stared at the monolithic castle. All the windows were lit like red, glowing embers. "How on earth am I meant to get in there?"

"There's only one way." Lainie's expression darkened beneath her hood. "You go up to the front door and you make Morgomoth believe you've joined his side. You already look the part."

"You can't be serious."

"The citadel is heavily guarded. That's your only option. You'll never get in otherwise. You'll never get close to him, and that's what you need to do if you want to unite the blades and kill Morgomoth."

I didn't reply, too overwhelmed by the risk that waited for me. Pretend to allege myself to Morgomoth. How would he not see straight through that? I'd defied and rejected him so many times.

Another question floated to the forefront of my mind, the answer like a bobbing apple that was difficult to catch. Why had Morgomoth tried to kill me when taking my life would end his too? Or had he worked out a way to break our connected life sources? I was certain Isgrad was dead, which meant...

Morgomoth has worked out a way to rupture the link.

It was one-sided, no doubt. If I killed him, I'd still die.

Bastard.

Even if I did follow Lainie's advice and stride up to the front door, if I somehow convinced Morgomoth that I'd joined his side, he'd never remove that tether I had to him. It would be his way of keeping me on a leash.

I'm still going to die.

Lainie strode ahead, launching herself into the arid desert. "We need to keep moving. We've already lingered here too long, and they could—" Her shoulders stiffened. She wheeled around to face me. "Wait. Your radio."

"What about it?"

She dived, slipping her hand through my cloak.

"Hey. Invade personal space much?"

She tugged the radio free from my waisted harness and dropped it on the ground.

"What are you doing?" My nails dug into my palms hard enough to leave crescent marks. "What's wrong?"

She stomped on the radio, breaking it into black chunks in the sand. "This is how they knew there was an intruder. They detected a magic signal that wasn't their own. They traced it."

She looked at me, eyes glittering with dread. "We have to get far away from here. They could already know our location."

"What about mapographics?" I raised the tablet, hoping to providence that Lainie wasn't about to seize it from me and destroy it too. "It's a prototype," I revealed, as though that would somehow make a difference.

She shook her head. "I don't know. Better to trash it just in case."

It wasn't the news I wanted to hear. Being able to detect the heat signatures around us would have warned me if rebels drew near, but then, if they were tracing the mapographic, keeping it was counterproductive. I dropped it in the sand and smashed my heel into the glass, cringing at the sound of its shattering surface.

Lainie and I didn't talk as we continued our trek through the sweltering heat, squinting through sweat-blurred eyes. Sometimes, we found ourselves walking through narrow valleys with steep sides, our shoulders brushing the rocky facades; other times, we hiked along the edge of canyons.

At some point, maybe after three or four hours of walking, my body finally caved to exhaustion. Lainie had packed waterskins, which I'd gratefully sipped from, but I hadn't eaten a proper meal in hours. One more step, one more shallow breath, and I was positive I'd collapse right there in the sand.

"Lainie." Even my voice sounded hollow. "I have to stop. I need to rest."

Her eyelids were slipping lower and lower too. She leaned over, hands on her knees, squinting ahead. "Over there. See that slit in the canyon? We can rest there."

We followed the sandy track between the rocks. On any other occasion, I would have been impressed by the rock formations that formed the canyon, the walls a natural fresco of pinks, reds, and oranges. We found a place where the canyon wasn't quite so narrow to rest and ate tinned food and dry meat. I drank my entire waterskin dry.

"We'll sleep till evening," Lainie announced. "And then we have to get moving."

I nodded, the only movement I could manage. All I cared about was closing my eyes and drifting into the dark.

I dropped onto my sleeping mat, ignoring the way the wind travelled through the canyon. The sound was like an injured, wailing ghost.

Rest wasn't in the cards. I found myself in another memory. Briya was standing over the workbench, cutting herbs. The silver-thorned witch stood by the fire, gently stirring a potion in the cauldron. Thick, heavy smoke billowed from the surface. Nothing had changed in the cavern, but more time must have passed since the last memory, because young me was sitting in the rocking chair, reading a large book. I must have been around five. My hair was shoulder-length and curling at the ends, starting to take the same form as Briya's.

Young me raised my eyes to my mother. "When's Daddy coming home?"

Briya exchanged a nervous glance with the witch before replying. "Not for a while yet, sweetheart. He's… working."

That's one way of putting it, I suppose.

"Why?"

"Because that's what adults do. They work."

"Is that what you're doing?"

Briya rubbed the beading sweat from her forehead. "Yes."

"What are you making?"

Young me was very persistent.

"A spell."

"What kind of spell?"

It was the silver-thorned witch who answered. "One that will swell your tongue if you don't stop asking questions, girl. Have you finished that chapter?"

Young me shook my head.

The witch tsked. "I want it finished. Your exam is tomorrow morning."

Apparently, the silver-thorned witch was home schooling me as well as taking responsibility as my nanny.

Exams at five years old. She's a tough teacher.

I returned to my book, dutifully reading, until a steady pair of footsteps echoed from the stairs.

"Daddy!" I was out of my chair and bolting across the cavern, running into Isgrad's arms. He picked my small body up, squeezing me tightly before settling me on the ground again.

He tapped my nose. "Can you go to your room and continue to study? The adults need to talk."

I pouted at him and made a face, but a stern look from the witch had me picking up my book and disappearing through a fissure. A second later, the cleft in the rock wall closed up.

Isgrad rubbed at his tired eyes. He moved to the workbench, examining all the chopped herbs. "Is this dinner or part of the spell?"

Briya shook her head at him, but she was smiling. "The spell, of course. Did you find the last ingredient?"

"It cost me." He removed a golden orb from his coat pocket. It was the size of an egg, but its surface was fleshy with a coarse fuzz. Its skin glowed, the radiance like sun rays in the early morning. This had to be the fruit of the melencicata tree. Isgrad had found it.

Briya released a tense breath. "Cost you how?"

"I had to seek help."

"From General Kravis? I thought we'd agree to only keep him informed when there was no other option?"

An unshakable tightness squeezed me. So, my parents had approached General Kravis for aid, and it turned out he'd agreed.

Isgrad's remarkable blue eyes narrowed, and I knew he didn't want to answer this question. Feared answering this question. "No. Not him. It's worse."

Briya wrinkled her nose. "Not my mother?"

A pair of heavy footsteps resonated from the stairway. A second later, a younger-looking Commander Macaslan stormed into the cavern.

"Briya," she announced, her voice thick and charged, with just a hint of disapproval. "I think it's time I meet with my grand-daughter."

CHAPTER 22

My grandmother!

My effing grandmother was Commander Macaslan. Surprise latched on to me but was quick to turn into something stronger. Irritation seethed through me, cutting my insides up like ribbons. All this time, that woman who had been cold and uncouth, who had watched me with impatience and antipathy, was my living relation. All this time, she had known and never said a thing.

My *legal* guardian. Now it made sense. She hadn't just been chosen by Chauvelin when he'd dropped me in Brendlash Orphanage. She'd become guardian by family magic.

Grandmother.

Granddaughter.

She's known—all this time.

And never said a damn word to me.

My hands were trembling by my sides, my rage rising into something ugly and hostile. I felt betrayed. Tricked. Made a fool of.

I thought about my lineage.

That means I'm related to Macaslan's sisters too.
Macha and... Melvina Raskovitch.
Providence help me.

All this time, Macaslan and Macha had known. My blood pounded in my ears, and my face burned. Why had they let me think I was alone and had no one? Was it because they knew I wasn't going to live long? Did they just see me as a weapon to defeat Morgomoth? A necessary sacrifice to be made?

I wanted to kick something. No, I wanted to tear my hands into Commander Macaslan and demand the truth. I was furious and dazed and feral, but I couldn't do anything but watch the memory play out.

Briya stared at the commander with icy reserve. "Hello, Mother."

Macaslan strolled into the cavern, inspecting the witch's home with an air of distaste. "This is where you decided to raise your child. I'd hardly call it appropriate."

Briya stilled, her expression cold and hollow. "Until Morgomoth is asleep, it's the safest place."

"The safest place would be at Tarahik where she belongs. Where *you* belong."

I noticed she didn't include Isgrad in that comment.

Briya sent a stern glare at Isgrad, as though to say, *"See what happens when you involve my mother?"*

She turned to Macaslan, the light dying out of her eyes. "Tarahik is dangerous. There are too many casters who could learn the truth about Zaya... who would want to use her for their own gain or surrender her to the Council of Founding Sovereigns for a reward. She'll grow to be a powerful necromancer. She's far better here where there are no eyes to watch her."

The commander never diverged from her brusque manner. "And what will you do *if* you succeed with this ridiculous plan?

What happens once you trap Morgomoth in a sleeping curse? *If you trap him?*"

"We will," Isgrad cut in.

Macaslan ignored him, her fuming eyes turning on her daughter instead. "Briya, I came here for you and Zaya. Come home. *He*"—she tossed Isgrad a livid stare—"passed you over once before. He will do it again. Men like him cannot be trusted."

"Men like me?" Isgrad sank his teeth into his lower lip, his face darkening with anger. "Is this why you helped me find the fruit? To take away Briya and my daughter?"

"To protect them," she snapped. "That potion will take another five years to fully brew." She gestured around the cavern. "You cannot expect a mother and her child to live in these conditions."

"Mother, that is enough." Briya's shoulders shook. "I'm staying here, and so is Zaya. Thank you for helping Isgrad find the fruit, but it's far too dangerous for you to remain at the cavern. Please return to Tarahik. I don't want you here."

Her voice broke on that last word.

So, mother and daughter didn't get along, just as grandmother and granddaughter didn't get along. I supposed there was some kind of irony in that. Commander Macaslan was a powerful woman who held everyone's respect, but she lacked what really mattered: family love.

The commander's face went uncharacteristically white. "This is no place to raise a child."

"And what would you know of it?" Briya's voice was viciously harsh. "You let nannies take care of me. Weeks would go by without me seeing you even once. You were a poor mother, and you have no right to judge me."

Macaslan's nostrils flared slightly, but she held back her disappointment, the way I so often recognised when she'd been infuriated with me. "Can I at least meet her before I leave? Just this once."

Briya replied with an exhausted-looking nod. She eyed the silver-thorned witch meaningfully, who'd been standing beside the fire the entire time, silently assessing the family drama.

The witch nodded with a small, tolerant smile. I wondered how she felt about her cavern being considered unfit to raise a child.

The fissure opened in the wall, and Briya led her mother toward my bedroom. Young me was sitting up on a bed, reading that large volume.

Before the commander could disappear through the cleft, Isgrad grabbed her wrist and spoke with quiet venom. "This will work. Once my brother is asleep and locked away in a tomb, Briya, Zaya, and I will be leaving this continent and never returning."

Macaslan's eyebrows went up. Her voice was whisper thin. "The problem with hope is that it leaves you with nothing when you fail. You will be the death of my daughter. I feel it in my bones."

She tugged out of Isgrad's grasp.

He stepped back, startled by the coldness on her face.

"You are dooming your family," she said with heavy condemnation, then strolled into the crevice.

Smoke and darkness closed in, the memory shifting into another.

I stood in the black crystal chamber, the mirrors that adorned the walls and ceiling reflecting the images in a multitude of directions, making me think I was in a mirror funhouse, something I'd always wanted to experience at a carnival, though I doubted very much that I'd have the desire to anymore. Not when it would remind me of Morgomoth's throne room. The jaded marble floor reflected the torchlight, flames spottily dancing across the surface.

In the centre was that perfect swastika symbol, held by a griffin and eagle, adapted from a time when our human ancestors had suffered under a reign of fascism. I'd had to look it up to understand its meaning.

Willieth was sitting on his throne, looking like an insolent prince who had been denied a crown. I was surprised one hadn't been made for him. His pale skin lacked life, his white-blond hair hanging past his shoulders now. The strands were the colour of ice. His handsome face was all sharp angles and hard lines, providing him with a permanent sneer.

The double doors to the throne room opened and Isgrad walked in. He bowed low. "You called for me, brother."

Willieth looked up as though waking from a pleasantly cruel daydream. He smiled, but it lacked kindness. "I have heard that we have a traitor in our midst."

Isgrad went very still. I didn't miss the bolt of panic that flashed through his eyes, which he was too slow to hide. I was positive Willieth saw it too. "I have combed each of your most loyal dissidents and commanders," Isgrad answered, enunciating each word clearly. "I would know if one of them was not true to you."

"I am not talking about my rebels." Willieth's blue eyes never blinked. He let out a dark chuckle, but he had one hand braced on the armrest of his throne, his knuckles whitening with suppressed fury. "I am talking about my family."

"I don't understand."

"Do you not? Should I show you, dear brother?"

Willieth clicked his fingers. A swarm of dissent rebels entered the private chamber, twenty in total, and stood in line at the walls, barricading Isgrad in.

Isgrad's throat bobbed. "What is this?"

A further three rebels entered the room. Two dragged a woman who'd been covered with a hood, her naked arms scratched and bleeding. She must have put up a fight, her white dress torn and ruined. She was *still* putting up a fight. She kicked and thrashed, screaming at her captors. The other guard carried a child, a girl no more than seven.

My body went heavy, like I had irons strapped to my feet.

Me.

Isgrad's skin went pasty, and his forehead gleamed with sweat.

Willieth laughed, a high whining sound that lacked humour. "Surprised, are we, dear brother? Not as surprised as I was to discover that I had an extended family. A niece. And a sister-in-law too." He clicked his tongue. "You did make an honest woman out of her, did you not, Isgrad? Ah, but I see no ring."

Willieth waved his hand again, a silent order.

The rebels raised the hood from their captive. Briya had been badly beaten. Her left eye was swollen from a punch, her lower lip cut and bleeding. She never stopped struggling, never stopped fighting. One of the dissidents kicked the back of her knee and she went down, hitting the floor hard. Briya's captors stood over her, pinning my mother to the cold marble.

A deep swell of rage swirled in Willieth's eyes. "I am surprised to see you alive, Briya."

"Stop this," Isgrad growled. "Willieth, please. I'll do anything. Just... let them go. I'll serve you. I swear it."

"Oh, we are long past that point." Willieth's voice was as toxic as a snake's hiss. "I always knew there was someone in my ranks who was a traitor. Imagine how devastated I was when I learnt it was my own brother."

His face shone with angry fervour, and the room began to tremble with Willieth's terrible, uncontained power. Shadows and smoke closed in. Wraiths. Their essences took form. Wispy darkness with spine-chilling grins. Their cries caressed every surface of the throne room. Coldness danced across my skin, making me shiver.

Isgrad took a step toward Briya, but two rebels broke from their line and seized him by the arms. A third dissident came forward, placing an athame-sabre dangerously close to Isgrad's neck.

"All this time," Willieth continued. "All these years. It was my own brother who worked against me. The person who I loved most. Who I admired and looked up to."

Isgrad flinched like he'd been physically struck. "Willieth... please...."

"So many secrets coming to light. My own brother working with the Haxsan Guard, the very people who terrorised and crushed us when we were young. How could you do it, brother? Can I even still call you that?"

Isgrad's hands were clenched at his sides. His blond hair slipped over his shoulder as he struggled, and an angry flush crept over his cheeks. "You stopped being my brother the day you died. You didn't come back the same. I regret ever asking the witch to help me resurrect you. I went against nature that day. I should have just let you... remain dead."

Willieth's blue eyes were blazing. They took on a new colour, wet and crimson. He wiped at them, almost surprised by the smeared blood on his fingers. Blood tears. His cheeks were streaked with them. "Traitors cannot go unpunished," he declared with cold apathy.

He nodded at Briya's captors. One of the rebels looped a short bola around her neck and pulled tight. She gasped, making horrible panting sounds. The rope cut into her slim neck, the soft underside of her jaw swelling. Her eyes bulged so wide that I thought the pupils might burst.

"Stop it." Isgrad was screaming, one of the worst sounds I'd ever heard. "Willieth, stop! Stop!"

Willieth barked an order full of savagery. "Get it over with."

The dissident placed his hands on either side of Briya's head and, with one swift move, twisted her neck like he was opening a bottle top. A snap crackled through the air. Briya toppled to the floor with a heavy thud, her neck protruding at an unnatural angle. Her eyes were still wide, held in a final expression of stunned surprise.

The scream that erupted from Isgrad splintered my own heart. It was worse than witnessing my mother's death. He fell to his knees, his arms still detained by his captors, and wailed. He turned his hatred on his brother, his blue eyes now a pool of frozen rage. "You are a monster. A bloodthirsty sociopath. Curse you. Curse you a thousand years."

Willieth stood from his throne and stepped down the dais.

Isgrad wailed again when he realised where his brother was heading. "Don't you dare go anywhere near her. Leave her out of this."

Willieth knelt beside young me. I was breathing hard, staring at Briya's broken body, my eyes glassy and unfocused. I was in a trance. I was in shock.

He gently stroked my cheek. "Pretty little thing, are you not?"

I didn't move. Perhaps witnessing my mother's murder had traumatised me too badly to feel anything.

"Leave her alone." Isgrad was thrashing and writhing. One of the rebels kicked him in the spine. He fell to the floor, his chin hitting the hard surface. He tried to crawl toward me, but the rebels stood on his hands. One of the men drove the athame-sabre down, right through Isgrad's shoulder, the tip scoring the floor below. Isgrad screamed, filled with terror and agony. His face turned blue-purple with what must have been a sheer effort to not pass out.

Willieth glared with soul-deep loathing. "Now, while I have you pinned literally to the floor, I am going to explain how this works. Your daughter is now mine. I sense the necromancy inside her. I sense how powerful she is. She will be my ally. My apprentice. My loyal family where you failed. You will become nothing but a distant memory to her. She is my daughter now."

Isgrad panted through gritted teeth. "I will kill you. I will tear you apart and feed you to your own lycanthors. And I will watch with a smile on my face."

Willieth roared his laughter with cold mirth. "I die, you die, remember? I am assuming our little child here is connected to the same life source." He gripped my shoulder, a gesture that appeared predatory. "You would not want to do anything that will harm Zaya, would you?"

Hearing my name on Willieth's lips sent icy pinpricks along my skin.

Isgrad snarled. "Don't touch her."

Willieth took my little hand, leading me toward the throne. He bared his teeth at his brother. "You will live the rest of your existence in a cell until I can create a counter curse to sever our connection. And then you will die. That is a promise." He turned to his rebels. "Take him away."

The dissidents dragged Isgrad across the floor. Blood spilled from his shoulder, a river of red trailing after him. He couldn't fight anymore. His lips were pale, his breathing coming out in soft, wheezing spurts.

"One last thing," Willieth taunted. "Your silver-thorned witch is dead. Her cavern is destroyed. You have no allies."

Isgrad was choking on blood now. His head drooped as the dissidents hauled him away.

Watching it brought on a surge of tears.

My parents had defied fate, and just as the silver-thorned witch had warned, they'd paid the price.

My eyes were still wet when I woke. Despite how humid it was in the cavern, I was shivering. What the memory had revealed threatened to snap me. I had witnessed my mother's murder, seen my father's imprisonment, and learnt that I'd been stolen by Willieth. I recalled what Vulcan had revealed back at the Otturin Cave.

"Your parents were dissent rebels. They believed in Morgomoth's cause and were willing to sacrifice anything to resurrect their fallen master… even their daughter. That's why you're here now, Zaya—to complete the ritual. They never cared for you."

So many terrible lies and half-truths. Even Macaslan and Darius had lied.

Macaslan.

My grandmother.

It still enraged me.

"Zaya." Lainie's voice wasn't at all sleepy beside me. She shifted onto her elbow, alarm settling on her face. "There's someone here," she whispered.

I shot upright, startled by the silhouetted figure that entered the canyon. My heart skipped erratically. Disillusioned thoughts to run bombarded my mind, but fleeing would be useless. We didn't stand a chance of escaping him.

Jad emerged from the shadowed entry. "Hello, Zaya."

CHAPTER 23

S *hit.*

"Surprised to see me?" Jad strode into the canyon. Dropping his rucksack on the sand, he leaned against the cavern wall, distancing himself from me as far as possible. He'd changed his clothes, too, and wore dissent regalia, probably stolen from the outpost. There was exhaustion all over him. His shoulders sagged. His eyes were heavy. But fatigue didn't deter him. He glared at me, pissed. "That was a stupid game you played back there."

"It wasn't a game," I snapped. "You were meant to lead the others back to the beach. To safety."

Oh providence. Where are they?

Not outside, I hope.

Jad's breathing turned ragged. "I swore to Macaslan and Darius that I would get you into Morgomoth's stronghold, and I intend to do that."

Then you'll die, I wanted to shout, but I couldn't find it in my heart to say the words.

I crossed my arms sulkily. "How'd you find us?"

"The radio. It had a tracker. I managed to trace it, found it in pieces, and then followed your trail through the desert to here."

Trail?

I thought the wind would have blown evidence of our footsteps away. I was sure it had, but Jad had lycanthor strength and could see what others could not. I wouldn't be surprised if he'd smelt our scent through the heavy gusts and winds.

Lainie twisted around on her sleeping mat. "What happened at the outpost?"

Jad's hateful gaze never left mine. "That stagma killed everyone, then flew off, probably in pursuit of you."

"Me?" I shook my head vigorously.

"There's an ancient bond between casters and stagma. You save a stagma's life and the creature becomes loyal to you. It hasn't occurred in centuries."

"I haven't seen it."

I was pretty certain I wouldn't miss a white-gold stagma flying the skies after me. Hopefully, the creature had flown far away from Orthrask, living a new life somewhere safe.

Jad just shook his head and rubbed his hands over his face.

"Are the others okay?" I dared to ask.

"As safe as can be. I made sure they were restocked with supplies before they left. Marek's leading them back to the beach. Macaslan and Darius are aware."

"Are they… mad with me?"

"Not as much as I am."

I flinched, feeling like I'd been doused with icy water.

I looked at Jad, really evaluated him, and a nasty suspicion pressed over me. "Did you know Macaslan is my grandmother?"

Please say you didn't.

It would be the worst of betrayals if he had.

I studied his face, looking for the sure signs that he knew, but his gaze shifted in surprise. He shook his head. "I wasn't aware. But it makes sense. There are... similarities."

Judging by his gruff demeanour, he wasn't happy that this particular information had been concealed from him either.

Join the frigging club.

Lainie's jaw dropped. "Macaslan is your grandmother?"

I nodded, trying very hard to keep my cool.

Grandmother.

It sounded spiteful in my head.

I could see questions forming in Lainie's eyes, but she wisely didn't say another word on the matter. Maybe she sensed the animosity rising from me.

Unbearable silence rippled through the canyon. I couldn't stand the way Jad's eyes continued to cut into my own like daggers.

"So, what now?" I demanded, looking between the pair. "You just drop me off at Morgomoth's front door tomorrow morning and pray for the best?"

Lainie inhaled a steady breath. "Not exactly. Morgomoth still thinks I'm on the ULD's side. And Jad could easily pretend to be Trajan. We could take you in, say we convinced you to ally with Morgomoth. If he believes us, he may let us remain at your side."

"Do you really think he'll buy that?"

My mind shifted back to the memory.

"She will be my ally. My apprentice. My loyal family where you failed. You will become nothing but a distant memory to her. She is my daughter now."

Maybe it could work.

One thing I had discovered about Morgomoth: he was cruel, vindictive, and a psychopath, but he prized devotion above all else.

Maybe deception is the only way to win the game.

I thought about the spell in the Bone Grimoire.

Tomorrow, I might be standing right before Morgomoth, begging for his trust, and I still have no idea how to solve the riddle.

Jad stared at the shadowed wall ahead. "We can strategise in the morning. Right now, all I care about is sleep." His dark brows narrowed. "Oh, and Zaya."

I looked up, expecting more hostility to be thrown my way. What I did not expect was a jet of fire. It landed on the ground at my feet, then circled around me like two hissing vipers. My body, my rucksack, and my sleeping mat were barricaded inside a wall of roaring flames.

Lainie gave a little cry and backed away.

"What the hell?" I cried, fury rising from the pit in my stomach.

Through the fiery tendrils, I saw Jad's lips twist into a nasty smirk. "My surety that you won't run. Goodnight, Zaya."

And with that snide remark, he lay back on the sand and went to sleep.

THE FIRE WOULD HAVE BEEN perfect on a winter's night, but all it did was keep me lathered in sweat for the next two hours. Too wired up and unable to sleep, I took the Bone Grimoire out of my rucksack and studied the spell.

Salted water, a drop you will need
Earth and spirit, forced to bleed
Shadows and dark, summoned alive
Glimpse death to survive
Hope will come, pass, and fade
Create the almighty Interitus blade

Find the Kingdom to grieve and mourn
Where the dusk will meet the dawn.

IT STILL MADE ABSOLUTELY no sense to me.

Salted water, a drop you will need.

That has to be the ocean, right?

I'm frigging kilometres out from the ocean.

I looked at the next line.

Shadows and dark, summoned alive.

I racked my brain, but there were no answers. My head was strewn with too many cobwebs from my past to concentrate on this.

Lainie had mentioned that the Grand Masters might help.

They did write the bloody riddle, so yes, they can darn well assist.

I returned the Bone Grimoire to my rucksack and lay down on my sleeping mat, glaring at the flames that whipped around me.

Keep your eyes closed. Just try to drift to sleep.

Hopefully, I would wake up in the Isla Necropolis, get the answer from the masters, and be out of there before Morgomoth even got an inkling of my presence.

Stupid, gullible, wishful thinking.

Because I did drop to sleep, only I found myself in another memory.

The dungeon was a dark, miserable place. Filthy water dripped from the ceiling, pooling between the cracks in the stones. The walls were rough-hewn and jagged, parts of it obscured in a jelly-green growth. I didn't even want to know what that was, or why it had been picked at, like someone had desperately been eating it. The cell wasn't large. It had one small barred window, too high for anyone to possibly see anything but the night stars or the sun during the day if they were lucky, and a thick stone door that I assumed was bolted from the outside. The worst part, though, was the wintry cold that seeped from every surface, making me feel like icy claws were running down my back. For a prisoner, that sensation would have been constant.

A magic trick, surely.

A man lay asleep on a wooden shelf, which appeared to have half rotted. His dissent uniform was wrinkled and stained, and his fuzzy beard held traces of the last meal he'd eaten. His blond hair was knotted past his shoulders and thin. Pale skin, colourless lips. Even his bare feet were blue. The tips of his toes were yellow where blood circulation was poor.

I shimmied forward. Sorrow chiselled into my soul.

Isgrad.

Judging by how he looked and the smell, he'd been imprisoned for a while. Maybe even a few years. He'd lost weight, his cheeks gaunt. I imagined I'd feel his teeth if I pressed against the sides of his mouth. Someone had placed a bowl of water on the floor by his sleeping shelf, as though Isgrad was no better than a dog.

A scream ricocheted from somewhere deep in the prison. Isgrad startled awake. He scrambled into the inky-black corner, raising his hands to either hide or shield his face.

"No. No. No. No," he mumbled.

There were nasty abrasions along his thin arms. He'd been tortured—repeatedly, by the look of things. I couldn't tell if they'd been inflicted with a blade or a whip.

A screech hollered outside the door.

I bunched my hands into fists, my own terror escalating.

That sound reminded me of Gosheniene, right before prisoners were lowered into the punishment cells to be feasted upon by the lycanthors.

"No. No. No," Isgrad moaned.

He started clawing at the wall, a desperate animal caged in and trying to get out.

Footsteps thundered outside the cell. The metal latch slid back, and the door opened with an elongated creak. A shadowy figure emerged. The newcomer carried a torch, the flames sending flickering shadows across the walls.

They stepped into a shaft of moonlight that spilled through the barred window and examined Isgrad with a judicious stare. "Do not be alarmed. Are you Isgrad?"

My father tipped his head up. He peered between his splayed fingers, never removing his hands from his face. "Who… who… who wants to… know?"

It crushed my heart hearing that. Years of prolonged silence had made it difficult for Isgrad to speak.

The man was dressed in a dissent uniform. He was wiry but athletic looking, his tanned face appearing through a curtain of light brown hair. He strolled closer and knelt by the sleeping shelf, pointing at Isgrad's badly slashed arms. "May I?"

When Isgrad didn't immediately flinch away, the stranger gently took his hands and inspected the wounds. "I'll bring an antiseptic potion and clean these. They're not deep and will heal on their own, but I just want to make sure there's no bacteria inside the cuts. Who did this to you? Was it your brother?"

The torchlight made Isgrad's eyes watery blue. He nodded. "My… pun… punishment… for betray… betraying him." He fixed his gaze on the mystery man and shivered. "Who… are… you?"

"My name is Clarence Chauvelin. I'm a doctor, of sorts. I have contacts on the outside. I'm here to get you out."

"Out?" Hope laced that single word, but like a drop of water on a hot day, the prospect of freedom quickly evaporated from Isgrad's face. There was nothing but madness and darkness in this cell. It wouldn't allow him to anticipate or wish for anything.

"Yes, but it will take time. You are weak, and we need to build your strength up. Have they been feeding you?"

Isgrad offered a half-hearted nod.

"Not well, it would seem. You look terrible."

My father managed a bitter, strained grin. "I… I'm… a spell-rock… addict. Haven't… had an… antidote… in a …while."

Now I understood why he shivered and sweated. Not because he was cold and feverish from illness but because he was suffering from withdrawal.

Clarence took out a small glass phial from the pocket of his uniform. "Courtesy of the silver-thorned witch. It's a potion to make you stronger. It's going to take some days to work. I'll keep bringing a glass to you every day until you're fit enough to finish what you started."

Isgrad was holding his breath. "She's… alive?"

"Yes. The witch was badly injured when the dissent rebels ransacked her home. It's taken her this long to recover. This long for her to finish and brew that spell. It's ready." Elation had filled his voice. "The witch has partnered with Commander Macaslan and a senator from the Council. Darius Kerr is his name."

"Why… would a… sen… a senator… help?"

"Darius is working against the Council of Founding Sovereigns. Macaslan too. She wants her granddaughter out of here."

"They sent… you… here to… help me?" Isgrad's eyes started filming.

Clarence looked down at the stone floor. "Not initially, but I'm here to help now."

"My… daughter?"

Clarence bit his lip. His voice was hoarse as he said, "She's being groomed by Morgomoth. Zaya is never alone, always in *his* company, or Vulcan's, or Melvina's. They never let her out of their sight. Zaya has witnessed some horrible scenes. Atrocities have been committed before her very eyes. I don't know how the child stays so strong. I'm sure it's her I hear crying every night through the walls."

Isgrad dropped his head in his hands and silently wept.

"We'll get her out. Once you're strong enough." Clarence pointed to the barred window. "Look to the night sky. As soon as the silver-thorned witch is able to, she'll bring you the spell that will hex your brother into a sleeping curse."

Clarence pulled away, but Isgrad clawed at his arms, keeping the man close. "When?"

"Soon. After you've recovered. I have to go. There are guards doing their rounds. I can't be seen in here."

"No. Don't… leave. Please… my dau… daughter. Don't… go."

Clarence stopped by the door, his voice a tight whisper. "I'll be back tomorrow. Drink the potion I brought you. Get your strength back."

"Don't… go."

But Clarence had already slipped into the passage, closing the door firmly behind him. The latch was drawn, and Isgrad was left alone in his cell again, blanketed by darkness.

The memory changed.

It was still night. I couldn't be certain how many evenings or days had passed since the encounter with Clarence. Isgrad sat on his sleeping shelf, staring at the wall ahead. He'd put on some muscle, his skin less ashen and his hair no longer resembling a dirty haystack. There was still an emptiness in his eyes, though. I wondered when he'd last smiled. Would his lips even remember how to do it?

A noise drew him to the barred window. It was heavy flapping, the swift undulations outside sending the cool night air into the cell. Isgrad climbed from the shelf and stumbled to the window. A rickety desk that looked half termite-eaten had been abandoned in the dark corner. He dragged it under the window and clambered on top, straining his legs to balance. There on the window's ledge were two potion bottles. One contained a liquid so eternally black that it had to be dark magic, the other a crystal-white potion that glowed silver.

I knew in my heart that the black potion was the hex destined for Morgomoth. The other potion, though, I didn't have an inkling what that one was for.

There was an envelope beside it. Isgrad read the note inside. A tear streamed down his cheek.

I heard the beats and flutters of wings and looked up to the window. Flying into the sky, its white wings catching the moonlight, was a phoenix.

CHAPTER 24

I jolted out of sleep and found myself staring at shadows. The circle of flames Jad had cast around me was out, doused like it had been hit with freezing water. A silvery trace of ice and frost remained in a perfect loop, as though I'd been caught in an ancient fairy ring. I was covered in a cold sweat. The temperature in the canyon continued to unnaturally plunge, causing my teeth to chatter.

There's a wraith present.

Somewhere.

I stared into the pitch-black shadows, as though it hid some ageless beast on the verge of climbing out. My heart rate soared, my insides roiling.

Jad remained mercifully asleep, his face serene, yet there was tension in his posture, as though he, too, could feel the unbalance of magic that rippled through the canyon. His hand was gripped tightly around his athame-sabre, poised for attack at the slightest sound. Lainie was asleep but shivering in the cold, her breaths clouds of white. I tugged on my cloak and gently laid another blanket on top of her, then turned to the shadows and waited.

"I know you're there. Make yourself known, please."

The darkness ahead remained undisturbed, and yet I sensed something watching. It moved at the same time I went to grab my cast-shooter. Pathetic, really. Cast-shooters couldn't protect me from ghosts. The shadows closed in, rippling like cool, black waters. It clustered around me from every direction, caressing my skin with icy fingers. I felt the wraith behind me. Coldness sponged the back of my neck.

Not daring to breathe, I slowly turned around.

The ghost with the long brown hair hovered above the ground. Her white dress flowed as though submerged in water, her hair moving like reeds, concealing her eyes. All I saw were her lips, so pale that they looked like they'd been dabbed in ice. Her swollen neck was bent and spotted with painful abrasions. I thought she'd been hanged, but she'd been suffocated, her neck snapped. I could still hear the crack of bones, that terrible sound sending her into this eternal doom.

Briya.

Mum.

Her wispy fingers cupped my face. I gasped, my skin burning from the icy touch. She drew back, sadness shifting across the thin shape of her lips. She bowed her head and drifted back through the canyon, the darkness and cold ebbing away with her.

"No, wait. Please don't go."

She stopped.

"Why did you come here? What are you trying to tell me?"

Raising a secretive hand, she beckoned me to follow.

An ache of panic rose in my stomach, but I mentally pushed it aside, refusing to be afraid. This was my mother. She wouldn't hurt me. I could trust her.

Double-checking that Jad and Lainie hadn't stirred, I climbed onto my feet and silently followed Briya into the dark slit of rock. She was a beacon guiding my way, her ghostly essence sending a washy illuminance across the stone walls. The canyon narrowed, the rock-strewn ravine now glistening with ice, as though I'd been transported from a barren desert to the beautiful, dangerous ice caps of the north. The stones beneath my feet were coated in frost, but my boots managed to find traction. Somehow, I didn't think that had anything to do with skill. It was magic preventing me from tumbling on my arse.

Briya floated around a sharp bend ahead, her white dress like a ghostly bridal gown behind her. My insides tightened. I was worried she'd disappear and I would never see her again. As balanced and smooth as I could manage on my feet, I reached the bend and turned into an enormous ice cavern.

The bright blue colour of the cave reminded me of large ocean waves that had frozen solid. I felt like I'd been carried to the deep mystery of the sea. Icy stalactites drooped from the ceiling, resembling crystal chandeliers not even the grandest palaces could compete with. But that was nothing compared to the silver-white phoenix that stood atop a natural stone plinth in the centre of the cavern. The bird watched me with curious eyes before unfurling its impressive wingspan. Ice and wind coiled around it, as bright as silver stars. When they fell like a glistening waterfall, the phoenix had transformed. I was staring at the silver-thorned witch. The queen of winter.

She was beautiful, not old and haggard as she'd appeared in the memories but strong and ancient, imbued with power I didn't even dare to try and understand.

Her lips formed into the loveliest smile, but they held a trace of sorrow. "Hello, Zaya."

I swallowed. The freezing air burned the back of my throat. "Hello."

Briya had disappeared. It disappointed me that she'd only been present to function in this small service. To bring me to the silver-thorned witch.

"Will you come back?"

My mother didn't answer.

The witch must have guessed what I was thinking, or she could mindread—a terrifying thought—because her facial muscles strained, but it was gone in an instant, her expression returning to a placid mask. "I am truly sorry for the task that has befallen you, Zaya."

"Is that why you're here?" I could barely get my voice past a whisper. "Is that why you've been following me? To help?"

If that was the case, where had she been all these years?

Her crystal-white eyes, flecked with blue, were sparkling. "I wanted to be there for you, but after Morgomoth's dissidents attacked and destroyed my home, I was badly injured. I transformed into a phoenix, my spirit animal, and spent the following years recovering. I must return to my animal form every few days now. My caster body can't function correctly without me doing so."

"Were you... cursed?"

She nodded. "I did it myself, so Morgomoth may never find me again. A phoenix symbolises endless life. Death can't touch or even dream of understanding it. In my phoenix form, I'm safe from him."

The tightness in my chest abated. "What are you?"

Spirit animal?

I'd never heard of such magic.

"I am from the time just after the change. I'm a keeper of the balance, a servant to fate. I've always been right and fair in my sight of the future, but your father and your uncle were my first failing." Her white hair flowed around her youthful face, which had turned sombre and cold. "It's my fault that this happened. I had been so determined to bring necromancy back to the world, to restore the magic balance as I'd been guided to do, that I ignored all the warning signs. Isgrad was meant to be the wielder of necromancy, but he was afraid, and I didn't take sympathy on him as I should have. I made a terrible mistake telling him that he could renounce the magic that night. At the time, I believed necromancy wouldn't forsake him because he was destined to have it. I was blind and a fool."

I recalled the memory, feeling like I was free-falling into darkness all over again. "You promised Isgrad on your magic that he could renounce necromancy. That's an unbreakable pledge. Why didn't you die?"

"Because I'm ancient. Modern magic doesn't apply to me. I lied to Isgrad, but in the end, that falsehood only backfired on me."

And me, I wanted to say.

And Briya.

And Isgrad.

Even Willieth.

As much as I feared and despised Morgomoth, he'd only been a young boy who'd had no choice when necromancy had been forced on him.

Providence, I was so tired. Not just physically but emotionally too. I was tired in my bones and my body. So many secrets. So many lies. I didn't think I could stand any more enigmas from the past. I deserved honesty. I wanted transparency. "Are you here to help me kill Morgomoth or not?"

The witch's face turned grave. "I'm here to help in whatever way I can, but mostly… I'm here to save Isgrad. He took on a task which he did not finish. Now that responsibility has fallen onto you. The least Isgrad and I can do is assist you to defeat Morgomoth."

I froze, hardly daring to believe what she'd revealed. "Did you say Isgrad is… alive?"

She nodded. "He's a prisoner here on this island. If my visions speak the truth, I believe he's locked in the cells in the Vrabkor

Citadel. Isgrad's life is linked with Morgomoth's. He will not risk anything happening to Isgrad, only so that he can remain alive and strong himself."

"But... I thought Morgomoth severed the connection. I thought...."

Isgrad isn't dead?

My father is alive.

The witch remained poised and still. She looked like she'd been chiselled out of alabaster. "The link remains. The three of you are connected to the one life source. If one of you dies, so will the others."

My nausea returned. "But Morgomoth has tried to kill me so many times. Melvina wanted to sacrifice me to wake him from his sleeping curse."

I scrambled through all my memories, none of it adding up.

"Did he?" The witch watched me with a coy smile. "Did Morgomoth ever really try to kill you, or did he just attempt to make you his prisoner?"

"He tried to kill me with the Neathror and Larthalgule blades at the Isla Necropolis.""And did this happen physically or in your minds?"

"What difference does it make?"

"He can't harm you in dreams. If he tried to hurt you, to cut you down, it was only so you would be trapped to him forever."

"And Melvina Raskovitch?" My voice shuddered out of me, leaving me feeling raw inside. "She definitely wanted to cut me up and spill my blood. Vulcan agreed. They said my blood had to be drained for Morgomoth to wake from his sleeping curse. They told me I had to die."

The witch cocked her head with a bold smile. "Spells can be misread. Why do you think Vulcan looks sickly and on the verge of death? Morgomoth is punishing his lieutenant for the terrible mistake he nearly made. He's draining Vulcan's life bit by bit.

Eventually, Vulcan will become nothing more than an animated corpse."

I stilled at the horrible visual her words had created.

"Morgomoth wants you by his side," she resumed. "He'd rather his brother and his niece siding with him, but he understands that you have chosen to be his enemy and are willing to end your own life to destroy his. He'll keep you and Isgrad imprisoned as long as he can until he discovers how to sever the connection."

"And once he does, he'll kill Isgrad and me?"

I trembled as clarity struck. "What if I died now?" I unsheathed my athame-sabre, the blade deadly cold in the frigid air. "What if I...?"

Took my own life and ended it all this very second.

Isgrad would die, yes, but more importantly, Morgomoth would be dead too.

I looked at the blade, imagining thrusting it into my chest. It would be beyond excruciating, but I'd do it. I'd suffer a painful death if it meant defeating Morgomoth right now.

"Do not be ridiculous." There was something wary in the witch's gaze, but it disappeared too fast for me to be certain for sure. "If you do that, you doom everyone who's in Orthrask. This place can't remain standing without necromancy. The moment you, Morgomoth, and Isgrad are dead, this island will sink to the bottom of the sea. There are casters on this island who are trying to flee. Men, women, and children who joined the ULD out of fear, who then saw the true colours of the organisation and are now desperate to abscond. They must have a chance to reach the beaches and the Haxsan Guard ships. Your friends must be given the chance to survive. That was your reason for leaving them, remember."

Fear and rage mixed in my blood. Once again, the world had proven totally unfair.

"Zaya, why do you think Morgomoth is so intent on uniting the Larthalgule and Neathror blades?"

I stared at her, struggling to keep my volatile temper at bay. "Because the Interitus blade will give him complete dominance over everyone, both living and dead."

Her expression tightened.

It took me a moment to read that look. "That's all the blade does, right?"

She watched me with a bird-eyed stillness. She and Macha would have gotten on brilliantly in another life. "The blade does as its wielder commands. Whatever the wielder wishes."

Astonished silence swept through my brain. "Are you telling me the Interitus blade can sever the connection?"

"If that's what is desired, yes."

I nearly fell to the cavern floor. If I could solve that riddle in the Bone Grimoire, if I could work out the spell to unite the Larthalgule and Neathror blades and create the Interitus blade, did that mean I would have the power to sever the connection and kill Morgomoth?

A small seed of hope was planted inside me, blossoming into something beautiful and wild.

Could I live?

The silver flecks in the witch's eyes swirled like liquid steel. "It is possible. It's one of the three futures I've seen for you."

I didn't care that she had read my mind.

Didn't care how invasive it felt.

"And the other two?"

"You die," she revealed. Her voice sounded heavy and broken.

I pressed my lips together, holding back that awful fear that tried to snake its way inside.

One out of three. Not great odds.

But still, I had an inkling of hope. A grim sort, but I'd hold on to it.

I eyed the witch. "You want to help me and Isgrad?"

I had to hear her say it again. I had to know she was an ally and was going to stick around. Not just transform into a phoenix and flap away.

She watched me, as though she were weighing every idea, thought, and desire in my head. "Yes."

"How are you with riddles, then?"

Her lips parted into a soft grin. "The spell is a riddle." It wasn't a question. "The Grand Masters were sneaky."

"Are sneaky," I corrected.

She raised her fine white eyebrows. "You've seen them?"

"In dreams. They say I'm the one controlling my visits... that it's my subconscious taking me to them. Twice, Morgomoth has appeared and has nearly...."

I struggled to finish the sentence, remembering the way he had nearly captured me, the terror in my heart when he'd brought those two blades down, determined to tether me to him forever. "I must be too afraid to return because I've never seen the Grand Masters again."

The witch's jaw tightened. "I don't believe the Grand Masters would help you solve the riddle. They made the spell that way for a reason, to ensure the bearer of the Interitus blade was worthy."

"I don't feel worthy," I admitted, straining to keep my composure. "I feel weak, and pathetic, and utterly useless."

The witch settled her gaze on me. "Riddles are never what they seem. Perhaps the spell is not supposed to make sense until the right moment."

"If that was a pep talk, it didn't inspire my confidence."

I felt more deflated than I had before. "Briya has been sending me Isgrad's memories. I've been seeing important moments of the past. Parts of my parents' story."

It had to be Briya. Her ghostly presence had appeared in the woods when Isgrad and Willieth were young. She had suffocated me—a very unmotherly thing to do—in my chamber at the Black Palace so I would continue to see my father's history. Why she had to do it that way, I didn't even want to know. Ghosts were mysterious entities.

The witch smiled. "I think your mother guided you, but I don't think she was responsible alone."

"What do you mean?"

"You are the necromancer. It's your subconscious drawing you to the answers you seek."

I pondered that for a moment. My subconscious. If that were the case, it made sense that I only slipped into these memories when I was sleeping.

"What have you seen?" The silver-thorned witch seemed to watch me with bated breath.

I told her, summarising everything I had witnessed so far.

Her face was drawn, perhaps not proud of some of the memories I'd referred to. She drew forward, standing tall before me. "There is only one piece left of the story for you to witness. Close your eyes, Zaya. Take charge and summon those memories to you."

My breathing had gone jagged again. "I don't know how to do that."

Her lips curved. "Yes, you do. Just tell your necromancy what you want."

I cursed inwardly. The damn witch was just as much of a riddle as the spell in the Bone Grimoire.

"Fine."

I closed my eyes.

I want to see the last memory. I want to know how it ended. I want to understand what happened to Isgrad.

It couldn't be that simple, surely.

I opened my eyes to tell the witch how stupid and foolish it was to expect magic to work like that, but she wasn't there. Or, to be precise, I was no longer in the cavern.

I wheeled around, recognising the damp stone floor and the green algae on the walls. I was in Isgrad's cell.

I was in the memory.

CHAPTER 25

Willieth must not have bothered visiting Isgrad in his cell;
otherwise, he'd have done something about seeing his
brother so... healthy. Granted, Isgrad's beard was still the length a
caveman would be proud of, and his hair was a shaggy mess that
would need to be cut to remove the permanent knots, but he'd
built muscle again. His face was no longer thin but strong and full
of colour. Even his eyes held resolve, the emptiness I'd seen in
them in the previous memory gone. Whatever the potion was that
Clarence had brought him had worked.

Isgrad was sitting on his sleeping shelf. He twitched his right
heel up and down, the slap of his boot the only sound in the
otherwise silent cell.

He glanced at the barred window "Come on," he muttered to
himself. His hands were so tightly fisted together that I wondered
how his fingernails didn't cut his palms. "This needs to work.
Where are you?"

Relief sparked in his eyes at the bloom of light that sped across
the dark sky, burning as bright as a meteorite, the clouds lit in a
golden-orange glow. Caster-fire.

A sound split the air outside the cell which froze me to the spot.

My mouth went dry a second later when I realised what it was. Shouts and screams full of mindless terror. The cries came from every direction.

Isgrad was on his feet, pacing his cell. He didn't look alarmed. He didn't even look afraid. He knew what was happening.

The caster-fire was a signal.

But for what?

A rattling latch slid back and the cell door was flung open, the screams doubling in volume. Clarence staggered into view, his arms and face flecked in blood. He was dressed in battle armour. The thick straps around his chest were equipped with sharp-looking knives and hex-grenades, and the hilts of two athame-sabres gleamed above his shoulders. He had a pair of impressive cast-shooters holstered at his sides.

"You're late." The vein in Isgrad's neck was pulsing. "You were supposed to get here before the signal."

Clarence unsheathed one of the sabres from his back and handed the weapon to Isgrad. "I got here as fast as I could. General Kravis is leading the attack. The Haxsan Guard have already infiltrated the castle. It's a bloodbath out there."

"That wasn't part of the plan."

"That wasn't part of *our* plan. General Kravis had other ideas."

More screams and grisly cries escalated from outside the cell.

Clarence swore. "Do you have the potions?"

Isgrad tapped his cloak pocket.

"Then let's go. There's no time to lose."

My blood pumped fiercely as I followed the pair into the passage. A hex-grenade must have gone off somewhere close because the floor bucked, nearly tossing me off my feet, and chips of stone pelted down from the ceiling. The torches flickered. The guards, if there had been any, had long abandoned their posts. Or maybe they'd been called to defend against the assault.

Isgrad's eyes widened in alarm. "Where's my daughter?"

They were halfway to the exit when an explosion ripped through the passage, the shockwave knocking us to the floor. Fire and stone rained down, the end of the passage—where Isgrad's cell had been only moments before—now an inferno of steaming debris and smoke.

I shook my head to clear the dizziness away. The memory couldn't hurt me, but it didn't prevent me from hearing that stab of white noise that accompanied the aftermath of a detonation.

Clarence stumbled onto his feet, panting heavily. "Are you all right?"

Isgrad was coughing. His face was saturated in sweat, and even his hair looked grey from the ash and dust. "I'm fine. Damn Kravis. He wasn't meant to lead the attack until after we were out."

Clarence helped him onto his feet. "Commander Macaslan will keep true to her word. The carrier-hornet will arrive soon. We have to be there on time. The pilot won't wait."

Navigating the prison's passages, the pair followed the swinging overheads, the electricity struggling to remain on with each boom that ricocheted through the castle. Clarence and Isgrad scaled the steps up to the main floor.

It was worse than I'd imagined. Dissent rebels were fiercely locked in battle with Haxsan Guard soldiers, the skirmishes scattered and violent. Everywhere I looked, my senses were greeted with yelling, screaming, and gore. The floor and walls were smeared with blood. Some of the trained killers were just a blur of movement as they hacked and sliced.

Clarence had to shout over the clash of weaponry. "This way."

We sprinted around the battle, dodging the blood splatters and sprawl of corpses, and ran up two flights into the heart of the castle. I had to tug my collar over my mouth to subdue the smoke that scorched my throat and nostrils. The thickening veil of fire was worse up here.

Through the windows—what was left of them—and the holes in the walls that steamed like craters, I saw caster-fire bearing down on the castle. Projectiles. Hex-grenades. Cannons. General Kravis was going all out to destroy the stronghold and seize his prize.

For a man who'd spent years incarcerated, Isgrad's tenacity remained strong. "Where's Willieth?"

"In the main hall." Clarence's eyes were dark. "He has Zaya. He knows he's surrounded. He knows you and I helped coordinate this attack. I fear what he's planning to do to her."

Before Isgrad could answer, a noise that was separate from the thunderous rumble of the battle below sliced the air. The hewn wall beside Isgrad was in burned tatters, allowing him to glimpse into the smoke-filled night. Descending toward the castle was a carrier-hornet. Its celestial shield protected it from the caster-fire that wreaked havoc across the sky. Despite how fast the hornet moved, though, the aircraft still dipped and buffeted as it tried landing on what must have been the helipad above.

Clarence drew in a startled breath. "I need to make sure he doesn't leave." He pointed to the passage ahead with a shaking finger. "Down there. That's where you'll find Morgomoth."

"Go" was all Isgrad said, already running. "And wait for us."

Clarence silently nodded. He hurtled up the next flight, disappearing around the corner on the landing.

Isgrad flew down the passageway, shielding himself from the scalding wind, the fires burning bright. The floor swayed as more explosives hit the castle. He came to the door of the main hall, which had been left ajar, as though open in a welcoming gesture.

Isgrad's eyes flashed resentfully. "Cocky bastard."

He slipped inside. I ducked in after him, my eyes taking a

moment to adjust to the poor light. A muscle twitched in Isgrad's cheek. The room's black-panelled walls gleamed, the long onyx table shining in the torchlight as though it had just been polished. There was a portal at the end of the room, the mirrored surface rippling like waves. Sitting before it at the head of the table was Willieth. His smile was cold and lethal. Next to him, young me was asleep in a chair, my skin so deathly pale that even my tiny freckles could be seen from here. Was I asleep? Or had Willieth done something much worse to me?

Isgrad swallowed back a tight sob.

"Hello, brother." Willieth's eyes raked over him slowly, fastening on the athame-sabre he held. An impalpable look crossed his face. Irritation, hurt, betrayal—I couldn't tell which. "Well done for instigating this little attack. I admit it caught me unprepared."

"What did you do to Zaya?"

Willieth stood from the table and prowled slowly forward. "Nothing. She is asleep. An induced sleep, mind you. I did not think it would benefit her to see the bloodshed her father caused. I am a very protective *uncle*."

Isgrad gritted his teeth.

Cold despair spread through me. Willieth wore his own battle armour, the hilt of a long athame-sabre protruding from the top of a waisted sheath. "You did not think this *little* assault could stop me, did you?" He pointed to the portal behind him. "I have outposts, hideouts, spies, and loyalists all over the globe. And I have control of the dead. I cannot be defeated."

He clicked his fingers. The sound was an audible snap in the hall.

Screams resonated from downstairs. The castle trembled from a new surge of power that shook its foundations.

Isgrad's expression was the image of devastation. "What did you do?"

"Raised the dead. My soldiers fight for me, even after death."

The sound of violence and bloodshed downstairs sent a metallic taste up my throat. Uncertainties tumbled through me, but all I could do was watch the memory play out.

Isgrad drew his blade. "You son of a bitch,"

Willieth threw his head back and laughed. "We do have the same mother, remember?"

"Yes, one you murdered."

"For you," Willieth seethed. "I removed her from the picture for you. Because she kept you in the cabin when you wanted to leave. You hated our mother. I killed her for you."

I choked back my disgust. Willieth really was a true psychopath. His childish need for his sibling's love had never left him when he'd been remade with necromancy. If anything, it had made him obsessive. I could see it even now in the way he watched Isgrad, as silent and cunning as a stalking wolf, wrangled with the desire to protect and possess. Was that why Willieth had built an uprising? Because of Isgrad's misguided teenage views about the world?

I think Isgrad might have realised it at that moment, too, because his face drained of colour. "Willieth—"

"I am not Willieth anymore," he roared. The dining chairs splintered, wood flying everywhere as his uncontained magic ruptured across the room. "I am Morgomoth. Stop being foolish and put your weapon down. We cannot destroy each other. You try to kill me, and you kill yourself and your daughter. You lost before you even started."

He returned to my comatose body and placed a tight-fisted hand on my shoulder. "The portal will not be open for long. Come with us. I will forgive your former solecisms if you allege yourself—"

Isgrad charged, eliciting a war cry. Willieth wheeled around, drawing his own athame-sabre, the blades giving an almighty clang as metal struck metal. I watched, horrified, as the rivalling siblings moved across the floor in a blur, feinting and slicing at each other. Isgrad cried out when the tip of the blade cut his arm, his dark sleeve soaked by blood. He snarled like a wild animal, his face twisted in rage as he attacked and blocked, over and over, his sabre singing.

Numbness spread through me. I wished I could stop this. They were going to kill each other.

A spasm of battle frenzy contorted Willieth's features. He struck again, his blade carving the back of Isgrad's leg. My father cried out but managed to turn and block the next aggressive blow. The pair were in a dance, their fight both graceful and dangerous. Isgrad was getting pushed farther and farther into the corner, Willieth's blows raining down harder and harder. I stared incredulously, my chest heavy. Isgrad was trying to reach into his pocket. This was it. He was endeavouring to get the spell.

A rumble shook the castle, so excruciatingly loud that it seemed like the earth had split open to swallow the castle whole. Both men were knocked backward as the ceiling collapsed. Storage tanks rolled from the level above. Oil pooled out, spreading across the floor in a black sea. From what I could tell, upstairs had been some kind of armoury and a place where fighter jet fuel was stored. It had likely been protected by magic shields, but those had long burned out after the castle was attacked.

Willieth slipped in the black oil. He landed hard on his stomach, struggling to get back onto his feet. Each attempt only spread the black liquid farther across his body. He finally found traction and loomed over his brother, looking like a monster that had crawled out of a bottomless bog. His eyes darkened, the storm in them churning like thunderheads.

Isgrad had fallen against the wall, cornered. He reached for his athame-sabre, which lay on the floor too far away for him to grasp. He gasped with breathlessness, spitting blood. "You can't kill me, remember?"

Willieth smiled. "No. But that does not stop me from hurting you."

The sword hurtled down, each moment suspended in time, drawn out in aeons.

Willieth halted. A choking cry parted from his lips, his eyes becoming impossibly wide. Isgrad scrambled away, staring at his sibling with confusion. I went rigid all over, my own head screaming and thrashing at the sight of the small girl who stood by the edge of the oil slick. Young me. My eyes were still red and cloudy from sleep, my hand outstretched where I'd dropped the torch.

Now I understood why Willieth never made the maiming blow. Bright flames had licked across the oil to surge up his legs. He tried patting them down, but the flames simply transferred to his arms. Willieth was covered in oil, and the fire went over him like he was kindling. He screamed, his howls of pain gory and gruesome. Smoke billowed around him. The crackle of fire grew to a roar.

"Daddy?"

Young me was in shock.

Isgrad sprang to his feet and pulled the long tablecloth free. He draped it over Willieth's body and dragged his brother out of the oil, rolling him on the floor until the flames went out.

"Daddy?"

"It's okay. Just… don't look." Isgrad dared to lift the cloth. He grimaced and dropped it again.

"Daddy."

Isgrad leapt toward me and wrapped his arms fiercely around my small shoulders. "You're okay. Just in shock."

There were tears streaming down my face. "I thought he was going to hurt you. I'm afraid of him."

"I know. I am too."

My mind groped to understand what madness I was truly seeing.

I did this to Willieth.

I'm the reason why he looks....

Footsteps pounded outside the door. A moment later, Clarence entered. He took in the oil and the deformed figure beneath the tablecloth. Smoke still wafted from the burnt bundle. "Providence, what happened? Is that… is that who I think it is? Is he dead?"

Isgrad's face was drenched in sweat, his hands coated in bits of burnt skin and fabric. "No. He's very much alive."

I shivered. What had become of Willieth was a fate worse than death.

"The pilot is leaving in three minutes," Clarence clarified. "I can't convince him to stay longer. This castle is about to burn to the ground."

Isgrad was still holding me tight. He looked into my face, at my tear-stained blue eyes, so very much like his. His smile was sad. "I need you to drink something for me. Do you think you could do that?"

He brought out the silver potion from his pocket.

"What is it?" My little voice was small but curious.

He squeezed my shoulder. "This will stop you from being afraid. You don't want to be afraid anymore, do you?"

I nodded, my auburn curls shaking around my face.

Isgrad popped the bottle open and brought the glass phial to my lips. "Drink it all. Don't leave a drop behind."

I drank it all. When I finished. I blinked, my face tightening, my eyes growing heavy. "It tasted… funny."

They were my last words. I lost consciousness. Isgrad caught me before I could hit the marble floor. He squeezed his eyes shut, tears leaking out from the corners.

Clarence prowled forward. "What did you do?"

"What was the right thing to do." Isgrad lifted me, passing my small body into Clarence's arms. "Take her away from here. She has no memory of this place or the atrocities she's witnessed. No memories of even me or her mother."

Clarence stared at him. "What was that potion you gave her?"

"A memory charm. Permanent memory loss. It's for the best. Now she can live a normal life." He eyed Clarence sternly. "Take her somewhere far away. She can't go to Tarahik. I don't trust General Kravis."

"The girl's grandmother. What if—"

"No. I don't trust anyone at Tarahik. Zaya just needs to disappear." There was pain in Isgrad's voice.

Clarence nodded, but the shock never left his face.

A tremor went through the castle. The walls rumbled, overwhelmed by the pressure that tore the edifice down.

"Go," Isgrad snapped.

Clarence left. He spared Isgrad a reluctant look over his shoulder as he disappeared out the door, taking me with him.

I fell to my knees, the shock of what I had witnessed breaking my heart.

My own father was the one who took my memories away.

Isgrad returned to the smoky heap on the floor and rolled what was left of the tablecloth out. The sight was horrible. Willieth's flesh had melted away, revealing blackened bones. His breathing had turned into hollow, desperate pants. He couldn't stare at Isgrad. He no longer had eyes, the burnt spaces unsettling to look upon.

Impossibly, Willieth's agonised breathing formed into words. "Cannot... kill... me."

"No, I can't," Isgrad admitted. "But I can make sure you remain asleep. Permanently."

He forced Willieth's mouth open, the teeth now crisped and

stubbed, and brought the phial with the black potion to his lips. Willieth sputtered and choked, the sound horrible as the mixture slithered down his throat, hissing against his cooked airways. He went limp, the very slight rise and fall in his chest the only indication of movement.

Isgrad held his brother's body with a grip like iron. I didn't know if he looked at Willieth's remains with guilt, anger, or a mixture of the two. "You're Haxsan Guard property now, Willieth. Rest in hell, brother."

CHAPTER 26

I opened my eyes, wiping at the tears that had worked their way into the corners. The silver-thorned witch watched me with intense curiosity, and I knew, either by her own magic or somehow by mine, that she'd witnessed everything I had. My throat burned with emotion. I had always wondered why Morgomoth didn't have a proper body. Why he was made of bones, fire, and shadow. I thought it had been his dark necromancy that had slowly devoured him over time, but it had been me. I'd set him alight to save my father.

Isgrad.

An energy that was equal parts anger and understanding ignited inside me. Isgrad had been the one to take my memories away. It hurt that he'd robbed me of that. I had no recollection of that time with my parents. Only fleeting scenes from the past, all tainted by tragedy.

I understood why he did it. Isgrad had wanted me to live a normal life. He'd taken away all the pain and horrors I'd experienced in Willieth's charge, stripping me of who I was and where I'd been, but it had backfired. You couldn't fight your destiny, only prolong it. Eventually, you *would* walk the path set out for you.

The witch inclined her head, having the decency to appear bashful. "There are many regrets I carry about the part I played in all of this. I made that memory charm, but I left it up to Isgrad to decide whether to give it to you. I am sorry for what you're now going through."

My edge of panic had dulled.

Providence help me, I really have accepted that my life was never my own to lead.

I'd been put on this earth to fix a problem. The Interitus blade could sever the connection, but I knew in my heart when I defeated Morgomoth—if I defeated him—my own death would be swift. Call it intuition. I knew it was coming. Once—*if*—I completed this task, my purpose on this earth was over.

I inhaled a sobering breath. "If we're going to find Isgrad, then we need to move—"

A strange buzzing filled my head, silencing my words.

"What's wrong?" The witch sounded distant.

"I don't know, but there's something—"

Pain enveloped me. I thought I might have been screaming, but I couldn't hear my own voice over the agonising stabs that ripped through my muscles. It started in my head, moving down my spine and into my gut. My legs trembled. Weakness tugged at my arms. I felt like I was being shredded into ribbons inside.

"Zaya."

That voice rattled through my body as though it wanted to snap all my bones.

"Morgomoth … he's in my head," I told the witch.

I gasped, trying to summon my magic, trying to build walls and banish him from my mind, but it was useless. I couldn't open my eyes. Couldn't ask the witch for help. The pain was suffocating.

Morgomoth's laughter was poison. *"Look what my revenants discovered."*

The images he sent bore down on me, cutting into my very soul.

No, I wanted to cry, but the terrible agony had me pinned like a moth to a board. I saw my friends running for their lives through the scorching desert. The Four Revenants herded them from the sky on their stagma. The beasts sent jets of fire from their cavernous jaws and then dived, their massive claws snaring Marek and Talina by the handful. Another pivoted for Bronislav and Annaka, easily snatching them from the ground. The creatures shot up into the sky, my friends taken away like mice caught by hawks.

"Annaka Vandergriff's invisibility charms were powerful, but I resurrected the stagma to hunt on smell alone."

The next image was worse. Marek was lying on a flagstone floor in a cell. His face was a mosaic of purple-black bruises, the bone crooked at the bridge of his nose. He breathed wheezily.

Another cell. Bronislav was leaning against the wall. His cheekbones were split and bleeding. His left eye had swollen so badly that his eyebrow had disappeared in the black shiner that took up the left side of his face. His head drooped before he toppled to the ground, passing out from exhaustion.

A new image. Annaka this time. She was awake, barely. Her eyes kept shutting, but she blinked them open, staring through the narrowly spaced bars that looked out to the torchlit passage. "Hey, you bastards," she cried, but no one answered her. She rattled the bars, or attempted to. They'd been sunk so deeply into the stone floor that there was no chance of moving them. I gasped at the wounds along her wrists. Painful-looking welts dotted her skin. At some point, she'd been restrained with manacles infused with fire magic.

Another scene materialised. Talina was curled into a ball in the corner of her cell, silently crying. Out of all my friends, she'd been the one I worried about most. Talina wasn't built like the rest of us. She had courage and bravery, yes, but she didn't have the strength or stamina to put up a fight. She was a healer, not a soldier. Something passed across her emerald eyes. Defeatism. She'd resigned herself to her fate. Talina had given up.

"This is your final chance."

I knew from the icy conviction in Morgomoth's voice that he meant it.

"Surrender yourself and your companions at Gondalesh Tower by midday; otherwise, your friends suffer a worse fate than death. I will kill and resurrect them. Their souls will be forever bound to me. Always serving me. Always a part of me."

His hateful laugh was the last thing I heard. Morgomoth's magic let go and I fell in a heap on the sand, gasping for air. I hadn't realised I'd been holding my breath.

"He has them," I revealed at the witch's alarmed stare. "He's going to… if I don't surrender…."

I couldn't bear the thought of my friends becoming a part of those tortured souls who were forever tethered to him.

The witch knelt by my side. She gripped my arms to steady me. "Tell me everything. From the beginning."

I did, my voice so frantic, my thoughts such a chaotic mess, that I had no idea how she managed to follow.

Unable to keep my guilt bottled up, a fresh wave of tears glistened in my eyes. In the end, my decision had been no better than Isgrad's choice to wipe my memory. I had left my friends, thinking that being as far away from me as possible was the right course of action to keep them safe, but all it had done was leave them on their own and unprepared. Of course Morgomoth would send his revenants after the people I cared about and loved the most. In the end, I'd pretty much offered my friends up as sacrificial lambs.

I lowered my head, trying to keep the dizziness at bay. I had a very bad feeling that Morgomoth had known all along what I'd planned. He'd been watching me with a predatory grace, stealing glimpses through the connection. He had said *"surrender yourself and your companions."* That meant he knew I travelled with Jad and Lainie. He'd possibly even seen the silver-thorned witch.

The ULD's cause might have been weakening, but Morgomoth was not. If anything, he was growing stronger.

If he gets his hands on that spell, he'll succeed in uniting the Larthalgule and Neathror blades.

There was no doubt in my mind that Morgomoth was cleverer than me.

I have to solve it first.

The silver-thorned witch continued to watch me, her expression yielding nothing. "Go wake your friends. You need to travel as soon as possible. It's past three in the morning, and it will take you hours on foot to get to Gondalesh."

I stared. My body had been trembling as everything had broken down inside me, but there—the tiniest spark of hope. "You... you want me to go to Gondalesh?"

I thought she'd yell at me to stay on my course. The citadel wasn't far. It would be counterproductive to not go to Vrabkor when I was so close.

She shook her head. "Morgomoth is playing a game. There must be a reason why he needs you at Gondalesh." Her gaze travelled to the cavern wall, but she wasn't looking at it, not really. I knew from the contemplative glow in her eyes that she was focused on something. "I must fly to Gondalesh."

My throat closed up. "Wait, you're leaving?"

I'd seen what she was capable of. She was a powerful witch. Honestly, I'd prefer that she remained by my side.

"I have to see what's happening... work out if it's a trap. I'll be back. I will find you."

She transformed, her silver-white wings sending soft undulations across the air as she glided through the cavern, circling back once as though in a parting gesture, and swept down the canyon.

I sat there for a moment, trying to collect myself, attempting to get my thoughts in order. When I returned to the canyon, Jad was awake. He sat on his sleeping bag, his black eyes assessing me with mistrust.

"How did you put the flames out?"

I lifted my head haughtily, not in the mood for his dark attitude. "Necromancer, remember? I have ghosts who help me."

I'd let him figure out the rest. Judging by the way he was staring at the ice ring, which was fast starting to melt around my sleeping mat, that was exactly what he was trying to work out.

I knelt down beside Lainie, gently nudging her awake.

She blinked the sleep out her eyes. "What's wrong?"

Alarm settled in her gaze when she saw the fear in mine.

I told them what Morgomoth had shown me.

Jad's reaction was exactly as I'd expected. "This is the reason why we should never have parted ways. You did this, Zaya. *You.* You made this happen."

I slammed my anger right back at him. "You think I don't know that? I'm hating myself right now. I don't need you adding to it."

His eyes took on a tinge of red around the edges. He looked capable of sending the entire canyon up in flames.

Lainie began packing her things, her face now sallow.

Jad surveyed her with an agitated glower. "What is Gondalesh?"

She flinched at the name. It must have been bad if she was more afraid of it than the Vrabkor Citadel.

Experiences are what make people fearful.

She'd been there before.

Lainie brushed her thumb across her cheek, either wiping

254

away sleep she'd missed or an anxious tear. "It's a prison tower and the place where Hadar conducts her experiments. The tower travels deep beneath the island. That's where the cells are kept, next to the furnaces."

"That's where our friends are," I confirmed.

Jad's brows narrowed. He zeroed in on Lainie again, his voice so demanding, it would have given Commander Macaslan a run for her money. "What happens there?"

Seeing the dread in Lainie's eyes made my own heart accelerate. "Terrible, despicable things. Most of the prisoners are dissent rebels who tried to flee and were caught. There are kidnapped politicians and spies too. The underground cells are built into a network of lava tunnels. Prisoners are chained and left to burn in the fires when the volcanoes erupt. Or worse, they're selected for Hadar's experiments and they become chak-lorks."

Dear providence.

No wonder she was terrified of returning.

Jad grabbed his rucksack, not looking remotely impressed.

"There's more." Lainie spoke so softly that I barely heard her over the gusty winds outside the canyon. She was staring at Jad. "Gondalesh is ruled over by Vulcan. It's his home."

WE'D PACKED up our provisions and were on the road in less than ten minutes. *Road* being a figurative term. We spent most of our time hiking over steep ridges, climbing over rocky terrain, and trekking across desert pavement, the loose pebbles uncomfortably loud beneath our boots. Lainie was the only one of us who had a watch. She assured me we were making good time, despite the challenging landscape. Jad had brought a watch to the island, but it hadn't survived the attack on the outpost. He'd nastily informed me that it had been melted down by stagma fire. I wished the stagma had melted his prickly attitude instead.

If the knowledge that Vulcan reigned over Gondalesh disturbed him, Jad never said a word about it. He kept his distance from me, ever vigilant as his eyes scanned the terrain, on the lookout for any hidden dangers. Lainie walked beside me, her head down, her face protected by the hood.

"Are you okay?"

She looked up. Worry filled her eyes. "I wasn't supposed to be at the outpost. I fled Gondalesh. Going back there will be...."

Lainie didn't deserve my sympathy, not after what she'd done to me and the others. Returning to Gondalesh was her just reward, and yet it didn't make me feel any better seeing her get her comeuppance.

"You don't have to go," I said at last.

"Are you releasing me from my oath?"

I didn't like the way she sounded so hopeful.

"No."

I couldn't trust her, not ever again. That magic oath was the only surety that she wouldn't betray me. She'd left me to die once before. It would not happen again.

"Then I have to go, don't I?" she snapped with an attitude that grated at me.

Before I could say a word, she walked ahead.

None of us spoke after that. Hiking was slow, but judging from the way Lainie kept looking at her wristwatch, the hours were ticking by fast. We stopped to eat, no longer than ten minutes at my insistence, then continued our lengthy slog through the desert. The volcanic cloud cover blotted out the sun, making it darker than ever. We didn't dare use our flashlights, even though we desperately needed to.

The phoenix never once made an appearance, which left me feeling nervous and gutted. What if Morgomoth knew the silver-thorned witch was here? What if he'd forewarned Vulcan and the witch had been trapped, now held prisoner in a cell, or worse, strapped in chains in the lava tunnels?

I was impatient to arrive, never given a moment of reprieve from my anxious thoughts until we crested a sharp peak. There it was in the valley below—a tower half concealed by copious smoke, a megalithic stone structure that pierced the sky. It was nowhere near as big or grandiose as the glimpses I'd caught of the Vrabkor Citadel, but it was still intimidating. It surprised me that Vulcan had decided to live in Gondalesh. A lava-front home with volcano views wasn't my idea of luxury living.

"Get down," Lainie cautioned in a low voice. "They have lookouts."

We dropped, lying on our bellies on the narrow cliff that overhung the ridge to monitor the tower. At least, Lainie and I did. Jad slid down the ash-slicked slope and shuffled behind a boulder. He fished out his binoculars, surveying the stronghold.

There was activity below. The massive doors to the tower opened, stone scraping over stone, the noise sending a flurry of shivers across my skin. A legion of chak-lorks filed out. They marched across the bridge that connected the tower to the mountains. No, not just a unit—an entire army. They kept coming, a line of chak-lorks armed to the teeth, their weapons and armour clanging in time with their heavy footfalls. The storm clouds seemed to roll in with a vengeance behind them.

I could barely stomach to watch it. "They're recently turned, aren't they? This tower is where Morgomoth's dead soldiers are created."

Lainie didn't answer. I knew the silence meant yes.

My spine locked. "How are we going to sneak in there?"

I doubted there would be a back door that was conveniently left open.

Lainie turned to me to speak, but a long *whoosh* sliced the air, catching both our attention. Jad cried out and was flung back-ward. Bile surged up my throat. He landed on the pebbled ground, a projectile wedged in his shoulder. It resembled a barbed spear used to kill whales.

"Oh providence," Lainie muttered. "They've tranquilised him with silver."

She gripped my arm before I could launch myself down there. My heart was in flutters. She was right. The weapon was coated in silver. My vision tunnelled. I couldn't tell if Jad was conscious or if he'd passed out. His wet, laboured breathing didn't help.

Silver will kill him.

He has to have an antidote in his rucksack.

I had to get down there. I had to save him, even if getting close meant he'd suffer. It was worth the price.

I struggled, breaking free of Lainie's hold, but this time it wasn't her who grabbed me.

A hood was fastened over my head. Judging by Lainie's cry, she'd received the same treatment.

A harsh voice ran across my ears. "We've got them."

CHAPTER 27

The hood must have been imbued with a sleeping sedative, or a spell that stripped me of my senses, because when it was taken off, I was kneeling on a burgundy rug, my legs aching from being in the same position for too long. Lainie was beside me, blinking the hex out of her eyes. A trio of dissent rebels stood behind us, as still as sentinels on watch.

Stationed along the right wall were several chak-lorks. Their skin was pliant and rotting, their crimson eyes insatiable with hunger. They watched Lainie and me with voracious interest. One of them even salivated, the viscous thread dribbling down their chin, making a sticky paste on the carpet.

My magic was screaming inside me. The creatures might have been animated by necromancy, but my powers could sense how tortured the souls were inside, how desperate they were to escape their broken bodies. The feeling was growing, becoming an impenetrable wave with no release, just continuously building. Never ending.

"Where are we?" I managed to whisper, trying to focus on anything besides the terrible sorrow that tormented the dead.

The room was spacious and appeared to be some sort of formal sitting area. Everything was made of black stone, even the long polished table. The chairs positioned around it were elaborate enough to be thrones. Gothic-inspired windows revealed the volcanic landscape beyond, the Vrabkor Citadel in the distance appearing through a storm of ash clouds.

Lainie's face was tight with fear. "We're in the Gondalesh living quarters. This is where—"

A solid kick was delivered to her lower back, and she fell onto the rug with a startled cry.

"No talking, you filthy traitor," the rebel behind her spat, this time striking her into the side of her ribs.

My fury spiked, but before I could say or do anything, a door opened and a man prowled in. My stomach hitched. The silver-thorned witch wasn't kidding about Morgomoth's punishment. Vulcan looked like a walking skeleton. His skin was sickly pale and so thin, all his bones protruded from his hands and face. His dissent uniform hung off him, as though there was no flesh beneath it. I wouldn't have been surprised to learn he was half a ghost. Morgomoth was feeding off him, drawing in his flesh and soul.

Vulcan's black eyes raked over me slowly. A nasty curl shaped the corners of his lips. "My, what a sight you look. Orthrask hasn't been kind to you."

"You should stare in a mirror sometime," I fired back. "Where's Jad?"

I had no idea how much time had passed. Would they have given Jad an antidote for the silver? Was he somewhere in this tower, strapped down to an operating table while Hadar conducted more wicked experiments? My head felt leaden and foggy at the thought.

Vulcan smiled. "Trajan is safe. He's recovering."

"That is not his name."

"Oh, but it is. And when he wakes up, he will have no memory of you or the people he believes to be his friends."

Vulcan pulled out a chair and seated himself at the table. "It should be your own predicament that you worry about, Zaya. Our ULD troops are positioned along every coast of this island. The Haxsan Guard ships now float idly in the sea, too afraid to approach. Your friends are in cells below this tower, soon to be transferred to the lava tunnels. I can prevent that last event from occurring. Surrender yourself and the spell and your friends will be released. I'll even portal them to one of the ships if you'd like."

"What's the catch?" I was breathing hard. My voice came out sounding shaky.

"No catch. You simply have to come with me to Vrabkor. You will either join Morgomoth and give him the spell, or… he takes the spell from you and you live the rest of your life as a prisoner. If he decides not to kill you with the Interitus blade, of course."

"Doesn't sound like much of a choice."

Something wasn't right. He kept looking out the window, and apprehension clouded his face. I couldn't work out if he was afraid of something that was about to happen or fearful that it wasn't.

My head was spinning. I'd been so close to Vrabkor. Why would Morgomoth force me all this way here to Gondalesh if he only intended for me to return in custody to the citadel?

"What's going on?" I remarked, fear slicing deep beneath my navel.

Beside me, Lainie exhaled a lengthy gasp. She'd figured something out.

Vulcan looked steadily at me, the conniving smile never leaving his lips. "Look out the window and you'll see."

Outside, the world ignited with fiery light, too bright to comprehend for a moment. An unfathomable rumble echoed across Orthrask, the magic radiant and powerful. In the distance, Vrabkor was surrounded in rippling black magic, as though it had been transported into a dark snow globe. It burned so brightly that red lights popped behind my eyes and I had to look away.

"A celestial shield," Vulcan informed me. "It turns out that Darius Kerr and the commander are intending to not only attack on the beaches but to strike us from the skies. Morgomoth needed time to prepare."

Every emotion in the world seemed to churn within me at that moment. It took copious amounts of magic to create a celestial shield. Normally, at least a hundred casters were required to build a single dome. Morgomoth had created one on his own. Sending me here when I'd been so very near to his front door had been his way of distracting me while he created this barrier. It was a way to ensure that when he did finally have me in his citadel, either willingly or as a prisoner, neither carrier-hornets nor fire-crusaders could attack. We'd be protected in that dome, giving Morgomoth the time to perform the spell and unite the Larthalgule and Neathror blades. He'd not only planned everything cunningly and resourcefully but with perfect precision.

Vulcan's voice cut like glass. "You have lost, Zaya. It's time to go to Vrabkor. There's a portal waiting for us."

He reached his hand out for me, expecting a favourable answer.

"Swear it on your magic that my friends and Jad will be returned to Darius and Macaslan, or you get nothing from me."

His face hardened, and I could tell it took every ounce of his control not to lunge at me right there. He erupted in cool laughter. "You are not in a position to bargain."

I need a way out of this.

I need help.

I need…

The dead.

My eyes settled on the chak-lorks. Since the moment the hood had been removed from my head, their pain and suffering had engulfed me.

If I'm feeling this, then does that mean… I'm connected to the chak-lorks?

Can I in fact…?

I concentrated on my necromancy, imagining it like dark shadows twisting around the dead, summoning their attention.

"What are you doing?"

Vulcan sounded afraid.

I smiled, sending more magic, imagining it like a ribbon of thread flowing into the chak-lorks, linking them together as my own small army. The floor shook. Some of the light fixtures hanging from the ceiling started to swing. A sort of murmur ran through the dissidents behind me, and then they were shouting as the build-up of pressure made all the windowpanes explode. Glass splintered across the room like a hailstorm. It had been stifling in the room, but now the temperature dropped, plunging into the negatives.

I prayed my command would be obeyed.

"Attack Vulcan and his rebels. Help Lainie and me escape."

The chak-lorks' growls were wild and primitive as they loped across the room, claws out to dismantle, teeth chomping down. Five went for the dissent rebels. The other three zeroed in on Vulcan. He drew out his athame-sabre, slicing and stabbing, but trying to maim what was already dead proved impossible. The chak-lorks simply reattached their severed limbs and continued their assault.

"Come on," I cried to Lainie over the roar of the battle.

We sped past the skirmishes and were nearly at the door when a hand latched on to my shoulder, tugging me back so hard that I swore my arm was about to be ripped from its socket. Unbelievably, Vulcan had beaten the odds, the chak-lorks headless on the floor behind him.

"You little bitch," he snarled.

I received a searing blow to the side of my head. Agony throbbed in my temple, my legs going out beneath me. I landed hard on the floor, unable to push back the dizziness that closed in. Vulcan was glaring over me, wearing his usual trademark smirk. He brought his fist down again, but before he could initiate the strike, something silvery and white flew in from the window, travelling at the speed of a shooting star. The phoenix dived for Vulcan's face, slashing with its beak and claws. He screamed and flailed his arms, but the bird merely attacked his fingers.

I stumbled onto my feet, my blood fizzing with adrenaline, and followed Lainie out the door into a dark passage that seemed to have no end.

"This way." Lainie careered around a corner that I would have entirely missed. "What's the plan, anyway?"

"I'm still working on it," I confessed. "For now, we need to find the others and get them out through the portal."

She nodded, leading me swiftly down a stairwell. "The cells are underground. The portal is on level two. Are you okay?"

I panted. A coppery taste had filled my mouth. I wiped a hand over my lips. It came back smeared with blood. Vulcan had hit me harder than I'd thought. "I'm fine," I lied.

"How long have you known you could control chak-lorks?"

"Just discovered it."

It would have been a hell of a lot more useful if I'd figured it out earlier.

Screams resonated below, instantly making my heart feel like it was trying to slam out of my chest. We entered a large hall where dissent rebels were in fierce combat with chak-lorks. The reek of blood permeated the air, and a jolt of shock ran through me. I hadn't just controlled the chak-lorks upstairs. Apparently, I'd summoned every single one in the building to fight.

It was a bloodbath. The undead leapt onto their opponents,

tearing and feasting into flesh. The rebels swung and sliced their weapons with useless effect. When they fell, they didn't remain dead for long. My magic animated them. They sprang back up like puppets, their eyes glazed as they turned on their comrades.

I gasped at the butchery occurring before my eyes. The Grand Masters had told me I was stronger with their necromancy, but I didn't realise how powerful that meant I'd become. Perhaps I was a worthy opponent for Morgomoth after all.

"We've got to keep going," Lainie breathed into my ear. "The lava that flows through the tunnels is on timed intervals. If the others have been transferred to...."

She didn't need to finish for me to understand. Gondalesh was trembling like a rocket about to take off, which meant the nearest volcano had erupted.

The lava will be flowing.

We darted around the battle, taking a second flight down-stairs, twisting around more passages that were a maze of black stone and granite. We arrived at the entrance of an arched tunnel. The other side was lost in eternal darkness.

Lainie reached for her flashlight and switched it on. The light spottily bobbed through the black ahead. "This is it."

Lamenting wails echoed along the tunnel walls. The dead were down there. I could feel it in the marrow in my bones. They were souls trapped where they'd died, forced to grieve and wallow in pity, never a saving grace in sight.

Another sound ripped through the dark. It was a long, mournful howl.

I sensed my pale face flush. "What else is in these tunnels?"

Lainie fiddled inside her rucksack, removing a cast-shooter that she loaded with silver bullets. She handed the weapon to me, along with a short athame-sabre that appeared to have been coated in silver. "Lycanthors."

"Are we expecting to encounter them?"

"I certainly hope not, but it's best to be prepared."

A hot wind came up from the tunnel, stirring my sweat-lathered hair. It smelt of rotting meat and bone.

"Here goes nothing." Lainie stepped into the tunnel.

I followed her into the blinding darkness.

NOT A HINT of moisture existed in the tunnels. The stench of sulphur irritated my nose and throat. I was surprised Lainie knew her way through the maze of passages. When I asked how she was so familiar with the earthen lanes, she wasn't forthcoming with the information. I questioned if she had at some point led inmates down here, then decided I really didn't want to know the answer to that.

She's on my side now. That's what matters.

Only because you made her promise on her magic, a snide voice responded.

The flashlight revealed some horrific sights. Many of the walls were smeared with red stains, and a few times we came across burnt bones that had been pecked at, jagged toothmarks scored into the surface.

Lycanthors must come down here to feast on prisoners' barbequed remains.

These bones had been dragged here at some point and then left when there was no more meat to be devoured.

The mental images this conjured made me want to heel over and retch.

Lainie and I didn't talk, too afraid the slightest whisper would echo.

Somewhere, either to our left or right—the acoustics were

muddled—another growl ricocheted through the dark. It had sounded close.

Lainie and I looked at each other but didn't say anything.

This is a good sign. If lycanthors are in the tunnels, then that means there's no fear of lava.

Not yet anyway. As soon as I no longer heard their grisly hollers, then I knew I had something to worry about.

"The cells should be just down here," Lainie revealed, speaking so quietly that I had to strain to hear.

My palms itchy with nerves, I followed her into an alcove where a passage branched off to the left and another to the right.

Lainie pointed to the left. "The prison cells." She aimed her flashlight to the right. "The lava tunnels."

"The left it is, then."

In and out, I told myself, hoping it would be that easy.

Please let my friends be in the cells. Please don't let them have been transferred to the lava tunnels.

I just wanted to get them out, then start my search for Jad.

"Well, that's one spot of luck." Lainie bent down, picking up a set of keys. There was blood on them. "Looks like the guards left their post."

"They either ran or…."

They'd been eaten.

Lainie shone her light once again down the left passage. We stepped into the prison, our boots scraping along loose rocks. It was a series of hewn cells with flagged stone floors, barred with a single door for access.

Lainie's face turned pallid. "They're all empty."

All empty except for one. Hunched in the corner was a familiar form who I didn't think I'd ever have the misfortune of seeing again. The once beautiful woman's kimono was stained with blood and filth. I scented urine in the air. She must have wet herself. That, or she'd been forced to squat in a corner. There were no toilets in the cells.

Even that pristine skin that she'd powdered every morning to ghost white now held a greyish hue, making her horrible scowl that much more apparent.

"Hello, Toshiko." I'd hoped to sound mocking, but my voice was laced with pity.

Her gold eyes gleamed with hateful recognition.

CHAPTER 28

This was the price Toshiko had paid for slipping up. For letting me escape. Her loyalty to Morgomoth had led her to this end, behind bars and wrapped in chains, with nothing but dry hay to rest on.

"Well, don't just look at me," she spat. Her voice was no longer refined but throaty and rasping, as though she hadn't sipped liquids in days. The dirt along her cheeks was smeared with tears, making her skin appear hollow beneath her eyes. She rattled the manacles that were fastened around her wrists with such force that I thought she might snap her bones. "Get. Me. Out."

"And why on earth would I do that?" I took a step forward, showing a bravado I didn't feel. "You had the Black Palace set alight. You killed the Council of Founding Sovereigns. The fires spread to Muiren. You murdered thousands of people. Being locked away is what you deserve."

The celestial shield around Muiren protected it from outside harm, but on that occasion, the danger had come from the inside, and the shield had retained the fires in the dome. People's skin would have melted right off, or people simply would have lique-fied on the spot. The imagery was far too horrible to dwell on.

Toshiko was eyeing the keys in Lainie's hand. Her lips pulled into a cruel smirk. "Don't play the self-righteous card with me. You hated everyone in that palace... in that city."

"I did not."

I might not have agreed with the system in place, but that didn't mean I wanted the Black Palace or Muiren destroyed.

Toshiko's voice was deadly cold. "This is a war. Sacrifices are made. People die."

I dropped into a crouch to get a better look at her, to see the true madness on her face.

She watched me with the intensity of a striking cobra. "Do you really think Senator Kerr and Commander Macaslan are any better? Have you asked them what they intend to do if they defeat Morgomoth and the ULD? Who will be the rulers of the new reign?"

She laughed at my blank stare, the sound a merciless echo that trailed up my spine. "Oh, Zaya. Be careful, for we are all rolling the dice and playing the game."

I backed away, afraid of what she hinted at. Her words returned my reservations. Darius and Macaslan hadn't done anything to stop the fires at the Black Palace. And they hadn't been forthcoming about why.

Toshiko grinned, wide enough for me to notice that some of her teeth were missing. "Be careful who you trust" was all she said. Spittle slipped down the side of her chin as she laughed.

For having been such a cultured, refined woman, it was unnerving to see how she'd done a complete one-eighty.

What horrors has she seen down here?

I stood tall, refusing to look shaken. "Where are the other prisoners?"

She let out a little snort. "Where do you think?"

I heard Lainie's breath catch. Her skin was so ashen, it looked like white stone. "If they're in the lava tunnels…."

Then we have limited time to get them out.

"Let's move," I instructed. I led the way back through the prison.

"Wait," Toshiko cried. "Give me the keys. Let me out."

I whipped around, swallowing the urge to call her every foul name under the sun. "You told me to be careful who I trust. And I don't trust you. Goodbye, Toshiko."

She deserves this.

It didn't matter why the ULD had put her here. She was locked away, punishment for the terrible crime she'd committed, but a part of me didn't feel right walking away. Guilt rattled my mind, my consciousness telling me that leaving her here was just as monstrous an act. Once I found the others, I'd come back and let her out of the miserable cell. She could find her own way back to the beach, though. My mercy ended there.

Her voice trailed after me. "I heard your thoughts when I looked into your eyes, Zaya. You are no killer."

It was an effort to prevent my knees from buckling as her raucous laughter echoed along the cells. It was the sound of someone who knew they were triumphant.

"Consider yourself lucky that I'm not," I fired back, surprised by the hostility in my voice.

Lainie and I followed the beam of the flashlight out of the prison and entered the tunnel to the right. The lava tube twisted endlessly, as though it were a labyrinth designed to confuse and disorientate us. The air smelt burnt. Fang-sharp stalactites protruded from the ceiling, forcing us to curl our bodies in unnatural angles to slip past. Steam rose from the ground, my skin slick from the stifling temperature. The most terrifying part, though, was the metal bar that ran along the wall. Manacles were attached at intervals.

This is where prisoners are chained, waiting for the lava to end them.

I sensed magic pulsing along the bar and the shackles, the only thing preventing them from melting. The fact that the manacles hung limply meant—

No. I can't afford to think like that.

I kept going, my blood roaring in my ears. More lava conduits joined the passage ahead. This place really was a damned maze.

"Talina," I cried. My shout resonated forlornly down the tube. "Marek. Bronislav. Annaka."

Lainie held my stare, her tone icy. "What are you doing?"

"There's no way we'll find them in all of this without their help. If they're down here, they'll hear us."

But something else had heard my cry. A series of lonely, hungry howls resonated from the conduits, growing higher and sharper.

Lycanthors.

A dark shape hurtled past the conduit ahead, too quick for me to see clearly, but I suspected I already knew what it was. Any longer here and we'd be herded and hunted.

A shout broke through the air somewhere to my right. "Zaya! Over here."

Marek.

My heart started beating furiously. He had sounded afraid.

I tore in the direction of his voice. The beam from Lainie's flashlight crisscrossed shakily as she sprinted behind me, the visibility poor, but I managed to follow that thick bar, turning left, then right, and left again as Marek continued to cry out. I bolted down a second conduit and came out to a cavern, the rocks all blackened and worn as smooth as silk, but there was no time to marvel at the geological wonder. Chained against the metal bar was Marek.

His eyes shone with relief when he saw me, which quickly turned to panic. "Bronislav's hurt."

Next to him, the soldier was lying limp against the cavern wall, his hands chained. A pool of blood leaked beneath his left trouser pant, his calf half torn, the meaty chunks ripped and slashed. He'd been bitten by a lycanthor. I ran to him, but there wasn't a lot I could do for Bronislav to stop the bleeding. He needed serious medical aid. He needed Talina.

I spotted her tied at the opposite wall. She was so thin, she looked like she'd lost half her body weight since I'd last seen her. Her long braid hung limp over her shoulder, greyed from ash and soot. She smiled when she saw me, but her eyes showed fear.

Next to her, Annaka was passed out. My mouth dried. She reminded me of a beautiful flower that had wilted in the hot sun.

"She kept us invisible for as long she could," Talina revealed. "But it wasn't enough. The lycanthors smelt us. One of the mongrels bit Bronislav. They would have killed us all if the place hadn't started rumbling." She went rigid all over. "The dissent rebels chained us and left. Zaya, what's happening?"

"The lava is coming," I confirmed, hoping not to startle her further. "It's okay. You're all right now. We're getting you out of here."

"We?"

That's when she saw Lainie. A thousand unspoken emotions spread across Talina's tear-streaked face, but it dulled to a resentful surprise. The time to reconnect would have to come later.

Lainie unlocked Talina's manacles and then worked her way across the cavern, unchaining each of my friends. The ground and walls shook again. I braced my legs, finding purchase. The ripples and tremors continued, like a piece of Orthrask had shifted. I wouldn't be surprised if the volcano's eruption had severed the island.

Marek, despite his wrists being burnt raw from the cuffs,

picked up Annaka's crumpled form. "Talina, Lainie, I need you to help Bronislav. He's not going to be able to walk on his own. Zaya, you can guide us out of here, right?"

I nodded, fairly certain I remembered the way.

With only one flashlight between us, though, this was going to be a game of the blind leading the blind.

We followed the sloping tunnel ahead, the inky darkness seeming to slither around us. Three figures appeared like apparitions through the torchlight, barricading our path to the conduit beyond. I sensed my friends go tense behind me, their stress becoming an energy that was palpable. My body locked tight when Vulcan stepped out of the darkness. His face was viciously cut up. The phoenix had left his cheeks and forehead looking like they'd been scraped over by a cheese grater. Next to him, Hadar lumbered out of the murky shadows, her cane dragging over the floor. The sound was as skin crawling as nails down a chalkboard. She watched our little group with a grin that made my insides feel like jelly. She was probably delighting in the fact that she had more victims for her wicked experiments.

But the worst shock was the last person who emerged from the gloom. He moved with the silence and stealth of a wraith. His blood-red eyes stared into my own with fierce adversity.

Jad.

No.

Trajan.

He had his athame-sabre drawn, the blade pulsing with fire magic.

My courage shattered.

I'm too late.

Behind the trio, four lycanthors appeared. The beasts were twice the size of any wolf. Their fur was matted with blood, their powerful muscles rippling beneath raised hackles. They dropped to their haunches in a low crouch and gnashed their teeth, their foul breath filling the cavern.

Vulcan's smile promised violence. "Kill them all except for Zaya."

The lycanthors lunged at the same time a boom shuddered through the earth.

It all happened impossibly fast. The groaning mountain was distraction enough for a figure to zero in from the side and slice through a lycanthor's heavily muscled neck. The severed head dropped to the ground with a wet plop, the creature's lengthy tongue hanging from its open jaws.

I watched, shaken and petrified, as Trajan moved like lightning, cutting down the next lycanthor, then the next, until the final beast gave out a barking, whimpering growl and sprinted away, deciding better than to take on a fiercer opponent.

"Trajan," Vulcan snapped with blinding fury. "What are you doing?"

Yes, what is he doing?

Because Trajan was not on our side. He wasn't designed that way.

Trajan turned to me, fire magic crackling around him. He stood like a soldier waiting for his next order.

No. Not possible.

But I knew the moment I looked into those crimson eyes, which were hungry with the need to kill and destroy, that he was my weapon to wield and command. I had control of the dead in Gondalesh. Trajan's soul was mine.

I couldn't prevent a smug smile from slipping onto my face when I glared stonily at Hadar and Vulcan. "He doesn't take orders from you. I killed Trajan with the Neathror blade at the Isla Necropolis. Whatever monster you made is dead inside him. And I control the dead in this tower." I stood like a pillar of steel as I pointed a damning finger at the pair. "Attack."

Like a summoned spirit, Trajan charged. Vulcan drew out his own weapon and met the attack with an ear-shattering parry. They struck and lunged at each other, equally matched, moving across the floor in a blur, sparks raining from their sabres.

"Go," I shouted.

Lainie and Talina carried Bronislav between them, the soldier conscious but struggling to walk. They had just reached the conduit's entry when Hadar barricaded the exit. She lifted the crook handle from her walking cane, revealing a blade as thin and pointed as a rapier. For such a slender, debilitated woman, she moved swifter than I could comprehend. She plunged the blade straight through Lainie's chest. Lainie's eyes flew open in astonishment. The end of the rapier protruded from her upper back, her dissent uniform soaking quickly in blood.

Hadar tore the weapon out. "That is the price traitors pay."

Talina was screaming, one of the worst sounds I'd ever heard. Lainie fell to the ground with a heavy thwack, and I knew there was nothing that could be done to save her. She was already gone. Her eyes stared glassily at the ceiling, still wide with surprise. One second, she had been here... and the next, her life was snuffed out. Like she'd meant nothing to the world.

I charged, my necromancy unfurling in a blaze of white-hot anger. I struck with my athame-sabre, but for the second time, I'd underestimated Hadar. She deflected my blow, her strikes both smooth and fast. I parried her attack. All my training returned, my arms and legs moving with skill, but Hadar hit faster and stronger. She must have had a potion running through her veins. It was the only explanation for how she could move at all with such a profound limp.

She knocked aside my next blow and whacked her arm straight into my chest. I went flying, flipping over and over again until I hit the wall. The loud crack alerted me that several ribs had snapped. Pain snaked its way into my sternum, impeding my breathing.

My athame-sabre had landed with a hollow clang at Hadar's feet. She kicked it, sending it skittering out into the conduit, lost in the ageless dark.

"Run," I cried breathlessly at Talina.

She was holding up Bronislav, barely. The pair had managed to make their way to the exit while I'd fought Hadar.

"Go," I urged, seeing the hesitance in Talina's eyes.

I saw what plagued her. She'd lost one friend. She didn't want to lose another.

"Save Bronislav."

That seemed to get her moving, her healing instincts kicking in. The pair slipped away into the conduit. Marek was right behind them, still carrying Annaka. Hadar had no intention of letting more prisoners leave. She swung her rapier, the blade singing as it sliced the air, ready to make a clean cut through Marek's neck.

My scream ran thick and fast through my body. There was nothing I could do, though. I was going to witness another friend die.

A war cry resonated from the conduit. Talina emerged, carrying my athame-sabre. Before I could stop to appreciate the absurd sight of Talina appearing with a weapon, she swung the blade with perfect precision. Hadar's head was severed clean off. The force threw it across the cavern as though it'd been hit with a baseball bat. I watched, shocked, as the rest of her body toppled to the ground.

Talina was breathing hard. "Oh providence," she muttered. She dropped the sabre, stunned by her own daring.

Even Marek looked startled, his face pallid.

"Go," I snapped at the pair of them. "Get out."

The cavern juddered, the walls and floor lurching as though a fire-crusader had just taken off. Stones and stalactites plunged from the ceiling.

Marek flinched. "We can't leave without you."

"And I can't leave without Jad."

Trajan and his father were still locked in battle. I had to end this feud once and for all.

Marek took note of my hardened face, the resolve in my eyes. I knew from the way his shoulders tensed that he understood there was no stopping me. He carried Annaka out of the cavern, practically dragging Talina out with him, despite her pleas for me to leave too.

A moment later, they'd disappeared in the dark.

Panting hard, I got onto my feet.

I turned to the father-and-son quarrel, wondering if the three of us would survive this.

CHAPTER 29

It pained me that Trajan was fighting under my influence, but it was also amazing—in a frightening way—to see the speed and skill with which he fought his father. If Jad was in there, I recognised no sign of him. Trajan was a killing machine, his face twisted by darkness and rage, his mind utterly gone. Vulcan skilfully dodged and parried, administering his own lethal blows, but it was never to kill, only to defend himself. He wanted Trajan by his side, not dead.

I guess he isn't as callous a bastard as I thought.

It was evident who had taught and trained Trajan to fight. The pair knew exactly where the other would strike, anticipating and blocking every attack.

Damning hatred filled Trajan's eyes, the colour in them liquid fire. Something inside me broke in that moment, and I knew if Trajan killed his father, there would be no coming back for Jad. I'd believed his wrath had been the result of the Bone Grimoire, but now I knew that had never been the case—not entirely. Trajan's soul, lingering in Jad's body, had been playing a tug-of-war in his mind, influencing his emotions. Trying to take full control. Trying to push Jad out.

Trajan was winning. If he killed his father, that would be it. Trajan would remain. It would be Jad moving on to the otherworld.

My heart clenched inside my chest. As much as I hated Vulcan, as much as I believed he deserved death, it couldn't be by Trajan's hand.

"Trajan," I cried, the air leaving my lungs.

His eyes snapped to mine, a spasm of fury contorting his handsome face, his lips curling back from his teeth. I could tell just from the way his chest rose and fell that he was fighting every urge to charge toward me and fling his blade across my neck. Only my necromancy was making him behave like a dutiful soldier.

Vulcan had also stopped fighting. He slewed around, his icy control cracking. "What have you done to my son?"

What I should have had the courage to do days ago.

I summoned the full strength of my necromancy, opening that doorway to the world beyond. I was the passage to the other side, the power in my veins making my blood feel as hot as fire. When I'd first opened the doorway for the sea serpent, the magic had been wholesome, promising peace and harmony. But this time, something else waited on the other side. It was a place full of shadows. Faces of impure, adulterated evil stared back. The souls were nothing more than skin on bones, the slashes over their bodies festered. I shivered, remembering the old saying "death by a thousand cuts." Apparently, whatever place this was, it was literal. Blood dribbled from their lips as the tormented souls reached out, ready to drag anything they could to the burning pits beyond.

Trajan froze, breathing hard like he'd been running. "No," he whispered.

His grip tightened savagely on his blade.

The ire had died on his face. Now he just looked… afraid.

"You can't do this to me," he shouted, his voice so similar to Jad's that I knew it was a ploy to unnerve me.

But I wouldn't be deterred. "Goodbye, Trajan."

I mentally cut down the barrier that held back the demons, because I was certain that's what they were. They charged in a storm of shadows, leaping on him. I heard the swish of tapered claws, heard Trajan's screams as his soul was detached from Jad's body. I let out a stifled cry. Everywhere the demons touched set fire to Trajan's soul. Black blood spurted from his wounds, monstrous power leaking out of him. His red eyes glared at me, as though he could slice me apart with just his hatred. He released a feral howl, scratching at the ground as the demons dragged him away from Jad's unconscious body. The sight made something deep inside me churn.

He's not hurt.

He's free.

Free.

The doorway to the other side was something physical now that stood beside me. I glimpsed twisted bodies inside, some burned beyond recognition, strapped to instruments of torture, writhing and screaming as they were repeatedly afflicted with jagged-tooth blades. The demons hauled Trajan through the door. He clung to the solid architrave, but he wasn't strong enough to wrangle himself free.

"I hate you," he cried. "I will haunt you until your dying day, and then I will drag your pathetic soul here into this underworld. I will tear you apart. I will force—"

His fingers slipped.

I curled my hand into a fist, closing the doorway with a snap. The last thing I saw was the light dying in Trajan's eyes as hands submerged him into a boiling vat of fire. The doorway disappeared.

I released a shuddering breath. That was a place I prayed never to see again.

"What did you do?"

The voice sliced at me like a blade.

Vulcan was seething. He raised his bloodstained sword. "What did you do to my son?"

Son? Like he had any fatherly rights.

He stalked toward me, dangerously slow. "You killed him."

"I did not. I banished the demon you and Hadar created. Jad is alive. Your son is alive."

"That"—Vulcan pointed at Jad, whose face had turned so pale that, if it weren't for his chest rising shallowly, I would have mistaken him for dead—"is not my son. That is a weakness. That is a coward. Where is Trajan? Where did you send him?"

My fingers tingled, ready to rally my necromancy again. Opening that door for one more soul wouldn't be hard. "You already know. He's eternally damned."

The ground shook, nearly toppling me off my feet. The cavern was rumbling so dangerously now that the lava flow couldn't be far. The sensible thing to do would be to run, but I couldn't leave Jad. And I couldn't leave Lainie's body behind either. She deserved a proper sendoff, surrounded by those who loved her.

I have to defuse this situation fast.

In those frantic upended seconds, Vulcan rushed at me, hurtling his sword. Destroying me would kill Morgomoth, but I saw the burning hatred in his eyes, saw that his only endeavour was to murder me, saw that the consequences be damned.

I pulled my cast-shooter out, aiming it at his chest. "These are silver bullets."

My warning didn't deter him. He swung his blade at the same time I pulled the trigger. He dived to his right at the last second, dodging the bullet, his athame-sabre just missing my left arm. He lunged again. I leapt back, evading the swings that came from every direction. I fired my pistol. Again. And again. It didn't matter. Vulcan had the dexterity to avoid every shot.

He laughed when a hollow click filled the air.

I'd run out of bullets.

"How unfortunate." He lashed out with a debilitating kick, hitting me right where my broken ribs already throbbed. I heard them crack farther, the split slicing at my ears. This time, the sapping pain spread from my ribs to my shoulders and down my arms. I sank to the floor, biting back my scream. I refused to show how badly hurt I was.

Vulcan stood over me. There was nothing remotely caster left on his face. He looked like a demon from that place beyond. I wouldn't have been surprised if he transformed into a lycanthor right there and ripped me to ribbons with his teeth.

He raised his sword. "You killed my son. And now. I. Kill. You."

He drove the athame-sabre down.

There was a clang, followed by a roar.

Holding my breath, I watched Jad strike at his father. Golden flamelight erupted from his athame-sabre. Jad was renewed and energised, rising like a phoenix. Flames burned around him. He fought his father, the pair moving so fast that all I could do was stare with hazed disbelief.

The mountain groaned, rocks and gravel raining down from the ceiling. Jad and I looked at each other at the same time lava spilled from every crack and fissure. Streams of molten rock gushed from the conduits.

This was it. The island had spoken. Orthrask was angry.

Vulcan was screaming. I gasped, tasting something sickly at the back of my throat. A boulder had landed on his leg, severing it from the knee. What was left of his lower leg was a mangled appendage of blood and bone. His other leg was also firmly pinned. There'd be no way to move it, even with Jad's strength.

Vulcan realised it too. "Curse you both," he snapped. "Curse you. I hope you both burn."

"No, Father." Jad said the words with a cool, calm menace. "It will be you who burns."

From every conduit now, a deadly pyroclastic flow moved at an insane speed.

"Go," Jad shouted at me.

He picked up Lainie's body, sprinting toward our one and only exit. I hurried after him, coughing against the toxic gases that had filled the cavern. I looked over my shoulder and wished I hadn't. The lava surged over Vulcan. It devoured his legs first, then his torso. His screams were worse than the demons I'd heard from the otherworld. His eyes found mine, and despite the excruciating pain he must have been under, he silently mouthed words I recognised. *"You will burn."*

His eyes glazed over before they, too, were submerged in boiling magma.

I followed Jad down the rocky tunnel, feeling the heat gushing over my shoulders. Everything was illuminated by the lava, a small blessing showing us the way. I was glad Jad remembered, because I had no idea. My legs were aching, but it was nothing compared to the stabbing torture that cut through my ribs. I had to blink to keep myself from passing out.

Just a bit farther. Just a bit farther.

I hope.

Embers showered around me, the thickening veil of smoke threatening to overwhelm my nose. We must have passed the prison because I heard a woman's shrieking cries.

"Let me out. Let me out."

Toshiko.

I had entirely forgotten her.

I had no idea if she'd spotted us running past. I didn't think so. The smoke was too heavy. She was just shouting on the off-chance that someone was still down here.

Oh providence. I don't have the keys.

"Keep running," Jad demanded, seeing my hesitation.

In the end, my sense of self-preservation won.

Goodbye, Toshiko.

I sprinted past, hurtling through the tunnel, my body going beyond a place of pain, my mind now in control and focused on one thing: getting the hell out of here. I willed strength into my legs, following Jad through the last tunnel and up the stairs into the safety of Gondalesh. I turned to see the lava flow rushing up the flight like an inland tsunami. I shut the door, relieved when the magic spells that protected Gondalesh triggered, shielding us from a burning death.

I slumped to the ground, the pain in my ribs now unbearable. I heard shouts and cries but didn't have the energy to see who it was. Hot tears slid down my face. I couldn't fight the dizziness that greeted me with open arms. I surrendered, lying on the floor, giving in to the darkness that came crashing down.

I STARTLED AWAKE, trying not to wince at the pain that lanced through my ribcage. I was in a bedroom, lying on a canopy bed, swaddled in bandages. Curtains blocked the fiery landscape outside, leaving me crowded by shadows. A single candle had been placed by the side table, not providing nearly enough light. I tried to sit up, but everything hurt too much, and I dropped back onto the pillows, exhausted.

Where am I? How did I even get here?

I became aware of a beeping noise and realised there was a

pulse oximeter clipped onto my forefinger, alerting someone that I had woken.

The door to the chamber opened.

Talina emerged, carrying clean bandages and potions. "You're awake."

She ambled over to the bed and sat on the mattress next to me. "How are you feeling?"

"Like I got kicked in the ribs and nearly melted down like a marshmallow."

I strained to sit up again.

"No, don't." She pressed her hands against my shoulders, gently forcing me to lie down. "Your ribs were broken, but I've healed them. It will take time for the pain to go away, though. You're very bruised. You need to remain still."

"Where are we?"

She pressed her lips together, her posture stiff. "We're still in Gondalesh… up in one of the higher levels. We think this might have been where Vulcan lived. There are many rooms. It's like a penthouse."

Her river of honey-blonde hair ran past her shoulders, cleaner than I'd seen in days.

"How long have we been here? And where are all the rebels?"

Surely they wouldn't let us stay. We were in danger. We had to get out. Before we were surrounded. Before we were taken prisoners once more.

I tried to move, but Talina pressed me back against the bedsheets. She draped another blanket over me. "You can't walk. The last potion I gave you numbed your legs. You need to rest."

"I can't rest without answers."

She sighed gruffly. "We've been here for just over a day."

"A day? But Morgomoth—"

"Nothing has changed. He waits behind the citadel, protected by his shields. Marek has communicated with Darius. Tomorrow evening, a brigade will be travelling from the ships through the portal here to Gondalesh. The Haxsan Guard forces will attack Vrabkor tomorrow at midnight. It will be a distraction for you... so you can enter the citadel and...."

Kill Morgomoth.

I vaguely remembered Vulcan saying something about a portal here in Gondalesh.

"What about all the rebels?" I repeated.

Another beat of silence.

Talina's shoulders sagged. "They're all dead. Every one of them. Your necromancy took over the entire tower. The rebels all fought until they died, then rose to fight the living. When you collapsed, the dead returned to being... well, dead."

Shame burned on my cheeks. The dead were not weapons. They deserved peace and respect, and yet I'd used them for my own gain. Granted, it had been to save my friends, but it still didn't deter the guilt that gnawed inside me.

Talina shifted on the bed. "Our orders are to remain here and recover. Darius and the brigade will be arriving this evening."

A brigade. How many Haxsan Guard soldiers was that? At least four thousand.

I tried to move, but the pain in my ribs nearly made me faint. Even breathing hurt. "What about the others? Are they okay?"

"They're fine. Recovering and glad for the rest. Annaka is awake and back to her usual annoying self. Bronislav's leg is healing. Marek is trying to work out how to connect the portal to our ships. That witch—if that's what she is—is helping him."

I nodded. "The silver-thorned witch."

So, my friends had met her. At least that spared me having to try and explain her mysterious appearance.

"And Jad?" I released a shuddering breath.

Regret flickered in Talina's gaze. "He's fine. There's no hatred inside him anymore. He's back to being... Jad."

Why had she hesitated?

Why couldn't she look at me?

Talina wiped at her eyes, and I expected the worst. "It's nothing bad," she confessed. "Not with Jad, anyway. He's preparing one of the rooms."

Preparing?

"For what?"

Talina made a choked sound. "For Lainie's funeral."

Her tears ran freely now.

Lainie. The girl who had betrayed us, then turned her back on the ULD and decided to help us instead. She had paid for it with her life.

Damn my pain.

Talina needed me now.

I sat up, wrapping her in my arms. She buried her face in my shoulder and wept. I silently cried with her.

CHAPTER 30

I 'd worked out quickly in my life that I hated funerals. I'd been
to enough of them at the Brendlash Orphanage to understand
that goodbyes were not final, that grief and mourning lingered on.
Many of my peers had died in that place from sickness and
neglect. Even though Brendlash had been one of the better
orphanages in the provinces, it still didn't have enough staff to
cover all the children and teenagers who were housed there. And
there'd been many of us. War did that.

There were countless military funerals at Tarahik too. Sometimes they were public for all to attend; other times they'd been
private at the request of the family. Always, every day, the seven
memorial rooms in the castle had been in use. At one point, I'd
heard that there was a three-week waiting period. So yes, I'd learnt
to hate funerals.

This one proved not to be the exception. This one was the
worst. Jad had really done a commendable job at such short
notice. He'd found an expansive stone chamber where candelabras
hung on the walls and had built a pyre out of whatever wood he

could find, mostly furniture he'd torn apart with his bare hands. In the centre, on a bed covered in black satin and red-fringed pillows, was Lainie. Her skin was white, her hair a cloud of black around her face. She wore an elaborate white gown that went all the way up to her neck and covered the gaping death wound. Her lips had been painted red and her cheeks tinged with a touch of rouge. She looked beautiful and at peace. I was certain I had the silver-thorned witch to thank for it all.

We didn't have flowers—none grew in Orthrask—so we used candles instead as we gathered around the pyre. I held Talina's hand, my heart aching as she cried. Best friends since school, Talina had known Lainie the longest, and she was feeling the loss acutely. Marek flinched every time he heard Talina's mournful sobs, and I knew it took all his effort not to drape his arms over her in a protective hug. Bronislav and Annaka hung back by the wall, their heads bowed. They hadn't known Lainie, but they'd wanted to pay their respects.

Jad started the ceremony, beginning with the eulogy that all Haxsan Guard soldiers received. He was doing it for Talina and me, because I knew no way would Lainie have ever received the proper funeral rite from the Haxsan Guard. Not after what she'd done. They would have given her the traitors send-off, which would have seen her thrown to the lycanthors in the labour camps. I shivered at the grim prospect.

We stood there, silent and unmoving as we listened. When Jad finished, he brought forward a wooden torch, which he ignited with his own fire magic. I could have sworn the flames had stars dancing in them, rising and cascading like fireworks. It was beautiful magic. Fitting for Lainie.

He held his torch out to Talina. "For you. When you're ready."

His gaze found mine, the touch of ours only brief before he

departed. I watched him go, wishing I had the courage to chase after him. To simply… talk. Talina had been right. There was no hatred in Jad anymore. That madness had left when I banished Trajan's soul to the otherworld. But the distance between us, the unspoken words, the continuous loss and pining, it had to end. I was destined for a fate just like Lainie. I had to learn to let Jad go. So I remained by Talina's side, choosing to be a supportive friend instead.

The others left, too, leaving me and Talina behind in this stone-cold room.

She drew in what sounded like an agonising breath. "Is she okay?"

I looked at her, not understanding.

She sniffled. "Has Lainie found peace? Is she with Edric?"

She stepped up to the pyre and wrapped her delicate fingers around Lainie's pale ones.

I quelled the urge to cry. Honestly, I had no idea. I didn't want to summon Lainie's spirit, too afraid of what I might discover on the other side. I remembered the fiery pits, the indescribable wailing of the tormented, the demons who tortured with jagged weapons and fire.

I had read an early history text that had survived from the human age. It had described a place where the sinful went after death: murderers, traitors, liars, and thieves. At the time, I'd thought it was just a fable to keep the ancient population in check. Now, I wasn't so sure. It seemed all stories held an element of truth.

"She has found peace," I said, hoping it wasn't a lie.

Talina made a murmured sound of appreciation. "She wasn't a bad person. Lainie had her faults, but she… she was lost. She was just searching for a better way. Surely that didn't make her a wicked person?"

"It doesn't," I agreed, but my stomach hollowed out. "So many casters turned to the ULD in search of the exact same thing Lainie was after. And just like Lainie, it was out of fear. That isn't a sin. The real evil is Morgomoth."

She looked at me, her green eyes full of dread. "You will defeat him, won't you? I can't bear to lose another friend."

I didn't say anything. I couldn't promise what she hoped to hear.

Talina let my silence go. She focused on Laine, her face drowning in grief. "Life is so precious. No one seems to understand that until something like this happens. I don't want to waste my life fighting anymore."

I whipped my head to her. "You have many friends who love you. One, in particular, I believe wants to be more than just friends."

Talina's back went ramrod straight. "Marek is interested in Annaka. He's—"

"Interested in you. And don't give me that look." I pointed at her. "You love him; otherwise, you wouldn't have decapitated Hadar like a barbarian."

The memory still made me uneasy. Talina had become someone else at that moment. A woman fiercely protective of the people she loved, willing to take a life to save them. It just went to show that we could all commit terrible acts when love and loyalty called for it.

"You don't want to waste your life, so go and talk to him," I encouraged. "There's been enough death around here."

If the girl lying on the pyre wasn't a call to action to reach for everything life had to give, I didn't know what was.

Talina nodded with slow wonderment, as though some newfound assurance had dawned on her. "Will you help me with one thing first?"

"Of course."

She raised the torch. "Together?"

Lainie's pure white gown gleamed like starlight as we set the pyre alight. The flames flickered to life. Wispy smoke floated up to the oculus in the ceiling, beautiful embers flowing up with it, reminding me of fireflies in a night sky. In the end, Lainie hadn't received the proper burial rites. There was no firing of cast-shooters, no flag or bugle calls, but this itself was a magical send-off for her soul.

Talina and I held each other as we watched the flames and said goodbye to our friend.

I sat in a grandiose dining room. The rectangular table was made of polished ebony, already set with silver utensils, china plates, and long-stemmed glasses. This must have been where the leaders of the ULD, those who reported solely to Morgomoth, conducted their meetings. There were no windows in the room, just stone walls that were thick and impenetrable, probably so no one could eavesdrop. I doubted even Bronislav's supersensitive hearing would pick up on anything through the walls. Candelabras had been lit. A crystal chandelier cast silvery light around the room, giving the impression of beauty. That's all it was. This place was a home to evil. I sensed the darkness seeping in from every surface. If walls could talk, I wondered what cruel tales they would speak of.

Grim-faced, I slouched in my chair and tapped my foot nervously. Marek had gone to the portal to meet Darius and Macaslan. They'd be arriving any minute. I actually hoped the portal wouldn't work, but that was a fool's dream. The silverthorned witch was too clever. She'd easily manipulated its magic.

I was so furious with Darius and Macaslan, so utterly hurt and betrayed that the commander had kept her real identity from me, and livid that the senator had known and lied about it. I didn't know how I would behave when they arrived. Judging by the way my heart was skipping erratically, it wouldn't be good.

After several heavier seconds where my lungs felt like they'd collapsed, they appeared with an entourage of tense-footed officers. Darius was dressed in Haxsan Guard armour, looking every part the unconquered warlord as he sat at the head of the table. He smiled at me, but it was thin and lacked cordiality. Commander Macaslan took the seat next to mine. There was no emotion in her teal-grey eyes, just determination and grit. I wanted to yell at her right there and then, but I bit my lip and kept my cool.

After the meeting, I'll yell at them both until I'm blue in the face.

Marek was present. So was Jad. Again, seeing Jad brought on that feeling of loss and heartache. It crept in, devouring me on the inside. When he'd been possessed and under Trajan's influence, it hadn't been any less easy to love Jad, but it had been easier to let him go. Now, the real Jad had returned, and so had the feelings I'd bottled away.

It doesn't matter. Not when I have the Bone Grimoire and the Grand Masters' power.

If Jad had feelings, if he had ever loved me, they had been doused like flames with water.

Fighting the quivering sob that rose in my throat, I focused on the war council. The casters in this room were now the most influential and powerful leaders in the world—excluding Morgomoth, of course.

Darius braced his arms on the table and began. "Our ships are two kilometres off the coast. Not only are the beaches protected by dissent rebel forces, a dead army, and stagma, but there are creatures in the sand that could swallow our troops by the mouthful should we attempt to make a landing."

I shuddered inwardly, remembering the worm and its razor-sharp teeth.

The senator shot to his feet. "An assault on the beach will now prove fruitless. Our only option is to attack the Vrabkor Citadel directly."

Murmurs circled around the room.

"That's impossible," an officer said with a cold edge. "The citadel is protected by a celestial shield. We might as well be firing at the sky for the good it will do us."

There was a mutter of agreement around the table.

Darius raised his hands, waving away the disputes, urging everyone to settle down. "For Morgomoth to even conjure a shield means he is not undefeatable. There are weaknesses in this new land. Weaknesses in his citadel that he's trying to protect behind the shield."

"It's true," a new voice started.

The silver-thorned witch stood by the far wall, her ice-white dress decorated with thorns and silver gems, making her look like a queen of night and winter. I hadn't even realised she was here. She appeared in her younger form, perhaps knowing that physical strength, as well as ancient wisdom, would be required.

"I've completed several flyovers of the citadel," she continued. "I've risked getting as close to the shield as possible. Morgomoth has prepared an army to defend his fortress. He wouldn't do that if he believed his citadel was unconquerable. He might have created this land and built himself a kingdom, but he's also caged himself in it."

"Which is why we must attack and end this now," Darius resumed. "We can carry out airstrikes from the ships. We can bring our troops through the portal. It will give Zaya the chance she needs to slip in unnoticed and kill Morgomoth once and for all."

There it was. The nervous flip-over in my stomach.

I still had absolutely no idea where to find the Larthalgule and Neathror blades, or how to complete the spell to unite them. All this could be for nothing.

In one of the chairs, a council member stiffened. "That still doesn't answer the question, Darius. How are we supposed to infiltrate a celestial shield?"

The senator was smiling. "With our own dead army."

Startled gasps ran through the room.

My eyes went so wide, I wondered how they didn't bug out of my head.

There was no smile on Darius's face now. I'd never seen him appear so serious. "The cargo holds of our ships are filled with chak-lorks. The creatures are subdued for now with spells. Zaya can control them. She can command the dead to destroy the shield. They'll be the first assault on the Vrabkor Citadel. The Haxsan Guard will be the next."

Silence filled the room. I guessed everyone was privately deliberating on whether it was possible.

A fluttery sickness found its way into my gut. I had only recently discovered that I could control chak-lorks. How could Darius have learnt that so quickly?

My gaze wandered to Marek. He avoided looking at me, but judging by the way he went rigid, he knew I was watching him and that I'd connected the dots. He'd used that handheld mirror. He'd reported everything to the senator.

Is everyone deliberately keeping me out of the loop?

Decisions were being made for me without my consent. Lies were being told, the truth always kept just beneath the surface.

I stood, feeling like a trespasser who shouldn't be here. Who wasn't really welcomed. Someone here for appearance's sake, to just carry out the actions ordered of them.

Before I knew what I was doing, I was stepping out of the room.

"Where are you going?" Darius wasn't angry, but his voice didn't sound impressed either.

I stopped in the doorway, feeling every muscle inside me spasm. I was so damn tired. I hadn't stopped since the moment I'd been plucked out of the Gosheniene Internment Camp. I'd witnessed cities destroyed, been tormented by the dead, and chased by all manner of monsters. I'd been cursed under a sleeping hex, used as a political symbol for propaganda, and been held captive numerous times. I was over it.

I just need a frigging break.

I stormed away from the council, refusing the calls to come back. The floorboards thudded beneath me, footsteps approaching fast. I thought it might have been Marek checking to see if I was all right, but I was surprised by the person who greeted me.

Commander Macaslan stood tall and proud, watching me with thinly disguised disappointment. "You did not have permission to leave. That council meeting involves strategic—"

"I don't want to hear it," I snapped, my temper boiling. "You'll make the plans without me regardless, so just tell me afterward."

I turned away.

"How dare you—"

My self-control cracked. "No. How dare *you*. You're my grandmother, and you never said a damn word about it. You let me believe I had no family. You let me believe I was alone."

The light in her eyes, as sharp as steel, guttered out. Her face went pale with surprise, the colour of white moonstone.

"I know who my parents are," I resumed. "I know who Morgomoth is to me. Why did you never say anything?"

She clenched her jaw, her lips forming into a thin line of challenge. "How did you find out?"

"The dead like to tell the living's secrets. Explain."

"Because I had no choice." She sounded like she was struggling to keep her voice steady. "Your parents made it clear that they wanted me to have no part in your life. My relationship with my daughter was a strained one. I never approved of Isgrad. I knew a relationship with him would only bring Briya ruin. In the end, it was worse. It brought her death. Isgrad wanted you to have a life where you knew nothing and no one from your past. Bringing you to Tarahik, where the ULD would know you were my granddaughter, was too dangerous. I agreed. *Reluctantly.* I swore on my magic to be your legal guardian, to support you financially until you were independent, but to have nothing to do with you."

My ears were ringing, my blood fired up. "Clarence left me in an orphanage."

"Where you would be safe. Where you could start a new life."

"And a lot of good it did. Look where we are now."

The commander stared like a vengeful queen, looking capable of wielding storms. "That first night I saw you, I begged Briya to return to Tarahik and bring you with her. I would have done anything to have raised you, but I'd sworn an oath to stay out of your life. It wasn't until Melvina and the ULD started hunting you that I had to intervene. I protected you in the only way I knew I could."

My hands twitched at my sides. I couldn't stop trembling. "Darius knew. If you were under an oath not to say anything, why didn't he?"

"He was sworn to secrecy."

A dull, pounding headache started at the back of my head, the aftermath of discovering too many secrets. I needed rest. I needed to get away from this woman.

Macaslan's eyes grew dark and haunted. "You are so very much like Briya. And as stubborn as I am."

I walked away. She could report back to Darius what she

liked. I was breaking apart inside. Tears pricked my eyes. I was angry because I'd been lied to, but mostly it was because I'd learnt that I'd never truly been alone. And now, with my ill-omened task hours away, I felt like I'd been robbed of that too.

CHAPTER 31

I sat cross-legged on my bed—my borrowed bed. I had no idea
who this room once belonged to, but judging from its appearance, it had been someone who hated colour. Black tapestry
curtains. Black rug on the otherwise bare floor. Clean wooden
furniture varnished in ebony polish. It reminded me of Lainie.

I closed my eyes, refusing to let emotion get the best of me
again. I would always associate the colour black with her. She'd
been a complicated person, and if auras were a thing, I imagined
Lainie's would have been as thick and shadowed as the deepest
abyss.

Yes, looking into the dark would be a struggle from now on.
I'd see Lainie in it. Always.

I lit the candles on the bedside table to suppress the shadows
in the room. Unzipping my rucksack, I gingerly removed the
Bone Grimoire like it was a prized possession. The smooth ivory
spell book, decorated with finger bones and symbols of the sun
and moon, seemed to stare back as though it were mocking me—
as though it knew I had no chance of working out its secrets.

"Why do you have to be so frigging complicated?"

No way would I hide the grimoire in my mind again. Having it physically present was risky, especially because I didn't know all the Haxsan Guard soldiers who'd started arriving through the portal in droves. But hiding the book in my mind would have been riskier still. Last time, Morgomoth had been close to uncovering it. I couldn't let that happen again.

I opened the book and flicked to the spell that was impossible to work out. A desperate need to solve the riddle pummelled through me, but my mind ran blank. A small voice in the back of my head teased that I wasn't clever enough or worthy of the task. It was a joke to even think I could defeat Morgomoth. Lunette, Edric, Colonel Harper, Lainie—they'd all lost their lives for nothing. All of this would be for nothing. Tomorrow at midnight, when Darius and I led the attack, we'd be leading lambs to slaughter.

Irked by my defeatist attitude, I dropped back onto the bed and stared at the ceiling.

Do not cry. Do not cry.

These days, I felt as stable as a broken earth dam, all my emotions gushing out of me. I shut my eyes, then opened them, certain in that split moment that I'd caught a flash of movement in the corner. I sat up, trying to see in the shadows.

I wasn't alone. The room had gone cold. A chilly moisture had settled over my skin, my breathing becoming clouds of white vapour.

"Show yourself, please."

Gondalesh had been the home to dissent rebels and lycanthors. Who knew what malevolent spirits might linger here?

Frost formed in spiderwebbing cracks across the ceiling. Pressure built in the room like a charged electrical storm. I was surprised the windows didn't explode.

A figure glided out of the dark. Her white dress glistened with ice, moving as though it were floating in water. Her brown hair flowed around her face like reeds, never allowing me to see her eyes. I didn't want to. I didn't want to see the pain that would be inside them. Her neck didn't sit right. The bone bulged at the side where it had been snapped, the skin abraded from the rope that had strangled her.

"Briya."

Mum.

She floated soundlessly back into the dark. A second later, a lock clicked, and my door creaked open with a groan. An invitation to follow.

I swung off the bed, hid the Bone Grimoire beneath my mattress, and hurried into the darkness. I paused in the doorway. The hall outside was quiet, not a soul in sight. Briya glided ethereally to the opposite end, the torches flickering as she passed. She took the stairs to the right, the long train of her dress rippling like a silver river behind her.

She has something to show me.

I can trust her.

She's my mum.

I moved silently down the hall and took the stairs. Thanks to the time it had taken for magic to heal my broken ribs, I hadn't had the opportunity to explore Gondalesh. The flight joined with another that went up like a spiral stairway in a lighthouse, only instead of a beacon above, there was more darkness. Briya was always just too far ahead for me to keep up, disappearing around the bends. She was a flash of white light that teased me to follow.

I should have brought a candle or a flashlight, because the higher I ascended, the more difficult it became to see, the shadows closing in like silent wraiths. When I reached the top of the stairs, a chill wind nipped at my face. There was a door. Simple, made of wood. Only it had five locks in place, as though the people in Gondalesh had feared what was on the other side. Hanging on a hook beside the door was a set of keys. Five in total.

Okay, Briya. You want me to open this door.

She was no longer present.

At least, I couldn't see her.

I should turn away. Find Darius or Macaslan. Make sure I'm not alone.

But I was still too angry at the pair, and my nerves were too excited to turn back now.

I grabbed the keys and released each of the locks. My fingers rested on the dust-smothered doorknob. I couldn't hear anything on the other side, which somehow made it even more terrifying. I swallowed and turned the knob. A wheezing whine escaped the door. It was a square room with solid black stone, no bigger than four metres all around. There was a single bed in the corner, a bucket to its right, and a tray of food that looked days old. A man lay on the floor. His back was to me, but I could see that he was breathing.

Dear providence. This room is a cell.

I rushed forward, intent on working out if he was injured... or tortured. My hands closed around his shoulders to gently turn him over. Dark shadows lined his eyes. His face was veined and paper-thin from lack of nourishment, but I recognised those ocean-blue eyes.

A startled gasp worked its way from my throat.

Isgrad.

But not entirely Isgrad. His white-blond hair was streaked with black, as though it had undergone a very bad dye job. His nose was angled as another's. Even his lips weren't quite his. Though the contours of them were somehow familiar.

I backed away, recognition shooting into my gut.

No. Not possible. Not possible.

Because I was not only looking at Isgrad but a conjunction of two people. I'd heard of spells used to glamour a caster, making them appear as someone else entirely. The magic had been banned long ago, but here it was in plain sight. Only the spell was wearing off.

My heavy scuffle had woken him. His eyelids fluttered, his features tightening when he saw me. He knew who I was. The shame in his eyes spoke words.

"Zaya." He licked his parched lips. "This was not the way I wanted to meet you again."

That voice. So much like Isgrad's.

And yet so much like his.

His head fell back onto the floor. I thought he might have passed out again, but I wouldn't let him remain unconscious for long.

I wanted answers.

Needed them.

"Colonel Harper," I snapped. "Wake up."

WE'D ASSEMBLED in an opulent living area. Commander Macaslan was staring at Isgrad with blatant fury. *Huh*, I wanted to scoff. Now she knew what it felt like to have secrets kept from her.

After the discovery I'd made, I found Darius and Macaslan. Marek and Jad had brought Isgrad—Colonel Harper... providence, I didn't know what to call him—down here. Now he was wrapped in blankets on the couch, silently eating soup that someone had found in the kitchens. He wouldn't look at me, but I couldn't stop studying him. All this time, the colonel had been Isgrad. I thought back on our first meeting in the commander's office the day I'd arrived at Tarahik. He'd been distant and indifferent, like he hadn't wanted me there. And yet that first night, when I'd been trying to find my room and had been separated from Millie, nearly plunging to my death by Adaline's trickery, he'd been there. Following me. Saving me. He'd been the first one to find me after I'd discovered Lunette's frozen body in Shadow's Wood. He'd been the one to get me out of Tarahik through the portal when General Kravis had come to arrest me. Now those acts of kindness, even though they'd been delivered gruffly, made sense.

There was something horribly violating about all of it, though. Once again, I had been deceived, the truth withheld.

Jad and Marek stood by the far wall near the arched doorway. Marek was staring at Isgrad with gape-mouthed wonder. Indeed, it was startling to see the glamour transform and slowly morph the colonel's features into Isgrad's. There was no sign of black in his hair anymore. It was pure blond. Even his nose had changed, less crooked and sharper. I didn't know if the magic was breaking apart because his secret had been discovered or because Isgrad was letting it fade.

Jad watched my father with stone-faced resilience. It was difficult to define what the captain might be thinking. He wasn't impressed, that was for sure. His heavy frown told me so.

Darius chuckled low in his throat. "Well, this is a surprise."

Macaslan's eyes never left Isgrad. She said only one word, her voice tearing into him like a vulture's talons. "Explain."

Isgrad placed his empty bowl on the table. He regarded us all with equal parts reservation and wariness. I wondered if the soup now tasted like lead in his stomach. "It's a long story."

Darius's amusement dimmed. "We have time to hear it. Was Eduard Harper even a real person? Or did you make him up?"

Macaslan flinched. It must have been difficult to realise that the person you'd trusted the most, who you'd believed was dead and who you'd mourned over, was in fact alive and someone completely different from who you'd thought.

Oh wait. I do know how that feels.

Isgrad clasped his hands firmly on his knees. "You have to

understand that I only wanted to protect my daughter without getting in the way. I had lived for years thinking Zaya was safe, trying my hardest not to seek her out, telling myself that she was better off without me or her memories. It was a struggle every day. So, I forced all of my energy into my earth magic, trying to build my strength, trying to forget my former life. I moved around a lot, but everywhere I went, there were whispers that the ULD were growing strong again. Without my brother... without a leader, I thought the ULD would crumble in time, but I was wrong. In my brother's place, Vulcan Stormouth had taken control of the ULD."

His cheeks heated resentfully. "I had to put myself into some very dark situations to find out information, but I couldn't risk anyone knowing who I was. I found a caster-witch who was able to sell me a glamour for a hefty price. The potion never ran out. It changed my appearance... made me into someone different. I was fine with it. I was happy to look in a mirror and never see my real face again. But maintaining the glamour, drinking that potion every day, came at a cost. I am a spellrock addict. The tonic I took to lessen my withdrawal systems did not mix well with the glamour. There were days where I was bedridden, unable to move."

I recalled the night on the *Velorosa* when I'd discovered Colonel Harper—no, Isgrad— in the midst of a seizure. It had been a terrifying moment and one that hadn't made sense at the time. It was clear now. He'd been drinking that black potion to maintain his glamour, only it hadn't combined so well with the spellrockabis tonic that was already in his system.

Isgrad continued his story, his voice rattling out of him. "I spent months talking to former dissent rebels who'd turned spy. Traitors. Assassins. Cut-throats. I spent many evenings tracking down thugs and socialising around fighting pits, learning about what Vulcan had planned. Word was that he had Melvina Raskovitch searching for a girl. No one was able to tell me the full details, but rumour had it that the girl was the key to awakening Morgomoth. It had been years since I'd cursed Willieth under the sleeping hex. I didn't care what General Kravis or the Council of Founding Sovereigns had done with his body. All that mattered to me was that Zaya remained safe."

He stole a look at me. My expression couldn't have been good because his gaze dropped. "I wondered if the necromancy running through Zaya's blood would be the key to breaking Morgomoth's curse. I sought out the silver-thorned witch, the only caster who could possibly have known. I looked for months to find her, but she'd entirely disappeared. Some said she was dead. One evening, in the backstreets of Hedmeer where I was hiding out, I heard the news that a caster girl at the Brendlash Orphanage had been killed by ice. My contacts in the ULD informed me it was Melvina who'd committed the murder. That she'd killed a girl named Adaline. A mistake. But then came more dreadful news. Another girl had been arrested for the crime. I saw her name and face in the papers. I knew it was my daughter being sent to the Gosheniene Internment Camp."

He knotted his fingers, sounding almost apologetic when he looked at Macaslan and Darius. "I had instructed Clarence Chauvelin to assign you both as Zaya's legal guardians, just in case something like this occurred. I knew you would both do your best to get her out of Gosheniene. But it took so long, and every day I grew fearful that Melvina and Vulcan would get to her first. I knew I had to work to get Zaya out of there. I needed to be in the picture again to protect her, but from a safe distance. So, I had papers forged. I stole the identity of a young colonel named Eduard Harper, who'd served in Vukovar and had been killed in action, his body never found. Before his death, he'd been transferred to Tarahik, so I went in his place instead, pretending to be him."

I was listening to the story, feeling as though my life were on the edge of a precipice, staring into the dark below. Now I'd seen what was hidden in those shadows. It was tearing toward me, wanting to pull me down, wanting to drown me in the past.

Macaslan folded her arms, devouring Isgrad with her stern glare. Darius had been listening the entire time with a restless understanding on his face, as though none of it truly surprised him. Being a sensitive, I wondered if his magic had alerted him all along to the fact that Colonel Harper was never really who he said he was. It was the kind of thing the senator would do. He was a man of mystery and secrets, only revealing his cards when it suited him.

Isgrad's mouth twitched. His voice was directed at the commander, but he didn't look at her as he said, "You never would have allowed me into Tarahik if I'd arrived as myself."

"You're damn right, I wouldn't have," she seethed. "My daughter died because of you. I lost the first years of my grand-daughter's life because of your selfishness."

Darius stood now. He stepped between the pair, raising his arms to defuse the tension. "Let's try to keep this conversation friendly, shall we. Isgrad is admitting the truth now. His appearance might have changed, but he's still the same person. Still your friend and ally."

Macaslan looked like she wanted to take off her shoe and throw it at him. She wheeled around and, just like I had earlier from the war council, stormed away. The commander slammed the door behind her, making me jump.

Like grandmother, like granddaughter, I suppose.

Isgrad let go of a troubled sigh. "The rest, as you know, is history. I worked with Darius and Macaslan to get Zaya out of Gosheniene. She was transferred to Tarahik, where I could keep watch."

A fine job you did.

I thought of all the danger and near misses that had crossed my path.

Isgrad dropped his head in his hands. He looked wrecked.

For a long moment there was silence in the room, only interrupted when Jad hitched his shoulders.

The captain's voice held a gravelly edge. "What happened to you after the *Velorosa*? How did you end up here in Gondalesh?"

Isgrad looked up. He made a slow assessment of us all, and I knew I wouldn't like what I was about to hear. "That evening on the *Velorosa*, before Zaya unleashed the Dark Divide, Willieth sensed who I really was. When we were trying to flee on the tender, a wave swept me away... though it wasn't really a wave. I was surrounded by chak-lorks. They kept me under the water until I passed out. When I woke, I was in that room upstairs."

Jad's striking black eyes darkened. "Why would Morgomoth keep you here? Why not imprison you in his citadel?"

Isgrad let out a wretched breath. "Because I don't think he could stand to see me. Willieth is...."

"Obsessed with you," I finished for him. "All he wanted as a child was your love and approval. The necromancy turned that into a fixated desire to possess you."

Isgrad silently nodded. "Not just me, Zaya."

The composure I'd held on to shredded.

I knew he was right.

CHAPTER 32

There were more questions. Darius wanted to know every detail about Isgrad's life before he'd become Colonel Harper. I tuned them out, trying to soothe the burning ache that had started in my chest and worked its way up.

All this time, Isgrad had been alive. Since the moment I'd arrived at Tarahik, my father had been close, keeping a watchful eye over me but never intervening. I didn't know if that made him brave, determined, or a coward. It certainly spun my emotions all over the place.

So. Many. Secrets.

Lost in my sea of troubled thoughts, it took me a moment to realise Jad was staring. For so many days, I'd seen nothing but hatred and revulsion on that impossibly handsome face, but now it held sadness, and regret, and… I didn't dare breathe.

Longing.

I swallowed, a tap dance of heat running through my veins. Warmth climbed over my cheeks. A rushing sound snapped in my ears. I looked away, trying to douse my own intense feelings. I'd

310

built a wall between us—hell, I'd assembled an entire stronghold —to protect myself. I'd accepted that I'd lost Jad. I'd made my peace with it. But now that Trajan was gone and Jad was free, everything I'd constructed had been unravelled with a single look.

It can't happen.

There was a reason Jad remained standing halfway across the room, never daring to get close. For him, the Bone Grimoire's magic made me as toxic as acid. Touching me would be like touching poison.

"Zaya?"

I jumped, attempting—and not succeeding—to hide how flustered I'd become.

Darius scrunched his brows into a frown. "Are you all right?"

"Fine," I lied, straightening in my seat.

"I said we'll leave so you may have time to talk to Isgrad. I'm sure you must have questions for your father."

I nodded, keeping my eyes trained on the floor.

"Are you sure you're all right?"

I opened my mouth to speak but decided against it. I didn't want Jad to see my overly hot skin. Or hear how badly my voice shook.

I heard Darius say, "Come along," followed by steady footfalls as he, Marek, and Jad made their way toward the exit. My eyes stole a final glance at the captain. He lingered in the doorway for a moment, as though he could sense my gaze on him. It felt like I'd been kicked in the stomach when the door closed with a heavy click, as though Jad, too, was putting up a barrier, shielding himself from me, keeping his distance.

It hurt more than I wanted to acknowledge.

I focused on Isgrad, knowing neither what to say nor do.

"You must have a million questions," he said at last. He watched me with a nervous anticipation.

I stood, ready to unleash a verbal flogging.

I wanted him to hurt. I wanted him to know how angry and upset I was. I wanted to loathe him for his deceit, but I couldn't find the strength to do it. My legs were swaying beneath me, and I dropped into my chair again. A foreign emotion inundated me, colliding with my wrath like a mudslide. Childishly, I wanted to run to his side, to be coddled by a parent, to be protected.

"I don't expect your forgiveness," he started, almost slurring his words in haste. "All of this... it's been my fault from the beginning. I killed my little brother. If I'd just accepted my actions instead of trying to find a way to correct them, none of this would have happened. And now it's you who is paying the consequences."

His expression contorted into one of self-disgust. He dropped his head in his hands and silently wept.

My blood stilled. The sight of his tears was too painful to bear. "It was the silver-thorned witch who started this," I corrected. "She misread the signs. She admitted it to me."

He looked up through bloodshot eyes. "You've seen her?"

"She's here in the tower. She came to Orthrask to find you... and, I think, to try and help me. She blames herself."

"We're both to blame. We made a mistake that evening. We turned Willieth into a monster."

And there it was, the true guilty verdict. I was only a part of the shame that plagued Isgrad. What really tore him apart was what he'd done to his brother.

His throat bobbed. "I often wonder what Willieth would have been like if he'd been allowed to grow up."

I tried to envision it. I imagined Willieth as a stout young man. As handsome and as unconventional as a bohemian artist. Likely a soldier in the Haxsan Guard, and a real catch with the ladies. He would have been best friends with his brother. Kind. Caring. Compassionate.

Necromancy had destroyed that possibility.

I felt like I'd been pushed off that precipice again, tumbling through a night sky. If Willieth hadn't been corrupted by necromancy, then there'd have been no need for me to be born to fix Isgrad's mistakes. It was another sign that I was destined for one purpose.

Destroy Morgomoth.

Then die.

But I didn't want my life to end. I wanted a future. Why couldn't I have a chance to connect with Isgrad and Macaslan and have a family?

My conversation with the witch came spiralling back. She's told me that I had one chance out of three to survive. One tiny chance. I would fight for it.

"I need your help," I started in a small voice, trying my best to muster courage. "If I can unite the Larthalgule and Neathror blades, then I can sever the connection with the Interitus blade. We could kill Morgomoth and survive. We can end the ULD. Help me achieve it."

A tight smile crept along his mouth. "You have your mother's impulsiveness, your grandmother's strength, and my temperament. You also have Willieth's kindness. If anyone can defeat the greatest necromancer the world has known, it's you."

I balked at that.

Willieth's kindness?

Though I supposed he had been a benign child at the start.

"I will help you. You won't be alone." Isgrad's blue eyes were now alight with cobalt fire. "I need to confront my brother. *We* need to finish this."

That small flower of hope started blossoming in my chest again—just a sprout, but it was there. "I have the Bone Grimoire. I've read the spell to unite the blades... memorised it, actually, but it's a riddle I can't work out. I asked the witch."

"And what did she say?"

"That it's a riddle for a reason. That I won't understand it until the right moment. I don't even know what *that* means."

Isgrad smiled weakly. "It means to have faith. You'll work it out when you need to."

"And what if I don't? My mind is linked with Morgomoth's. Every waking second, every small moment I manage to sleep, I'm terrified he'll take the book from me. That he'll solve the riddle and unite the blades and everything will be over."

Isgrad leaned forward in his seat, his face a mask of stern contemplation. "The grimoire… is it a real, physical object?"

"No, not anymore. Not exactly."

I explained what had happened at the Isla Necropolis, how the Bone Grimoire chose both Morgomoth and me, dividing the Grand Masters' magic equally among us. I told him about the Grand Masters and how they were trapped with the book's power, now a permanent part of me and Morgomoth.

"They seem so sad," I admitted. "They're just wraiths. Trapped and unable to move on."

"Then perhaps you could do something about it."

I stared, unsure of his meaning.

Isgrad's voice was thick and strange. "Do you want this power the Bone Grimoire has granted you?"

It was the first time anyone had asked me that question. I'd had to acquire the magic. It was expected of me. It was the only thing that would save us. But did I truly want it?

"No," I confessed with a heavy heart.

"The book is a part of you, as are the Grand Masters. You have the spell. You said yourself that you memorised it. If you fear Morgomoth obtaining the grimoire, then renounce the magic. Destroy the book. Send the Grand Masters to the otherworld. From what you've said, it sounds like that's what they need. To move on."

The breath died in my throat.

Can it really be that easy?

I thought about it some more. Uncertainty bit deep. "But what if the magic doesn't leave Morgomoth? What if his half remains with him? Aren't I just weakening myself?"

"It's possible, but the mind link will be gone. And what Morgomoth wants most is that spell. Without the book, there is no chance he'll succeed in obtaining it."

A knock sounded on the door.

The silver-thorned witch appeared, lovely in her white silk gown, her crown of crystals and thorns making her appear as ageless and ancient as a goddess. "I'm sorry to interrupt, but Isgrad, you're required in the war room. The war council wants information about your brother."

"Duty calls," I said, feeling only slightly relieved that my presence hadn't been requested.

I eyed the pair meaningfully. "No more secrets. No more schemes or strategising behind my back.

"No more secrets," Isgrad agreed. "Think about what I said. And goodnight, daughter."

I froze, unsure how to reply to that.

"Goodnight," I said stiffly.

I sped down the hall, wondering if I should have called him Father. There was so much more I wanted to know from him. Questions I had about Briya. About his own mother and Willieth.

But it would have to wait, because right now, I had an appointment with the Grand Masters.

I HELD the Bone Grimoire to my chest as I settled onto my bed and listened to the empty silence around me. I closed my eyes, willing myself to fall asleep. I needed to see the Grand Masters. Get in and out of that mind-created necropolis, before Morgomoth realised I was there. That was the plan.

Huh. Like I'll be that lucky.

The silk sheets were comfortable to rest on—what the humans would have called heavenly—but it still took time for the swift black waters of sleep to submerge my mind. At long last, I woke up in the Isla Necropolis. The chamber was the same way I'd left it, except this time the frescoes were bold and bright with colour, as though centuries of dust and sediment had been removed from them. The runes on the ceiling glowed with luminant power, like a pale pink dawn rising out of the night. In the centre of the chamber were scattered bones, which looked like they'd been scavenged by vultures and wolves. I understood what had really occurred, though. Morgomoth had torn the plinth apart when he'd tried and failed to capture me. This was the result of his explosive anger.

I shivered and moved away.

"Zaya Wayward," the ghostly voices called, the sound intrusive in my head.

I stared at the five Grand Masters on the dais, or what was left of them, the red cloaks billowing behind them. No skin. No flesh. Except for the pale ivory jaws and the stitched mouths, there wasn't even a hint of bone. Wraiths. The realisation was like cold fingers trailing up my spine.

The Bone Grimoire had made the journey with me, still tucked in my arms. I stepped toward the dais. In the steeliest voice I could manage, I said, "I have come to return this to you. I don't want it."

Please let this be the right thing to do. Please don't let this backfire.

The Grand Masters didn't answer for a long time, but the

temperature in the chamber plunged, as though someone had opened freezer doors.

"The Bone Grimoire is a gift. To return it would be ungracious."

There was no kindness in their tone, and it really did make me feel like an insolent child.

I held my ground. "I have from the book what I need, and now I'd like to give it back to its true masters. I want to help you move on."

More silence.

Harsh laughter filled the chamber. It sounded like crows cawing. *"Move on? That is a luxury not afforded to us. We are cursed. While the book exists and contains our magic, we will always be. We cannot move on, as you so plainly put it."*

I was breathing hard, scrambling for words, not wanting to lose control of the situation. "Then destroy the book yourselves. You created it. You did it for a virtuous purpose, but while there is a necromancer like Morgomoth in the world, the Bone Grimoire will never be used for good."

Not a sound was uttered, but I felt their eyes on me—if they even had eyes—watching me, their curiosity stirring from the gloom. *"We cannot leave our brothers and sisters."*

I thought about the souls that were a part of Morgomoth. There was no worse fate than to be tethered to him. To make up a portion of his body where there was no flesh. "If the Bone Grimoire is destroyed, surely your brothers and sisters would be free too."

It was a big gamble.

"You are asking us to risk it?"

I heard the desperation in their voices, their need for freedom, to flee this place. I just had to push that little bit more.

"It's the magic from the book, *your* magic, that Morgomoth and I took. If the book doesn't exist, if you take the magic back and destroy it, then you'll all be freed."

Please. Please. Please.

The tension in the chamber was becoming palpable, like I was in the midst of a galactic storm. Alarm sluiced through my veins, flushing up to my chest with pounding effect. To sweeten the deal, I summoned my magic. The doorway to the place beyond appeared beside me. This time, it was an arched entry filled with incandescent light so bright, I could barely stand to stare at it.

I approached the dais and placed the Bone Grimoire on the lowest step. "It's up to you. This chance may never be offered to you again."

Especially if I die.

Especially if Morgomoth wins.

I waited, sensing their hesitance, their reluctance, their yearning.

Silence. The anticipation was killing me.

"*Zaya Wayward. We agree.*"

"You do?" I wished I hadn't sounded so surprised.

Their pitiless laughter was a bass rumble through the chamber. Winds tore at their cowls, revealing their monstrous faces. Red eyes that reminded me of exploding stars. Teeth as sharp as rodents'. "*It may be you who comes to regret this decision.*"

They flew from the dais like a ghostly cavalry, their cloaks rippling as though they were bringing a crimson tide behind them. And just like a wave, they rushed toward the blistering white light, crossing to the other side of the door.

Without them here, the chamber collapsed. The frescoes imploded like they were made out of breadcrumbs. The columns bowed under the weight of the ceiling, which came plunging down. The floor gave out. I was thrown, falling, slamming into bits of debris, my teeth clacking so hard that—

It was the scream that woke me, so loud that it shattered the windows and scattered the furniture. I raised my arms, shielding my face from the splintering wood and glass. The curtains flapped in the hot breeze, sulphur and fire congesting my airways.

That scream, that roar of rage, had not been in my head. It had travelled across the entire island, causing all of Orthrask to shudder.

In that instant, I knew Morgomoth had realised what I'd done.

CHAPTER 33

I scrambled off my bed, tugged on my boots to avoid the mosaic of shattered glass on the floor, and ran into the hallway. Others had the same idea, the passage full of chatter and panic. Some soldiers were pulling on their uniforms, armed with cast-shooters and athame-sabres, others looked like they'd slept in their Haxsan Guard attire, ready for battle at a moment's notice.

Is that what's happening?

Battle?

Everything was in disarray. There were shouts and orders to get in positions.

Positions?

I shouldn't have walked out of the war briefing.

Macaslan and Darius must have instigated a plan should Gondalesh go under attack.

I hurried through the slew of people to Marek's room. He'd know what to do. Before I even had a chance to knock on the door, though, it popped open. Talina peered her head out, half dressed.

I froze.

I must have the wrong room.

Her cheeks instantly coloured, but her voice held a hint of annoyance. "Is it bad? Are we under attack?"

I met her stare, unsure why she looked so flustered. "I don't know. That's what I'm going to find out. Do you know where Marek is—"

There was a flash of movement behind her.

I stilled, doing a double take. That was definitely Marek I saw naked to the waist on the bed, nothing but a sheet covering his lower half.

"Talina." I didn't know whether to be shocked or embarrassed. She'd clearly taken my advice and talked to Marek. Apparently, more than talked. No wonder she didn't want to heed the call for formation.

"The pair of you better get dressed," I urged, no longer able to contain my sheepish grin.

She glared up at the ceiling and shut the door.

I made my way down the remainder of the hallway, still smiling. I was happy for Talina and Marek. After everything they'd been through, after everything they'd endured, they deserved this chance together. To see where it would take them. Life was too short not to.

My good mood evaporated the moment I hit the stairs and saw the soldiers assembled on the lower level, ready for whatever army was amassing outside.

Have I doomed everyone?

Was destroying the Bone Grimoire and breaking the connection to the Grand Masters' power enough to make Morgomoth act?

Has he brought his forces upon us to destroy us all?

Somehow, I managed to keep breathing as I pushed through the soldiers. I found Macaslan and Darius in the war room, listening to reports from various officers who arrived one after another, all of them wearing the Infinite Eye bordered by a star on their left shoulders. That was the insignia for the night watch.

I took it as a good sign that they remained composed, but there was still a nervous mix of momentum and anticipation in the room, everyone geared up for whatever may come.

On the table, holographic maps were on display of the surrounding land. Orthrask was silent. There was no approaching army rolling in. The churning in my stomach settled a little, only for my heart to collide with my ribs when I spotted Jad. He was listening to the reports and passing out orders. Our eyes locked. It sent a flash of heat through me that I ruefully tried to dismiss. Now was not the time to let emotions get in the way.

I found Isgrad standing over a mapographic, his eyes scouting the landscape.

"What's happening?"

He inhaled a sharp breath. "Nothing. For now." He sounded like he could hardly believe it.

"It's a false alarm?"

"Looks like it, but we're increasing the watch, just in case. Something happened at the citadel. Morgomoth's anger shook the entire island."

I plastered on a blank expression, but I wasn't fast enough. He saw the flash of guilt that ran across my face and connected the dots. "You destroyed it, then?"

"Destroyed what?" a new voice demanded.

We both spun.

Commander Macaslan stared at me, colour flushing up her neck as her eyes darkened. They were no longer like storm clouds but exploding embers, threatening retribution.

I swallowed the sickly taste that lined my throat. "I destroyed the Bone Grimoire."

"You did what?" She drew herself up to her full height. With a black cloak draped over her shoulders and a pair of athame-sabres strapped to her sides, she looked more menacing than any warrior queen had a right to be.

No way. No way was she allowed to preside over me now and judge my actions. Not after the secrets she'd kept.

"The book is gone," I announced in a voice teeming with steadfastness. "The Grand Masters' magic is finished. I sent them to the otherworld. And before you get narky with me, I have the spell to unite the Larthalgule and the Neathror blades. Morgomoth doesn't have a chance of finding it."

"You should have discussed this with me first. And Darius. We should have been involved in this decision."

My strength to hold back had been as delicate as ice. It was cracking. If she wanted a grandmother-granddaughter fight, she'd get one.

"That is enough," Darius intervened. He stood between us, shaking his head with disappointment. I didn't know whether it was directed at me or the commander. "What's done is done. Nothing can change it. Morgomoth is furious, but he hasn't led an attack. We need to work with each other and trust each other; otherwise, our plan will fall apart. Understand?"

His eyes trailed over everyone in the room.

Trust?

Pity that couldn't have been our motto from the beginning.

Macaslan looked like the blood was roaring in her head. I wondered if she'd ever been publicly reproached before. I didn't dare tell her that the idea to destroy the Bone Grimoire had come from Isgrad. That would have been like throwing petrol bombs into an already raging inferno.

Darius wasn't finished. He raised his voice for all to hear. "We will reconvene tomorrow morning to discuss our strategy for the assault on Vrabkor." He looked meaningfully my way. "This time, it's expected that you will attend the session. The whole session. Dismissed."

That last word was directed at me alone, because everyone else continued their discussions, planning their tactics should another event occur throughout the night.

The pressure released from my chest. I walked out of the war room, holding my head high, refusing to look at Macaslan. I hadn't gotten far in the hall when footsteps sounded heavily behind me. I turned… and stopped dead in my tracks.

Seeing Jad's black eyes skim my face sent fire across my cheeks. My stomach did that annoying flip again, and I had to look down at my feet to inhale a calming breath. It didn't work. In his presence, everything inside me was stuttering. I had worked so hard to forget him, to convince myself that what could have been would never happen.

"Once this is all over, I never want to see you again. I hope you die in that place."

Trajan's words. Not Jad's. But they still hurt.

He stared at my arm and swore. "You're injured."

I looked down, surprised to see I was bleeding. I must have been cut when the window in my bedroom exploded. It wasn't deep, and the gash wasn't large. I'd never felt the pain until now. Awareness made it sting.

"It looks worse than it is. I'll find a first-aid kit."

I turned to walk away, but his voice stopped me.

"You're shivering too."

Damn. He'd noticed.

"You did just see what happened in there, right?" I pointed back to the war room. "The commander verbally attacked me."

I had every right to be shaken up after that incident, even if that was only half the reason why I was trembling.

He watched me with that perceptive gaze that made me feel like a window had opened to my soul.

"I'm fine," I lied. "I'm not hurt. My room is a mess, though."

It looked like a tornado had gone through it. I thought about all the glass and broken furniture and wasn't in the mood to clean it. "I'll find a couch to sleep on tonight."

There had to be a private lounge somewhere in this enormous fort.

"Take my room. It's on the other side of the tower and stayed mostly intact." He pointed down the hall behind me. "Down there, the last door on the right."

"Won't you need it?"

He laughed softly. "Captains don't get much sleep on the eve before a battle. Take the room. And clean your arm."

Before I could thank him, his face twisted into a frown. "Have you seen Marek? I can't find him anywhere. Darius has ordered him on watch."

I went silent, unsure how to proceed with that answer. Talina had shut the door in my face. I figured that meant she wasn't finished with Marek. Not for a long time.

"He's... occupied." That was probably the nicest way I could put it. "You'll need to find someone to replace him."

"Occupied?"

Do I really have to spell it out?

"Talina," I said, feeling my skin blaze. It had nothing to do with how overly warm and stuffy it was in the tower.

That earned me a surprised glance, followed by an uncharacteristic smile. "Well, that's something else that often happens on the eve of a battle." Jad looked pleased for his friend. "I guess I'll leave him to it."

"Probably wise."

I, for one, would not want to walk into that room again anytime soon.

Jad didn't leave. I didn't either. We stared at each other, my insides tumbling into a free fall. It didn't help that I'd put the mental image of what our best friends were doing in our minds. Each silent moment only seemed to ramp up the tension.

I became aware of just how close we stood. My breath shook out of me as realisation struck.

The Bone Grimoire was destroyed.

The Grand Masters' magic was renounced.

And that means...

"We're free of the curse," I blurted, my pulse fluttering all over the place.

Jad stared at me, that look cracking the armour I'd mentally worn. His gaze dropped to my lips, and every nerve in my body lit up. I could have stood on my toes and kissed him right then, could tell that he wanted me to, but instead I looked away.

Conflicting emotions weighed me down.

One chance out of three.

The likelihood that I would die tomorrow was high. I couldn't do that to Jad. I couldn't love him and then die on him.

Keep your distance.

But I couldn't. His eyes had me pinned in place, the desire in them reflecting my own. He pushed closer to me, his warm hand cupping my cheek, gently stroking the skin there. The sensation sent fire and heat all through my body. His breathing changed, his mouth only a small space away from mine.

"Zaya...."

The plea in his tone unravelled me. My control, my reasoning, all of it slipped away as I leaned forward, my mouth colliding with his. The kiss was hot and urgent and full of need, the days of built-up yearning no longer able to be denied. Jad's arms encircled me as he deepened the kiss, his tongue pushing against my own, his fingers trailing gentle lines along the small of my back. I was on a high. An addictive rush. I ran my fingers through his dark hair, soaking up the ecstasy of our kiss, amazed that even that simple movement could make him shudder.

"Excuse my interruption."

I pulled away, startled by the voice, mortified when I realised who it was who'd caught us.

Commander Macaslan glared at Jad like she wanted to peck his eyes out. "Captain Arden, you are required in the war room."

I'd never seen Jad look so rattled. His lips were swollen, his uniform ruffled, his cheeks still heated from our kiss. Jad was five years older than me, but right then he looked as nervous as a teenager who'd been caught trying to sneak into his crush's bedroom.

The commander turned her sharp eyes on me. My face flushed under her stinging gaze. "Go to your room and get some rest. *You.*" Her voice was as harsh as a razor on Jad. "Come with me."

Unable to disobey a direct order, Jad followed Macaslan across the hall. Before he disappeared in the war room, though, he stole a final look at me, his eyes invoking something as powerful and hungry inside me as our kiss had. A promise of more to come.

I turned away, deciding it would be way too dangerous to take him up on his offer and use his room, but I found myself drifting down that way regardless.

Go to your own room, Zaya.

But I didn't want to clean up the mess that waited for me there. Besides, it would be dangerous to sleep in a bed that could have glass in it. What if I missed a piece and cut myself in the night?

And Jad said he wouldn't be using the room. I doubted Macaslan would let him out of her sight again after what she'd witnessed. Not that she had any right or say in the matter.

I found Jad's room. It was more spacious than mine and must have belonged to one of the ULD's commanding officers. There was a canopy bed draped with black fabric, the silk sheets fit for a king. Judging by how tight the sheets had been tucked, I didn't think anyone had ever slept in the bed. I checked the wooden armoire. Empty. Just as I'd expected. No one had occupied this room. I sat on the bed. The window had been blown out, the glass shards scattered beneath, but other than that, everything remained untouched.

He told me to use the room.

Jad said he wouldn't be getting any sleep tonight.

I wondered if my grandmother was wrangling with him right now, as deadly as a stagma about to spit fire.

I looked at my hands. They were filthy. Even my clothes were smeared with dirt, some stains so dark that I knew it was dry blood. When had I last showered? I realised it had been on the *Crown of Glory*. That felt like an age ago. The most hygiene I'd acquired since then had been what I could achieve with wipes, deodorant, and a toothbrush. How had Jad managed to touch me when he'd smelt clean and amazing?

I wandered into the adjoining bathroom and peeled out of my clothes. In the shower, I cranked up the water to the highest heat, appreciating the steam and warmth for a full ten minutes before I slathered my skin in soap and cleaned the cut on my arm. After that, I massaged shampoo into my scalp, aghast at how dirty the water became as it went down the drain.

I found a spare toothbrush in the cabinet under the sink, cleaned my teeth, and wandered back into the bedroom. There was a wardrobe in the far corner. Luckily for me, a white nightdress was inside. Actually, there were quite a few dresses and dissent uniforms, the clothes femininely tailored.

I stood corrected. The bed wasn't suited for a king but a queen.

Fine by me.

Dressing quickly in the nightgown, I flung myself into the bed beneath the silk sheets, savouring the softness of them against my skin. It was already dark in the bedroom. The only light was from the broken window, the curtain blowing agape, the glass underneath glittering against the purple and white flashes that lit the sky outside. The thunder was almost comforting. When I closed my eyes, I imagined I was falling softly to sleep against the sounds of a summer storm.

I WOKE some hours later to the click of the door gently opening. My entire body went rigid as someone, definitely male, slipped inside and started stripping down.

Shit.

Does someone else think this room is empty?

After a moment's consideration, I decided I needed to say something.

"This room is occupied."

The person jumped, nearly toppling into the armoire, and swore. A light blinked on.

I stared, my mouth ajar. My eyes roamed over Jad's half-naked body, his trousers hanging low over his waist. My cheeks coloured, and I immediately went tense under the sheets, embarrassingly aware how revealing my nightdress was.

"Zaya, what are you doing in here?"

What...?

What am I doing here?

"You told me I could use the room," I said too fast, my words a stumbling blur.

His face went blank, but his eyes glinted with recollection. "I didn't think you actually would. Not after your grandmother caught us."

Providence, he was right. I should have gone back to my own room. Should have dealt with the mess. What had I been thinking?

You know exactly what you were thinking, a small voice inside me teased. *You were hoping for this.*

I swallowed, again experiencing a wave of intense longing. My eyes trailed the low curve of Jad's stomach, all the way up the hard, sculpted muscles of his abdomen to his chest.

Providence save me.

I have to get out of this room.

I realised the absurdity of it all now.

Mortified, I climbed out of the bed. "I'll leave. I'm sorry."

I was halfway across the room when he reached for my wrist. "Your grandmother is down the hall. She'll see you. She knows this is my room. And I don't fancy facing her wrath again."

I understood what he implied. It wouldn't be a good look if I left now.

Grandmother. Not commander.

So she did have a firm word with him.

If Macaslan saw me leave this bedroom, she'd probably throw Jad into a pit full of lycanthors.

He was still holding my wrist. His touch sent an electric current through me, and I saw that touching my skin affected him just as badly. His chest was rising and falling, and I wondered if his heartbeat was fluttering like my own. I thought about what might happen tomorrow, that it might be my last day on this earth, and decided I didn't want to spend the night alone. I didn't want to be alone any night I had left.

"Jad—"

But my words were cut off as he wrenched me against him, his lips crushing mine. His hand tangled in my hair, then moved down my body, sliding over my skin. His kiss consumed me, hungry and powerful and devouring. I ran my hands over his chest, a tremble rippling through him, and I didn't object when he swept the nightdress over my head and tossed it aside on the floor. Jad lifted me in his arms and carried me to the bed, gently laying me on the sheets.

If I wanted to put a stop to this, now would be the time, but I trusted Jad. Nothing in the moment felt more perfect than this. I ran my fingers along the waistband of his trousers, pulling them down. I could feel the pounding pulse in his neck as I trailed kisses across his skin. He brought his lips back to mine, his tongue brushing against my own. I arched my body, startled by how easily it made him groan. He lowered himself slowly, every touch, every movement sending fire through my veins, our bodies wrapped together long into the night.

CHAPTER 34

I woke up more refreshed than I had in months, my body pleasantly sore. Jad was asleep beside me, his eyelids fluttering every so often.

I watched him sleep, my mind playing over the memory of last night. I wished we'd caved to our needs much earlier, before the Bone Grimoire, before the sleeping curse and the Dark Divide, but fate had never been on our side back then. It wasn't on our side now. One night was not enough. I didn't want to die. Not if this was the future. Not if it meant I'd wake up beside Jad every morning.

He stirred, his eyes opening slowly. His lips formed into an idle smile, and he leaned forward, pressing our mouths together in an intoxicating kiss. My blood heated, warm and sweet and wonderful, my skin tingling all over. I didn't know how long we remained that way, kissing and tangled up each in other, hands exploring.

Knowing this moment couldn't last forever, I pulled away. "What time is it?"

Outside, Orthrask was a perfect vision of fires and storms, making night and day impossible to define.

Jad checked the small clock on the bedside table. "It's 10:00 a.m."

"10:00 a.m.?" I repeated incredulously.

Everyone will be looking for us.

I made to move, but Jad gathered me into his arms again.

He brushed a kiss over my temple, his voice a whisper against my skin. "Relax. The war council isn't meeting until twelve. That's Darius's way of ensuring people get their proper rest."

I let my head fall back on his shoulder, trying to soothe the anxiety that had worked its way into my stomach. Tonight, we would strike the Vrabkor Citadel. In a few short hours, we would either be victorious or conquered.

"I'm afraid," I admitted.

If I didn't defeat Morgomoth, if the battle ended in bloodshed and he won, what would become of the world? What would happen to Jad? To Talina and Marek? To all my friends? From the moment I'd woken as a ten-year-old in the Brendlash Orphanage, not a clue who I was or where I'd come from, my life had been a lonely one, but in the last several days, life had gifted me with a grandmother and a father. And it had brought me Jad. They were worth fighting for, but not having solved that damned riddle, the true meaning of the spell still elusive, made me terrified that I was leading everyone to their doom.

Jad cradled me against him, his fingers tangled in my hair. There was a tremulous note in his voice. "I'm afraid too."

"You are?"

I couldn't believe it. Jad had been involved in his fair share of battles. He was an experienced soldier, brave and undefeated. The scars along his body were a story of every obstacle he'd overcome.

His face went stark. "I'm always scared. But more so now."

More afraid after everything we'd shared.

I pressed a kiss on his lips. "How do you overcome fear, then?"

He smiled sadly at me. "You don't. You just have to enjoy the moments life gives you, appreciating that they might be your last."

I considered that. "Well, if that's the case, we have two hours to spare. How should we appreciate the time?"

He caught the hidden suggestion in my words and pulled me on top of him.

AFTER SHOWERING and changing into a pair of slim-fitted trousers and a shirt, I snuck out of Jad's room. I wasn't ashamed— I would have happily walked hand in hand with him, stealing kisses—but I feared if Macaslan saw, she might very well skewer Jad with a lance. He'd told me about the little discussion they'd had, which only increased my aggravation with her. Macaslan didn't have any right to intervene. Grandmother or not, she should stay out of our business.

Gondalesh was a hive of activity. More Haxsan Guard soldiers had arrived from the portal, and there wasn't a quiet space to be found in the tower. The warriors were armed, their postures relaxed for the most part, but still the stronghold carried a tension that was oppressive, like we were in the midst of a deadly storm. Everyone was braced and ready for an attack.

At five minutes to twelve, I joined the stream of generals, commanders, and intelligence officers who entered the war room, feeling 100 percent out of my depth. Jad was there. He was back to being the captain everyone honoured and respected, his impassive face a far cry from the flames that had sizzled in his eyes last night. My blood sang remembering it.

More officers entered the room, and I lost sight of Jad as I was wedged into a corner. The spacious chamber was still not enough to accommodate all of us, and we were forced to stand shoulder to shoulder. Darius and Macaslan stood at the front, presiding over the assembly.

The senator cleared his throat and started the briefing. It turned out that all evening, a dozen alchemist casters and the silver-thorned witch had performed a series of enchantments on the portal. Not only had they managed to connect several conduits from each of the warships to the main gateway, but they'd opened a second access outside Vrabkor's celestial shield. It meant we wouldn't be enduring a long hike to reach the citadel. Better yet, if the battle did go against us, our forces could flee, using the portal to travel at the speed of light across Orthrask to the ships.

I would be leading the first attack, or at least my necromancy would be used to send the first wave of chak-lorks through the celestial shield. The goal would be to bring the shield down. The second wave would be the fire-crusaders, which would fly in from the ships to drop their bombs. And finally, the third wave would see the Haxsan Guard soldiers charge onto Vrabkor, attacking and slaying whatever foe they met on the frontlines. Isgrad and I would be using the distraction to buy ourselves time to sneak into the citadel.

It sounded so easy when Darius explained it, but I knew—I suspected everyone knew— that the plan was far from concrete. Anything could go wrong.

"The attack will be at midnight," Darius informed us. "Rest. Prepare yourselves. Ready your troops. You need to be in formation by the portal at half past eleven tonight."

Except for shuffling feet and a few murmurs, there was silence.

"That will be all."

There was a swift exodus from the room. I hung back, waiting until everyone had departed and there was only me and Darius left. He was looking over a set of mapographics that reflected Orthrask's scanned terrain.

The senator's face was as hard as stone when he heard me approach and peered up. "You disagree with the plan, don't you?"

I wrestled with the right words to say. "I don't know if it'll work. If it does, and I do get inside that citadel… if I defeat Morgomoth, I need you to promise me something."

He gave me an assessing look. "This sound serious. Perhaps I should call for your grandmother."

"She's to know nothing about this."

He stilled. "Oh? And what exactly is this about?"

Sweat broke out along my brow the longer he looked at me. "What I'm about to ask stays between us. I need you to swear on your magic that you will do this."

"I'm not in the habit of making promises that I can't keep."

"Please," I begged, feeling a stirring behind my eyes.

I didn't know whether it was what he saw in me then—the struggle, the desperation on my face—but he leaned back against the table and crossed his arms. I wasn't sure if his smile was mocking or full of pity. "Tell me what it is I'm promising."

IN MY ROOM THAT EVENING, I sharpened my athame-sabre and loaded my cast-shooter. My weapons set, I focused on cleaning the mess from last night. Glass crunched under my boots. The furniture looked like it had been ransacked by looters. It turned out my room had been damaged the worst. I'd gotten the brunt of Morgomoth's wrath.

I sorted through the debris, not because it needed doing—I doubted I'd be returning to this place again after tonight—but because I needed to do something. I had to keep my mind occupied; otherwise, the sensation that a swarm of hostile bees was buzzing in my stomach would start all over again. Jad was in another council meeting. Talina and Marek were doing... well, I didn't want to know what they were doing. Annaka and Bronislav? I'd inquired about them at the makeshift hospital ward that had been set up in the lower levels of the tower. They were still in recovery and unable to receive guests. I guessed that meant they weren't taking part in the attack on Vrabkor. I was pleased about that. That was two less friends I had to worry about.

A knock sounded on the door.

"Come in."

Talina entered. She was smiling, but it was laced with worry.

I raised my eyes at her. "Finished with Marek, have you?"

She stilled for a moment, then levelled a playful glare at me. "You can't talk, Miss Wayward. You were seen leaving the captain's bedroom this morning."

I smirked. "Really? I thought I'd been discreet."

Her low laugh rippled through the room. "You? Discreet? You would suck at being a spy."

My lips curled upward. I was surprised by my pealing laughter. I couldn't remember when it had last happened like this. Certainly not since before Tarahik.

Talina must have been thinking the same thing, because her gaze flattened, serious again. "How are you feeling about all of this?"

The question sent a spurt of unease through me. I knew what she was asking.

"Fine, I think. As good as anyone could be who's about to go to war."

A war where winning was entirely dependent on me.

No pressure.

A whirlwind of emotions shifted over her face. "They're

putting a dinner on in the main hall. I came to see if you would like to go." She sounded hopeful.

My scalp prickled and my fingers went tingly at the ends. The nervous energy had spread into my gut. "I don't think I could eat even if I wanted to."

The optimism vanished from her eyes. "Right, well... I'm leaving Gondalesh soon, so I just thought—"

I drew in a short breath. "You're leaving?"

"After dinner. The healers have been ordered to return to the ships and prepare the hospitals on board. Annaka and Bronislav have already been moved there."

I knew what this was now. This was Talina's last chance to spend some time with me in case....

"Don't you want to share this time with Marek?"

An awkward colour sprang to her cheeks. "I've seen enough of Marek to last me a lifetime."

A grin curved my lips. "No, you haven't."

She laughed. "You're right. I haven't."

And then the waterworks started. Tears streamed down her cheeks. "I said goodbye to him. Now all I can do is pray to providence that he doesn't get hurt... or die." A heavy sob worked its way out of her throat.

"Oh, Talina." I barrelled forward, wrapping my arms around her, comforting my poor friend in her time of need. I cried long and hard myself. I didn't want to say goodbye. I didn't want her suffering like this. She'd already lost Lainie. I couldn't stand for her to lose Marek either.

In the end, neither of us went down to dinner. We sat on my bed and talked, like two girls who were parting ways to attend colleges on the other side of the world, not about to be separated by war. We both started crying again when the time came for her to leave. I hugged her, savouring the moment.

She looked at me, her green eyes luminous. "Remember to

eat. You'll need your strength. And don't you dare die. If you do, I'll never forgive you."

I wiped at my eyes. "I'll try not to."

And then she was gone. The door closed behind her with a resounding boom, as though announcing an important chapter had ended in my life.

I REMAINED IN MY ROOM, watching the clock tick. It moved slowly and yet too fast toward 11:00 p.m. I should have tried to get some sleep, or have eaten something, but my anxiety was paralysing.

Maybe I'll go outside? Try to be around people?

No. That will just make it worse.

The tension in Gondalesh would only serve to reinforce the truth with a damaging impact.

In just a few short hours, I might be dead.

I paced the room, feeling more and more like a caged animal. At ten minutes to eleven, I changed into my Haxsan Guard uniform. I sheathed my athame-sabre, two short blades, and holstered a pair of cast-shooters at my sides, then stared at myself in the fragmented mirror. The cracks reflected a broken girl. Looking at her eyes, I saw the tortured soul inside.

At 11:15 p.m. I left my room, making my way down the various passages and flights that led to the portal. There were other soldiers too. No one spoke. No murmurs or barbs or jokes like there usually had been in Tarahik. There was only determination, seriousness, and grit in people's eyes. Some held the poignant realisation that what waited on the other side of the portal was either victory or death.

I took my place in the line. In the great hall ahead, ribbons of blue light gleamed like droplets of rain in a sunrise. As I approached the radiance, though, I saw my first glance of the portal—a gigantic aperture, the surface ebbing and flowing like delicate waves in an ocean. A horrible bout of sickness swept through me. It reminded me of the doorway to the other side, as though the otherworld knew we were doomed and was greeting us with open arms.

I watched the soldiers enter the portal in droves. I hadn't yet stepped into the great hall when a hand grasped my fingers, wrenching me into what appeared to be a broom closet. It was too dark for me to tell, and besides, my attention was quickly taken by Jad. He pressed a final stolen kiss on my lips. It was delicate at first but grew into something more intense and hungrier as our mouths tasted and teased. I pulled him closer, savouring the feel of his lips on mine. It was a kiss that consumed me and, for a short while, obliterated my anxiety. But the moment we reluctantly drew away, the dread returned twofold.

Jad's breathing was heavy. He had both hands cupped beneath my jaw, and even though his callused fingers held me gently, they were trembling. That was what startled me the most—that he was afraid.

"We'll see each other again soon," he said softly.

We both knew he was lying.

"Whatever happens, I love you." I drew him into a second, longer kiss that ended far too quickly.

"I love you too."

And then he was gone, the door closing with a click behind him.

I lingered in the closet for a moment longer, regaining my breath, summoning my strength to tackle the task ahead.

So much to lose. So much at risk.

Please. I want to live.

I didn't know who I was asking.

Providence. Fate. Magic itself.

A heavy weight settled in my stomach. That sensation only amplified when I snuck out of the closet and stepped into the great hall to face the portal. The soldiers ahead disappeared in the swirling, dipping folds of its surface, and then it was my turn. The wind that derived from the portal was so strong that it took my hair out of its braid, tangling the ends around my face.

Panic. Fear. Love. Hope.

It all swept like an avalanche through my soul.

The portal was glowing blindingly white now, as though it knew exactly what it could take from me.

I stepped up to the dais, closed my eyes, and let my frail body float into the spinning eddies.

CHAPTER 35

I emerged into a world of fire and shadow, struggling to calm my racing pulse. Ahead, lit by devastating flashes of lightning, was the Vrabkor Citadel. Gondalesh was a resort in comparison. Vrabkor was built into the mouth of a volcano, rising in an array of soaring towers and piercing turrets. It was a black monolith of evil. I could feel the darkness in the very ground I stood on. Smelt death and suffering in the air.

The Haxsan Guard troops stood in formation, staring out at what the humans would have called an unholy landscape. Darius and Macaslan had certainly accomplished a sizeable combat brigade, which had been divided up into tactical units and waited on the knoll.

"Cadet Wayward."

A soldier crossed the flat-topped hillock, his face streaked with sweat from the abominable heat. His lips were moving, but it took me a moment to make out the words.

"Cadet Wayward," he repeated.

No one had ever addressed me with that title before.

His brow furrowed. My hesitance must not have inspired his confidence. "This way, please."

I followed soundlessly, the tension inside me seeping into terror. The soldier led me through the units, their whispers dying as I passed. From what I could glean, Darius and Macaslan had organised the units in a wedge formation. I wished I'd paid more attention during the war council. Hell, I wished I'd paid more attention in my field navigation and tactical classes back at Tarahik.

I arrived at the front line. Darius and Macaslan assessed the scene, looking like a king and queen united in bringing us a swift victory. My grandmother gave me a stern glare. If she was worried about my task ahead, she didn't reveal it. A flash of silver at her side revealed her athame-sabre, the runes already alight, the sword fuelled with her magic. Her eyes returned to the citadel, and she bared her teeth. She looked as vicious and capable of destruction as a stagma. My grandmother was certainly not a woman I'd want to oppose in a battle.

Isgrad slipped toward me and said in a voice too soft for the others to hear, "You can do this. I have faith in you. And I will not leave your side. We do this together."

My guts twisted all over again, but I forced a small smile. One day, after all of this was over, I hoped we'd have time to make a real connection. I wanted a chance to know Isgrad and... maybe feel comfortable enough to call him Dad. We could give Briya the proper memorial she deserved, because I was certain Isgrad had never been granted the chance to mourn and say goodbye to her.

If I survive.

The thought loomed over me.

The stillness in Darius's face alerted me of movement ahead. Our entire army seemed to pause with surprise. The dark ebony smoke that had crossed the land and hindered our view disappeared, revealing the enormity of what we truly faced. The volcano stood in a large hollow, as though the ground had fallen out from the earth, as though the entire landscape around the citadel had given up and died. Rivers of lava streamed down the sides of the mountain, creating a moat of liquid fire in the sunken ground. The celestial shield enclosed Vrabkor in an impassable barrier.

And behind that barrier stood the enemy lines, crawling with black shapes. The sheer size of their number caused my legs to turn to water. Morgomoth's army was an assortment of chak-lorks and dissent rebels, the clangs and clashes of armour and weapons a war-hammering drumbeat. Stationed ahead of our front lines were our own chak-lorks, or what Darius had referred to as the first wave. A ring of dark stone had been fastened around their necks. I could hear the creatures biting and growling, but they never stepped out of line.

I passed Darius a questioning look. "What are the collars for?"

He turned his gaze away from me. "They're halo-binds. The alchemists created them. The halos incapacitate any wearer. It was the only way we could capture the chak-lorks and control them without relying on your necromancy."

Something inside me bristled at that. Again, that feeling that there was more he wasn't saying afflicted me. It would have taken an entire production line to create that many halo-binds. It would have taken months. How long had Darius suspected that this war was going to occur?

"It's time," the senator announced. "We need to bring that shield down."

Orders were barked across our unified army. My eyes found Jad, who stood in front of his own unit, shouting commands. Again, I was trapped in warring emotions: fear and love. I fought to tear my gaze from him; otherwise, I'd crumble apart, unable to conjure my magic.

My heart hanging by a thread, I summoned my necromancy.

It burst from me in rippling light, blinding, powerful, and invigorating. I heard a few startled cries, but I focused on the magic, sending it in a wave down the valley. It latched on to the chaklorks, sinking into what was left of their flesh. I had access to their bodies, but at the same time, their minds pressed down on me. Sorrow and anguish. Some were screaming. Screaming and begging to be released. Their bodies were a prison.

"You will be free," I promised, hearing the conviction in my mind. *"One last fight and the otherworld awaits you. Now destroy our enemy and bring those shields down."*

My army of corpses charged, hissing and snarling like savage wolves. A rumbling vibrated through the ground that made every nerve in my body tingle with fright, and the hairs along my arms rose in stiff dread. The chak-lorks breached the shields. I couldn't say it was a bloodbath—the dead didn't bleed—but the screams and frantic howls, the tearing of flesh and cracking of bones as the two dead armies merged was what nightmares were made of.

I had never seen how chak-lorks destroyed celestial shields. They rained hell upon the barrier, breaking it apart with their arms, hands, and teeth. I was startled that the shield had already started to fragment just by our lines crossing the boundary, as though it were made of nothing more than smoke.

Our army cheered.

This is too easy.

Morgomoth would never create a celestial shield this weak.

Darius raised a radio to his mouth and barked an order into the receiver.

A sound more menacing than thunder crackled across the sky. I looked over my shoulder to see a mass of black fire-crusaders hurtling forward in a V-formation. The second wave. I knew the fighter jets could travel long distances in a short amount of time, but across Orthrask at this fast rate was impressive. The jets were loud enough to silence a storm as they sliced through the air. The first blast hit the shield. A trail of fire gushed down the barrier, the ground inundated by shock waves. Explosions rippled across the sky, volleys of caster-fire sending sparks and smoke over the shield.

My breath hitched. "I don't like this."

"I don't either," Isgrad admitted. He was staring at the battle, his face bone white.

"It's almost like Morgomoth wants us to break the shield down."

This is a game. He's planned something.

Anxiety swelled in me.

"The shield is a distraction," I shouted too late.

Screams bellowed from our forces at the rear. I turned to Darius and Macaslan at the same time darkness swept in from the horizon. A galactic storm the size of the island raced across Orthrask, pinning our army in like cattle surrounded by rising floodwater. Lightning flashed, the echoes of thunder reverberating through my skull. I searched for Jad but couldn't find him in the sea of terrified faces that looked up into the formidable storm.

We can't pull back.

We can't even turn around.

The storm was everywhere, coming from every direction. Dissent rebels charged from the churning darkness, waving athame-sabres and cast-shooters. It was impossible to size up their unending army. We were vastly outnumbered and unprepared. A hail of bullets rained across the Haxsan Guard forces. From the skies, winged creatures flew down. Fear made it feel like my organs had liquefied inside me.

Winged chak-lorks.

The creatures' leathery, dark wingspans ran from their shoulders right down to their ankles, allowing them to easily manoeuvre the heavy winds. No doubt, they were Hadar's last creation and her final gift to Morgomoth.

Water chak-lorks. Fire chak-lorks. And now air chak-lorks.

Morgomoth had employed them with perfect timing.

The winged chak-lorks plunged, soaring through the Haxsan Guard like torpedos. Men and women were thrown from the ground where they stood, ripped apart or tossed metres across the battle. All around me were the screams of the dying. Blood sprayed, falling from the skies like rain to make a terrible paste on the ground.

I saw Macaslan locked in a wrestling match with four dissent rebels. She struck and sliced at her would-be capturers, decapitating heads and cutting off limbs. Next to her, Darius stabbed one dissent rebel and snapped the neck of another. He brought his sabre down, beheading the bodies so the dead couldn't rise, before he efficiently moved on to his next kill.

A jolt went through me when I recognised the athame-sabre ablaze in flames. Jad struck at his assailants. Marek was beside him, dispatching any adversary, either chak-lork or dissent rebel, that approached. Our enemy seemed to recognise Jad as the leader of his unit and came tearing toward him like feral beasts. And like a savage animal, Jad retaliated. He met their blows, swiftly enacting his vengeance. Two enemies. And then four. And then six. On and on they kept coming. Jad had to be tiring. He ducked a near-cut to his arm, rolling agilely onto his knees, then sliced his athame-sabre right through the legs of his opponent. Jad moved on to his next foe, then his next, cutting them down one after another. I lost sight of Jad and Marek among the fighting and gore. I tore forward, desperate to see where they'd gone, but a hand latched on to my shoulder.

I was jerked back with enough force that I nearly lost my footing.

Isgrad clenched his teeth, which looked peculiarly white amid the ash and soot that gusted the air. "We have to go to the citadel. This is our only chance."

I knew he was right. The celestial shield was destroyed, parts of it plummeting like an imploding star. Digesting the full weight of what I had to do, I silently nodded and ran with Isgrad down the valley. Thick clouds of black vapour pressed down on us, the flames and smoke torturous on my lungs.

We reached the bridge that ran across the moat. Up close, the molten rock below was expansive. More like a river than an actual moat. Huge power surged over the earth as more explosions rippled through the battle. The bridge shook, knocking me flat. Isgrad landed next to me, shielding his face as rocks and burning embers spilled over us. Orthrask was responding to the destruction that wracked its surface. In retribution, it had inflicted an earthquake from deep underneath.

"Come on." Isgrad pulled me onto my feet.

Fires and smoke belched from the volcano, but we carried on, sidestepping bits of the celestial shield that showered down like hail. I blinked the black spots out of my sight. I could not afford dizziness now. I could not afford to think about Jad or the others I loved. All that mattered was reaching the black doors that waited at the end of the bridge—the door that would grant us entry into Vrabkor.

A powerful roar cleaved the world. Isgrad shouted at me not to look back, which of course meant I did. At first, it was the rancid smell that alerted me to their presence. Stagma surged from the maelstrom of darkness, shooting jets of fire onto the battle that raged above the ridge. Lainie had said the dissent rebels captured the creatures, killed them, and let Morgomoth resurrect their bodies. He'd made them into weapons. And fight they did. The stagma's claws snared Haxsan Guard soldiers by the handful. They flew into the air with their gigantic wings flapping so fast and strong, I felt the undulations from here. They either feasted on the soldiers or dropped their captives with bored interest before diving to repeat the process all over again. It was horrible seeing men and women fall to their deaths, their screams drowned out by wet thwacks that sounded like fruit splattering.

Isgrad's eyes sparked with anger.

Good. We'll need that rage to fight Morgomoth.

We continued, our progress slow across the bridge, the seismic activity forcing us to take cover on the ground more times than I wanted to count. We'd nearly made it halfway across the bridge when something formless lunged from the sky. There was no time to shout a warning before the winged chak-lork gripped Isgrad by the shoulders. He cried out as the beast's talons burrowed into his flesh and tore him off the ground.

I screamed, reaching out for Isgrad's legs, but it was too late. The creature ascended, rising up the citadel until Isgrad became only a speck in the air, and then… nothing. He was gone. I could no longer see him.

No. No!

This was Morgomoth's doing.

He'd taken Isgrad.

Which meant he's been watching us all this time.

Isgrad was his final bargaining chip.

I can't do this.

Not alone.

Self-doubt paralysed me. It stilled my heart and thinned my blood. I couldn't breathe.

Ahead, the doors to Vrabkor shuddered open in mocking welcome.

I have to do this.

Otherwise, everything will be a waste.

Darius and Macaslan's plans had been obliterated before they'd even started.

I'm the only one who can finish this now.

Before more fear could incapacitate me, I barrelled forward. My own fire was burning inside me now, the only thing I had against the rising apprehension, which was trying to probe my mind with nightmare darkness. The dark was my fear. I had to hang on to that light. My necromancy. The only weapon I now had.

I reached the black doors. They were at least ten metres high, decorated with skulls, thorn carvings, and serpents.

I can do this.

I will do this.

I ran inside.

Behind me, the doors slammed, sealing me in darkness.

CHAPTER 36

My breathing came out in shallow gasps. I scrambled for the small flashlight that was secured to my belt, but my hands were trembling so badly, my fingers seemed to slide over every surface except for the button. Wherever I was, it was ominously quiet, which only served to make me panic more. When the coldness rushed in, I knew I wasn't alone. I sensed something—no, *somethings*— drawing closer. I fumbled for the flashlight again.

Come on. Come on.

Got it.

The flashlight came alive, the light bleeding into the darkness ahead. I stood in a great hall that was rotunda-shaped, the walls made of solid black stone that reached higher than my flashlight could reveal, making me feel like I'd been closed off in an oubliette. Faces stared out, heightening the tension that had become as taut as wire in my body. Not real faces, thank providence. Demonic, gargoyle-like façades, grinning at me with incisor teeth. At the back of the hall, a sprawling staircase led to the citadel's upper levels.

I stepped toward the flight at the same time a shadow rose to my left. Another came from the right, then another. Four in total, advancing slowly from various directions. A hiss that was both snakelike and breathy sent a piercing chill across my skin. The beam from my flashlight wobbled. I recognised the forms as they stepped into the flickering rays. Cloaked figures, the robes as dark as the loneliest abyss.

The Four Revenants.

They closed in like a pack of prowling wolves, carrying blades of steel that tapered to a thin point.

They will not kill me.

They couldn't. Not while my life was still linked to their master's. But that didn't mean they couldn't capture me. The revenants soundlessly approached, sabres poised to attack. Beneath their cowls, ivory bone and razor-sharp teeth appeared, their eyes orbs of black that disappeared in the hollows of their cheeks, as though the darkness in their souls had bled out.

I unsheathed my athame-sabre.

The monsters charged with vicious speed, and my training kicked in. I swung my sabre, blocking their attacks, then spun to parry the next blows. Their black eyes met mine with brutal menace. I clenched my teeth, defending and blocking. The flashlight had long fallen from my hand and had sputtered out. The only light source now was from the runes that glowed from my athame-sabre, which seemed to be burning like a sunrise ascending over a peak. The revenants snarled, their shrill cries ringing through the room, so piercing that I thought my eardrums might burst. They pulled away from the searing light, their bony fingers clawing at their eyes as though they'd been permanently blinded. They couldn't look at me.

A moment later, I understood why. It wasn't only my athame-sabre glowing like sunlight but all of me. Rippling brightness filled the room, as radiant and dangerous as lightning. This was not a remnant of power left over from the Grand Masters or the Bone Grimoire. This was my necromancy, charged to its full strength, enveloping me and the entire room.

My anger fuelled it. The magic continued to build until I could see nothing but light myself. It was all around me, pressing down with unrelenting strength. I thought about Jad and the way he conjured fire from his fingers, and I concentrated on doing the same. My magic raged so fiercely that when I could no longer hold it, I sent the searing light across the room. The revenants didn't have time to pull back. The light engulfed them, their shrieks of agony making my gut curdle. Light shot out of their eyes. Their fingers were burning, turning into crisps, their bones blackened.

I sensed rather than felt the door to the otherworld open beside me. A second later, I knew what place fate had deemed worthy for the revenants. The demons scuttled on all fours, crossing the room like spiders. They latched on to the revenants, dragging them across the floor. Unlike Trajan, the wraiths didn't score their nails into the stone to prevent being hauled into the otherworld. They no longer had fingers to do so. The demons lugged the revenants to the otherworld. The door closed with a resounding boom, the wicked screams suddenly cut off, leaving the room in silence once more.

I collapsed onto my knees. My magic dimmed, exhaustion replacing what had been the burning strength in my heart.

Keep going.

You have to.

For Isgrad's sake.

For everyone's sake.

I inhaled deep breaths, and then I was back on my feet, pivoting around to the stairway. The revenants had been a distraction, a way to tire me out, but damned if I was done yet. Isgrad was right. I had my mother's impulsiveness and my father's temper—and my grandmother's tenacity. Morgomoth was going to meet the full brunt of my magic.

I climbed the stairs. My body throbbed, my head spiralling with desperation and fear. I dreaded to think about the kind of torture Isgrad might be suffering at this moment. I pushed more force into my legs. Up and up I went, this black monolith of a citadel seeming to have no end. Every so often, I heard the raging battle outside and saw through the windows the cruel, bitter landscape. Orthrask was besieged in flames, the two armies opposing each other in endless destruction. Somewhere in that hellhole was Jad.

End this.

On I went. Every so often, dark shapes loomed in passageways and antechambers. I was halfway up one staircase when something whirling and dark flew at me. The impact knocked me against the wall, my teeth chattering hard. Pain jarred up my spine, but I blinked through the cloudiness, grabbing the athamesabre I'd dropped. The creature shrieked from above, its ungainly limbs bearing down. A chak-lork. One of the winged creatures that I had no control over.

It had brought friends.

They reminded me of overly large cave bats as they dived from the ceiling, lashing out with lengthy claws. I veered at the last second, swinging my blade. I sliced at wings and legs. Snarls and howls of pain filled the stairway, but I didn't stop. I couldn't kill these creatures, as Morgomoth's necromancy would just make them rise again, so I aimed for their heads, ruthlessly cutting through rotting tendons and bones. Their blood sprayed in every direction; I tasted it on my lips and felt it stringing through my hair. The light blazed inside me again. I drove the magic forward, catching the chak-lorks mid-flight like they'd been struck by lightning. A roiling mass of flames ignited the creatures. Their bones popped like wood in a crackling fireplace, and their rotting skin melted right off. What was left of them fell into piles of ashes on the steps.

So they can *be destroyed.*

My eyes stinging with sweat, I kept going. My legs screamed at me, and I had to harden my will to make it up the last flight.

I have to be nearing the top, surely?

I found a window and looked out. Dizziness clutched at my mind. The land was very far below, strewn with billowing smoke. I scrambled back from the window.

Yes, definitely not far.

Which meant….

I arrived at a door. Red light poured out, as though whatever hid inside that room contained the citadel's beating heart. I advanced slowly, terror and reluctance surging through me, but I couldn't turn away. Not now. I couldn't let the self-doubt and the fear win now that I was this close.

Dread flooded my veins, my body both too hot and too cold at the same time. Summoning a final bout of courage, I entered the room.

MY EYES TOOK in the magnificent chamber. It was more impressive than the Black Palace, the Isla Necropolis, and Tarahik combined. Dark wood floors, as black as a river at midnight, gleamed against the torchlight. Polished ebony walls reached up to a ceiling where crimson flags hung from rafters. Each flag was embroidered with the United League of Dissent's insignia, a griffin and eagle holding a swastika. For as long as I lived—which might not be for much longer—that symbol would always inspire fear.

On a dais sitting on a throne made out of bones was Morgomoth. He wasn't a king presiding over the room but an emperor of a new realm. His skeleton was as black as burnt firewood, the wraiths that made up his body swirling in and out of the smoke and flames.

He tapped his thin fingers against the armrest with bored impatience, raising what remained of a scarred brow. "My esteemed niece *finally* arrives. Have you had enough bloodshed yet? War is a nasty business, and not something I particularly enjoy participating in."

"I'm not your niece," I retorted, throwing acidity in every syllable of the word. "And you started this war."

This only made him smile. "My plans were simply to bring you and your father here. To sort out this mess among ourselves. It was you, Darius, and your grandmother who began the attack. When you took over Gondalesh and killed my lieutenant and my scientist... well, I had to retaliate." His grin deepened with twisted enjoyment. "You are attacking my kingdom. I am merely defending what is mine."

"You are trying to destroy the world."

"No. I am trying to make it a better place for casters." His eyes were black and glinting. "Did you ever stop to consider what I would do once the humans were eradicated and casters were free? I would create a single shield across the earth, keeping us all safe from the elements. No more provinces. No more Free Zones. Just one kingdom. United."

"Where we would all suffer under your rule."

I glanced around the enormous tower room, but there was no sign of Isgrad.

Morgomoth stood. His voice came out in a hiss. "If you are looking for your father, let me assure you he is perfectly safe. For now," he added in a heinous undertone.

He snapped his fingers.

Next to his throne, Isgrad materialised. Some sort of invisibility charm had kept him hidden. Two winged chak-lorks had their claws fastened in his shoulders. The blood spilled down Isgrad's arms, and he barely had the strength to look up from the ground. His blue eyes went straight to me. There was concern and exhaustion inside them. Bruises had started forming on his cheeks, and his lower lip was split open. He must have put up a damn good fight.

Panic crept over me again, so intense that it made my ears buzz.

How can I save him when he's trapped like this?

The thought must have been apparent on my face, because Morgomoth stepped down from the dais. With a flourish of his fingers, the doors slammed, trapping me inside the tower room. Another wave of vertigo struck. Telekinesis had been Vulcan's magic, and he was dead.

The silver-thorned witch's words came tearing back. *"Why do you think Vulcan looks sickly and on the verge of death? Morgomoth is punishing his lieutenant for the terrible mistake he nearly made. He's draining Vulcan's life bit by bit. Eventually, Vulcan will become nothing more than an animated corpse."*

The lining in my mouth turned slimy and bitter.

He absorbed Vulcan's power.

It had been a lethal mistake to think that renouncing the Bone Grimoire and the Grand Masters' magic would make Morgomoth weaker. He was stronger than ever.

Cold rage hardened his features. "Time and time again, I have given you both the opportunity to stand by my side and unite with the ULD."

Neither Isgrad nor I answered.

"We now find ourselves at a crossroads. Or a checkmate, if you wish. Not one of us can die without killing the other. I want our link severed just as much as you both want it. And I want this war to end."

He raised his hands, the Larthalgule and the Neathror blades materialising in his palms. I couldn't breathe. I felt like my neck was at the end of a rope and someone was pulling it tight.

Morgomoth's black eyes sliced into mine, and I saw that he had every intention of getting what he wanted. "Use the spell and unite the sabres," he demanded. "Conjure the Interitus blade."

I stood there, unable to move. My lips shaped words, but I couldn't seem to get them out. I recalled the witch's infuriating wisdom. *"Riddles are never what they seem. Perhaps the spell is not supposed to make sense until the right moment."*

Clearly, this wasn't the right moment, because the meaning behind the spell hadn't become apparent.

Morgomoth set the Larthalgule and Neathror blades on the ground before me. The bringers of life and death were both terrible but beautiful weapons. Their runes glowed and gave off heat. I wouldn't have been half surprised if the floor melted around them.

"Unite them," Morgomoth stipulated through clenched teeth.

"I can't. The spell is a riddle. Only the worthy can figure it out. And neither you nor I appear to be worthy of learning its meaning."

He sneered. I expected him to lash out, to hit me with a surge of telekinetic power, to fling me back against the wall like an annoying fly, but all he did was stare.

Arrogance and triumph shone in his levelled gaze. "Is that so."

Not a question. A statement.

Morgomoth laughed. It sounded like a deep-throated growl of enjoyment. "I suggest you decipher the riddle now. And quick."

He waved his hand. Another form materialised next to him, someone else who had been concealed by invisibility. From his robe, Morgomoth pulled out a silver blade, pressing it against his victim's throat.

The imaginary noose tightened, my gasp sending a spasm of

pain down my chest. My ribs had only just healed, but they might as well have been broken all over again for the agony the image ahead provided.

"The captain was a hard man to track down amid all that fighting," Morgomoth mocked. "It took ten of my chak-lorks to pin him down."

He pulled Jad by the hair. The captain's face was scratched and bloody. His nose bled in a scarlet streak over his lips that congealed with the dirt on his chin. His hair and clothes were crusted with dirt and ichor. He looked at me through heavy eyes, utterly spent from battle. I saw the apology in them and could barely stop the sob from working its way out of my throat.

Morgomoth's eyes were still fixed on me. "Unite the blades, Zaya. Otherwise, I'll sever your captain's pretty little head from his neck."

CHAPTER 37

I'd been afraid many times in my life. In fact, fear seemed to
have a permanent hold on me, as though it were a puppeteer
and I were attached to its strings. But I had never experienced
anything like this. It started in my stomach, the toxic sensation
spreading through every limb, muscle, and artery. This fear
brought me to my knees. Grovelling, tears spilling down my
cheeks, I begged for Morgomoth to let Jad go. Out of all of us,
Jad was the one who deserved to live. He deserved—no, he'd
earned—a second chance at life. He had sacrificed so much to
keep everyone safe, and this was how he was to be repaid—with a
knife to his throat.

Morgomoth had been five steps ahead of me and Darius this
entire time, calculating as he moved all his pieces across the chess-
board. Jad was the final piece. Morgomoth knew he was the one
person I'd sacrifice anything for.

"Unite the blades. Now." He drove the tip of his dagger into
Jad's neck, eliciting a small cry from the captain. Blood spotted his
skin, but that was nothing compared to the sound of sizzling
flesh. Morgomoth's weapon was pure silver. Even the slightest

touch would spread that toxin through Jad's body. It wouldn't be enough to kill him right away, but it would draw out the slow, painful end.

"Don't do it, Zaya." Isgrad was struggling against the winged chak-lorks. The creatures held him back, digging their claws farther into his shoulders, delighting in his growl of pain. One of the creatures sent a violent blow across Isgrad's cheek, knocking his head back. The impact had been so hard, I was surprised Isgrad didn't spit out any teeth.

Rage swivelled inside me, drowning whatever clarity was left. I crawled toward the blades. The runes burned so brightly, I wondered how the weapons wouldn't sear my skin when I touched them. Sweat ran down my back, pooling between my shoulders.

We might have all been holding our breath when I gripped both hilts.

"Riddles are never what they seem. Perhaps the spell is not supposed to make sense until the right moment."

I thought about the spell, combing over each word.

Salted water, a drop you will need
Earth and spirit, forced to bleed
Shadows and dark, summoned alive
Glimpse death to survive
Hope will come, pass, and fade
Create the almighty Interitus blade
Find the Kingdom to grieve and mourn
Where the dusk will meet the dawn.

STILL, its meaning was elusive. I couldn't work it out. Jad was going to die. Isgrad and I would live the remainder of our lives as prisoners on this providence-forsaken island until Morgomoth figured out how to sever our connection. And Morgomoth would win this war. We were all doomed because I couldn't piece a frigging riddle together.

I closed my eyes, feeling them sting with tears, the burn sliding all the way down to my throat.

Tears!

I wiped a bead of it from my cheek, which amalgamated with the dirt and blood on my fingers.

Salted water, a drop you will need.

I had thought it literally meant seawater, but tears were salt too.

Earth and spirit forced to bleed.

Outside, rivers of molten rock were streaming down the sides of the volcanoes, the earth and land tormented by dark magic. And in the caster world, magic was often referred to as spirit.

Shadows and dark, summoned alive.

That had to be Morgomoth. He was literally made of darkness.

Glimpse death to survive.

My eyes travelled to Jad, his once-tanned skin now the colour of white bone. The poison was spreading through him faster than should have been possible. The only way to even remotely save him now was to unite the blades and pray I could find a healer in this cursed land.

Hope will come, pass, and fade.

I couldn't deny that those emotions had swept through me like a fire-crusader dropping bombs.

Create the almighty Interitus blade.

Yes, but how?

Find the Kingdom to grieve and mourn.

I was living in it, thank you.

Where the dusk will meet the dawn.

That one stumped me. The sun rising and setting couldn't be further times apart from each other.

I stared at the beautiful yet deadly athame-sabres in my hands. Larthalgule, the giver of life, was embellished with red serpents, dragons, and demons. It looked like a key to the otherworld— that place of fiery pits and never-ending torture. The other blade, Neathror, the bringer of death, was adorned with onyx gems that reminded me of black snake scales. It was nowhere near as magnificent as its sister blade, but it possessed its own kind of dark beauty.

How on earth do I unite you?

The blades throbbed in my hands, as though they sensed the other's magic and hummed with the urge to be joined. At the end of the Neathror hilt was a symbol I hadn't noticed before. A sunset. The bringer of death, symbolised by the sun going down. I turned the Larthalgule blade over. There, just like Neathror, it had a sun rising. The giver of life, illustrated by the new day.

Where the dusk will meet the dawn.

It can't be that easy, surely?

I realised now that the spell had never been an enchantment. It hadn't even been a riddle but rather a prophecy. The Grand Masters had been foretelling this moment.

No wonder they had sounded so smug.

Even the silver-thorned witch, in her own mysterious and implicit way, had hinted at it. *"The spell is not supposed to make sense until the right moment."*

Calming my growing excitement, I slowly brought the hilts together, holding my breath as the rising sun united with the setting one. For excruciatingly long seconds, nothing happened.

Morgomoth lost his infinite patience. "You didn't do it properly. You—"

Light exploded, a wall of flame searing across every wall in the tower room. The force threw me backward, my entire body spasming from shock and pain as I landed hard, my ribs screaming in the process. It felt like I'd broken a few of them again. I groaned, swallowing the blood in my mouth. The heat burned hot at my back as I rose slowly to lean on my elbows, my legs still frozen by shock.

The blast had knocked Isgrad from his knees. He was lying on the floor, looking dazed. Blood dripped from a cut on his forehead. Behind him, the winged chak-lorks that had held him captive were on fire. Their shrieks were horrible to hear as the flames tortured and burned them with unrelenting strength, reducing them to a melted black gunk on the floor.

My eyes met Morgomoth's. For a second, there was stunned surprise in his, but then the flamelight reflected off the bones that made up his face, his rapt expression terrifying to behold. On the floor was a new sword. Its hilt was shaped like a silver stagma with slitted red eyes, the cross-guard its vast wingspan. Down the double-edged blade were runes that were golden and alive, now giving off a heat that made me feel like I was standing at the edge of a fiery crater.

I had done it. I'd created the Interitus blade. Made something I thought would be impossible.

I glared at Morgomoth with soul-deep hatred. "You have your weapon. Now let Jad go."

The dark smile that flitted across his lips cleaved me in two. "No."

And with that final word, he drove his silver blade into Jad's gut.

I screamed, watching the captain's body plummet lifelessly to the floor, his eyes wide and disbelieving, the dagger still sticking out grotesquely from his abdomen. He stared at me, and his lips parted softly. I thought he might have said a silent apology, forgiveness for not being strong enough. And then his eyes closed.

My scream pulsed through my ears, drowning out every other sound. My ribs groaned in agony, all of them feeling like they were splintering into small pieces. I had watched Jad be shot by his own father. Seen him barbarically experimented on by Hadar. I myself had stabbed Trajan with the Neathror blade. Jad had been through so much. Survived so much. And in the end, all it took to defeat him was a silver dagger.

I didn't know if he was dead or dying. All I knew was that the rippling, boiling rage inside me couldn't be contained. My magic unfurled, white light bursting from my eyes, my ears, my skin, my scream so viciously loud that it shattered the very walls of the tower room. They came down like they'd been hit by a catapult, exposing us to the red sky above. I had completely destroyed the tower. The shards of what remained resembled melted-down arches on a crown.

In that moment of madness, I didn't hear the *whoosh* of a sword cut through the thick air until the last possible second. Morgomoth had the Interitus blade. It was coming directly for me, too fast to block or even attempt to shield myself or dart away. I saw the purpose in Morgomoth's eyes, the eagerness to destroy, the elation that he had won. He brought the sword down, ready to slice me apart. Ready to sever the link that tethered our life forces.

One chance out of three.

It seemed fate was not in my favour.

I braced myself, waiting for the pain, waiting for death.

Something dark flew at Morgomoth, preventing the Interitus blade from making its mark. My heart caught at the sight of Isgrad with his own rusted athame-sabre. It was a dissent weapon, the blade still sticky with black ichor, which meant it must have belonged to one of the chak-lorks. Isgrad charged, lunging and slicing at Morgomoth, the pair engaged in a dance of dangerous sibling rivalry. The tower shook. The entire world shook. Isgrad must have been using his earth magic to make the citadel unstable, to give us a fighting chance.

"Flee," he yelled at me over his shoulder. "Leave my brother to me."

But I couldn't.

Not without him.

Cold hatred shone in Isgrad's eyes. His face was as pale as death as he strained to destroy the monster that had caused him such heartache. Morgomoth launched at him, pounding his elbow so hard into Isgrad's nose that I heard the bone crack. Panting through gritted teeth, Isgrad yelled at me again to leave and lunged at his brother.

One chance out of three.

Isgrad was giving me that opportunity now.

I could run, but it wouldn't be right.

I couldn't leave him.

Or Jad.

I was still too sore to get up on my feet, so I crawled toward Jad. He was barely breathing. Above us, the sky was a roiling mass of flames and darkness. Volcanic lightning sent blinding streaks across the black cloud plumes. The ash was falling harder now, like rain. I brushed it off Jad's cheeks. He managed to inhale what sounded like a laborious breath. His eyes were stinging with smoke and tears when he looked at me. He didn't talk, but I read the silent command on his face.

"Run."

I shook my head.

No. Never.

I stroked his grimy hair off his face. He passed out again, his body limp. I didn't dare look at the gash in his abdomen. If I did, I would surely break down, begging for my death to come swiftly.

A cry tore out into the night. Gut-wrenching sorrow filled me as Isgrad fell to the floor, hard enough that I wondered if he saw stars. His rusted blade was broken in two at his side. Morgomoth loomed over him. As Willieth, he had loved his brother. He'd idolised him. He'd wanted Isgrad by his side always. But there was no trace of brotherly love in Morgomoth's eyes anymore. He brought the Interitus blade down. Seeing it pierce through my father's chest was like experiencing it going through my own heart. Isgrad choked out a gasp of surprise, looking incredulously at his brother. Morgomoth wasn't done. He stabbed again in a frenzy, taking years of pent-up frustration out with every damaging blow.

A desperate sob broke from me. I thought I'd burned myself out, but that rage deep inside came alive again, responding like a feral animal. It wasn't only my magic pulsing around me, though. Light pooled from Jad's athame-sabre, which had mysteriously appeared at his side like it had been summoned. It wasn't ablaze with flames this time but runes that glowed as hot as starlight. I recognised the intricate swirls and patterns. They were the same runes that had marked the passages in the Isla Necropolis. The language of the dead.

Sheer, hesitant surprise worked its way through me. I had questioned how Jad's athame-sabre could summon flames. It was connected to his magic, yes, but I realised there was also necromancy in the blade. When I'd stabbed Jad at the Isla Necropolis with Neathror, it had killed Trajan, but the blade must have tainted Jad and his magic with necromancy too. A spark of hope flared inside me. The captain's athame-sabre was a necromancer's weapon, and it had answered to my call of wrath.

I curled my fingers around the hilt.

I will kill him, I swore to the darkness.

One chance out of three.

Climbing to my feet, I hurled myself at Morgomoth with a hoarse battle cry.

I didn't know who was more surprised, him or me. He must have seen the savagery on my face, or seen the powerful sword in my hands, because for a moment he froze, as though he were truly unsettled. The Interitus blade was still wedged deep in my father's body. He drew it out, meeting my blade in a deafening clang. Lightning and fire burst off the weapons in shards. I was a storm of destruction raining down, which made Morgomoth a sea of tumultuous waves rising in greeting.

He attacked, faster and stronger, and laughed. "I will enjoy killing you."

"I burned you once," I mocked with icy vehemence. "This time, I'll make sure there's nothing left of you."

He was too fast, and I was distracted by the rictus grin on his skeletal face. He slashed out with the Interitus blade, driving it into my shoulder. I screamed, agony ripping through me, my knees twisting as my body suddenly became too heavy. I was going to fall. If that happened, I'd never get back up again. Morgomoth realised it too. He tore the blade out. My blood spurted, the sight nearly making me go into a faint. Morgomoth swung the blade in a final deadly blow, intending to behead me.

Biting back the pain, I leapt that final crucial step out of the way, summoning the last of my necromancy. Heat blasted the front of my face, my athame-sabre aglow in flames. I spun around, charging toward Morgomoth faster than a shooting arrow, and hurled my blade right through his chest.

He bellowed, black blood dripping from his mouth. It wasn't only his roar that shattered my ears. The wraiths who made up his body screamed, not with pain but with joyous glee. They detached themselves from him, drifting up into the night like smoke. Morgomoth yanked at them, trying to keep himself intact, but the ghosts simply went through his fingers. He was nothing but a skeleton now with a bit of flesh in a robe. Wind slammed into him from all directions, shredding and gashing.

I remembered my promise—that I would leave nothing left of Morgomoth. The athame-sabre wedged in his chest must have understood that vow, because the flames licked over his bones, cooking and melting. Then the blade disappeared. Light glowed over Jad's body. The weapon had returned to its master.

Now, there was a smoking hole through Morgomoth. I could see right through him to the fouled land beyond. He slumped to the ground. Grunting from what must have been excruciating pain, Morgomoth crawled toward Isgrad's body. When he could no longer crawl, he dragged himself, dark threads of his blood streaming through the ash. He reached for Isgrad's hand.

How dare he? After everything he's put us through.

I charged forward, intending to crush his fingers into dust, but stopped the moment he twisted around to look at me. It wasn't Morgomoth's black eyes that stared back, but Willieth's blue ones.

"Isgrad," he muttered. The name on his lips sounded choked.

A final trickle of blood pooled down the side of his burnt face, and then the life went out of him.

The heaviness in my legs disappeared, the numbness in my body fading away. I ignored the pain in my shoulder and knelt beside my father. Isgrad was breathing, but his body was cold. His chest resembled pummelled meat. So much ash had fallen over him, it was almost as though nature were trying to bury him. His eyes opened, staring into my face with sad intensity. And, I realised, with pride.

He raised his hand, dragging his soft fingertips across my cheeks. "Your mother waits for me now. I'm going home."

I nodded, soothing, reassuring. It was all I could manage.

"I will see you in the next world," he told me.

And then he was gone.

CHAPTER 38

I didn't know how long I stared at Isgrad's lifeless body. One second, he was alive, on the verge of becoming an important part in my life. The next... just an empty shell. We hadn't known each other. Not really. But I'd wanted that chance. It was something else that had been stolen from me. I reached down and closed his eyes, making him appear more peaceful, like he might be sleeping.

A cold brush of fingers gently ran down my cheek, the same place where Isgrad's had touched only moments before. Lunette materialised beside me, cloaked in golden light. She was beautiful, her alabaster skin smooth and resplendent against the radiance that glowed around her. I started to believe the humans' ancient stories of angels and their heavenly glory.

She smiled, her eyes holding me with purpose. *"You know what must be done now."*

I nodded, but damn, I was so tired.

Lunette took my hand. Her fingers felt surprisingly solid against my own. Warmth spread through me, energy lighting everything that had turned dark inside, filling me with a last bout of strength.

Her smile never left her face, even as she faded away.

Pain radiated down my entire shoulder, blood running down my arm, but Lunette was right.

Just one more task.

Trembling, I got onto my feet. The Interitus blade remained where Morgomoth had dropped it, the runes on the metal so hot that they'd melted the ash around it. I picked up the athame-sabre, drawing in a lungful of air, my legs complaining with each slow step it took to reach the edge of the tower. Below, Orthrask had become a scene of carnage and blood where the battle still raged. Only the living fought. The chak-lorks and stagma, whose bodies had been reanimated by Morgomoth, were once again life-less heaps on the blood-soaked ground.

So much death. So much destruction.

The volcanoes that stood in a ring of fire around the citadel streamed lava, the smoke casting a shadow of death across the accursed land. This place was a scar on the earth. A place that needed to be buried under the sea.

From my holster, I took out my cast-shooter and fired a jet of blue fire into the sky. It erupted like a firework, blue light flashing across the roiling clouds. That was the signal for Darius. I'd made him promise that once he saw the blue flame, he would instruct the Haxsan Guard forces to pull back. I would not allow another life to perish.

The order must have been received, because like a cloud of black locusts, our armies regrouped and fled through the portal. What remained of the dissent rebels pursued, but it didn't matter anymore. Soon, they would learn that their side had lost—that the United League of Dissent no longer existed. They would soon understand that they had nowhere to run.

"Zaya."

I turned to find Jad staggering toward me. He clutched at the wound in his abdomen, as though by holding it, he could prevent the blood from spilling out.

I stumbled to his side and wrapped an arm around him to support his weight. "You shouldn't be moving."

I was surprised that he could even stand.

He passed me a sad smile. "Lycanthor strength, remember? I'm using the last of it so I can remain by your side. Till the end."

Hot tears slid down my face. Jad knew all along what I'd intended to do, and he wanted to be with me when it happened. His arm draped over my shoulders, and we slowly floundered our way to the edge of the tower.

We looked out over the poisoned land. There was no escape for us, not with the injuries we'd sustained. I could see it on Jad's face, the acceptance that we would die in this tower. His breathing must have become an effort because I had to prop him up, using my side to keep him balanced.

Hurt and fatigue clouded his eyes. "Do it."

Summoning that last will of strength Lunette had gifted me, I drove the Interitus blade into the ground. I was its wielder now, and its magic—both life and death—had to obey me.

I didn't speak the words aloud. My throat ached too badly to even try.

"Stop this terrible war. End the United League of Dissent. Not its people but its philosophy and its dogma. Bury this land, never to be seen or raised again. And once Orthrask is gone, melt yourself into oblivion."

The earth groaned and quaked. In the distance, a wave of water billowed from every direction, sinking the vastness of the island. Gondalesh fell. Even from here, the deafening crash of the edifice as it collapsed reached my ears. All around us, the volcanoes folded inward, magma shooting into the sky in a last effort to destroy before they, too, were toppled by the overwhelming wave of water.

My mind drifted to my friends. I thought of Talina and hoped she'd been reunited with Marek on a ship, the pair locked in each other's arms. I imagined Annaka and Bronislav healed and recovered, standing at the stern and watching Orthrask subside into the sea. In the chaos and panic of commanding the fleet to leave, would Darius spare a moment to appreciate the sacrifice Jad and I had made? I believed he would. And my grandmother? Would Macaslan be crying furious tears, her stern heart finally breaking at the realisation that she'd lost another member of her kin?

Most of all, I thought about everyone who'd been taken from me. Adaline. Lunette. Edric and Lainie. Briya and Isgrad.

I'll be with them soon.

I held Jad as the Vrabkor Citadel trembled from its foundations. The volcano below us erupted from all the unstable magic, the devastating rumble overwhelming all other sounds.

"Will it hurt?"

Jad tightened his grip on me. "It'll be quick."

Thunder burst from the sky, lightning searing the agitated clouds. For a second, I could have sworn I saw a flash of white wings, but it must have been a trick of the light, and I soon forgot about it as scalding wind blew my hair in disarray, my skin popping with sweat.

Below, the plume of black smoke rose.

I stared at Jad. As filthy as he was, clothes torn, bruises and cuts lining his face, he was still the most beautiful person I'd ever seen. I pressed my lips against his, sealing us both in a final kiss. If I had to die, I couldn't think of any better way to meet death.

Even with my eyes firmly closed, I saw a flash of incandescent light, only this time it came with the wild beating of wings.

Maybe an angel has come to meet us.

But that thought too soon disappeared as heat and fire consumed me, and there remained only darkness and no feeling at all.

CHAPTER 39

I dreamt of claws and leathery white wings that glistened with gold. I was airborne, held by something I could neither fathom nor dare to describe. I couldn't see it. My eyes wouldn't open. But I sensed it take me away, rising higher, carrying my soul faster toward a blue light that was magnificent and as powerful as the sea.

Why had the ghosts never told me about this?

This must be the otherworld.

My final journey.

I found the strength to open my eyes. I reached upward, my fingers sinking into the azure glow. Its magic emanated through me, filling me with radiance. Too much. Too powerful. But also… freeing

I closed my eyes once more and happily let my angel take me to the light.

Pain shot through my shoulder when I woke. Or maybe it had always been there, and it was only when I opened my eyes that my body fully registered that I had an injury. A groan fled my mouth as I tried to move before I reluctantly dropped back onto the pillow again.

My mind was sluggish to catch up on what I was seeing. I was in a bed, swaddled in blankets. Tubes and bandages were attached to just about every part of me. A cannula had been inserted into my lower left arm, and I winced whenever I moved, feeling it tug inside me like a bug trapped underneath.

Okay. Not dead.

The pain that racked my body was affirmation that I was alive. The last thing I remembered had been… death.

I definitely died.

I remembered the angel.

A flood of images that I couldn't quite piece together ran through my mind. Gigantic wings that rippled with gold. Claws that felt like they were still enfolded around me. Searing blue light.

"You're awake," a voice cried from the doorway.

My heart leapt when Talina barrelled inside. She was in her nursing scrubs, and despite being on duty, she pulled up a chair and sat down.

Her face spread into an elated smile. "I'm so glad you're okay. You had me so worried. I thought you weren't going to…."

She didn't finish what she was about to say. Instead, she brushed away a tear that trickled down her cheek. "It was so close. We nearly lost you. There were six healers working on you night and day."

I tried to sit up a little higher, but my shoulder stung as I moved under the covers. "Where am I?"

"The ship's infirmary. We're on our way back to Vukovar. A place called Edradus. Zaya, stop," she insisted, gently pushing me back down on the bed. "You mustn't move. You might start bleeding again."

Again?

I decided I didn't want to know.

My scalp prickled, questions still lingering in my mind. "What happened? How did I get on the ship?"

"A stagma happened," another voice answered.

Marek had entered the room. He stood at the foot of my bed, looking down at me with a relaxed smile. I couldn't remember the last time I'd seen him appear so... carefree. He wore a Haxsan Guard uniform that was clean, his face and neck revealing only a few scraps and abrasions to indicate he'd even fought in a battle.

How much time has passed?

I looked at the bandages wrapped around my right arm. Days old, the edges crusted over from the dry acrylic.

My throat was parched. I greedily drank the water Talina offered me in a plastic cup. "A stagma?"

"It was rather incredible," Marek admitted. "Orthrask had nearly entirely disappeared in the sea. The portal was on the brink of collapsing, and then at the last possible second, this enormous white-and-gold stagma emerged. Its roar was so powerful, I thought it would rip the ship apart or even capsize us. It laid a small bundle on the deck, and then it flew off."

"It brought you and Jad," Talina emphasised. "Darius immediately ordered that you both be taken to the infirmary. There was such a rigmarole on deck of field medics and healers, of people asking questions and pushing to get closer, that it was impossible to even get nearby. People are saying it's a miracle."

I recalled what Jad had told me that day in the canyon. *"There's an ancient bond between casters and stagma. You save a stagma's life and the creature becomes loyal to you."*

So that's what happened. When Jad and I had faced certain

death, the creature had known. It had come. I'd saved its life, and it had repaid the favour.

Marek's face tightened, but not unkindly. "People have seen the stagma flying in the distance. It doesn't get close to the ship, but it's enough to alarm people."

"They don't need to be afraid," I confirmed.

I knew it in my heart that the stagma wasn't dangerous. Perhaps it remained near because it was bonded to me somehow. I'd given it life. Maybe by saving mine and Jad's, it felt linked to us.

Could such a magic exist?

My stomach sank. "Jad!"

I made to move, biting back the pain. My fingers dug into the sheets, but it was useless. All the tubes had me tightly strapped in. Not to mention, my legs were stiff and aching, as though I'd run a marathon. My hips actually felt like they might pop out of my skin.

Concern laced Marek's voice. "He's in the intensive magic ward. He's unconscious, but it's expected that he'll make a full recovery. Physically, at least."

A part of me choked on that news.

Physically?

Focus on the good news. Jad's okay.

But he and I would have scars that would stay with us long into the future. We had witnessed and experienced terrible atrocities. We had seen the aftermath of war and the devastation it caused. We had faced death. Accepted it. The mind didn't get over that easily. It would be hard to move on. If we ever did.

My throat felt scratchy. "Can I see him?"

Talina shot me an uncharacteristically stern glare that Macaslan would have been proud of. "You can barely stand, Zaya. Focus on getting better. As soon as we arrive at Edradus, I will personally see that you and Jad share a hospital room, if you wish."

I blinked in confusion. "You don't have that much persuasion."

"She does, in fact." Marek drew closer to her, draping an arm over her shoulders. He pressed a kiss to her temple. "My girl got promoted."

Talina was beaming. "I'm chief nurse. Well, on this ship, at least. Until they can find someone with more experience. Many of our medics died."

Her smile dropped.

I reached for her hand, entwining our fingers. "I think the role is perfect for you."

"I think it is too."

I tried to sit up straighter, cursing myself when I couldn't.

Talina let go of my hand to reach across to the bedstand. She poured more water into the cup.

I took it gratefully, savouring the feel of it against my dry lips and tongue. It had a sweet scent and a floral smell I couldn't pinpoint. Not like water at all.

"We're going to let you rest," Talina told me.

She left hand in hand with Marek.

A corner of my mouth stretched into a smirk. "So, you two are official now?"

Marek smiled, but it looked sheepish.

Talina's grin could have reached up to the moon. "Yes."

Good. At least I didn't have to skirt around their moping and pining for each other anymore. I was happy for them.

But I also felt....

"Talina," I mumbled, my voice a slur. "This isn't water, is it?"

"No," she admitted, sounding not the least bit guilty. "That was a sleeping potion. You need to rest. I knew the moment

Marek and I left that you would make a beeline for the intensive ward, so I took precautions."

Her smile was as smooth and sweet as honey.

Well played, I thought, then passed out.

THE SALTY BREEZE ruffled my hair. I stood on the deck of the mighty warship, watching the distance to the shore shrink as we steadily approached. It was early in the morning, the sun newly risen. I shouldn't have been out here. Talina would be furious, but the nurse on duty had taken one look at me when I'd woken from my nightmare, seen my pale face and sweat-soaked gown, and let me come up on deck for air. She waited now near the bridge, keeping a stout eye on me.

Huh. I've survived way too much bullshit to throw myself overboard now.

But she did have reason to be concerned. The nightmares had plagued me every time I slept. The dreams were filled with fire and demonic faces, fiery chasms and screaming ghosts. But out here with the sea calm and the new day tainting the horizon pink, I knew that's all the nightmares were. Just memories of the horrors I'd witnessed, my subconscious sifting through them, trying to make sense of everything I'd endured.

The dreams had started on the night I'd first been allowed to visit Jad. It had broken me to see him lying in the intensive magic ward, his face dull and pale, his arms and chest covered in tubes that transported magic nutrients to his body, keeping him alive as he slept and recovered. I hated hearing the rhythmic hissing sound of the ventilator pushing air into his lungs. It filled my own chest with a stabbing, all-consuming fear. The healers promised me he would be okay. That he would wake up eventually. They just couldn't tell me when.

"Thinking about the future?" a voice asked, interrupting my sad reverie.

Darius appeared, his hands loose by his sides. He'd forgone his Haxsan Guard uniform for a perfectly tailored suit, looking more like the senator I remembered, not the warlord who had both impressed and terrified me.

I stared out at the sea. "Something like that."

His brows rose, and he took up a place by the railing. "Thank you, Zaya. For what you did. I know none of it was easy. It was difficult for all of us. But it's over now. And I'm glad you're here." He swallowed, his voice taking on a hint of uncertainty. "I am sorry that you felt you needed to doubt me at times. I had to make some very hard choices. Choices that will haunt me for a long time, no doubt."

He peered down at the gently lapping waves, and I wondered if he was thinking about everyone who'd been left to perish when the Black Palace was destroyed.

The smell of salt filled my nostrils. The scent was calming. Soothing.

"I understand," I said at last.

We had all done terrible things for the greater good. We had all faced difficult situations and made the best of it as we could. That wasn't something to be punished for.

I pointed to the shore, where the glistening white towers of Edradus appeared. The city was like diamonds reflecting the sunlight. The nursing staff told me that Edradus was a spectacular city to behold. Apparently, it had seen its share of attacks by dissent rebels and chak-lorks, but its high walls had kept it safe, and the Haxsan Guard had managed to keep it secure, even after its celestial shield fell.

I cleared my throat. "What happens now? Once we reach Edradus. Is it really all over like you said?"

I didn't dare to hope.

Darius's gaze swept across the water to the city. "It can be over for you, Zaya. You've been through enough. But for the rest of us... the world has been left in a mess. There are people without homes. Humans living underground with no celestial shields to protect them. We have no government. No central rule, which makes the world just as dangerous as it was with the United League of Dissent in it. We need to elect new officials and quickly. We need to mourn and heal. And we need to rebuild. It will take years."

I didn't doubt him. I pitied the poor people elected to lead, but if there was a pair strong enough to tackle the task, it was Darius and Macaslan.

Disappointment rolled into my gut. My grandmother hadn't come to see me once while I'd been recovering. When I'd asked about her, Marek had searched in vain, reporting that she'd gone on board another ship to take command.

Not avoiding me. She has duties to attend to.

But it felt like she was sidestepping an important conversation that was no doubt going to have to occur.

"I'll help in whatever way I can," I told Darius, and meant it.

He bowed his head in an appreciative nod. "I'm sure you will. I'd be too afraid to say you couldn't."

I chose my next words carefully. "We will be all right, won't we?"

I'd removed Morgomoth from the scene. I'd begged the Interitus blade to destroy the United League of Dissent's principles but not it's people. I didn't believe I should have the power to change people's beliefs, which meant there were still dissent rebels out there. Marek had reported that most of the insurgents had disbanded, surrendering after Morgomoth fell. Some had been relieved to get away from the fascist force, realising Morgomoth had indeed used their fear against them. But there would always be rebels out there—casters just like Vulcan and Hadar—who'd be planning further uprisings and attacks, still holding Morgomoth up as a martyr. He might be gone, but what he'd done to the world would remain a scar on the earth for a long time to come.

Darius's anguished look confirmed it. "Time will tell."

There was a gasp behind us. My dutiful nurse had approached. She was staring up at the sky in both rapt and frightened awe.

I looked up as well. There, soaring through the clouds like it was dancing, was the white-and-gold stagma, its scales glittering in the sunlight. It bellowed happily.

I'm going to have to give you a name if you're going to keep hanging around.

Seeing the stagma inspired some hope in me.

If this creature could return from the dead and be content, then so could I.

CHAPTER 40

Edradus was a beautiful city made of white stone and glass, built into a mountain that overlooked the Adriatic Sea. It had a similar layout to Muiren, the white buildings, plazas, and towers rising up the dramatic rock outcrops, the Silver Palace proudly standing on the crest. They called it the City of Flowers, which was an appropriate title, because every building was decorated with hanging crawlers. Flower baskets adorned all the lampposts in sight, and there were incredible century-old banyan trees that were decorated with vibrant ribbons. The locals called them wish trees, and they were sacred to the city. In the mornings, I often liked to stroll among them, reading the wishes people had written on the ribbons. Sometimes there were prayers, or poems, or even drawings.

It seemed that the people who lived here had been encouraged to grow and maintain gardens, because every street corner, every façade, added to the city's luscious scenery. Edradus hadn't gone unscathed, though. When we'd made port and stepped down from the ship, a series of sparrowhawks had arrived to collect Darius, Macaslan, me, and a small band of officers. On the journey to the Silver Palace, I'd seen the devastation that had been inflicted on the city's outskirts. Houses were burned and ransacked. Streets were blackened by fires, right up to the defensive wall that had protected the rest of Edradus. One officer mentioned in a snooty voice that "at least the decent part of the city survived," meaning the lesser parts—where the serving casters had lived—didn't matter. I glared at him, and I was proud to call Macaslan my grandmother when she kicked him in the shins, apologising profusely that she hadn't meant to. His leg happened to be inconveniently in the way. The officer's comment was a stark reminder that we still had so much more than just recovery and rebuilding to tackle.

I'd insisted that Marek, Talina, Bronislav, and Annaka join us, reminding Darius of what part they'd played in this war. I did not want my friends living in what had been dubbed "the tent city" below the mountain, where refugees, the injured, and the dying were being brought on a daily basis, attended by Haxsan Guard soldiers and healers. My friends would be down there soon enough to work. We could afford them a little luxury to start with.

Jad? He'd been transported by air ambulance to the Silver Palace and left in the care of trained healers and medics. They'd marvelled at the miracle of his speedy recovery. His body had healed, thanks to his lycanthor strength, but still he slept. The silver-thorned witch and even Macha had assessed him a few times, connecting their minds with Jad's dreams. Whenever they came out of their trance, they assured me his mind was okay. He was just resting. My patience started to wear thin, and I worried everyone was lying to spare me more heartache. Every morning, afternoon, and evening, I'd sit in a chair beside Jad, holding his hand, talking to him, just waiting for those beautiful eyelids to peel open.

On the tenth day since our arrival at the Silver Palace, I woke in my huge bedroom, the curtains drawn back and the sea air caressing my face. It was the first time I'd slept in the canopied bed, because every evening I'd fallen asleep in that chair beside Jad.

Someone must have carried me in here.

There was a note on the gilded side table. I recognised the neat, handwritten text and held my breath.

Please meet me at the Providence Chapel at 10 a.m.
Sincerely,

Commander Macaslan

OH BOY.

What's this about?

She was probably going to reprimand me for not being involved in the recovery. She and Darius, along with Clorenzo, Macha, the silver-thorned witch, and other high commanding officers, had been working around the clock to put in motion the plans for post-war recovery. They had come up with strategies for long-term goals. I'd been present for one meeting that had included the restoration of human and caster health, but I'd heard there'd been other discussions around repairing war-damaged areas, rebuilding the Haxsan Guard without conscription, reconstructing our damaged economy, and more importantly, the correction of social inequality among casters and humans. So much work to do. It would take years.

It was half past nine when I looked at the clock. I dressed quickly in my Haxsan Guard uniform and braided my hair, then was out the door walking through the silver halls and passages to the palace's gardens. The Providence Chapel was an outdoor rotunda with a domed roof made of glass and white limestone walls. It reminded me of an elaborate mausoleum, surrounded by flowers and greenery.

I stepped inside, basking in the cool air. Candles and little tealights had been lit, small flames dotting every surface of the chapel, emitting a soft light that felt... peaceful.

Commander Macaslan was kneeling at the altar on a harrow, an eerie reminder of the time I'd found her praying to Saint Leandra after General Kravis's funeral—right before Toshiko had betrayed me and the sovereigns. I shook the memory from my mind, preferring not to dwell on the past.

I knelt beside Macaslan. "You wanted to see me."

My voice was averse and colder than I'd intended. She'd only visited me once since we'd departed the ship, and I was annoyed that she'd summoned me like I was nothing more than a regular soldier awaiting her orders.

Grandmother indeed.

She squeezed her eyes shut, as though she were trying to push through mental fatigue. When she opened them, her slate-grey eyes were full of tears. She handed me a taper. "I thought we could light a candle together for Briya and Isgrad. I never had the opportunity to give my daughter a funeral. I don't even know where she's buried. If she even *was* buried."

A choked sound worked its way out of my own throat. I had tried not to think about Isgrad or Briya since arriving at the Silver Palace. I hoped my parents were together now in the otherworld. All I had left of them were brief memories—just small, stolen moments I'd seen through the Dark Divide. Isgrad had died to save me, and I would be always grateful, but I hadn't known him. I'd never been given the chance. Now, all I could do was live my life where he couldn't.

I hadn't tried to summon my parents. Their souls were resting now and to do so would have been intrusive. In fact, I hadn't felt the presence of any ghosts since the events at Orthrask. It was like they'd been cut off. When I did reach out with my necromancy, I sensed the otherworld still tethered to our own but at a distance, as though the dead understood now that they could move on. The connection was calm, harmonised, at peace.

My hand found the strength to move. I took the taper, lighting two candles for my parents. Macaslan did the same.

"What happens now?"

"Now we give ourselves the time to grieve and mourn. And then—" Her voice sounded thick with emotion. "Macha and I would like the chance to get to know you. You are our family, after all."

"Do *you* actually want to, or do you simply feel inclined that you should?"

She gave me her obligatory stormy-eyed glare. "Of course I want to. You're my granddaughter."

"Okay, then."

This is going to take some work.

I couldn't stand the empty silence between us. She was an unyielding commander, but a conversationist she was not. "Will you rebuild Tarahik?"

She inhaled a steadying breath. "I don't know yet. There have been developments."

"Such as?"

"I've been asked to stay on here to help form a stable government."

"That sounds… like a lot of work."

"Indeed. Darius and the other officers have decided to enforce a system of government where the people will vote on who leads them. There will no longer be sovereigns but rather elected representatives. One each to speak on behalf of casters, humans, and lycanthors."

"And he's asked you to nominate yourself as a representative for casters?"

She nodded. "Not only me. There will be others in the running for the position. I will have to create a convincing campaign."

"It sounds perfect for you."

Actually, I couldn't think of a more promising leader.

Her gaze grew distant. "Time will tell, I suppose."

I passed her a wan smile. "Are you nervous about it?"

"I do not get nervous," she retorted.

But from the way she gripped her hands tightly together, I knew she was.

I pressed my lips together to deter my laughter.

This is certainly going to put her personality to the test. She's actually going to have to convince people to like her.

"And what will you do?"

The question stumped me. Watching Jad sleep every night, I had thought over and over about it myself. Did I still want to be part of the Haxsan Guard? Or were there other opportunities for me now? One thing I was abundantly clear on: When Jad woke up, I wanted to be by his side. Always. Where he went, I would go. I supposed my decision would be determined based on what Jad wanted.

Macaslan pulled an unpleasant face when I told her. "I don't think the captain will let you follow him around like a lovesick puppy. He'll want you to make your own decisions. *Your* choices are your own, Zaya. Don't let anyone else tell you or dictate what you should do. Especially those who love you most."

And then, surprisingly and to my utter horror, she leaned forward and pressed a kiss to my cheek. "Until you decide what it is you want in life, granddaughter, have fun. You've earned it."

And with those final words, she moved silently out of the chapel.

It was late evening when a knock sounded on my door. I rubbed the sleep out of my eyes and scrambled out of bed. I had reluctantly left Jad's side in the infirmary earlier that evening when the healers had kicked me out, demanding that I go seek proper rest and let them do their work. I'd become friends with one of the healers named Willa and had made her promise to come get me if something happened. Even if Jad so much as stirred.

Throwing on a red silk dressing gown, I opened the door. Nerves and anticipation bristled through my body.

I found Willa's beaming face on the other side, her cheeks pink from having run here. "He's awake. You must come now. He's asking for you."

She pulled on my hand. We barrelled down the passage, my bare feet struggling to find purchase on the polished floor. I didn't care when I nearly collided into a pair of Haxsan Guard soldiers who were on their way to the night watch, or when officers loitering about in one of the gaming rooms yelled at me to slow down and keep quiet. I outran Willa. I raced down the stairs, taking two and then three steps at a time, and sped through the crystalline passages to the infirmary. My hip slammed sharply into the frame as I rounded the doorway, but I didn't care. The burst of pain was worth it because there, sitting up in the hospital bed, his gaze still sleepy, was Jad.

He laughed softly, his eyes taking in my bedridden, ruffled appearance. "Red suits you."

With his long, graceful fingers, he reached out for me. I crossed the room and wriggled into the bed, pressing up beside him. I held his face in my hands, looking into his eyes to see if he really was all right, questioning if there were scars inside that he hadn't yet recovered from.

"I'm fine," he told me. "Just really hungry."

"You frightened me," I quipped, half-jokingly. "Never do that to me again."

"Now you know how it feels," he answered with an outright grin. "You've fainted and been knocked out more times than I can count. I thought it was high time I paid back the favour."

"Then let's agree that we don't let anything like this happen again."

Those dark eyes held a promise in them.

He kissed me lightly on the lips, but I wouldn't let him pull away. I deepened the kiss, the intensity picking up, passion and guilt warring inside me because I knew Jad still needed to rest. But rest seemed to be the last thing on his mind as he yanked me under the blankets.

The healers had the decency to leave the room and shut the door behind them.

It was another three days before Jad finally had the strength to leave the infirmary, and another two weeks until he was given the healers' clean bill of health to return to duty. We spent our days with Marek, Talina, Bronislav, and Annaka, attending to the wounded in the tent city or aiding in the search effort to find missing people and reconnect them with their families. Often, the results led to tragic outcomes. So many casters and humans had died in the war, we were left scrambling to discover where people had been buried. When that didn't work, I used my necromancy to track the souls of the departed. If there was one silver lining, it was that every soul I summoned was at peace, and while the knowledge couldn't hinder the grief or the despair of loved ones, at least it did provide small comfort.

I decided that was what I wanted to do with my life: console family members who had lost a loved one by giving them that brief connection with the dead. That had, after all, been the purpose behind the Grand Masters before they'd grown too powerful and been betrayed. When I told Jad that evening, our heads resting on the same pillow, he planted a soft kiss on my forehead and said he thought that was a great idea. We spent most of our evenings like that actually, curled up with each other, kissing until late in the evening—among other things—and waking early to help in whatever way we could with the reunification of Vukovar.

I enjoyed the routine we'd settled into with our friends, but it couldn't last. One morning, Annaka brought me down to the dockyard, barely able to contain her excitement.

Her smile was infectious, and she started dancing on her toes. "It's mine."

I stared at the massive warship. Its flag with the Infinite Eye—no longer a symbol of oppression but an emblem of hope—remained at half-mast, just like every other warship that was tied at the docks.

I eyed her inquisitively. "Yours... how exactly?"

"I'm the captain of this beautiful girl. VMS *Vengeance*. Isn't she magnificent?"

"Indeed, she is." I had gone positively rigid. "Does that mean you have an upcoming mission?"

I had enjoyed spending time with my friends in the Silver Palace and had dreaded the day when we'd be separated. I watched Annaka with nervous anticipation.

She must have understood the look on my face, because her smile dimmed. "There are people here who want to return home to Navask. And there are people in Navask who want to return home to Vukovar. There's an entire fleet of us heading out."

"When?"

"Next week."

THE FOLLOWING week came sooner than I would have liked, and I found myself once more at the docks, accompanied by Jad, Talina, and Marek, only this time, we were saying goodbye to two friends. Bronislav had been assigned to the mission too. Actually, he'd volunteered. He was a soldier, not a sailor, and after everything that had happened to him at sea, it surprised me that he'd be willing to set out on the *Vengeance*. But standing on the deck now, I caught the way he looked at Annaka, a sparkle in his eyes, and it all made sense. He'd grown close to her in the last several weeks, and I wondered if in the future... just maybe. Annaka had never said anything about Marek and Talina. She knew they were official, and if it hurt her, she didn't show it. I remembered her telling me that she had once lost someone whom she'd loved, and I hoped that in time, either Bronislav or someone else would fill that hole in her heart.

"Goodbye," I said, wrapping my arms around the pair in a final hug. "Be safe."

"Be safe," Annaka scoffed. Her eyes shone with amusement, which could only have meant trouble. "That's boring. The people on board my ship have survived a war. Now it's time for them to celebrate their new lives and live a little. There will be parties on the *Vengeance* every night."

Jad raised his eyebrow. "A fine captain you make."

"I'd be surprised if someone doesn't end up overboard," Talina muttered.

Annaka gave her a closed-lip smile. "I'll miss you too."

She and Bronislav waved goodbye as they ascended the gang-plank. Ropes were untied, the propellers spun into motion, churning the waters at the stern, and the ship lurched.

Talina, Marek, Jad, and I remained on the deck long after the *Vengeance* had drifted out of the harbour. We left when the vessel became a speck on the horizon, then disappeared with the setting sun.

OVER THE NEXT SEVERAL WEEKS, as preparations were in place for the elections that would form a new, stabilised government, more missions were announced daily. There were uprisings south in Vukovar. A few small bands of dissent rebels had gathered in guerrilla warfare to sabotage progress. They raided villages, ambushed the Haxsan Guard, and partook in petty conflicts in whatever desperate ways they could. Darius was confident that they couldn't inflict too much damage. They were too small in number—just loyalists to a cause that was dead—but he did want them answering for their war crimes.

That evening, on the balcony that connected to our room and looked out to the ocean, Jad told me that he and Marek had been assigned to the peacekeeping operation in the south. It was devastating news. I didn't want Jad to go. He'd been through so much. Didn't he deserve a break? Didn't we deserve more time with each other?

Jad wasn't one to eschew a direct order, though, and a few days later, I was once again saying goodbye. I walked hand in hand with Jad from the hangar onto the tarmac. Not far from us, Marek and Talina were already locked in an embrace, saying their private farewells.

We reached the carrier-hornet. My throat wobbled, my eyes filling with tears. It had been weeks since I'd last cried. I'd been filled with so much happiness and hope that crying now felt foreign.

Six months. How would I survive so long without Jad?

I looped my arms around his neck, sealing a final kiss to his lips. "You'd better come back," I warned. "You avoid danger. You don't get injured. And you do not die. Because if you die, I will send your soul to that foul place in the otherworld for leaving me."

He laughed and gathered me into his arms.

"I love you too" was all he said.

Talina joined me as Jad and Marek ascended the boarding ramp. I waved a tearful goodbye and was reminded of the day Jad and Marek's carrier-hornet had shot across the sky when they'd arrived at Gosheniene, when all of this had started nearly a year ago. So many things had changed for the better since then. *I'd* changed for the better.

I watched the carrier-hornet taxi down the runway, slow at first and then gaining speed. Lifting in a powerful takeoff, it soared into the sky and disappeared in the heavy clouds.

Talina leaned her head on my shoulder. "What happens now?"

I rested my cheek on her forehead. "Now we live our lives."

EPILOGUE

TEN YEARS LATER

ZAYA

I t was Ascension Day, and the celebrations in Edradus had gone on for a week now. There'd been festivals and markets, stunning pyrotechnic shows, but tonight was the big event. To mark the tenth anniversary of our rise from conflict to peace and unity, the best fireworks ever had been promised. Dragnor, the white-gold stagma who lived in the sea caves below the city and who was frequently seen flying around the Silver Palace, would be making a special appearance, likely performing fire magic, which the children would love. My bond with the stagma had only grown over the past decade. He was like an overly large pet, but really, he was Edradus's protector.

Conrith, my three-year-old son, was in raptures, running around the house with his toy plane, practically barrelling from wall to wall in excitement as he made loud engine noises. I rolled my eyes. I had no idea where he managed to get so much energy from. His obsession with planes had started the moment he'd seen a carrier-hornet and realised his dad was a pilot. Conrith wanted to be just like Jad. He looked like a miniature version of him, too, with his sun-kissed skin and ebony hair. He'd also inherited my husband's midnight-black eyes. It still irked me sometimes. After twenty hours of labour, Conrith had been born, and everyone had immediately exclaimed how much he looked like his father. I'd been the one who'd done all the hard work, thank you.

I set the table on the large balcony. We would eat out here tonight and watch the fireworks. Macaslan had already arrived, accompanied by Macha and the silver-thorned witch. The trio were always a sight to behold in parliament and had been dubbed the Triple Witches by the public, but not unkindly—more in admiration. After ten years, my grandmother still hadn't gotten used to her security escort, who stood at different corners of my house. They were never far behind her, even when she snapped at them to leave her alone.

Darius, who was already seated with his partner, Hector, laughed and reminded my grandmother that as president of the casters, she should be used to being shadowed. Macaslan just harrumphed and turned her nose at him, then froze when Conrith climbed into her lap for a cuddle. She patted his back awkwardly.

"Give him here," Darius insisted. He picked my son up and set him down on his knees.

Hector pulled faces, which set Conrith into hysterics.

Well, at least all this excitement will exhaust him, and Jad and I might actually be able to sleep tonight.

I returned to the kitchen, checking on the food. I wasn't the best with domestic duties, but I was an okay cook. Talina was the pro, though. Married to Marek with four kids and another on the way, she knew how to organise a kitchen, monitor children, and give instructions to the waiters I'd hired. It was Ascension Day, so of course I was paying them all double by the hour.

The doorbell rang, and a short moment later, Annaka and Bronislav arrived. I hugged them both and seated them together at the table, but it wasn't long until Annaka joined me and Talina in the kitchen.

She snorted when she saw Talina's round belly. "Providence, girl, are you pregnant again? I know the world needs repopulating, but that task isn't entirely dependent on you and Marek, you know. Next time, consider getting a dog."

Talina smiled sweetly. "It's nice to see you too. Here." She handed Annaka a plate of baked potatoes. "Put that on the table."

A loud belch cut through the melodic chatter from the balcony, and Bronislav excused himself.

Annaka rolled her eyes at us. "Can you believe I waited seven years to marry that?"

Talina's smile turned wicked. "Was it worth it?"

Annaka shrugged and returned to the balcony. "I'm still deciding."

But she planted a kiss on Bronislav's cheek and sat beside him, entwining her fingers with his.

Another knock on the door. This time it was Clorenzo and his two children. Livel and Sarith were in their final year at school and still bickered as much as they had when they were kids. They yelled and cursed at each other, not caring how high their voices escalated.

"Raising teenagers is hard," Clorenzo told me as I led them to the balcony. "You're lucky you only have the one child."

I smiled, filling his glass from a heavy crystal tumbler.

Well, do I have news for you all later.

Jad and I had decided to tell everyone that night that we were expecting our second child.

I checked the clock. Jad and Marek would have finished their security preparations for the celebration this evening and would be off duty by now. They arrived ten minutes later. Marek went straight to Talina, greeted her with a warm kiss, and then checked on his children, who were seated at their own small table, overrun with crayons and paper.

Jad took my hand and led me around a corner away from prying eyes. He kissed me long and gently, and I savoured the feel of his lips on mine.

"Come on," I said, reluctantly pulling away and leading him to the balcony. "We have time for that later. Let's go join the others."

We sat down at the table and started our Ascension Day celebration. I loved listening to the tinkering of our cutlery against plates, the clink of our wineglasses when we raised them in "cheers," and the joy in our conversations. It had taken years for the world to show the first signs of recovery, but for this, it had been worth it.

I thought about everyone who wasn't here. This was as much a celebration for them as it was for the living. Every time I'd tuned in to the otherworld, I felt nothing but peace, but this morning, there'd been something else tethered in that bond. Joy for the living.

Peace was such a fragile thing, and I knew one day—though hopefully not in my time, or in my children's time—that darkness would raise its ugly head again. But for now, all I wanted to do was enjoy my life with these amazing people and my husband.

We'd earned it.

ACKNOWLEDGMENTS

What a journey this series has been. I started writing the first book in The Wayward Haunt Series over ten years ago, and then, in the beginning of 2017, ditched my numerous drafts and started re-writing the entire story. Now, to see this series completed in 2024 is a dream come true.

There have been countless people who have invested their time and expertise into this story. A big thank you to Gillian, Stuart, Tom, Stacey, and the Brisbane Nightwriters for taking the time to read and critique samples from all four books. I always appreciate your feedback and the improvements that you make.

Thanks must go to my two wonderful critique partners, authors Shan L. Scott and Lisa McNeil. You ladies have been a big part of my author journey. Thank you so much for all your help, advice, feedback, and suggestions over the course of writing these novels. I appreciate all of it and will always cherish our friendship.

Thank you to my editor, Kristen Scearce, and final eyes reader, Kim Deister, who have both been so patient editing and looking over all four books.

Thank you to everyone who has read and provided a review for this book and the previous three novels in the series. I always value the thoughtful reviews and the time readers take to write them.

And finally, thank you, reader, for following Zaya's journey. I'm honoured that this story found a home with you.

XOXO
Cas

ABOUT THE AUTHOR

Cas E. Crowe is an admirer of all things spooky, quirky, and witchy. She enjoys writing YA and NA dark fantasy, horror, and romantasy stories filled with magic and adventure. Cas lives in Brisbane, Australia and, when she is not reading or writing, is often daydreaming about her next story or creating art with Photoshop.

www.casecrowe.com

BB bookbub.com/authors/cas-e-crowe?

a amazon.com/author/cascrowe

g goodreads.com/casecrowe

instagram.com/casecroweauthor

X x.com/CroweCas

f facebook.com/casecroweauthor

tiktok.com/@casecroweauthor

pinterest.com/casecroweauthor

LEAVE A REVIEW

If you enjoyed The Bone Grimoire, please consider leaving a
review on Amazon and Goodreads through the links below.
Authors depend on reviews to get the word out about their books.

Amazon
https://books2read.com/u/bM2DKB

Goodreads
https://www.goodreads.com/book/show/209045012-the-bone-
grimoire

NEWSLETTER

Sign up for Cas E. Crowe's Author Newsletter

Get access to
Author Interviews
Sample Chapters
Bonus Book Material
Book Recommendations
WIP (Writing in Progress)
Book Reviews
News and Social Events
Reading Lists
Exclusive Reveals
Upcoming Events
https://casecrowe.com/contact/

BOOKBUB

Follow Cas on BookBub to get notifications about upcoming releases, preorder availability, new book launches, and limited-time discounts.

bookbub.com/authors/cas-e-crowe?

Milton Keynes UK
Ingram Content Group UK Ltd.
UKHW011551290424
441792UK00027B/97/J

9 780975 613535